THE NIGHT COURT PRINCE

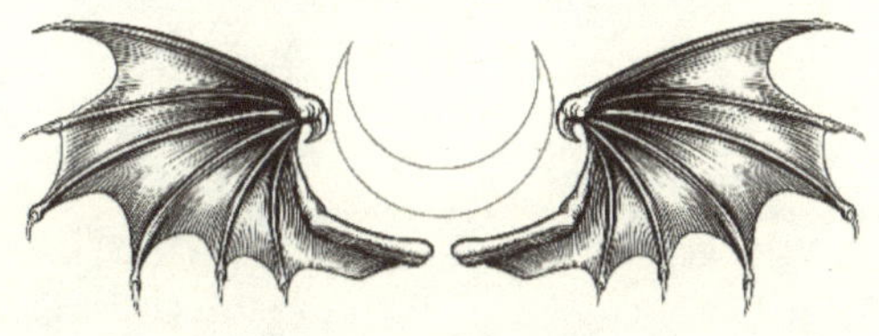

A HUNTING SAGA NOVEL

MELISSA SILVA

DEDICATION

For those who have loved and lost, there's light at the end of that dark tunnel, even if it takes you a while to get there.

TRIGGER WARNINGS

MM SCENES
SEXUALLY EXPLICIT SCENES
BONDAGE PLAY
BREATH PLAY
VIOLENCE
MENTAL HEALTH
MEMORIES OF CHILDHOOD ABUSE
ON PAGE DEATHS
NON-HEA ENDING
LANGUAGE
DRUG USE
ANXIETY
DEPRESSION
ALCOHOL

PLAYLIST

Wake Me When It's Over- Faouzia
Control- Halsey
Red Velvet (with Ari Abdul)- Jutes, Ari Abdul
Savage (feat. BIA)- Bahari, BIA
Chaos Control- Daktyl, Lily Kershaw
Easy to Love- Bryce Savage
World Gone Mad- Bastille
Burning Lines- Austin Giorgio
Go To Hell- Letdown.
Empty- Letdown.
Karma- Letdown
Afterlife- Evanescence
Dark All Day- Gunship, Tim Cappello, Indiana
Ticking Time Bomb- Elohim
Stargazing- Moonlight Version- Myles Smith
How Do I Say Goodbye- Dean Lewis
ALWAYS BEEN YOU- Chris Grey
LET THE WORLD BURN- Chris Grey
Love me- Ex Habit
All My Mistakes- Elvis Drew
Kill for you- Mandrazo, Mangusx
Watch It Burn- Oscen
Dirty Hands (Gone Mad)- Kendra Dantes
Let You Go- UNSECRET, Matthew Perryman Jones
Skin and Bones(Ballad)- David Kushner

COPYRIGHT

ISBN: 978-1-998500-25-3

CHAPTER 1

TAMZIN

"Fuck." I just had to go and let myself get distracted in the middle of a fight. The taste of iron in my mouth has me gagging and spitting out thick globs of the red liquid onto the sand covered arena floor. "That's your one," I mumble, pointing to the dickhead across from me. He smirks, bouncing around on the balls of his feet, watching me straighten myself back out.

The crowd around us cheers, hoots, and hollers, our names chanted and clinging to the thick air around us. The atmosphere is heavy, smoke and the scent of blood and sweat heavy in the air. I catch flickers of beer and whisky here and there, and I smack my lips together at the sudden need to drown myself in the sweet elixirs. Fuck, what I wouldn't give for a drink right now so I can get rid of the awful taste of blood in my mouth. The girl I saw in the crowd is gone, melding into the swarms of people crushing themselves closer to the cage.

"Look out!" Someone screams, drawing my attention to the fight once more.

Mother fucker. There I go again, letting myself get distracted, and it almost cost me my head this time. I barely ducked in time to not have my head literally cut off. "What the fuck is this?!" I scream out, tipping my head up to the suite above me, currently housing Kaliem, the fucking ringleader and owner of this not-so-fine establishment. "You said no weapons!"

The screech of the microphone rips through my eardrums, making me flinch and shake my head. "Did I?" He drawls, a soft chuckle drifting through the speakers.

The Fae in front of me snarls, launching at me again with that stupid fucking jagged blade. I have no idea how I didn't notice it before, or where the fuck he could have hidden it up until now. Maybe up his ass, he seems like the type. I smirk to myself, sidestepping him again and shoving him in the same motion. He stumbles, barely catching himself on the cage, and regretting it instantly. He howls out in pain, the magic of the cage sending electric current burning through his skin. Dark webbing laces up his arm from where he made contact, the skin withering and dying.

"Fuck," he croaks out, cradling the arm to his rapidly moving chest.

"You should have remember about the cage, *Daxton*." Fucking prick. I've always hated the guy, and apparently the feelings are mutual because he thought it was a good idea to challenge me to a pit fight. It's not *my* fault *his* girlfriend decided to sleep with me, but he thinks it is, so here we are. Who knew a girl he's only been dating for four months is worth a death match?

"Fuck you!" He spits out, his hand trembling as he tries to keep a steady grip on the blade.

"I would if I could," I chuckle. "I hear I'm a pretty good lay. You should know since Catia seemed satisfied when I was done with her."

That was definitely not something he wanted to hear. Do I regret it? Not really, no. It's not like this fucker means anything to me, and it's not like people don't know who I am or what I'm capable of, they're just too stupid to understand the difference between us. The Fae of the Night Court territory mostly have the same characteristics, but the royals are *more*. We've been through more, suffered more, are hated *more*. If they truly knew the struggles and pain we've had to endure, they may have taken pity on us…maybe.

Kaliem had to have been paid off to allow him in here with a fucking outside weapon. I'll have to deal with him later, but right now… I sigh, shoving Daxton again when he tries to swing at me. Fuck, he's so bad at this. I almost feel bad that I have to kill him…almost.

Gasps and screams erupt through the building, the Fae lights flickering for a moment before being snuffed out by the darkness engulfing every corner of the room. My eyes quickly adjust to the blackness, my sight snapping into place with the release of my abilities. I can see Daxton in front of me, clear as day, glancing around with panic and fear on his face. The darkness wraps around me, cradling my form as I slowly walk towards him in the shadows.

"You thought you could take me on?" I chuckle, my voice bouncing from every direction around him. He spins on the spot, eyes wide as he tries to pinpoint my location. "Idiots die, Daxton. You're an idiot for challenging me over something so stupid."

"I love her!" He chokes out. "You took her from me!"

"I didn't take shit. If she loved you, she wouldn't have sought *me* out. It's not like I tried to get into bed with her, she fell into mine."

"You're a monster," he grits out. "All you royal bloods are fucking monsters. Doing what you want, taking what you want."

Well fuck. How the fuck did he know what I am? I guess this power flare is a pretty good, logical guess. My bad. Not like it matters right now, he won't be able to tell anyone, and the crowd is too focused on the pure savagery of the match to clue in. "*I'm* not the one challenging a royal to a fucking death match." His eyes widen again. "Oh, you didn't know? Did Kaliem lie to you, or make you a promise you couldn't refuse?"

"I—I didn't know."

"Now you do. Only one of us is allowed to walk out of here alive, Daxton…and it won't be you."

I guess I feel a bit of pity, it's the only reason I give him a quick death. He would have been better off picking a fight in a bar or on the street, but he thought it was a good idea to make it official. The false sense of security that comes from an official match, even *if* it's still an underground ring that *shouldn't* be functioning. My blade hisses out of existence at the same time my shadows recede. Silence greets me from the crowd for a few long heartbeats. Then, cheers and screams erupt. My eyes drift up to Kaliem, his mouth gaped and his eyes darting between Daxton's now dead body and me. A sinister smirk pulls at my lips, and I slowly drag my thumb across my neck while my eyes keep his locked onto mine. Even from this distance, I can see the lump of his throat bob in fear.

Interesting turn of events. I thought Kaliem and I were amicable. He's let me fight here for a few years now, using the ring to blow off some steam whenever I needed it, since I hated being at home most nights. This just proved to me that something is off and he's after something. He set Daxton up, allowed him a weapon in a fight that shouldn't have them, and made him believe that he could win. I've never had to use my powers in this way during a fight, I've never had a need for it. I prefer to fight hand to hand if I can, not wanting to expose the sinister power that I've developed for being who I am.

The magic surrounding the cage hums, my eyes narrowing on Kaliem once more. I see his mouth move, his head tipping slightly to the side, speaking to someone outside my line of sight. I swear to the gods if he doesn't drop the ward—

The barrier falters, the sudden absence of magic making my skin prickle. I fight back the shudder building along my spine and head for the cage door, ripping it open before Kaliem changes his mind and attempts to keep me locked in here. It wouldn't do anything but piss me off. Something like this can't truly keep me caged in, not with the powers I have inside of me. The cage holds me during fights because I *allow* it. It looks better for the show he so obviously wants for the swarms of people that pile in here, dumping money left and right.

I stumble to the side, catching myself on the brick wall leading into the lower levels. "How could you!" Slowly I turn, my face betraying nothing, but my chest tightens at the tears streaming down Catia's face. "You didn't have to kill him."

"You clearly don't understand how this works, darling."

She shoves me again, but my feet stay planted. She slams her fists into me, and the one emotion I didn't want to feel, creeps up inside of me—guilt.

"I hate you! You're an asshole! You fucking murderer!" She keeps hitting me, waves of tears streaming down her cheeks as she sobs for a man I no longer know if she loved or not. "You fucking asshole!" She screams again.

"I'm sorry," I murmur, and I actually mean it. If Daxton hadn't challenged me within these walls, I would have never taken it this far. I would have pounded into him, taught him a lesson, but I wouldn't have killed him. If I hadn't, we would both be dead right now. I may hate my life, but I don't hate myself enough to want to die, especially because of some stupid fucking girl.

Her hands fall limply at her sides and slowly she turns, dragging her feet towards the cage until she's standing next to Daxton's body. She sways unsteadily and crumples to the ground, her knees slamming into the sand with a dull thud. She sobs—chest heaving sobs that shake her entire body as she drapes herself over his corpse, hugging him to her. She should have thought about the consequences of her actions. *She's* the idiot that threw it in his face. In her anger, she told him what she did, yet somehow, *I'm* the one being blamed. People really need to start taking responsibility for their own actions.

I turn away from the broken girl and freeze. The girl from earlier is down the hallway, hidden partially in the shadows. The faint Fae lights illuminate small features, her glowing eyes sparking like iridescent flames. My body moves on its own, my eyes locked on her unmoving and unblinking form.

CHAPTER 2

TAMZIN

I grunt the moment my back gets slammed into the wall. My teeth clink together, sending a rattling pain through my brain. "What the fuck do you think you're doing here?" My jaw twitches as I stare up at my brother, my chin lifting in defiance. "Answer me!" He snarls.

"What the fuck does it matter?" I mutter. "No one gives a shit what I do, Cam."

"Royals shouldn't be associating with the lower district like this. What the fuck is wrong with you?"

"Cute of you to think this is the first time," I snort, shrugging out of his grip. His hand drops away, curling into a fist that whitens with his anger. "Now you..." I sneer. "You shouldn't be here. The precious Prince, set to rise to the throne, shouldn't be seen with the scum of the Night Court."

"You're a Prince of that very Court, Tamzin. You need to start acting like it."

"Why? That illustrious crown will never grace this pretty head, so what difference does it make?"

"It's still your duty and your right."

It's not," I mumble. "I was the unhappy accident, remember? The abomination of the royal line."

He sighs, taking a small step back from me. I drop my eyes from his when I notice the pity in them, darting my gaze to the hallway once more. She's gone. The girl that distracted me earlier and who seems to be stalking me has completely vanished. I sigh, pushing off the wall and turning away from him.

"You better get home before father dearest notices you're missing. Plus, I doubt you'll want the crowd here to notice that the Crown Prince of the Night Fae is wandering about in the depths of hell." Glancing back at him, I take in his pathetic attempt at hiding his appearance. For a hole like this one, he stands out like a sore thumb with his fucking dress pants, polished leather shoes, and a random hoodie thrown over top. "Who the fuck dressed you? Or did you dress yourself in the dark? You look ridiculous."

"At least I'm not covered in dirt and blood," he snaps back.

"Have you looked around? *I* fit in here, especially covered in dirt and blood. You look like an idiot. Don't you own any jeans?"

He fidgets awkwardly, tucking the hood further over his head. "No. The sweater is yours, though. I don't own shit like this," he grumbles.

Fuck me, it *is* my sweater. One of my favourite ones, too. "Well, it's the least valuable thing you've stolen from me," I mutter, drawing his gaze back to me.

"Tamzin," he sighs. "That wasn't my choice."

"Of course not," I scoff. "Gotta do everything daddy says, even if it hurts the ones around you."

"Come home, Tam."

"I'm good, thanks. I plan to get drunk and get laid. You can run along though. I don't need to be supervised." I lift a brow mockingly. "Unless you're into watching, but I'm sure they charge extra for that."

"Resorting to paying now?" He snaps.

"Better than having the drama that comes with not paying." I nod towards Catia, who is now being dragged away from Daxton's body while she screams bloody murder. "That's the result of hooking up with someone I don't pay for."

"When are you going to grow up, Tamzin?" He sighs.

"The day you decide to grow some balls and stand up to dad," I grumble, shoving my hands into the pockets of my torn jeans. "Until then, leave me the fuck alone."

"We want you home," he says quietly. "We're family, Tam. We want you to act like it."

"I need to go collect my money," I grumble.

"Tam!" He calls out, but I'm already halfway down the hall towards the change rooms in the lower pit.

I fucking hate that he found out where I am. This was the one place I never had to worry about my fucked-up family finding me—used to be anyways. I'll have to lie low for a little while and hope that Cam won't come looking for me again. I'm surprised it was him that came. I half expected Dorian or Croh to come, since they're both sociopaths in their own right. Cam coming just makes me wonder what the fuck is going on at Court.

CHAPTER 3

TAMZIN

The door to the change room smacks against the wall. I don't react, keeping my back to the dumb fuck lumbering towards me. A stack of bills lands on the bench next to me. "Your winnings," Kaliem mutters.

"Care to tell me what that was about? I thought we had an understanding, Kaliem." I grab the money, shoving it into the duffel at my feet. The air crackles with tension, my shadows signalling that he's not alone. Slowly, I glance over my shoulder at him. His frown wrinkles his face, his lips pressed into a hard line, tugging the scar across his cheek into a deeper groove. The bastard needs a bath—or ten.

"It was a high stakes match," he says bluntly.

"High stakes?" I can't help it, I laugh, pulling myself to my feet to face him. His guards bristle next to him, stepping ever so slightly closer. Warlocks for hire by the smell of them, the echo of smoke and ether in the air. "I was unaware I was being put into a high stakes match against my will."

"If you want to play in the pits, you play by my rules, kid."

"Kid?" I snort. "You have the audacity to call *me* a kid?"

"You look like a kid."

The shadows writhing in the corners pulse with my rising irritation. “I’m not a kid,” I grit out.

“You would be wise to mind your tongue and know your place.”

“My place?” I snarl, stepping towards him. His guards shift in front of him, Kaliem sneering behind their protection. These dumb fucks have no idea who I am or what I’m actually capable of. I’ve done well to hide my identity from them—not like the royal family has any reason to show off their youngest, useless son. For years I’ve been sulking in the lower district just to get away from that life.

“Yes, your place. You work for *me*. I pay you to fight, and the fans come here to see you fight. High stakes mean more money, for the both of us, Eris.”

He flinches when I cluck my tongue and bend down to grab my bag. “You wouldn’t be pulling in half the money you are if I wasn’t fighting here.”

“That might be true, but I still have standards. If you can’t fall in line, I can’t allow you to fight. My men will escort you out.”

Grunts of pain and the sound of shattering bones echoes off the walls. Kaliem stares with wide eyes, his tawny skin going deathly pale as he stares at his so-called men lying in heaps on the floor. The cool lick of my shadows caresses my skin as I stare him down. “I can see myself out,” I say bluntly, no longer holding back the anger from my voice. “Cross me again and you’ll be joining them.”

He drops his eyes to the ground and steps back when I walk towards him. Poor fucker, even as a Fae himself, he’s still weak in comparison. His size makes up for his lack of power when it comes to intimidating others. He’s not weak, but he’s weak compared to someone of royal blood. Too bad he doesn’t know that, or he wouldn’t have the nerve to speak to me in such a way or threaten me the way he just did. Here, I’m Eris. A recluse Fae, a nomad, someone who *wants* to stay off the radar. Fighting in the pits obviously draws attention to me, but no one would expect a royal son to be in the most depraved part of the territory. I pushed myself as far out as I could go while still within the border of my territory.

It pisses me off that Cam found me out here. I thought I was being smart and keeping myself hidden well enough, but somehow, he fucking found me. Kaliem stumbles back when I push through him and head for the door. I don't even bother glancing back at him, he's probably shitting his pants right now, realizing I actually killed his two bodyguards like they were flies on the wall.

CHAPTER 4

TAMZIN

Nox jolts awake when I drop my duffel on the coffee table, almost falling off the beaten-up couch in his panic. "Fucking hell don't do that," he grumbles.

"Why the fuck are you sleeping out here? You have a bed."

"Yeah, about that," he mumbles, dragging his hand down his face. "I sort of have an unwanted guest that refused to leave after we...you know."

"Have you learned nothing?" I snort. "You're not supposed to bring your hook-ups home, you idiot. I don't need random people in my fucking apartment."

"Sorry, it was closer to the bar than her place. I didn't think she would stick around. I thought I made it pretty clear what this was."

"Do you want me to deal with it?" I sigh, hating that I'm being put into this situation, *again*. It's not the first time Nox has brought a girl home when he knows not to. He's lucky I even let *him* stay here, but it's easier to cover the rent when I have a roommate. Trying to stay under the radar means fending for myself and not tapping into daddy's vault of money.

"You would do that for me?" He asks, batting his eyelashes like a fucking sociopath.

"Stop that," I snort. "You need to learn to deal with your own problems, and by problems, I mean your fuck buddies, Nox."

"Taaaaam," he groans. "I'm not good at confrontation!"

Am I an idiot for telling this idiot who the fuck I am? Yes, yes, I am. It doesn't help that he saw me stumbling out of Court like a drunken idiot one night after I decided to toilet paper every single inch of the west garden. I played it off that I had a vendetta against the royals, but later on I had no choice but to tell him the truth. He's an idiot sometimes, but he can put two and two together when it's all in front of him.

"One of these days I'm going to pummel your ass," I sigh, slipping my jacket off and tossing it on the arm of the couch. "Was she good at least?"

He shrugs. "I have no idea. She passed out when I went to the bathroom. All we did was make out for a bit."

"Seriously?" He blinks innocently, pressing his lips together. I'm sure he's regretting admitting the truth since he just made it sound like they actually hooked up. "That's not saying much about you, you realize that, right?"

"I didn't do anything!"

"Maybe that's the problem," I snort. "You're a good-looking male, there shouldn't be any reason for you not to seal the deal, mate."

He huffs out a disgruntled breath, flopping his feet on the table. I stare at them for a minute, glancing back at him with a quirked brow. "What the fuck are those?"

He wiggles his feet, the rabbit ears on the slippers flopping around. "What? They're cute and they're warm."

"You would be warmer if you put more clothes on. What the fuck is the point of the slippers if you're walking around in your underwear?"

"Are you judging me on my fashion?" He clutches his hand to his chest in mock shock. "How dare you."

I roll my eyes and start making my way to his room to get rid of the girl. "You're buying me breakfast in the morning for this!" I call to him.

"Deal!" He laughs.

I shake my head, wondering how the fuck I ended up with someone like him in my life, and open the door. I frown, my eyes locked on the girl, not sleeping, but sitting up in bed, staring at me. She smirks, folding her hands on her lap and tilting her head curiously.

This can't be real. *Her?* Why the fuck is *she* here? I didn't get a good look at her in the darkness of the pit, but those eyes...I couldn't forget those eyes even if I wanted to. Light brown, almost golden, with that same iridescent glow that I saw in the hallway. The room is dimly lit, but the bedside lamp is enough for me to see how vividly red her hair is. Her strawberry lashes flutter and the smirk turns into a grin.

"Eris," she purrs.

I step further into the room, eyeing her warily. "You need to leave," I say bluntly, trying not to let my suddenly racing heart get the better of me. She's been on my mind since I got a glimpse of her in the ring.

"Do I?" She says in a lilting voice. "Hmm, I rather stay."

"My friend is too kind to ask you to leave. I on the other hand, have no issue kicking you out of *my* home."

"So, this is your place, not his?"

"Yes." She doesn't need to know Nox is actually my roommate and not some random friend that's decided to crash at my place, but if lying to her gets her out of my fucking house, I'll say what I need to.

"Do your friends make it a habit of bringing girls into your home without you knowing about them?"

"Not usually, but he slips up from time to time."

She smiles, uncurling her legs to stretch out on the bed, settling her hands behind her. My eyes move to her very bare legs. She's not naked, but she may as well be. A bra and panties tell me how far they got before she supposedly passed out. Something nags at the back of my mind at the whole situation, and it's enough for my guard to go up. I take a step back, anchoring myself with my hand on the knob again. I catch the slight narrowing of her eyes before she plasters that smile on her face again.

"Did you know Nox was staying in *my* home?" She doesn't respond, just continues to stare at me, like she's judging me. "Answer the question," I snap, putting more bite into the words to get my point across.

"I met him at Transcend," she shrugs. "How was I supposed to know I would be seeing you again tonight?"

"Get out before I physically throw you out."

I turn to leave and hear the bed creak behind me. "Do you not want to know my name?"

"No because I don't care," I lie. I *do* want to know her name because I want to know who the fuck she is. It can't be by chance that the girl that was watching me fight in the pits just so happens to come home with my roommate.

"You will," she says coyly.

I spin around, mouth open to snap at her again, but I stop short. She's standing now, and my eyes drift across every inch of visible skin. I swallow, dragging my wandering eyes back to her face. "Are you following me?" I grit out, swearing mentally at the audacity of the dick between my legs. Of *course* it's reacting to her, like a fucking savage beast. I didn't get nearly as much aggression out as I would have liked to while fighting tonight, but that fight against Daxton left a bitter taste in my mouth.

"Now why would you think that?" She muses, grabbing her shirt off the floor.

I sigh in relief at the fact she's covered enough to get me under control, but then she goes and turns her back to me, bending down to slip her pants over her feet in the most exaggerated way. Her pert ass sticks out in the process, a lacy thong flaring like a beacon for my cock. I grip the doorknob hard enough for the metal to bend in my palm, a loud crack resonating from the room. She glances over her shoulder, smirking again. Little shit, she knows exactly what she's doing and she's fucking playing me.

"I don't want to see you again." My voice is strained, fighting between a snarl and a dying cat, if you can believe it.

She walks towards me, stopping when she's right next to me. Her hand settles on my chest, and it's like I'm being electrocuted from that simple touch. "Now, we both know that isn't true," she coos, dragging her fingers lightly against my blood-stained t-shirt, her long pointed nails, tipped in ruby polish, scrape against the material in the sexiest way. I close my eyes, breathing through my mouth to stop myself from scenting her. If I pull in her scent, I'll be too tempted to track her, and the last thing I need is to be turning into a stalker. "Are you sure you want me to go?" I nod, refusing to look at her, even though I can *feel* her eyes on me. Those golden eyes that burn like a liquid sun, even in the dimmest of light. "Fine," she sighs, pulling away from me.

I don't move, don't breathe, don't even fucking think, until I hear Nox mumble a goodbye and the sound of the front door closing. My breath whooshes out of me in a hot wave, my body trembling from keeping myself coiled in a hyper state. "You good?" Nox calls out.

"Yeah," I say shakily, finally opening my eyes. "I'm going to shower and then to bed. Make sure you lock the door before you go to sleep again."

The last thing I need is that girl trying to sneak in here while we're both passed out. I shouldn't be judging her like that, but I can't shake this feeling that's been gnawing at my chest since earlier tonight. There's something about her; somethings I can't quite put my finger on. It's wishful thinking to hope that I never see her again, but I've been wrong about a lot of things in my life. I doubt my instincts are wrong about this girl, but it's not like I have to keep up appearances. She called me Eris, so she doesn't know my true identity, and I rather keep it that way. She's a walking red flag pretending to be sweet and gentle and very green, but I know better. I don't fall for the green, I hate green, the colour reminds me of puke, or baby poo, and I just can't stand the sight of it, so why would it be any different when it came to the warning flag flying high above the people I come in contact with?

I need a fucking shower and at least a few hours of sleep to cleanse this day from my mind and body. Wishful thinking, but it's the thought that counts, right?

CHAPTER 5

TAMZIN

I'm going to fucking kill him. Groaning, I cover my head with a pillow to drown out the sound of his stupid blender. Seconds later, the sound of *Sleep Token* comes streaming into my room at an obnoxious volume. I get tangled in the covers in my desperate attempt to bolt out of bed, regretting the quick movement when it causes my head to pound harder.

"Morning!" Nox says in a way too chipper voice the moment he sees me. A wide grin spreads across his face as he hits the button on the blender again. He points to an already full glass on the table. "Drink up, you need the vitamins."

"How did I end up with a health freak as a roommate?" I grumble, dragging the chair back to sit down. "You were supposed to *buy* me breakfast."

He rolls his eyes, and I sigh when blissful silence finally greats my ears. Well, not full silence since the music is still playing, but at least I *like* this music. "I'm not a health freak, I just feel like you need to take care of yourself a bit better. You can't live off chips and takeout, Tam."

"Says who?" I grumble, eyeing the concoction in front of me warily. "Why is this fucking bright red?"

"Oh, I used beets this morning!"

"Great," I say, not even trying to hide the sarcasm from my voice. He watches me carefully as I grab the glass and bring it to my lips. I should get an award for not outwardly cringing at the taste. "It tastes like dirt." His face falls, and he turns back to his own glass to pour the blender contents into it. Fuck, I'm such an asshole. I know he's trying, but I keep throwing these simple gestures in his face. No one forces him to cook or clean the house, but he does it without complaint. "It's not so bad once you get used to it," I add, taking another sip of it.

He sighs, keeping his back to me. "You don't have to drink it," he murmurs.

"How else am I supposed to get my vitamins?" He finally turns to look at me over his shoulder, and I hold up the glass to him in a mock cheers, gulping back half the contents in one go.

A small smile pulls at the corner of his lips, and he gives me a small nod. "A new job came in this morning," he says, turning to lean against the counter while he drinks his own dirt shake.

"How much?"

He quirks a brow. "You rather know the pay than what we're hunting?" He snorts.

I shrug. "I rather know the pay *before* I know what we're hunting. If it's not a decent amount, I won't even consider it, no matter how easy it might be."

"Fifty."

"Nox," I sigh. Fifty isn't *bad,* but I usually don't get involved in anything under seventy-five and he knows that.

"It's an easy enough job, Tam. A snatch and grab, nothing involving people."

"A snatch and grab? What the fuck are we stealing?" Stealing isn't part of our usual repertoire. Normally we get hired to hunt down criminals, or people who owe scarier people money. Depending on if they want them dead or alive, the price goes up substantially. Stealing just seems so...petty.

"It should be easy for you, considering." I frown. "There's an amulet at Court—"

"No."

"Tam—"

"I said no, Nox. Fifty is not worth it if it involves Court. The security alone—"

"Which you can bypass easily since you're *part* of court."

Anxiety blooms in my chest. "Who's the hire? If they're only offering fifty, knowing it should be easy for me, they know who I am. I don't like this."

He shrugs, draining the rest of his glass. "The message came in this morning, and they just signed it as Den. I don't know if that's a nickname or who it could be."

"We really need to start vetting clients. This is getting too dangerous."

"*This* is dangerous?" He snorts. "You don't even have to fight anyone. I can take care of the security system around the property and give you time to get through the barrier undetected, but at least if you get caught inside, they won't question it. You're one of them, Tam."

"I'm not doing it."

"Fine, then I will."

"The fuck you will. If you get caught breaking into Court you won't just be sent to the cells, Nox, you'll be killed. We do fucked up shit, but this is *beyond* fucked up."

"We need the money."

"We'll wait for the next request," I argue. "Something that will pay better for way less work."

"Requests have been scarce since the imperial sanction went out against bounty hunters. They still leave us alone, but it's put enough fear in the less deranged folks to have them not seek assistance."

"We don't need the money *that* bad." He rolls his eyes, grabbing the now empty glass from my hands to wash. "I won't let you go there, Nox."

"So, what do you want me to tell the client?"

"Say thank you but no thanks." He pulls out his phone, quickly typing out a message. It pings with a response almost instantly, and he frowns. "What?"

"They must really want this thing. They just increased the payout."

"By how much?"

"They'll give two hundred."

"Two hundred. From fifty to two hundred...that's fucking suspicious as shit."

"A little bit, yeah. If they were willing to do this much all along, why the fucking lowballing?"

I hate that this situation has now piqued my interest. I'm fucking curious who this asshole is and what they could possibly want with an amulet from my home. What amulet could they be talking about? "Give me the phone." Nox stares at me for a minute, but hands it over when my gaze shifts to a glare.

"A pretty boy like you shouldn't have a look like that in his arsenal," he chuckles.

"Pretty boy?" I snort, opening the message thread with the client. I don't recognize the number and there's only a handful of messages between them so far.

"Blond hair, blue eyes, skin-tone that would make anyone with a pulse swoon, and have you seen your jaw line?" He brings his fingers to his lips, kissing them and lifting them into the air. "Fucking divine."

"You're ridiculous," I laugh. "Is this your way of hitting on me?"

"Are you offering?" He grins.

"Ass is ass, and I'll admit, you have a decent ass." That shuts him up. Red scatters up his neck, all the way up into his face. "Don't dish it out if you can't take it," I laugh. I punch out a message to the client, hoping to fish for some details. He doesn't need to know whether or not I'm planning to take this job, but if I want information, I need to play it up like I'm considering it. Which I am, but it's because I *really* want to know what they're up to.

"What are you doing?"

"Getting details on what he's actually looking for."

"So, you're going to take the job?"

"I never said that."

"But—"

"Call me curious. Whoever this is, knows something I don't, Nox. I have no idea what amulet they're referring to, and how would *they* know about it and not me. It's my fucking house." Well, it *was* my house. It hasn't been for a few years now and I had no plans to go back there. A text comes back almost instantly with a rendered drawing of the necklace in question.

Nox: *You do realize that court is massive, correct? How do you expect us to find something so small in a place that's so large?*

Den: *Figure it out. This is why I've increased the payout. If you're incapable of doing such a task, then just say that. I reached out to your organization because I was told that you're the best.*

Nox: *Fine, send me all the details you have. Half payment up front, other half upon completion. Wire the funds into this account.*

I quickly type in our joint bank account and press send, handing the phone back to Nox. He glances down at the message exchange, rolling his eyes as he tosses it on the counter. "I thought you said you weren't going to do it?"

"I wasn't. I changed my mind."

"Thank you."

"Don't thank me yet. I still have a bad feeling about this, but I'm too nosey to pass this up."

"Do you recognize the necklace?" I shake my head. "They don't even have a picture of it, but the drawing is decent." He pulls his phone out again, zooming in on the photo that was sent. "It looks pretty ordinary. What could be so special about it that it's worth two hundred thousand?"

"I'm not sure. We have plenty of things with value in that home, some things dating back to the dark times. Maybe the necklace is worth a lot more than what they're paying us."

"Could it be magical in nature?" He asks, squinting and leaning closer to the phone. "It looks like there might be runes carved into it from the drawing." He startles when it goes off again, a smile creeping across his face. "The funds got transferred and he sent more info. "Apparently, it's an Enochian relic, so there should be a magical signature to it once you get close to it."

"It would be easier to track it if I *had* that signature already. Also, what the fuck? Enochian? I highly doubt my parents have Enochian relics just sitting around in our home."

"That's angelic, right?" I nod. "Angelics don't associate with Fae very often. Do you think it was stolen, or was it a gift?"

"I have no idea, dude. I don't even know if my mother has it or my sister."

"Your sister is pretty hot," he mumbles, scrolling through the phone, not realizing I'm glaring daggers at him at this point. When I don't say anything, he finally looks up, his instincts kicking in and forcing him to take a step back. “Easy, I’m just pointing out the obvious.”

My eye twitches in irritation. “Off limits,” I grit out.

“Why? Am I not *worthy* of your sister?” He snaps back, surprising me.

“She would eat you alive, Nox. I’m telling you to back off for your own safety.” That seems to surprise him, but an edge of doubt still tugs at his features. “Trust me, you don’t want to get involved with my family.”

“I doubt anyone of the royal family would give a peasant like me the time of day,” he laughs.

“You’re not a peasant, and what am I, chopped liver? I spend more time with you than I do anyone else.”

“Half royal is still peasant, and my royal lines are super minor,” he murmurs. “Couldn’t even have anything as significant as Night Court or Solar. Fuck, I would have settled for Lunar, too, but that wouldn’t be possible since they’re basically wiped out.”

Fifty years later and the horrors of that night still circulate through every Court on the continent. Probably the entire world now that I think about it. Darklings aren’t as rare as one might think, but most corrupted souls are just that, fully corrupted. Atlas didn’t fall completely into darkness by the sounds of it. He sought out the Solar Queen after it happened...after he killed her betrothed—his own *brother*. If he were truly corrupted, he would have forgotten about her, lost to the darkness that overtook his magic and his life. I wonder what he’s like, what he’s doing now after being banished from the Fae realms. The Night Court are more similar to Atlas than people realize. We live in darkness, are born from it, but our souls come out intact...if not a little bit damaged.

My life was never easy. I wish it were, especially as a child, but it wasn’t. I wish I had a normal childhood, one with love and happiness, with normal activities that someone of that age should experience. Instead, I was practically tormented, moulded into the being that sits here now, hating the life I've lived, and finally allowing myself to run from it. I can't escape—not really. It's only a matter of time before the King decides I've had enough time to throw my tantrum and summons me home. They'll have to drag me back there, kicking and screaming.

I don't even miss it. I know I should, and there are moments that I think about my family, but I can't justify going back there just to live through hell once more. It's not like they need me for anything. The youngest son—the useless one. Even Helia has more power than I do, and they give no respect to females...fucking assholes. Still so caught up in the old ways. She's the oldest of us, the first born, but she'll never see power within this Court. That line falls to Cam being the eldest son, the true heir to the Night Court throne.

I shake my head, trying to push the thoughts from my mind, and focus back in on Nox. He's watching me with a guarded expression, like he's waiting for me to physically implode. "Your lines are Star Court, are they not?"

He clucks his tongue, dropping heavily into the chair across from me. "Yeah. Bastard son to the douche bag Prince who couldn't keep it in his pants. I have a half-bastard sister, probably a few others, but she had the balls to kill the bastard for what he did." I frown. "You don't know? I figured someone like you would know what happened. Yeah, she killed him for raping her mother. I'm pretty sure she ended up at the Solar Court after everything was said and done. Taken in by the Queen herself. If she hadn't, I have no doubt she would have been executed for it. I never met her, but I'm pretty sure her name is Jacqueline."

"I try to stay out of Court business if I can help it, but I still hear things here and there in passing. It must not have been a significant loss, not like what happened to Lunar."

"Definitely doesn't compare, but insane none the less."

"I'm going to head out for a little bit. I'll be back in a few hours."

"Alright. I'm going to head to the store and pick up some food. We're running low on supplies."

"Sounds good, man, Thanks for breakfast."

"We both know you're going to pick something up at the Hub," he snorts. "But I appreciate you entertaining me."

He's not wrong because I feel hungrier than I did before consuming that shake of his. Heading back into my bedroom, I get changed quickly, tossing on a ripped pair of jeans and a faded grey T-shirt. I snag my favourite sweater off the chair on the way by and head out the door.

CHAPTER 6

TAMZIN

I'm regretting not grabbing my sunglasses the moment the sun beats against my eyes. A flash of red catches my eye and my line-of-sight darts to the alley next to our apartment. I chuckle when an orange tabby peeks out from behind the garbage bin, a long breath slipping from my lips. I'm way too on edge lately, but I have no idea why. No, I *do* know why. I've had this itching sensation crawling beneath my skin from the moment I laid eyes on that girl. That deviant, sly little fox, full of tricks and deception.

I shove my hands into the pouch of my hoodie and make my way down the road towards the Hub. The streets are already bustling this early in the morning, people going about their day, getting their caffeine fix before a long day at work.

The line in the Hub is asinine, long enough that I'm contemplating forgoing my usual breakfast sandwich and quad espresso and just going about my day. The moment I hit the counter I wish I would have done just that.

"Sorry about the wait, I'm new," the redhead laughs nervously, pausing when she finally lifts her eyes to meet mine. "What can I get you?" She asks, trying to hide the surprise on her face.

I stare at her, taking in every detail visible to me in the light of the sun streaming in through the giant windows encasing the place. "You work here?"

"Just started today," she smirks, lifting her chin in a way that makes my hand twitch on my thigh. She licks her lips, and it draws my eyes to them, to the perfect pout, the subtle bow of the upper one, and the thin sheen of gloss caressing them. "Are you going to order or...?"

Of all the places for this girl to get a job, she gets one at the one place I frequent at least four times a week. "Quad espresso and a sausage croissant, hold the tomatoes, heavy on the sauce."

Her lip twitches and her eyes drift down to the screen in front of her. She frowns, gnawing on her lip while her eyes keep flicking to the barista behind her.

"What's the hold up?" Someone yells from the back of the line, making the girl in front of me jump and then cringe when Kylo comes over to the register. My eyes drift to the name tag on her chest. Kalia. I want to say the name and taste it on my tongue, but I'll definitely look and sound like a creeper if I do that right now. She steps back nervously when Kylo motions to the register.

"Morning, Eris," he says cheerfully. "Sorry about this."

"It's no problem at all," I reassure him, not wanting him to fire the girl on her first day because she's struggling to figure things out.

"Come on!" The goon in the back yells again, my temple pulsing with irritation. My teeth grind together hard enough to have both Kylo and Kalia look up at me. "Hurry the fuck up!"

"Excuse me," I say quietly, my teeth gritted together as I turn towards the asshole who won't shut up.

I stalk towards him, the people in the line backing up when they see the death glare I'm giving the fucker. He realizes too late that he fucked up, staggering back, but not fast enough to avoid the fist that hits him square in the nose. Blood spurts through the fingers now holding his broken nose, spattering across the clean white tile floors.

Gasps and murmurs ripple through the building before settling into a hushed silence.

"You need to learn some fucking respect," I snarl, gripping into the front of his now ruined dress shirt. My nostrils flare, scenting the fucker. Human. Of course he's human. I shove him back, watching him stumble over his own feet to fall to the ground. "I would hate to see how you treat people you know when you have no qualms in treating strangers who are serving you like their worthless fodder." He cowers when I step closer to him. "If I catch you here again, it won't just be your nose that I break."

"What's your problem, man," he murmurs, his voice nasally and muted from what I did to his face. His face pales, eyes going wide when I let my powers pulse enough to know my eyes are glowing.

"Get out." It's a whisper filled with so much venom and the promise of death that the fucker actually pisses himself. He scrambles back like a petrified crab, tripping over himself as he shoves his way through the door and the growing line.

Sighing, I turn back around and head back to the register. "You didn't have to do that, Eris," Kylo sighs.

"Yes, I did. Guys like that deserve to be brought down a peg or two." He holds out my order to me, Kalia hiding behind him and peeking up at me through her lashes. "Tell you what, I have some time to kill. Let me just eat this really quick and I'll help you out."

"That's not necessary," he says quickly.

"I'm not expecting you to pay me, but I can at least man the kitchen while you finish training her like you're supposed to. Why would you pick rush hour to throw her into this?"

"We're not usually this busy, but we had an online influencer come in here a few days ago and now we've sort of blown up."

"You should consider hiring more staff, not just one new person. If this place went viral, this is just the beginning."

He sighs, waving me off to go sit down while they deal with the still growing line that's now out the door. Fuck, so much for this being my go-to spot. There's no way in hell I can handle waiting in a line like this every fucking time, and I sure as fuck don't want to get up any earlier to get here before the line forms.

I watch Kalia struggling from a table in the corner, smirking every time I catch her stealing glances my way. She quickly drops her gaze when I stand, snagging the plate and the rest of my coffee before heading in behind the counter. I grab one of the aprons lying on the inner shelf behind the counter and quickly sling it on. Kalia stiffens when I step in behind her, her body shuddering when my breath flutters the skin of her ear.

"Relax, little fox. If you keep panicking the way you are, you're going to give yourself a heart attack." She turns her head enough to glare at me, and I back away, hands up and a smile spreading across my face. "What's on the order?" I ask, shifting my attention to Kylo.

"Maybe I should—"

"You're better on the brew, Kylo. I know the menu. I've literally *eaten* everything on your menu."

"Fair enough," he chuckles, sliding the order receipt onto the counter. With that, I get to work, whipping out order after order until finally, the line dwindles down to a manageable number. "Thank you for helping," Kylo sighs, clearly thankful the breakfast rush is finally over.

I have no idea how they're going to manage lunch, where the orders are bigger with the possibility of the same number of customers in tow. "Maybe you should call Ridley in. She can help you guys out for the lunch rush, but I would still put out a notice to hire."

"I will. Thank you for your help today, Eris."

"No problem at all," I smile. "I might have to hold off coming here until the rush dies down a bit," I chuckle.

"Nonsense. Just shoot me a message before you come and I'll have your order ready for you by the time you get here. Free of charge for your help."

"I don't need you giving me anything for free. I didn't help you expecting anything in return."

"Do you mind if I take a break?" Kalia says quietly. "I could really use a smoke right now."

"Of course," Kylo smiles. "Take fifteen." She nods, scurrying off to the back room to grab her smokes before darting out the front door. "She's a sweet kid, and I hate that she had to deal with that on her first day."

"She'll survive," I snort. "I don't think she's as sweet as she pretends to be." He quirks a brow in question. "I met her last night." His eyes widen and I laugh. "Not like that. She was in Nox's room when I got home last night." I don't need to tell him that I know I saw her before that at the pit. "Do you know much about her?"

He shakes his head. "She just moved here a couple of weeks ago from the Autumn territory in Denton."

"Autumn? That's surprising. They don't associate with any other Court much, most definitely not Night. Who is she?"

Kylo shrugs. "No idea. I got the basic information off of her for a half-ass background check just to make sure she's not completely insane."

"What's the verdict on that?" I smirk.

He rolls his eyes. "She seems saner than you at least, and if I can handle you, I think I can handle her just fine."

"Fair enough," I laugh.

"Do you want a coffee to go?"

"Sure. Thanks, Kylo."

He pours me a steaming cup, giving me a kind smile as I head out of the shop and into the blaring sun once more. Kalia is leaning against the far wall of the building, one sneaker-clad foot propped up against it as she takes a long drag from her smoke. She doesn't hear me coming, startling when I snag the smoke from between her lips.

"Hey! I'm not done with that!"

I take a long drag, licking my lips with a quirked brow. She tries to reach for it, but I hold it out of her range above her head. “You better hope Kylo doesn’t realize what you’re smoking during break,” I tease. “Nice touch with the mint, but anyone who gets close enough to you will know the smell of nokweed.”

Surprise rips through me when she jumps up and snags the smoke back, shifting away so I can’t grab it again. “Only a sociopath like you would notice,” she grumbles, taking another heavy drag. “Scenting should be illegal.”

“Should it now?” I muse, crossing my arms across my chest. I study her features, which seem guarded now that we’re alone. She must have been putting on that green flag front to trick Kylo, and the gullible bastard fell for it. “So, *are* you an idiot, or do you just pretend to be?” She frowns, and I nod my head towards the coffee shop.

“I’m not playing him,” she snaps. “Have you *seen* that register? The stupid thing makes no sense. Tablets in shops are ridiculous.”

“They’re upgrades to the shit he used to use. Do you have a problem with technology?”

“It’s complicated for no reason,” she grumbles, letting the smoke from her mouth curl around her lips before she exhales completely.

“Tell me, *Kalia*.” Fuck, her name feels nicer on my tongue than I imagined, and her throat bobs, her eyes flicking up to meet mine. “Have you led a sheltered life? To have such an aversion to modern technology, I can only imagine.”

Her lips press into a hard line, and she quickly drops her gaze to the ground between us. “My parents have never been ones to enjoy change. Even after living for hundreds of years, they don’t *want* to integrate more than is necessary.”

“Technology *is* necessary, though. If we don’t integrate, we have to deal with mortal suspicion. Did you move here on your own, or did your family come with you?”

“I came alone. My family...wouldn’t move here anyways.”

She sounds sad admitting that. Does she not have a good relationship with her family? Are we more alike than I care to admit? The last thing I need to do is get involved with anyone, let alone her. I still have this nagging feeling, that our encounters aren't by chance, but I'm trying my best to squash it down and just let myself enjoy her company for what it is...a possible friendship. That's it—that's all it *can* be. If anyone found out who I really am, it would go one of two ways. Either they shy away from the fact I'm royalty, or they try to take advantage of it.

"Eris?" I shake my head, pulling myself out of my wandering thoughts. "Are you alright?"

"I'm fine," I say quickly, taking a step back from her to not only put distance between me and her, but the situation itself. I can't let myself be drawn to her, but it keeps happening. I didn't even realize I had stepped even closer to her while I was off in my own thoughts. "I need to go. I have some errands to run before I have to work."

"Oh, okay. Maybe I'll see you tomorrow then." I quirk a brow at the comment. "I took on as many shifts as I could for now, just to get a bit of extra cash."

"I'll see you later, fox," I smirk.

She frowns. "Fox? What's that supposed to mean?"

"Hmm, you'll figure it out, I'm sure." A faint blush scatters across her cheeks, and if it isn't the most adorable thing, seeing her flustered. It makes me want to keep teasing her just to see how far I can push her. She opens her mouth to say something more, but I turn and quickly get myself as far away from her as I can.

CHAPTER 7

TAMZIN

"I saw your fight last night in the pit." I turn to glare at Orion. He shrugs. "How you holding up?"

"I didn't know dealers gave a shit about *feelings*," I scoff, snapping my fingers for him to hand over the vial.

He sighs, sliding it across the counter and taking the money from me as he pulls back. "I've never seen you that shaken up after a fight, Eris. It seemed more personal than usual."

"The fight should have never happened. He was an idiot for a lot of reasons. For challenging me to begin with, knowing what my record is in that pit, and the fact he picked a fight like that over something so stupid."

"Was it stupid? He said he loved her."

"Look where that got him. If he would have confronted me on the streets I wouldn't have had to kill him."

"So, you would have let him live if he cornered you instead of an official match."

"I don't kill people for shits and giggles. They die in the pit or if I'm getting paid to do it, no other reason." I sigh, shoving the vial of helion in my pocket. "And of course if they threaten my life or anyone I care about."

Orion snorts, shaking his head. "It looked like the pit boss had it out for you during that fight."

"That obvious?" He nods. "I don't know what the fuck he's playing at. He has no reason to target me like that. I bring in a decent crowd and lots of money. He should be thanking me, not putting me into situations like that."

"You really should try to wean yourself off that shit. It's going to end up killing you," he says, nodding towards the bulge in my pocket.

"Coming from the guy who sells it to anyone who has the money to pay for it," I snort.

"I've known you for a while now, Eris. I just don't want to see you getting hurt."

"In my line of work, getting hurt is a given. I appreciate access to having an edge."

His brows furrow in confusion. "Do you use that during fights?"

"No. I try to keep the fights as fair as possible, but the pits aren't my job, Orion. I deal with a lot of unsavory people, so having better access to my powers is beneficial."

"You seem pretty strong for a typical Fae."

"Who said I was typical?" I grin. He laughs off my comment, like it's not the actual truth. "Pleasure doing business with you," I say, patting the counter and heading out before he decides to pry further.

I know using helion is dangerous and addictive, but my powers need the boost. The basics of my ability work just fine, but the stealth aspect isn't where it should be. Traveling through the void space takes a toll on me, and if I have any chance of succeeding in slipping into court unnoticed, I need the shit to boost that part of me. If I don't use it, I gas out after one jump, and I can't risk getting stuck in that fucking house or running into someone I don't want to run into.

I have a love and hate relationship with helion. The drug was developed a few years ago, synthesized in the same way float was made. I have no idea how it would affect a human. Float could kill a human, but it works on the system differently in comparison. Helion targets power, enhancing it beyond its normal level, even if it's temporary. Of course, dark world kind would trip over themselves to get it, but the side effects are a bitch to deal with. Little by little, it chips away at your life energy, burning through it by pushing it to its limits.

My phone starts buzzing in my pocket, forcing me to dig for it in the admittedly too tight pants. "Nox," I sigh. "I'm headed home shortly."

"Do you mind picking up some beer? I forgot while I was out and I'm in the middle of making dinner."

"Such a good roomie," I snort. "Sure, I'll head there now and see you in a bit. What's for dinner?"

"Steak and mashed potatoes. I figured I needed to make it up to you for the dirt breakfast."

A deep laugh rumbles from my chest, my cheeks hurting from the smile he's able to pull from me. "It wasn't *that* bad."

"I promise not to use beets again," he chuckles. "See you in a bit."

Fuck, I love him. Honestly, I don't know where I would be if I didn't meet him and become friends with him. He's been the one to keep my head above water, keeping the darkness inside of me at bay.

The first couple of years weren't the best, and I did lie to him to start. I denied what he saw when I stumbled out of court, not like it proved anything, and that was before they upped their security anyways. I think he saw right through me, but he accepted my answer and went about life with me like it didn't matter. It didn't matter, and he proved that later on. He didn't truly find out who I was until six months into living together. He heard me screaming in my sleep, bolting into my room to see if I was okay, only to come face to face with me in my full form. Not just the wings, but the power level that comes from those that are of true royal blood.

We can't hide our wings or what they represent. The leathery texture is a dead giveaway of two things. He was either living with a darkling, or a royal of the Night Court. The latter was less terrifying, and surprisingly, he accepted me for who I was. I trust him more than I do my own family. He accepted me—didn't judge me—and that's all I could ask of him. I wouldn't have blamed him if he wanted to leave, I expected him to, but he's gone above and beyond in making me feel wanted.

I blame myself for being so lost in my own thoughts that I don't notice the solid object I run into the moment I turn the corner. Well, not completely solid, if the squeak of surprise and the thud followed by a very unsexy grunt is any indication. I stare at her sprawled on the ground, rubbing her ass.

"Are you stalking me?" I chirp.

She tips her head up, eyes widening in surprise for a moment before settling into a frown. "If I were stalking you, I wouldn't be getting plowed into by you." I smirk at the comment and her cheeks flush at the hidden inuendo. "Pervert."

"You're the one who said it," I snort.

"Yeah, but *your* mind went there."

"So did yours if you clued in that quickly, so who's the pervert now? Do the thoughts of me *plowing into you* invade your little daydreams?" I hold out my hand to her, but she slaps it away, climbing to her feet on her own.

She wipes at her clothes with rough swipes, huffing out a disgruntled breath. "I don't think about you at all," she snaps.

Ouch. I guess this infatuation is only one-sided. Can I even call it infatuation at this point? Would I like to get into her pants? Absolutely, but I'm not going to allow myself to do that because I know better. Hook-ups are fantastic, but only with the guarantee that I'll never see them again. I can't form attachments, not with the high risk of someone finding out who I am. It's better for me and everyone else that she's not interested in me.

"My mistake," I murmur, stepping back from her when she turns to face me again. I step around her, trying to get as far away from this situation as I can.

"Eris!" She calls out, but I ignore her, lengthening my step so she's not tempted to follow.

CHAPTER 8

TAMZIN

"You're being pretty quiet." Nox's voice rips me from my thoughts, my glazed eyes focusing in on him across from me, a frown deepening the line between his brows. "Did something happen today?"

"No, nothing," I say quickly. "Sorry, I'm just feeling a bit drained today. I'm hoping to get everything in order so I can break into court tomorrow. I just want this job done and over with as quickly as possible."

"I got the layout on the security system today and the magical blueprints of the warding. I'll work on finding a weakness in the barrier in the morning so you can warp in without a problem."

"I shouldn't need more than a few seconds in the spells. Plus, any longer than that and it might bring attention to the witches within the walls." Who am I kidding, they'll probably know the instant those wards falter, even *if* it's only for a few seconds. This is so stupid. I really shouldn't have accepted this job, but curiosity really did get the better of me.

"We need to have perfect timing on this then. Once you're within range, I'll give you a countdown. How long do you think you'll need in order to find the amulet?"

"I have no idea. I wish I had more to go on than just the picture, but I should still be able to make it work. I'll have to push my tracking ability."

He frowns, settling back into his chair while he studies me. "What do you mean? Usually, you need a scent in order to track, so in this case, you would need the magical signature tied to the amulet."

Fuck, he's going to be so pissed. "I'll use a bit more helion to amplify that part of me." His eyes widen. "Don't start—"

"Tamzin! You can't keep using that shit! I thought you went off the stuff."

"I only use it when I need it, and for this, I need it, Nox. You know how unstable my warping ability can be."

"Have you ever thought that *maybe* the helion is making it so you can't actually gain control over that part of yourself? If you keep relying on a drug for control, you're going to end up losing control in the process."

I *have* considered it, but at this point, does it even matter? Right now, I don't have time to hone my skills. I never really had a need for it since it's not like we do a lot of snatch and grabs, and if I use the void on my own, I usually give myself enough time to recover before I have to use it again.

"I'll be fine, Nox," I say, hating seeing the worry etched into his features. This is the downside to friendships. Having someone to care about, and in turn, someone who cares about you, too. I never want him to feel responsible for my actions or my fate, but he takes everything I do to heart.

"Are you trying to die?" He snaps. "Nothing about this is fine, Tam."

"I'll be fine," I say again, fixing my eyes on his, willing him to understand. I've put myself in plenty of dangerous situations, and sure he's worried, but he seems truly shaken about the fact I've been using helion to gain an advantage over my power.

"Until you're not," he murmurs, dropping his gaze back to his plate.

I watch as he pokes around his food, shifting the potatoes around absentmindedly. "You're not telling me something." He stiffens, his fork clattering to the plate loud enough to make him flinch at the sound. "Nox."

"I never told you the truth about my mother," he whispers.

What truth? I knew she died the year I met him, I just assumed it was something to do with her pack. Nox is a rare occurrence. Hybrids of any combination were rare, but times have changed, and more are being created. Most supernaturals breed with their own kind, where some go the mortal route. He's extraordinary, Fae and shifter blood, melding into one powerful supernatural being. Hybrids like him are unpredictable in the sense no one knows what their powers will become. Will they take on all abilities, any of the weaknesses straddling either side of the coin? The strongest hybrid to this day is an archangel crossed with a shifter, her shifter soul being a true alpha. All the powers, and none of the typical weaknesses, she's a force to be reckoned with.

"I didn't know until it was too late. She got addicted to the stuff. Her pack was into some shady stuff and was handing it out to their members like a fucking energy boost. By the time I noticed the symptoms, it was too late. She burnt out...her heart gave out."

Fuck. He's got a personal tie to the effects of helion, and he's waited until now to tell me? He let me use it for the last three years, only making subtle hints on how bad it is. I already knew that. I went into it knowing full well what the side effects were, but I wasn't using it enough to warrant his concerns.

"I promise to be careful, Nox."

"I would feel better if you just stopped using it."

"I can't do that. Not yet."

"Why?! Why the fuck do you think you need it? You're strong enough on your own, Tam. You're addicted to it, and you won't fucking admit it to me!"

"I'm not addicted!" I snarl, flinching at the anger in my own voice.

He shakes his head, tossing his napkin down on his half-eaten plate. His chair drags back loudly against the tile floor. "Where are you going?"

"I can't do this right now," he murmurs, dumping his dinner into the trash. He says nothing else, and I just stare at his retreating back as he heads for his room. The door slams loudly, the sound resonating right into my soul.

The last thing I wanted to do was upset him. Nox puts up with a lot of my bullshit, supporting me in most of my stupid decisions. The guilt I feel in my heart is heavy, knowing that I'm causing him unneeded pain because of the helion. I can stop—I *will* stop—just not yet. I won't let it get to the point where I lose sight of myself.

I glance up when his door opens again, my mouth opening to say something, but stopping short when he doesn't even spare me a glance as he makes his way to the door. "Where are you going?"

"Out," he says in a clipped tone, grabbing his jacket from the coatrack.

"Nox—"

"I don't want to hear it, Tam."

He slips out the door, and the weight of my guilt presses down even further. Knowing him, he's going to Transcend again. He frequents the club more than I do. I was never a huge fan of places like that, preferring smaller pubs with live music versus the thrumming beats and sweating bodies that shove themselves into dance clubs. I have to be in the mood to go to a place like that, and as much as I'm *not* in the mood for it, I can't let our night end with him being angry with me.

CHAPTER 9

TAMZIN

The line up into the club is asinine, wrapping around the building like a warning sign to stay the fuck away. Sighing, I step out of line and make my way around the building into the alley, hiding myself in the shadows along the wall. Closing my eyes, I focus on what I remember of the layout of the place. I haven't been here for at least two months, but I doubt they've done any major renovations.

A scream of shock and surprise greets me when I pop in near the bathrooms, the vampire in front of me spooking enough that his fangs descend. "Sorry," I chuckle, patting him on the shoulder.

I sense his gaze on me as I walk past him into the bustling crowd in the club. I could have just wiped his memory of that, but he's supernatural and shouldn't be worried or surprised by something like that happening. My eyes close, the need to scent for Nox strong in my core, but I stop short, shaking my head. I shouldn't be here, not like this. He's probably going to be pissed off when he sees me here, knowing I don't come to this place willingly. He had to physically drag me the last time and thought better of it since.

I head for the bar instead, casually scanning the bouncing patrons on the dance floor. "What can I get ya?" The bartender asks. My eyes drift to him and he quirks a brow in question. My nostrils flare, scenting him, and he frowns. "What?"

"Nothing, force of habit. Can I get a pint of dark lager?"

"Sure," he says, giving me a tight smile.

Even with all the different scents of dark worlders in here, and even some humans, I caught his without a problem. Part human, part reaper of all things. I don't run into reapers very often, but the sickly scent of death associated with them is too prominent to ignore. I'm curious if his reaper parent actually parented. They don't often come into our world in their true form, resorting to possessing humans. It takes a lot of energy to pull themselves completely from their realm, a rift between worlds.

He slides over the glass, and I hand him a bill. "Keep the change."

He tips his head to me in thanks, giving me a real smile this time. I return it, grabbing my glass as I sit into one of the stools at the bar, turning it to face the crowd. My eyes scan the area over and over again, trying to pick up on Nox's dashing good looks instead of relying on my tracker senses. It feels like hours before I finally spot him, his dark hair gleaming in the strobing lights as he smiles and leans in towards a blonde female.

At least he's not sulking and is enjoying his night—even if it's away from me. He deserves to be happy, and I've been nothing but a miserable prick. He's always telling me to lighten up, to enjoy life while I can. I used to be more than what I am now, my family slowly squashing my spirit sort of ruined my personality, but I've been getting better. Little by little, my old self has started to show through once more, and that's because of him.

"Eris." I stiffen at the female voice next to me and slowly turn my head. She gives me a weak smile, pointing to the seat next to me. "May I?"

"I don't make the seating arrangements. You can sit wherever the fuck you want." I suck in a sharp breath when she climbs up onto my lap, facing me. "What the fuck are you doing?"

"You just said I can sit where I want," she chirps, a smile tugging at the corner of her lips.

This little shit. A sly little fox indeed. I lean away from her, chugging back the rest of my beer. "You know very well what I meant." She shrugs, running her fingers and those damn nails down my chest. "Get off."

"Is that what you want?"

"I'm saying it, aren't I?" She shifts herself closer, the heat of her radiating into my cock. "What are you *doing?*"

"Getting off," she gasps, gripping into my shoulder. My eyes widen, darting around to see if anyone is watching what the fuck is happening right now. Who the fuck *is* this girl?

"Kalia," I grunt, slamming my eyes shut, trying to tamper down the raging boner growing in my pants. "Stop," I grit out.

Surprisingly, she does. A whimper slips through my lips, and I slowly open my eyes to see her golden ones staring back at me in amusement. "So, you *don't* want me to get off?"

"Get. Off. *Of. Me*. Right fucking now." A puff of disgruntled air slips through her lips and she slowly slides herself off my lap. Gripping into my jeans, I rearrange myself, struggling to hide the still prominent erection straining against the material. "What the fuck are you doing here?"

"It's a club, what do you think I'm doing?" She says, settling into the stool next to me and calling over the bartender. "Can I get a vodka and soda water, and another drink for my friend here."

"I don't need you buying me drinks."

"I seem to be upsetting you on a regular basis, it's the least I can do."

The least she could do would be leaving me the fuck alone, but maybe that's too much to ask for. Seriously, her sudden presence is sending off so many warning bells, but she seems so unassuming. Gorgeous, but unassuming. I must be reading too much into this.

A hushed murmur drifts through the crowd, drawing my attention to the door. Ice settles into my veins at the sight of Dorian, Croh, and Helia walking in. Croh's eyes scan the club, and I turn in my stool quickly, ducking my head down.

"Do you have an issue with the royals?" Kalia asks. "I'm surprised they're here. I didn't think they socialized outside of court."

"They don't," I say quietly. "I need to go." I glance over my shoulder, noticing them beelining their way towards Nox. Panic hits me when I see his face pale, his eyes darting around frantically. How the fuck do they know him so easily? Have they been fucking watching me? I can't let this happen. I can't let him get involved with my fucked-up family. I bolt off my stool, shoving my way through the crowd towards them and hearing Kalia call out my name behind me.

"Nox Shepard," Croh murmurs, his deep timber voice carrying over the pounding music around us. Nox swallows, his wide eyes fixed on Croh's.

His eyes dart to me the moment I settle my hand on Croh's shoulder. He slowly turns to look at me, one of his perfectly shaped brows going up in surprise. "Leave him alone," I murmur. "Your issue is with me, not him."

"Eris," Nox says quickly. I shake my head, giving him an apologetic look.

"I'll handle this. I'm sorry, Nox."

"Eris?" Croh chuckles. "Too ashamed to go by your actual name, *Tamzin*." A couple of people closer to us gasp, leaning in closer to each other to whisper amongst themselves, no doubt about me being the reject son of the Fae royals.

"Can we take this outside, *please*."

He gives me a wicked grin but nods his head. Nox tries to follow us out, but I shake my head. I don't want him getting in the crosshairs if this goes sideways. Everyone parts, giving us space to make our way outside.

"You've been on your own long enough," he says once we're a few feet away from the entrance to Transcend. "Don't you think it's time for you to take responsibility and play your roll?"

"How did you find me?" I murmur, keeping myself a safe distance from them. My eyes settle on Helia, sadness creasing her eyes.

"We miss you, Tam," she says, her voice actually sounding sincere.

"No, you don't. I'm nothing but a nuisance to everyone, so what possible reason could there be to miss me?"

She opens her mouth to speak, stepping closer to me, but Dorian grips her arm hard enough to make her wince. She drops her eyes to the ground, submitting to his hold.

"You're an embarrassment to our house," Croh snarls. "Romping around in filthy holes like this one, among other things."

"Have you been following me?"

"Following, no. We've just been keeping an eye on you."

"No one knows who I am, or at least they didn't up until you opened your big fucking mouth."

"Watch your tone, *boy*. I'm older and stronger than you, and you will show me some respect."

"Older, sure. Stronger? That's still up for debate." My hands curl into fists at my sides, holding back the urge to throttle his ass just to prove a point.

"You *will* come home!"

"Make me."

He steps towards me, ice particles forming at his fingertips, but stops short just as I feel an arm slide through mine. Glancing down, I frown at the girl standing next to me. Her black hair, cut into a sharp bob, gleams in the light of the moon, flickering with a reddish iridescence. Who the fuck—

"We should get going, babe," she coos, tipping her head back to look at me.

My throat dries, clamping around the words I was about to speak. Those eyes...those ethereal golden eyes that have been haunting me for the last twenty-four hours. A crowd of people streams out of the club, Nox and a couple of other guys and girls coming towards us as well.

"It's getting late," Nox says. "We have a long day tomorrow, so we should head back." I glance back at him, flicking my gaze to the two burly Fae flanking him now, their arms slung across their female's shoulders. Nox has a girl with him, too, the one he was talking to when I first noticed him.

"This isn't over," Croh hisses, stepping towards me and gripping the front of my shirt in his fist. His ice spreads from his hand into me, and I'm fighting back the sting of pain from the frigid touch of his power.

Kalia grips into his wrist, and seconds later, Croh is flinching back, his eyes darting to her. "Don't touch him," she snaps, brushing the wrinkles from my shirt and settling her hand on my chest.

"Do you know who I am?" He says, his voice dripping with venom.

"Croh, we should go," Dorian murmurs, nodding his head behind me. A small crowd of people is now forming, drawn out here as word spread of three of the royal children being present in the lower district. "Father will be upset about this type of attention."

"Yes, run along home to daddy. I'm sure you don't want a royal spanking," I sneer, gripping into Kalia's hip and pulling her back a step, closer to Nox and the others.

"You *will* come home, one way or another."

"Don't threaten me," I growl, my voice dropping dangerously low as my shadows pulse around me. He grins a wicked grin, backing up closer to Dorian. Helia glances up at me, granting me a sad smile. "Helia," I whisper.

"I—" Dorian cuts her off again, yanking her back hard enough she stumbles over her feet.

Why the fuck did they bring her? Was it to torture me? To lure me with my need to protect my only sister. She's suffered plenty in all her years, having to submit to the archaic Fae way of life. Why wasn't Cam with them? He would have never allowed Helia to be treated that way, especially in public. He was the only reason I felt comfortable in leaving my home, at knowing he would protect her for as long as he needed to. This is not protection, it's fucking subjugation. I'm going to kick his ass the next time I fucking see him.

My eyes stay trained on their retreating forms, the breath I was holding finally escaping my lungs when they disappear from view. I can't keep the tremble from my body, but I look down at Kalia, still gripping my arm. I slip away from her, earning a frown and a pout from her beautiful face.

"A glamour?" I ask, waving to her hair.

"One of my many tricks."

"Why would you need to glamour yourself?"

"I don't need to draw their attention to me," she snaps, stepping back. "I was trying to help you without putting a target on my back." Her suddenly defensive tone has my skin burning with anger. She crosses her arms over her chest, perking her tits up in the barely there top. "*Tamzin*," she says bluntly.

"Eris," I correct.

She juts her chin towards the area where Croh and the others disappeared. "*He* called you Tamzin."

Fuck her and her Fae hearing. This is making me want to pack up all my shit and disappear from this place. "He was mistaken," I say carefully.

She lifts a brow. "A Fae Prince mistakes someone for his own *brother*? Why are you lying to me?"

"I'm not," I lie. "I'm actually quite flattered that my sexy bod and killer good looks were enough to trick the Fae brats."

"Ready to go?" Nox says, interrupting Kalia from whatever jab she was planning to nail me with next.

Glancing over to him, I notice the female he was with walking away with the others. "No tail tonight?" I tease.

“I think I have my hands full with you.” His eyes drift to Kalia. “Will she be coming? You look familiar.”

“Not tonight,” I say quickly, stepping towards him and draping my arm across his shoulders.

“Fucker,” she mutters as we walk away. I spare a glance back at her, her hair now back to its red hue and waist length.

CHAPTER 10

TAMZIN

"What was that about?" Nox asks the moment we hit our street.

"I'm sorry you were dragged into that. I didn't expect to see them there."

"I didn't expect to see *you* there. What the fuck were you doing at Transcend? You hate that place."

Guilt washes over me once again. "I wanted to make sure you were okay. I don't like being in a fight with you, and I know I hurt you, Nox."

"You did, but I always end up forgiving you. You didn't need to follow me."

"I did. It was the right thing to do. I don't know how Croh even knows what you look like. I don't know how they know *anything*. They must have someone watching me, it's the only thing that makes sense."

"What do you want to do about it?"

"I'm not sure. I don't trust them. Croh and Dorian least of all, and I don't like the way they're treating Helia."

"Still as hot as ever," he muses. I shove him playfully. He laughs, staggering to the side at the force of it. "You have to admit, I would be a better option for her to be hanging out with in comparison to your brothers."

"You would, I won't deny that, but she's still a Fae Princess of the Night Court and she would end up ruining you, Nox."

"Always my protector," he chuckles. "You didn't have to come to my rescue tonight either. It's not like Croh could have actually done anything to me."

"He could and he would. If he has his sights set on you, it's not a good thing. You need to try and lie low for a bit if you can."

"So, I can't go out without a bodyguard?" He smirks. "How did I get so lucky in having someone care about me *so* much?"

"You're ridiculous, but yes on all counts. Of course I care about you. You've been more of a brother to me than my actual brothers, and I don't want to see you getting hurt, especially because of me."

"Who was that girl? Pretty ballsy of her to step in like that. Croh looked about ready to kill her for touching him. I don't think I've ever seen a Fae Prince recoil from a female that fast, least of all one who was as hot as her."

I can't hide my smile at his comment. Of course he didn't recognize her. He was too focused on getting into her pants last night that he clearly missed the way her eyes glitter like a setting sun, how her irises have an internal glow to them, like molten lava trying to seep out from their rings. She could change everything about her body—every single thing—but I would recognize her instantly because of those eyes. I don't know if she didn't push the glamour to her eyes on purpose, or if it's something she just can't manage. I'd like to think the former, meaning she expected me to recognize her because of those unforgettable eyes.

"Just a random girl," I say, not wanting to make him feel like shit for not recognizing her with a glamour. He's not as psychotic about the details as I am. Yes, I'm admitting I'm psychotic, but it's not like I've *really* denied it.

"She seemed pretty into you. I'm surprised you didn't bring her home with you. Come to think of it, you haven't brought anyone home since that one girl. What was her name again?"

Catia. That was two weeks ago, and after what happened at the pit, I'm almost tempted to swear off women all together. I say that, but my mind wanders to the little fox in the club, climbing onto my lap and rubbing up against me because I don't think before I speak.

"I don't remember," I lie. I seem to be doing that a lot lately. Lying shouldn't come so easily, but I blame it on my upbringing.

"That's not like you. You usually remember everyone's name." He frowns, staring at me while he holds the door open to our apartment complex.

"Does it matter?" I sigh.

"If it really doesn't matter to you, it doesn't matter to me. I can't really say anything. I don't put a lot of effort into remembering my random hookups either."

I follow him into the apartment, quietly closing the door behind me. "Are we okay?" I ask, my heart thrumming loudly in my ears as I try to tamper down the anxiety that I feel in remembering why he left earlier.

He turns to face me, his eyes focused on mine. I squirm a bit under that scrutinizing gaze, hating how weak I feel in needing his forgiveness and approval. "For now," he says slowly. My shoulder droop. Not the answer I was hoping for, but I'll take what I can get. "Promise me you'll stop using."

"I will, Nox. I promise I will," I say quickly, and I mean it. I don't want a stupid drug to be the thing that comes between our friendship.

He strides towards me, wrapping his arms around me tightly. His grip trembles, but it's firm, showing me how much this whole thing means to him. He lost his mom to this stupid drug for fuck's sake, and here I am, using it like the rules don't apply to me.

"I'm going to bed," he mumbles, pulling back and trying to subtly wipe at his eyes.

"Hey." I grip into his arm, forcing him to look at me.

He laughs, trying to brush off the fact that he's crying. "I'm just emotional. I had too much to drink."

"Don't. Don't do that, please. There's nothing wrong with being upset or showing emotions, Nox." I say it and I wholeheartedly believe it. All my life I was told emotions were a weakness. That crying for any reason made me fucking weak, but it's the opposite. Showing emotion shows how strong you really are. It shows someone how much you care—that you've had enough of an impact on their life that they feel that strongly about you. I pull him towards me, wrapping my arms around him one more time. His sob gets muffled against my shoulder, and his emotions tear at me, ripping me apart from the inside out.

"I'll see you in the morning," he whispers, pulling back again with his eyes trained on the ground.

"Get some sleep."

I watch as he quietly makes his way to his bedroom, the urge to break something has me curling my hands into fists. I'm not angry at anyone but myself. No, that's a lie. I'm angry at Croh and Dorian and even fucking Helia. They came into *my* life and tried to ruin what I've built away from them. I've never asked them for anything, never had a need or desire to reach out to my parents for help. I've done fine on my own, earning my own money and carving my own path. I hate that I was born into that fucked-up family. Cam was the only one I really got along with, similar to me in many ways, but too chicken shit to do anything about the wrongs he witnesses.

The twins, Lex and Flynn, are no better than Croh, but they're more discreet about their hatred and cruelty in the public eye. Twin shadows of death, the assassins of the royal Court. I'm still waiting for them to show up on my doorstep like the wannabe reapers that they are. Their hatred for me isn't unwarranted, since the last time I saw them, I gave them twin matching scars. That was the last straw, the final piece in the puzzle for me to make the decision to leave.

Father thought they were stronger than me, too. Using them to force me into submission, but I refused to submit, refuse to bend to their hellish rule and the way they continue to corrupt the ideals of what a Fae royal should be. What I wouldn't give to be in a different house, one that appreciates the Fae within their realm and cherish their abilities and what they have to offer as citizens of the realm. King Paxton and Queen Guinevere are a joke, wanting nothing more than unwavering fealty, no matter the cost.

My mind doesn't want to settle, my eyes fixed on the ceiling above me. I can't help but smile at the glowing stars in the darkness, stickers that Nox thought were hilarious to put up in our rooms. I never had anything like this growing up as a boy, I mean, why would I? Born in the times before technology was created, living through different times has been an interesting experience. I love this world and its people. How much society has developed, even with the hardships that very society has to endure. Humans are fascinating creatures, though very few are as good as they portray themselves to be.

Within those glowing stars, two seem to shine brighter, morphing into halos of gold. She had no reason to come to my aid tonight, and it's not like she asked for anything in return. She gripped into Croh without a second thought, not even registering the danger she put herself in with that move.

Kalia. Who the fuck is she and where did she come from? I mean, I know she's from the Autumn territory, but why does it seem like our paths keep crossing? Maybe she *is* a stalker. I snort at the thought, rolling over onto my side and curling up against the pillow.

CHAPTER 11

TAMZIN

Looks like *I'm* the one turning into a stalker. I have no reason to be here, none at all, not after the massive breakfast Nox made this morning. He went all out, shoving plates of bacon, eggs, sausages, and even pancakes towards me with a giddy smile on his face. He's one hundred percent boyfriend material, and anyone will be beyond lucky to finally have him as the perfect catch.

The line into the Hub is still pretty long this morning, but I throw myself into it anyways, just for the chance to see her again this morning. I left things pretty miserable last night, snapping at her when I had no reason to do so. Of course she was curious about what happened. It would be weirder if she wasn't, since it isn't every day that the Fae royals randomly show up at a club and call out their brother who is hiding in secret from society.

I catch a glimpse of her red hair in the distance, my heart thrumming in my chest like a fucking teenager with a crush. I'm surprised to see Shahar behind the counter as well helping Kylo, her gothic aesthetic a high contrast to the clean, simplistic style of the Hub. She catches sight of me, smiling widely. She nudges her husband in the ribs hard enough for him to grunt out a breath of surprise. He looks over and I give him an awkward wave.

"Eris!" He calls out happily. "I thought I told you to message me for your order!"

"I—" I get shoved forward, bumped into by a small child, who almost got my wrath when I spun around to face her. Her wide eyes on the verge of tears at the fury in my gaze, squashed all my anger instantly. Shifting out of line, I make it over to the side counter. "I wasn't planning on coming. Nox made a big breakfast, but I thought I should stop in anyways just to see how you guys were making out."

My eyes drift over to Kalia, but she's ignoring me completely. She smiles at the customer at the counter, handing over some change and signalling for him to go over to the other counter to wait for his order. My eyes linger on her slender fingers, tucking a stray strand of hair behind her ear. That smile, no matter how small it is, lights up her face, bringing a glimmer to her eyes.

"We're doing okay. Kalia has improve a lot in just a day, so we're handling the influx a lot better than yesterday. I still called Shahar in to ease some of the strain. Do you want me to grab you a coffee at least?"

"No, that's okay. You still have a decent line."

"Eris, it's not problem at all, just give me a few minutes and I'll get you a quad espresso."

"Thank you," I smile. He nods his head and heads back to make my order. My eyes drifting to Kalia once again.

"Kylo told me what you did for her yesterday." I startle at Shahar's voice, snapping my head away from Kalia when I notice her turning to look at me.

"What?"

"That guy that was trying to start shit in here. He said you went feral on him and then ended up sticking around through the morning rush to help out. I really appreciate you doing that."

"It was nothing," I murmur, hating the fact that I feel my cheeks heat with embarrassment.

"You're not giving yourself enough credit, Eris. That was very sweet of you." Her eyes drift over to Kalia, a sly grin spreading across her face. "No matter what your actual motives may have been."

"What?"

"You're sweet on her, aren't you?"

No," I say quickly. "I just don't appreciate assholes treating people like that. She did nothing wrong. She's new and she was learning, and people need to learn patience when it comes to shit like that. What's the fucking rush? That's all people do theses days, rushing around and losing sight of what it truly means to live."

"Ah, you see the world for what it is then, something that should be enjoyed and not taken for granted."

"Life itself shouldn't be taken for granted. You would think the dark worlders would be the worst for it, having lives that last centuries longer than the mortals, but it's the humans I see doing it more often. They work and rush and run themselves into the ground. Fleeting lives that they don't even get to enjoy, it's fucking miserable to think about."

"That it is," she smiles.

"Your coffee."

I glance over to see Kalia walking up to Shahar, her eyes down as she holds the cup out to me. "Thank you," I murmur, taking the cup from her. My fingers graze against hers and she quickly pulls back, turning away without another word.

Kylo is watching her with furrowed brows, Shahar tipping her head in question. So that behaviour *isn't* normal for her. She's definitely upset with me, but I did it to myself with my fucking attitude. I slide a bill across the counter to Shahar, and she gives me a small smile.

"Have a good day, Shahar."

"You as well, Eris. Try and stay out of trouble."

I give her a mischievous grin. "Me?" I laugh. "You know that'll never happen." I give her a wave and one to Kylo as well. Kalia is watching me, her eyes betraying nothing of her emotions right now.

I tip my head to her, turning away without waiting to see if she acknowledges it at all.

CHAPTER 12

KALIA

It should be illegal to look that good this early in the morning. I thought after last night, he would try to avoid coming here—avoid *me*. I know I pushed it too far when I tried prying the truth from him, but is it so wrong for me to want to *know* the truth, and to hear it from him?

I came here for one reason, a stupid one at that, and one I wish I could get out of. I know all about Tamzin—the fallen Prince, the outcast of the Night Court. I knew it was him the moment I saw him at his apartment. I knew it was him in the pit. Others might be blind to the power that lurks beneath the surface of that perfect skin—that perfect fucking body—but I'm not blind. I'm good at seeing what others can't, picking up on the subtle tells that people try to hide.

"Kalia, you can take your break now," Kylo says, startling me out of my thoughts. I glance around, not realizing that the line has finally gone away, my body naturally going through the motions now. "Are you alright?" He asks, concern lacing his voice now.

"I'm fine," I squeak out. "Just trying to get used to the high pace of the place."

He chuckles, pulling out some supplies from one of the cabinets to prep for lunch. "I promise this isn't the norm. Usually, we get a third of what we've been getting in the morning. Business isn't slow, but it's definitely not *this*."

"I guess those influencers really loved the place," I smile, trying my best to edge him away from my stray thoughts.

"Apparently so," he chuckles.

"I'll be back in fifteen." I run back to the break room and grab my carton of smokes, darting out the back door into the alley.

That first puff hits me like a brick, smothering my senses in the luscious pull of nokweed. I can't believe that asshole was able to smell it even with the mint lacing I put into it. I smile, remembering the surprise on his face when he snagged it from me and took a hit. I'm sure he never expected someone like me to be smoking it, least of all during work hours. He would be even more surprised if he knew anything about me beyond what I've allowed him to see.

Playing the forward route doesn't seem to be granting me the attention I expected. I've heard the rumours about him, how easy he can be to get into bed, so I didn't expect him to be so...tame. After his reaction last night, I resolved myself to try the lesser route. Not one completely playing hard to get, but I know he's interested. Maybe he's actually shy and the rumours were false. He hasn't hooked up with anyone since that twat Catia from what I've gathered. I know he's unattached—a Fae Prince, hiding his identity, wouldn't get seriously involved with someone and risk them finding out who he truly is.

He's probably afraid of how I'll react in knowing the truth. Does he think I'll take advantage of him? It's not like he's living like the royals or with them in the center Court, so what advantage would there really be in trying to get him for his title. He's the youngest of six, a spec in the royal name. He'll never see the crown, not as long as all the others are still in existence. I like him better than any of the others, Croh being the worst of them, fucking prick. He dared to put hands on Tam for no fucking reason. I should have incinerated him for that, but Tam would have been upset with me. He needs to see me for me first. He needs to understand and make the choice for himself.

He could be so much more if he just put in the effort to do so, but he's off playing the stupid game of fighting in the pits, releasing his pent-up rage, and subjecting himself to the disdain of hunting. Such a shame. He deserves so much more for all he's suffered—for what they turned him into. I'll play his little game, for now.

CHAPTER 13

TAMZIN

"I'm in position," I murmur. The earpiece squeals loudly. "Fucking hell," I grit out, tapping the piece again.

"You good?" Nox's voice crackles through, clearing up the sound vibrating through my skull.

"Fucking earpiece had a reverb," I grumble. "Did you hear me?"

"Yeah, you're in position. Give me a couple of minutes and I'll let you know when you're clear to go."

I stare at the boundary to the compound, the magical barrier glittering in the night sky, hidden to the mortal eye, but felt by every supernatural within range. Looks like they've upgraded their defenses since I was last within these walls. Fuck, this is such a pain. The fact the barrier is so far from the actual compound is going to make it a problem. I have a lot of ground to cover once Nox weakens the wall enough for me to sneak through, but with my void jumping I should be able to get within the walls once I'm through.

"Once the barrier is down, you'll have ten seconds to get through. I don't know if the barrier will interfere with our communication though."

"Drop the barrier in an hour." I glance down at my watch. "At ten after, Nox, drop it. If I'm through, great. If I'm not—"

"I'm not leaving you in there," he snarls, and surprise radiates through me at his tone.

"There's nothing you can do if we lose communication. If I get caught, you go."

"No."

"Nox—"

"No, Tam. I'm not fucking leaving you."

"Guess I need to make sure I get the fuck out then."

"I wish you would have let me come with you," he sighs.

"You're safer at a distance. I didn't need them spotting you and using you against me. Stay where you are and I'll see you soon."

"Fine. The barrier will be down in a minute."

I grab the bottle of helion, dripping two drops under my tongue. The effects are almost instantaneous, its magic manipulation coursing through my veins like molten lava. I shudder at the feeling, dropping the visor on my car. Dark rings settle around my irises, bleeding into them for a moment before flaring with iridescent light. This is different from my natural power flare, the tone shifting to a subtle green, which shifts my blue eyes into an almost aqua tone now.

"Thirty seconds," Nox says quietly. I slip out of the car and make my way to the edge of the barrier. I can feel the ripple of power the closer I get to it, the heat of the magic nipping at my skin, pressing into me like a heavy weight. "Ten seconds." Taking a deep breath, I close my eyes, focusing in on his voice. "Five…four…three…two…"

"One," I sigh, opening my eyes and pushing through the barrier. It ripples and tugs at my skin, my teeth gritting together at the feeling of it trying to tear apart my skin. Fuck, this would have killed me if I tried getting in without it weakened. Leave it to Nox to merge technology and magic, creating a sort of magical virus that he can use like a computer program. It integrates itself into the magic itself. He's an idiot, but not when it comes to tech. Street smarts on the other hand…

The barrier ripples and flares behind me, the pressure of it snapping back into place rattling through my bones. There's nothing but static through the line now, a subtle hum that just amplifies the fact that I'm completely alone now. I move further away from the barrier, not wanting the use of my powers to trigger its sensors and alerting them of an intruder. I hope that Nox was able to keep the glitch in the system to a minimum, but if not, I definitely have less than the hour I asked for.

The contact, Den, sent all the information they had on the amulet. Apparently, it was sent over by the Autumn Court as some sort of peace offering, and it's being kept in one of the vaults. My father must not trust what it is, sensing the magic imbued within it and locking it away. I'm actually surprised he didn't have it destroyed, but it must be valuable enough to risk a possible breech.

My body is thrumming with power, coiled and on the verge of boiling over. I let it loose, allowing my shadows to swallow me up and carry me into the compound. I need to get as close as possible, and I picture the vault itself, willing my body to move where I need it to go. The air in my lungs rips out of me as my back hits the marble floor.

"Fuck," I grumble, pulling myself up to sit. I tip my head up, glaring at the gawdy golden doors in front of me. The material ripples with power, snapping out against the lingering remnants of shadow still cradling my skin. "Seriously?" I huff. The fucker really has trust issues if he has his fucking vault warded as well. I'm of royal blood, so anything and anywhere within this house should be accessible by me, and yet it's not. I really didn't want to have to do this, and I'll definitely be paying for it later, but they've left me no choice. "I'm sorry, Nox." Pulling out the vial of helion, I drip another two drops under my tongue.

I gasp, gritting my teeth at the influx of power burning in my veins. Normally, the effects last at least an hour, longer if you're not tapping into your powers and therefore your life force. The remnants from the previous drops are still in my system, the use of power to get in here not enough to drain the effects. Now? Now I'm fucking paying for it. I don't usually do more than two drops at a time, three if I'm desperate, but I'm *beyond* desperate right now. I can't risk being seeing or getting caught, and I have no other way of pushing through this barrier without Nox's help. He *can't* help me in here. I was on my own the moment I stepped onto the property, and I plan to keep it that way. The last thing I want is him running into the face of danger by coming in here.

My luck, he would run straight into Croh, and he would end Nox without a second thought the moment he saw him. I stagger to my feet, gritting my teeth as I step closer to the door. I don't actually remember much about the vault inside, and that could have also contributed to the fact I launched out of my void outside the place.

The ripple of spells snaps out against me when I step closer, and I close my eyes, drawing in a ragged breath to tamper down the edge of pain the drug is pushing through my system. A wave of power washes over me, my desperation urging me forward, ripping me into the void once more. The air feels electrically charge the moment I open my eyes to see the inside of the vault, loaded with treasure that would make the poor weep.

My lungs feel like they're in a vice, every breath feeling like shards of glass, but I push through it, not really having any other choice. I try to keep my focus, my eyes drifting to every piece of glittering gold and ornate silver in my path. My nostrils flair, trying to pull on any hint of magical essence in this fucking money pit. Closing my eyes, I force my senses to the one that matters right now. Magic. I need to feel for the magic, even if I don't know the exact signature that Enochian holds.

A tingling creeps across my senses, something unfamiliar, something that doesn't belong amongst all the other relics within. There. My eyes snap open, my feet moving of their accord through the rows and rows of jewels. The helion flares in my blood, pushing my tracker ability further until I come to a small box in the corner of the room. Slowly, I open the lid, my eyes widening at the amulet nestled within.

My hand trembles as I reach into it, carefully pulling it out. It looks almost exactly like the drawing, but the drawing is nothing compared to the real thing. The gemstone is beautiful, a rainbow obsidian surrounded by fine woven white gold. Runes are carved into the metal clamps encasing it, tiny fragments of diamonds wedged into random sections. It pulses with power within my palm, and I quickly shove it into my pocket. I check my watch, swearing when I realize how much time has actually passed.

How the fuck has it been almost an hour already? I got lost in the track, the helion blasting through my time without me realizing it. My body is still vibrating with power, and I pull on it now, launching myself into the void.

I scramble out of it a hundred yards from the boundary, my car glinting in the moonlight peeking through the clouds above. A crack of thunder rumbles through the earth beneath my feet, and I take off running. My breath wheezes through my lungs, but I push myself faster, glancing at my watch and watching the minutes tick down. Faster, I need to go faster. My lungs burn, my legs burn, my entire fucking body burns.

I feel it before I see it, the ripple in the barrier sending a current skating through the air. Glancing up, I notice the edges begin to waver. I glance at the watch again. 12:09. "Fuck," I huff, panting out ragged breaths as I push myself harder and harder, further and further. I watch the barrier waver in front of me, willing my body to keep moving. I close my eyes, pushing my body to its limits. The searing pain ripping and shredding at my skin has me gasping and grunting, but I keep going, collapsing to the ground when I feel the snap of power rip from me once again.

"Tam?! Tam?! Did you make it through. Fuck, please answer me! *Please!*"

The desperation and panic in his voice has my heart pounding frantically against my chest. I roll over onto my back, a heavy groan slipping through my lips. My hand trembles as I lift it to the earpiece, my heart breaking from the choked sob crackling through the line. "I'm here," I say breathlessly.

Another choked sob. "Tam," he whispers. "Thank fuck. Are you okay?"

"I've been better," I admit. A fork of lightning skitters across the sky above me, the sound of thunder vibrating through my body seconds later. The sky opens, a floodgate of rain falling from the ether above to pelt against my body. "Fuck," I grumble, shivering as the chilling rain seeps into my clothes right down to my bones. I welcome it, the cooling bliss of water calming the fire still burning in my blood from the drug.

"Did you get it?"

"Yeah," I sigh. "Send the text and set up a meeting. I want to get rid of this thing as soon as possible."

My teeth are chattering now, but I welcome the chill that's slowly creeping through my body as I sit up, dragging myself back to my feet. "Tam?" He says quietly. "How far did you push it?"

Guilt settles into me, my entire body shaking as I collapse into the seat of my car. "I'm fine, Nox."

"Okay." He says that, but I can tell he doesn't believe me, and that guilt pushes into me further and further, threatening to crush me into oblivion. "Let's get home."

"Okay."

CHAPTER 14

TAMZIN

"You look like shit," he murmurs the second we hit the elevator from the parking structure.

"I feel like shit." I can barely keep myself standing, leaning my body heavily into the railing of the elevator to keep myself propped up.

He clucks his tongue when my knees give out and I start to slide down the wall, and he quickly ducks himself under my arm, hoisting me back to my feet. My body feels like lead, my feet dragging with every step we take from the elevator to our apartment door. Nox grips into me harder, digging through his pocket for the key. This is one of the downsides to helion, especially in a dose like I took tonight. It's like you're literally feeling your life trickling away, bit by bit.

"You took it too far, Tam," he grumbles, nudging the door closed with his foot once we're through the threshold. "How much did you take?"

"I'm fine—"

"Stop fucking saying you're fine! *This* isn't fucking fine. You can't even stand on your own!"

"Yes, I can," I grumble, lurching away from him and regretting it instantly. My legs give out completely, my body crumpling to the ground like I have no connection to my limbs. "Fuck," I whimper.

"Idiot," he hisses. "Stop fucking lying to me." He drags me back up, grunting as he tosses me over his shoulder to carry me to my room like I'm a sack of potatoes.

"Put me down," I grumble, grunting when he drops me onto my bed like a dead weight.

"We're meeting with Den in the morning, so you need to get some sleep—let your body recover." I can barely lift my head as I watch him take off my shoes for me and then my socks. "Where's the amulet?"

"In my pocket," I say quietly, feeling embarrassed that he has to undress me like a fucking invalid. He tugs off my pants for me, reaching into the pocket of my jeans. The sadness on his face when he pulls out the vial of helion breaks my heart. His eyes drift to me, and I look away. He sighs, setting it down on my dresser before digging through the other pocket to pull out the amulet. "I have a chest that tampers down magic. I'll put it in there for now in case they notice it's missing and try to track it." Shoving it into his pocket, he helps me sit up so he can pull my shirt off of me and tugs the covers over my body. "Get some sleep."

"Nox?" I say quietly. He pauses at the door and glances back at me over his shoulder. "I don't deserve you."

A weak smile pulls at his lips, that sadness from earlier still showing in his eyes. "Maybe. Maybe not. I love you, man."

"I love you, too," I say without hesitation.

He turns off the lights to my room and closes the door, leaving it open a crack. I watch his shadow hovering just outside the door for a moment longer before it merges into the light from the living room. I sigh, my eyes landing on the bottle of helion on the nightstand. I definitely pushed it too far tonight, but I wouldn't have been able to do what I needed to without it. I wouldn't have made it into the vault, and even if I had pushed myself hard enough without it and managed to get in, there was no way in hell I was getting out of there.

I couldn't let that happen, especially after hearing the sadness in Nox's voice when he was frantically trying to contact me. Not after hearing the relief in that very same voice, the sob that escaped him in hearing that I made it out. He needs me just as much as I need him. He's my brother, one I've chosen and will do anything to protect. He's the reason I'm still fighting to have a life outside the confines of the Court, and I never want to be without him.

Something shatters in the kitchen. Closing my eyes, I pull on the last fragments of my power and scent the air, tasting Nox's aura. Pain, guilt, anger, sadness—every emotion swirling into one toxic fume that blasts into my senses. He's angry at me...no, he's angry at himself. Fuck me, he blames himself for what I'm going through right now. I can see how his mind works, the way he's playing out this scene in his head. If he hadn't have pushed to take on this job, I wouldn't have had to resort to the helion, and I wouldn't be lying in this bed, ready to fall into a coma for a few days.

It's not his fault and I would never blame him for any of this. This was still my decision. My curiosity is what spurred me into taking this job. My shitty needs are what pushed me to rely on an unstable drug. I'm the reason I'm lying here in this bed, feeling like my body is breaking apart bit by bit, not him—*never* him.

"Nox," I call out. He doesn't answer, and I wonder if my voice is too broken and too weak for him to hear me. I try to lift myself from the bed, but my arms shake under me, unable to bear the weight of my own body. "Fuck," I whimper.

The door sneaks open and Nox peeks his head inside. "Did you need something?" He asks, his voice sounding broken as well.

"Can you stay with me until I fall asleep?" I ask weakly. He frowns, opening the door a bit further. At first, I mulled over the request in my head in order to help him—to stop him from beating into himself for my stupid decisions. Now? I sort of like the idea of having him here with me. He's always *with* me, but the loneliness has gotten to me more than I care to admit.

"That's an odd request coming from you."

"You don't have to if you don't want to," I sigh, suddenly feeling a bit stupid for asking this of him.

"Why do you want me to?" I don't answer, curling further into my pillow. He takes another few steps into the room. "You can't be honest with me, can you?"

"I don't want to be alone right now," I admit. Hiding the truth won't get me anywhere, it'll just upset him more. He turns back around without a word, leaving my room. A shaky breath rattles through my lungs, the thought that I really fucked this up ripping through my mind. I see the light go off in the main area, his soft footfalls radiating through the silence in the apartment. I can still hear the distant sound of thunder, the storm slowly rolling over the city like a fleeting memory.

He comes back in a few minutes later, surprising me. I can see him in the darkness. He's changed into some sweats and a loose t-shirt, and my heart pounds heavily against my chest when he closes the door behind him. He crawls into bed behind me, letting out a heavy sigh.

"Thank you," I say quietly.

"You'll never be alone, Tam. I'll stay with you for as long as you need me."

"What if I need you forever?" I murmur, feeling my body relax further at the sound of his quiet voice.

"You won't. One day you'll figure things out, find yourself the perfect girl that brings out the best in you, find a life that actually makes you happy. Who knows, you might even get married," he snorts. "You'll get out of this prison you've called home and go on to do great things."

"You deserve all those things more than me, Nox. My life is basically forfeit because of who I am."

"The Court doesn't define you, Tamzin. Who you decide to be as a person is what matters. You'll find someone who doesn't give a shit who you are or where you come from. They'll see *you*—they'll see your soul."

Tears burn in the back of my throat. I try to swallow them down, but the burning progresses to my eyes, where tears begin to stream down my cheeks, soaking my pillow quickly. I don't think he realizes how much that means to me, how much his words burrow into my heart and soul to fill in the cracks that my own family created.

His warm hand settles between my shoulder blades, and a small sob slips through my hold. "You're enough, Tam, exactly as you are. You don't need to try and be more, especially not for others. Try and get some sleep."

"You'll stay?"

"Yes," he chuckles. "I'll stay."

I wish I had him in my life growing up, he would have made my life mean something and I would have had something more to fight for. I'll fight for him and this life we've created for ourselves, but the first step is getting myself off the helion.

CHAPTER 15

TAMZIN

I shift myself closer to the heat at my back, my eyes snapping open. Glancing back, I see Nox sleeping peacefully on the bed with his back to me, his dark hair disheveled across his eyes. My body aches with each small movement, and I'm regretting the fact I even have to get up this morning. I settle my head back against the pillow, closing my eyes and wishing for just a few more minutes of peaceful sleep. The bed shifts behind me and I fight the urge to look at him.

"Good morning," he whispers right at my ear. I shudder, feeling the heat of him pressing further into my back. "I know you're awake," he says, hearing the smile in his voice. His hand settles on my forehead, brushing my hair back from my face. "You feel a bit warm still. Do you feel okay?"

"I still feel like shit," I mumble. "Everything hurts."

"Stay here, I'll grab you some breakfast and some pain meds."

"You're too good to me," I whine, earning a laugh and a playful ass smack as he gets out of bed. I can't help but watch him as he strides across the wood floor, stretching his arms above his head with a cute squeal. Definitely boyfriend material. No, scratch that, he's fucking husband material through and through.

Half an hour later, he comes strolling in with his arms loaded down. I shift to get up, but he whistles, shaking his head. "None of that," he murmurs, his eyes narrowing on me. I sigh, nodding my head and shifting myself to prop up against the headboard. I flinch at the pain, letting out a small hiss of pain. "I can meet with the client without you," he says, setting a plate of pancakes down on my lap and a huge glass of orange juice on the nightstand next to me.

"No."

"Tam, it's just an exchange. You can barely fucking move right now. Here." He grips my wrist, flipping my palm up to drop two pills into it. He grabs the glass of orange juice and motions for me to take them.

"What time is the meeting?" I asks once I swallow them down.

"In an hour at the docks."

"I'm coming with you."

"Tam—"

"I'm coming with you! I'm not letting you go alone because I can't bear the thought that something will happen. We fucked with Court, Nox. We already know I'm being watched and so are you. I'm not risking you going alone."

"You're seriously going to fight me on this?" He sighs, settling into the bed next to me with his own plate of food.

"Absolutely. I'll feel better if I go with you. I don't want to sit here wondering if you'll come home or not." He glances at me from the corner of his eye and smirks. "What?" I sigh.

"We sound like a married couple," he laughs.

I smile, dropping my gaze down to my plate. "We act like a married couple, too," I chuckle.

"Almost," he snorts. "If we were sleeping together, it would definitely be accurate."

"I mean, we sort of did, if last night counts."

"Do you want it to count?" I shrug, suddenly feeling a bit embarrassed by this conversation. "Alright, *husband*, I'll let you come with me."

"Thank you."

The weirdest sound slips my lips when he grips into my jaw hard enough to make my cheeks pucker. I stare at him for a moment, my eyes widening when he smacks his lips against mine in a quick kiss. He lets go of me, laughing and smiling at my stupefied face, but I'll admit, all I can think about right now is the tingling across my lips. I lick them, tasting the sweetness of the syrup that lingered on his mouth and the mint from his toothpaste.

I've teased him before, but I never expected *him* to play into it this hard. He's never made it apparent whether or not he was interested in males as well as females. Maybe he's more like me than I actually realized. I haven't been shy. He knows full well that I go either way because I'm not focused on the sex of the person, only whether or not I'm attracted to them. Nox is *very* attractive. Not just physically, but his personality and his heart as well.

"Did I overstep," he asks, shoving a massive forkful of pancakes into his mouth.

His question jolts me from my thoughts, making me realize I've been freakishly quiet and I'm still staring at him like a deer caught in the headlights. I shake my head. "Not at all."

He gives me a crooked grin, triggering the dimples in his cheeks. "You're my first dude kiss," he laughs.

"Does that really count as a kiss?" I counter, wanting very much to show him what a real kiss from me would be like.

"Our lips touched, so yeah, it counts."

"Fair enough." I don't want to ruin our relationship by making this weird, so the last thing I should be doing is openly flirting with him. He's already allowing enough, and I'll accept it as it comes.

CHAPTER 16

KALIA

"Is everything alright?"

I startle at the sound of Kylo's voice right next to me, leaning away from his face coming into my line of view. "Everything is fine," I squeak out.

He lifts a brow. "You're acting jumpier than usual. Is something bothering you?"

I sigh, handing the customer his change while my eyes drift to the line and then out the massive windows. "Do you think Eris will be in again today?"

He laughs, the sound of the milk steamer drowning it out slightly. "He comes in quite a bit, but he doesn't have a set schedule as to when that is. He didn't message me for an order yet, so who knows." His phone goes off, and I watch him pull it from his pocket, a small smile pulling at his lips. "Guess he's coming in. He's picking up his order, and it seems like Nox's as well in ten minutes."

Nox. That's the roommate I went home with a few nights ago. I'll admit, he's attractive in the typical bad boy sense, but there's just something about Tam that I can't shake. He's perfect in a completely different way. He may look like a pretty boy but knowing the power and danger that comes with it, that's lying beneath the surface...there's just something different about *knowing* the danger is real with him. I didn't get that from Nox, he felt...safe. I know it was wrong of me to use him and lead him on like that, but I thought Nox would be my way into Eris's life—*Tam's* life.

Kylo finishes up the latte he was making and moves to get Tam's order ready while I help the next customer. I smirk as he cups the quad espresso. Only a sociopath would need that much caffeine to function. I quirk a brow when he starts prepping for a matcha latte, and he catches me staring.

"Nox isn't as big of a coffee drinker and Eris," he snorts. "He likes the healthier option with still a buttload of caffeine." He tosses a couple of chocolate muffins into a bag and sets everything down behind the side counter.

A few minutes later, I'm frowning when Nox comes bustling through the door, apologizing as he squeezes past the line. "Kylo!" He says happily. "Eris mentioned your booming business. How are things going?"

"Things are going great! I have your order right here," he says, lifting the drinks and muffins up onto the counter. Nox slides over a bill and gives him a huge smile, activating those dimples that had me sort of swooning when I first met him. His eyes settle on me and his smile falters slightly.

I quickly turn back to the current customer, my ears pricking when he lowers his voice. "You look familiar," he says, and I can feel his gaze fully locked on me now. "You're that girl from the other night."

"Sorry I fell asleep on you," I say quickly, glancing up at him.

"No worries," he says nonchalantly.

"Where's Eris?" Kylo asks, thankfully drawing Nox's attention back to him.

"He's in the car. He's not feeling too great this morning, so I told him I would run in for the coffee before we head out for work."

"Meeting with a client this morning?"

"Yup. We finished a job last night, so we're just finishing it up."

"Well, you two be careful. I would hate for something to happen to you guys, especially since Eris is one of my best customers."

"You're favourite customer, right?" Nox laughs.

Kylo laughs as well. "I wasn't going to say it since it would go to his head, but yes."

"I'll be sure to deflate that ego when it's necessary. Thanks again, Kylo. I'll see you later."

"Such a good kid," Kylo smiles. His eyes drift to me, and that damn eyebrow goes up again. "So, you hooked up with Nox?"

"Not exactly," I say quickly. "Nothing really happened, and it was just one night."

"Hmm, fair enough."

He gets back to work, ripping through order after order like it's second nature, but my mind is on what Nox and Tam could be up to. Did they have a bounty last night? For them to be meeting with a client this morning, it would be the only reason. Fuck, why do I have to be working right now? I rather try and find out what they're doing, who they're meeting with, what could possibly be going on with Tam for him not to come in here himself. Is it because of me? Did Nox lie when he said he wasn't feeling good? Does Tam not want to come in here because *I'm* here?

Anger rises up inside of me, the feeling burning through my veins and heating my body in a way that's making me uncomfortable. "Can I take a minute?" I ask, turning to Kylo. I'm struggling to catch my breath, and he frowns, but nods his head. I scurry around the counter, darting past the line of people into the blazing sun. The air is cooler than it has been, and I drag in sharp gulps of it, trying to calm myself down. My eyes get drawn to a gleaming car, Nox's dark hair ducking through the door. Tam. Tam is sitting in the passenger seat, sunglasses dropped over his eyes. A tightness pulls at his mouth as he smiles at Nox, grabbing the cup of coffee from him before Nox slides into the driver's seat. He *does* look awful. His normally tawny skin looking a bit pale and sickly, and I swear I saw him flinch slightly when he snagged the bag of muffins.

New anger surges through me. I swear if someone fucking hurt him—*No.* I shake my head. I can't let my anger take over my senses. I drag in a few more harsh breaths and turn back into the building to get this workday over with.

CHAPTER 17

TAMZIN

Nox stays pretty quiet as we make our way to the docks, but I can feel him stealing glances at me as I stare out the window, watching the city streets stream by. "What?" I grumble, not bothering to look at him.

"You still look pretty pale. Here, have my muffin, too."

"I'm okay, just feeling a bit tired still, that's all."

"You're taking a nap as soon as we get home."

"Yes, dad," I grumble.

"It's daddy, get it right."

I snort, finally pulling my gaze away from the window to look at him. "So, you're my daddy now?" I muse.

"Aren't I? I take care of you, bail you out of shit, and I love you, so..."

I smile, shaking my head at the audacity, but I have to admit, he's definitely a daddy. I sit up straighter in my seat when we hit the docks, noticing a single vehicle parked out near the pier. "Think that's them?"

"More than likely." Nox slows the vehicle down, inching it closer and closer to the car and the single occupant inside. He parks about ten feet away from it, throwing his hand across my chest when I move to get out. "Just wait." He pulls out his phone, shooting out a text to who I assume is Den, the client. "Yeah, it's him," he murmurs.

We both glance up when the driver steps out, clad in dark wash jeans, bright fucking white runners, and a dark hoodie with the hood thrown over their head. My eyes narrow, trying to focus in on them, but they don't turn to face us. Nox leans over the center to grab the box from the back, carefully pulling the amulet out.

"You can wait here."

"I don't know if that's such a good idea."

"You're here, which is what you wanted. It's just an exchange, Tam."

I nod, and he slowly gets out of the car. Den keeps his head down right up until Nox is standing in front of him. Nox shows him the amulet, and Den pulls out his phone. Nox's phone pings in the cupholder and I glance down to see the confirmation of wire transfer for the remaining balance. I let out a long sigh of relief, glancing back up at them. Nox is partially obscuring Den from view, but even from here, I see Den lift his head to look at Nox. Nox's back stiffens, and then he's stepping back, throwing the amulet towards Den. It clatters to the ground, Den making no move to pick it up.

My eyes widen when I get a look at Den's face and I'm staggering out of the car before I even realize I'm doing it. Nox turns to look at me when he hears the door close. "Get back in the car!" He snarls. His voice is laced with anger, not fear, maybe a small edge of panic, but he's not afraid of him. He's pissed, as am I. What was the point of all this? Why the fuck did he go to these lengths for a fucking piece of jewelry? "Now, Tam!"

I shake my head, bracing against the front of the vehicle as I stare at my brother in my fucking hoodie again. His brows furrow, concern lacing his features when he notices my body shaking at the effort to stay standing right now. He moves to step towards me, but Nox steps into his path, shoving him back.

"Stay away from him," Nox growls.

"I'm not going to hurt him. He's my brother."

"That didn't stop your asshole siblings the other night," he snaps.

Camden frowns, his eyes drifting between us with confusion clear on his face.

"Croh and Dorian paid me a little visit the other night at the club. They had Helia with them," I explain.

"What?" He says, true surprise lacing his words. "What the fuck for?"

"I could be asking you the same thing. What's with all the redirection, Cam? What the fuck is going on?"

"You didn't want to talk to me at the pit. I figured getting you to do a job would be the next best thing to try and get you to talk."

"We have nothing to talk about," I murmur, shakily sitting into the hood of the car.

"Are you okay?" He asks, stepping towards me again, but again Nox shoves him back.

"That's far enough. You will not go near him."

He glares at Nox, eyeing him in a way that shows him weighing his odds. "Call off your hound, Tamzin. I'm not here to hurt you."

"He's not my hound. He's my best friend—my fucking *brother*."

"Brother," he snaps.

"More of a brother than you've ever been."

Hurt flashes across his face, but he puts up his hands and steps back. Nox rushes towards me, his hands moving across my body to check me over. "I'm okay," I murmur, patting him on the chest.

"What's wrong with you?"

"I overdid it last night trying to get that hunk of metal for you. What did you think was going to happen if I had to get into Court?"

"You should have been able to walk right in," he says carefully.

I snort. "With that amount of warding? No way. It was bad enough on the outside perimeter, but the vault barrier was a bitch, too."

His frown deepens. "Barrier? You shouldn't have been denied access."

"Well, I was. I told you, I'm not *welcome* there, Cam."

"But father said he wanted you home."

"Did you ever think he wanted me home to trap me? To contain me? To fucking *imprison* me? I'm the reject, Cam. He doesn't *want* me."

"Tam I—" He steps closer, but Nox spins and glares at him, placing himself between me and my brother. "What do I have to do to prove to you I'm not here to hurt him, I just want to talk."

"You can talk from a distance," Nox snaps. "Back the fuck off."

Cam tips his head, backing up to pick up the amulet from the ground. "Was this all a ruse?" I ask, hating that I fell for something so stupid.

"Not entirely. I wanted the amulet because of its origin."

"Okay?"

"It was a gift from the Autumn Court, but it still should be worn by someone of the Autumn Court." He turns to look at me, sadness pulling at his features. "I'm getting married. I've been paired with one of the Autumn daughters. Father accepted the gift but locked it away the moment he had the chance. I want to give it to her."

"Why would he—"

"He doesn't trust anyone from other Courts, never has, as you well know."

"What's with the marriage?"

"A power play of course. He thinks he can have more control if he marries me off to one of the main houses. I'm surprised they even agreed to it. Though, I'm also surprised he's not holding out for Solar."

"What?"

"You didn't hear? The King was murdered. I think someone poisoned him or something."

Fucking hell, what is going on with that Court? That's a betrothed and a husband now that the Queen has lost at the hands of someone else. There has to be something going on behind the scenes there, and now I'm even more curious about the whole thing.

"Maybe you should be thankful he's not trying to pawn you off to that Court. With the Queen's track record, you wouldn't last a month."

Cam's face softens. "Come home, Tam."

"I have a home and it's not with you."

"Will you come to my wedding at least?"

"When is it?"

"It's set for the end of the month."

"Do you actually like her?"

He shrugs. "I haven't talked to her all that much. She stops in at Court once in a while, but she refuses to stay on the grounds until she absolutely has no choice."

"Wait, is she traveling back and forth from Autumn?"

"I'm not sure. I doubt she wants to be there longer than she has to as well. Autumn Court is archaic. Everything around them has evolved and changed, but the King and Queen refuse to accept those changes. I may hate our parents as well, but at least they've accepted the changes of time."

"I'll go, but only if I'm allowed a plus one."

Cam's eyebrows go up in surprise. "I wasn't aware you were with anyone that warranted your attention beyond a single night."

"There's one." My eyes drift to Nox, who senses me looking at him and turns enough to watch me over his shoulder. "I'm sure the rest of court will be pissed off with whoever I decide to bring, but especially with who I have in mind." Nox smirks, turning back to Cam.

"Why are you *trying* to piss them off further?"

"It's what I do best. Also, I don't appreciate you breaking your promise is keeping Helia safe. Dorian was cruel to her, more so when she tried speaking to me directly. Get your brothers in line, Cam."

"They're your brothers, too."

"You know I can't do anything without repercussions. I'm trying to stay under the radar, meanwhile they're tracking me. I don't fucking appreciate that, Cam. If they find out where I live, I'm going to lose my shit."

"I'll talk to them," he sighs.

"You better, and no more of this bullshit," I say, waving towards the amulet. "You have our contact info, and we have yours, so no more secrecy."

"Will you actually talk to me if I reach out?"

"It'll depend on my mood, but I'll entertain the idea." I push off from the car, gripping into the hood again as I make my way around it to the door. Nox moves quicker, getting ahead of me to open the door for me. "Thanks," I sigh, groaning as I drop into the seat.

"I'm sorry my request pushed you this far, Tam. It was never my intention for you to weaken yourself in this way. I promise I had no idea about the barrier. If you need anything, please just reach out to me."

"I think you've done enough," Nox murmurs, shutting the door before I can hear what Cam says, but I see his lips moving as Nox steps towards him.

Cam shakes his head, his eyes widening and his lips moving faster now. I catch bits and pieces when his voice lifts in volume, but Nox says something that has Cam's eyes darting to mine through the windshield. The next second, Cam is staggering back, his hand at his jaw and his eyes blinking rapidly to clear the quickly forming tears. Fuck, Nox just lost it. I can't believe he just punched him, and now I *really* want to know what the fuck was said between them. Nox says something else, his body coiled in anger and his arm swings back to point towards me. Cam gives him the barest of nods, backing up to give Nox space as he moves around the front of the car. His eyes meet mine and the air in my lungs freezes at the look of pure fury in his subtly glowing eyes, his power flare barely contained by willpower alone.

"What happened?" I ask as soon as he sits down and closes the door. He grabs his phone, probably checking to make sure Cam sent the money, and throws the car into reverse, backing off the pier. He stays silent, ignoring my stare until we're back out on the street. "Nox?"

"Nothing," he mumbles.

"You punched him. You punched the Crowned Prince of the Night Court, Nox."

"And?" He whispers harshly, swinging his gaze to me. His eyes are still glowing, flaring brighter with each passing second. "He deserved far worse than me just punching him once."

His grip on the gearshift tightens, the leather squealing at the pressure and his knuckles turning white. "Hey," I whisper, settling my hand over his. His grip loosens slightly, thank fuck, since I really don't want to replace the gearshift if he breaks it. "I don't want you losing yourself to anger because of me. This isn't like you."

"He put you at risk for a fucking stupid reason, Tam."

"So, will you be my date to the wedding?" He turns to look at me, his brows going up in surprise. "What?"

"I wondered if that was where you were going with that comment," he snorts. "Are you sure you want me to meet your parents?"

I roll my eyes, pulling my hand back from his. "I can't think of anyone else I rather drag to an event like that. I know I'll be in good hands with you," I smirk.

"That's my line," he laughs.

"Oh, I have *very* good hands."

His gaze darkens, and I'm not sure if I'm imagining it or not, but I swear his eyes flick to my lips for a second. "So I've heard." The drop in his voice sends a shiver skating up my spine, and that ever-present edge of embarrassment creeps in again. I'm walking a really thin line right now, and I'm not sure if it's wise for me to tip over to the other side.

"I'm good with my mouth, too." Fuck me and my fucking mouth. I'm physically cringing at the fact I just said that out loud, loading the inuendo on fucking Nox of all people. What is wrong with me? I close my eyes and turn away from his heavy stare, but I feel it burn into me as I stare out the window.

"I'm sure you are," he chuckles, thankfully dropping the conversation and allowing the silence to fill the car all the way back to the apartment.

He helps me once again, but I'm definitely feeling better than I was earlier. "I'm going to crash for a bit," I murmur, balancing myself on the wall as I make my way to my room.

"Do you want some lunch first?"

"Maybe just a shake."

"You hate my shakes."

"I don't *hate* them. Some are just better than others."

"Are you sure?" I nod, slipping into my room. "Alright!" He calls out.

I flinch with every scrape of clothing over my skin, hating the way the jeans feel, and the restriction of the t-shirt. I settle for just a pair of thinner flannel pants, crawling into bed just as Nox knocks at the door.

"You don't need to knock," I sigh, shifting the pillows behind me.

"I didn't want to catch you if you were indecent."

"You've seen me naked plenty of times," I argue, but I note the flush of pink creeping into his cheeks.

"Here."

I take the glass from him, eyeing it up suspiciously. I take a small sip, surprise radiating through me. "It's good," I admit, taking a larger drink from the glass.

"It's got a ton of protein in it, but I used some bananas and peanut butter to flavour it to your liking."

"I appreciate it." He stands and waits for me to finish it, taking it back once the glass is empty. "What are you up to today?"

"Nothing at all, so if you need anything, just call out." He squeezes my shoulder and turns to leave. My mouth opens and closes a few times, no words coming out. I feel like a needy little shit, wanting him to stay with me again like he did last night. I have no right to ask that of him, but I'll admit, it was nice having the company. He flicks the light switch, turning to look at me one last time before closing the door.

CHAPTER 18

TAMZIN

My throat burns like a sun-scorched stone. Blinking away the sleep pulling at my eyes, I slowly prop myself up in bed. I fumble for my phone, my hand searching aimlessly on the nightstand for it, and hiss out a breath when the screen light burns into my retinas. "Fuck," I grumble, tossing it back on the nightstand. It skitters dangerously close to the edge, stopping short before falling to its doom.

I slept the entire day away and most of the night. I'm actually surprised Nox didn't come in and wake me at all, especially for dinner, but maybe he thought it was better to let me sleep. Of course he would know what's best for me, he always does. I flop my gaze to the side, to the empty space beside me, and slowly run my fingers over the cool sheets next to me. I'm so fucking tired of being alone.

I don't want to be alone, but I have to be. Anyone who gets close to me ends up hurt, or worse. I've lived my entire life in darkness, never knowing what love really was. My mother never loved me, my father even less. Helia wasn't as bad when I was still a boy, but the hatred from the others caused her to shut down, and in turn, push me away as well. I would give anything to just...*be loved*—truly loved. The love only a mother can give, but that seems so out of reach for me when my own mother despises me. Why did she even have me if all she wanted was for me to disappear? I was a *good* kid, and maybe that was the problem. They didn't want good, they wanted submissive. Fucking pawns for them to manipulate and control, even their own flesh and blood.

My eyes grow heavy again, and I curl myself back onto my side, letting the pull of sleep drag me under.

***

"Please stop!" I sob, my body trembling with fear and pain. Another crack of the whip cuts through my back, drawing out a broken scream from my lungs. Warm liquid heat coats my back, my skin burning like a hot flame licking at the tender flesh. "Please, dad!"

"You will learn to be silent! You will learn to take it like you're supposed to."

Another crack of the whip slices through me, and it feels like my body will break in two from the force of it. I crumple to the ground, the chains around my wrists biting into the skin like a sharp knife. I can't feel my legs anymore, the weight of my body too much for me to handle.

I want to die. I don't want to die. I want to die. I don't want to die. The thoughts battle with each other, and at this point, I don't even know which one will win in the end. I want the pain to stop—I know it'll stop if I just die, but I want to live. I want to have a real life, one where I'm not being beaten for being different from my siblings, for not manifesting my powers when father expected me to. What did I do to deserve this?

Hot tears stream down my cheeks, my broken sobs and pleas going unanswered and my screams slowly fading into raspy choked breaths when even my torn throat betrays me. My heart is beating frantically, trying to keep me alive, but threatening to kill me on my next breath. Heat burns through my veins, the burning sensation spreading through every cell in my body, building and building, until I finally break.

***

"Stop!" I scream, lurching up in bed, my power pulsing out of me in a heavy wave, plunging the already darkened room into an even heavier darkness. It presses against my skin, my lungs, my very soul. Air saws through my lungs, sweat clinging to my heated body, and the weight of my wings tear at my shoulders in agonizing protest. I can't breathe—can't pull in a proper breath to try and calm me from the nightmare I've relived for the last hundred years. That memory is branded into my very soul, and it'll follow me into the ether in death. Tears stream freely down my cheeks while choked sobs try to claw their way up through my throat. I hear a thud, and frantically peer through the darkness, but it won't stop—it won't go away.

"Tam!"

"Nox," I whimper, his name sounding more like a plea than anything else.

I feel him clawing at my shadows, tearing through the heavy veil that's erected around me. I whimper again at the feel of his arms wrapping around me so fucking tightly, it feels like he's trying to hold me together with is own body. I claw at his back, sobbing harder than I've sobbed in a long time.

"Shhh, I'm here. You're okay, Tam. You're not alone. No one's going to hurt you, okay?"

I let his scent blast into me, opening up all my senses until I'm drowning in him. The heady scent of pine, and mint, and earth. I found comfort in his smell the first time I scented him, and I still find comfort in it now. Nox *is* comfort. He's my anchor, a lightning rod drawing me to him, taking all I have to give and withstanding it like the beacon that he is.

"I—I can't—can't control—"

"Shhh, it's okay. You won't hurt me. It's okay, Tam, just breathe."

"I'm sorry," I say weakly, gripping into him harder.

He tightens his hold further, and I can't tell if his body is trembling from emotion, my own trembling, or if I'm hurting him with my power. "Don't ever apologize to me for this. There's nothing for you to be sorry for."

"I'm such a fuck up," I sniffle. "I can't keep a hold on my shit."

He slowly pulls back, but only far enough that he can look at me. My shadows have receded enough to bring the natural darkened light back into my room. "You haven't had one this bad in a while. Did the shit with Cam trigger you?" His face shifts to one promising pain depending on my answer.

"I don't know. I would think it's more from the fact I was back *there*. Being in that house doesn't make me feel good, Nox."

"Let me get you some water." He must notice the panic on my face as he gently unhooks my fingers from his shirt. "I'll just be a minute, and I'll leave the door open so you can see me, okay?" I nod, keeping my eyes trained on him as he walks through the living room into the kitchen. The light from the fridge flares to life, now clearly showing how disheveled Nox looks. I catch a glimpse of some pillows and a blanket on the couch before the light from the fridge gets snuffed out. "Here," he says, holding out a bottle to me.

I take it from him gratefully, chugging back half the bottle in my desperate attempt to ease the burning in my throat. "Were you sleeping on the couch?" I finally ask.

"I didn't want to get too far from you in case you needed anything."

"Nox," I sigh. "You didn't need to do that."

"I know I didn't, but I wanted to. It's still early, so try and get some rest, Tam."

My hand launches out to grip his arm, my heart beating viciously against my chest. "Don't go," I plead. "Please. *Please* don't go."

"Alright." He grabs the bottle of water and sets it down on the nightstand before going around to the other side of the bed. He settles into it behind me, gently touching my wings. "Just breathe, Tam."

I nod my head, trying to calm myself down enough to try and pull the stupid things back in. Nox was never afraid of my wings—of what they looked like. He actually finds them sort of cool, which is saying a lot about him. He rubs at my back, his warm hand gently stroking between my shoulder blades. The touch relaxes me, grounds me back to him, and after a few more breathes, I get enough semblance of control to draw them in. My next breath rattles out of me, my body suddenly feeling more exhausted than it did moments ago.

"Come on," Nox whispers, dragging his hand down my arm and gripping into my fingers gently. I let him tug me back, and I settle into my pillow facing him. My breathing is still too quick, too panicked, but seeing the dim glow of his eyes in the darkness, the outline of his features staring back at me, helps calm me down. My eyes flutter closed when he gently brushes my hair back, his long fingers soothing and calming. "Do you want to talk about it?" He says quietly, almost hesitantly.

Slowly I open my eyes to see him watching me with a worried frown on his face. "Why does my family hate me?" My voice cracks on the words, the hesitation to express these thoughts clearly apparent. "Ever since I was a boy, they've done everything to break me, and I just don't...understand."

"I don't know, Tam. It doesn't make sense to me because you're an amazing person. Your kind, caring, funny, giving—everything that's good in this world." Tears burn the back of my throat. "I know you didn't deserve any of the pain you suffered."

"I just wish I could escape these nightmares."

"Was it the same one as last time?" I nod. "You don't have to tell me if you don't want to."

"I have a few different ones that my mind likes to cycle through, but this one is always the worst one. My father...he used to beat me, almost everyday, but this time he chained me up. He used a whip on me until I bled, until my body gave out. He was so *angry*, hating the fact I hadn't manifested my powers yet, when my other brothers had all gotten theirs by my age."

"How old were you?"

"I was ten. He got what he wanted though, he pushed me until I broke, and my powers manifested that day. I had no control over them, and I almost killed him—I wish I *had* killed him. If I had, I wouldn't have had to continue to suffer even *after* that day. I thought my manifest would finally mean he was done with the torment, but if anything, it just got worse. I manifested with normal wings, if you can believe it," I laugh, no humor in the sound. "None of my siblings manifested in that way, the darkness was already well ingrained into their very being."

"You manifested with your soul intact," he says, cluing into what I'm trying to say.

"I did. I held on for so long, hoping it would just get better. It didn't."

"What did they do to you, Tam?"

"My soul broke when I was twelve. I had a dog..." I smile at the memory of Harbinger, the black great Dane that followed me around everywhere, the only one who loved me as I was. "I came home to Lex and Flynn ripping him apart." My eyes slam closed at the memory, the whimpers and screams from my best friend, suffering a fate he never deserved. "He was innocent. The only thing he did wrong was loving me. The only soul on this planet that loved me no matter what and he suffered for it." My voice breaks, a choked sob slipping through my hold.

Nox grips into me, pulling me into his chest to wrap his arms around me. "I'm so sorry," he murmurs, tucking my head under his chin.

"That was the day I changed. I lashed out, ripping into Lex and Flynn for what they had done. I was going to kill them, but father showed up and stopped me before I could do more than damage his precious sons' faces. He punished me for that. That pain pushed me to develop a second ability, one with more raw power and ability to damage." I snuggle further into him, trying to cling to his warmth as it seeps into my now chilled body. "I'm broken, Nox, so fucking broken. You would be better off not knowing me or being near me, but I just...I can't let you go."

"You're not broken and I'm not going anywhere. I'll always be with you, no matter what."

CHAPTER 19

TAMZIN

"I have enough food," I sigh as Nox shovels another spoon of eggs onto my already overflowing plate.

"You need the energy," he argues. "You've been through a lot over the last few hours. Are you sure you're feeling okay?"

"I feel better than yesterday. I can't stay in bed all day."

"You could if you wanted to."

"Well, I *don't* want to. I need to move around and do shit."

"You're not planning to go to the pit again, are you?"

"Maybe later," I mumble, earning a glare from him. "You know I need to handle my anger, Nox."

"That pit is going to end up getting you killed."

"I've done fine up until now. You don't have to worry about me."

"Do you use while you're in the pit?"

I shake my head. "No. I don't even use my powers when I'm down there. The last time was the first time it happened." His eyes widen. "Oh, yeah. Kaliem let my opponent use a weapon, which isn't allowed. I had no other choice if I planned to walk out of there."

"What if he does it again? What if the next time you don't realize in time?"

"I'm not *weak*, Nox."

"I never said you were, but is it so wrong for me to worry about you?" Guilt settles into me at the look of pain on his face, and I drop my gaze from his. "Tam," he sighs, dropping into the chair across from me. "I can't help but worry."

"I know, I'm sorry for making you worry."

"We got another request this morning," he says, and I'm thankful for the subject change. "I can tell them we pass if you're not up to it."

"No, it's fine. What's the payout?"

"Three hundred. The bounty is some guy named Calvin Dean. Dead or alive was the only guideline." He pulls out his phone and scrolls through the message. "Apparently, he runs an ability trafficking ring off the outer district, and they've done what they can to bring him down legally, but the guy is squeaky clean on the outside."

"Wait, is the client actually law enforcement?"

"Sounds like it," he snorts. "I love that they're trying to take down hunters, but now they're having to rely on us to do their job. Apparently, supernaturals have been going missing every week, but they've been trying to keep it under the radar. No one notable has gone missing, but that almost seems worse since they're targeting lower class and the vulnerable."

"Get all the information you can on this guy."

"It might take me a day or two to get enough to find out his routine, but I'll get it."

"Great. Have them send half the funds into the account."

"Already done," he smirks. "I was tempted to ask for more since I had suspicion it was the guard involved."

"Have they notified human authorities on the matter?" Nox shakes his head. "Why the fuck not?"

"If it's involving supernatural, you know they don't want the humans involved unless absolutely necessary."

"I wonder if Court knows," I mumble, shoveling a forkful of eggs into my mouth.

"Do you want me to contact Cam?"

"No. If they don't know already, I don't want them finding out about what we do."

"But Cam already knows. Do you think he would tell your family?"

"I have no idea what the fuck he'll do, but I don't want to risk finding out."

"Alright. Why don't you go talk to Hawk and see if he's heard anything in the underground about this guy."

"Yeah, I'll do that after I grab a coffee from the Hub."

He settles back into his chair, a smirk tugging at his lips. "Speaking of the Hub, I see the girl I brought home is working there."

"Is she?" I say, trying to play it as cool as I can while my heartbeat skips erratically.

A sly grin spreads across his face. "You're going to tell me you didn't know?"

"The night she was here was the first time I saw her," I lie. "That girl only started working there a few days ago from what Kylo said."

"She looked disappointed when I went to pick up our order."

"Really?" His brows shoot up in surprise. "I mean, did she say anything?"

"I fucking knew it," he snorts. "She didn't really talk to me. She barely looked at me. Kylo was worried that something was wrong with you, but I just told him you weren't feeling very good." He gets up, stretching his arms above his head. His shirt rides up, drawing my eyes to the smooth skin and toned abs. "I'm going to get started on this, and I'll probably head to Transcend tonight to unwind. I need a drink or ten, and I need to get laid."

A twinge flutters through my chest at his words, something akin to jealousy. "Okay."

"Do you want to come with me? I know you hate the place, but I don't want to leave you here alone to sulk."

"I'm not going to sulk."

"You need to get laid, man. You're way too tightly wound lately."

"Yeah," I mumble. "Maybe you're right." He pats the table and saunters off to his room to get changed, my eyes once again trailing after him.

He's been way too good to me these last few days, but I think his actions have been skewing the relationship I have with him. He's my friend—my *best* friend—my fucking brother. I won't risk that by testing the waters and seeing if there's something more going on between us.

I polish off the rest of my breakfast, and I'm just finishing off the dishes, when Nox comes back out, freshly showered, with his laptop gripped in his hand. He settles onto the couch, the sound of keys clacking filling the room. I sigh, trying not to read too much into the sudden silence between us, and head into my room to take a shower myself.

The heat of the water beats into my skin and muscles, doing a somewhat decent job in relaxing the tension that's built in them over the last few days.

I change into some faded jeans and a long sleeve henley, eyeing the helion on the nightstand. I pocket it before I convince myself otherwise and snag my wallet on the way out.

"I'll see you in a few hours."

Nox blinks, shakes his head, and rips his gaze away from his computer. "Oh, okay. Be safe."

"I will." He smiles and drops his eyes back to the computer, typing away at a speed that is beyond human.

The streets are a bit quieter this morning, the morning rush having already passed since I slept in longer than I usually do. The walk to the Hub is quicker, too, my body moving on its own. My steps stall when I walk in, the line not as big as it has been, but that's not what has me coming up short. Kalia isn't here, Ridley in her place behind the counter. By the time I get to the counter, I've lost hope that I'll see her today.

"Morning, Eris!" Ridley says in her bubbly voice. "The usual?"

"Just the quad, Ridley." She nods, punching in the order. I hand over some cash and shift in front of Kylo, who's eyeing me with a weird expression. "What?"

"Are you feeling better this morning?"

"Yeah, just a weird bug yesterday."

I lean slightly past him, trying to get a glimpse into the breakroom, but it's empty, too. "She's not in today."

"What?"

"Kalia. She's not in today. She had some appointment she had to go to later this morning, so I just gave her the day off. She'll be back in tomorrow."

"I don't really care either way."

"Don't you?" He muses. "I see the way you watch her, I'm not blind."

"It's annoyance and curiosity more than anything."

"She seems like a nice girl. Maybe you should pursue her in a formal manner."

"She's *not* nice. She's good at putting on this fake persona to fool you, but I've seen her out in the wild." His eyebrow creeps up in curiosity and I sigh. "I've met her a few times. She was at the pit fight I was in a few nights ago, and then at Transcend when I went looking for Nox. She's up to something, but I can't figure out what."

"Well, she's nice to me and Shahar, and she's learning quickly, doing everything we ask of her. She's shown us no ill will, and she seems like a good kid."

"Have you gotten a read on her power or anything? Her aura?"

He shakes his head. "Either she's a lower-level Fae or she's hiding her aura from me. I can't get anything substantial from her."

This girl just keeps getting more and more complex. I *felt* what was lying beneath the surface when she stood up to Croh. There's no way she's a lower-level Fae because a lower-level would have cowered in his presence...unless they're stupid. I mean, she *might* be stupid, but her clever act has sort of proved otherwise.

"Here's your order," Kylo says, snapping me out of my thoughts. "Hopefully your day today goes better than it did yesterday."

"You and me both."

I give him a small smile, grabbing the cup from the counter. "See you guys later!" I call back.

"Bye, Eris!" Ridley says, her voice always so chipper. I don't know how the girl does it, living everyday seeming so happy. I wish I had even an inkling of the joy she feels in just waking up in the morning.

Walking the streets gives me time to think, the caffeine settling into my system like a puzzle piece fitting into place. I don't *want* to think, since my thoughts keep drifting back to everything that's happened the last few days. I shudder at the memory of last night and the fucking nightmare plaguing me once again. I've been doing better, and I thought I had it under control, but that's clearly not the case. I could have seriously hurt Nox in my uncontrolled state, but he pushed through my power, literally clawed his way through my physical form shadows to get to me—to comfort me.

If I were a better male, one who wasn't selfish and stupid, I would leave him—slip out of his life to let him *live* his life in peace, but I can't. I can't lose him yet, and I'm going to cling to the normal he provides me for as long as possible.

The further I walk, the less people I see. A lot of people don't linger around the Hollow—the worst part of town. It's like it's been completely rejected, which it has. This is where I ended up getting the helion, though I didn't have to go as far into the hole as I do now. Hawk likes his business at the heart of it all, running his own ring of questionable endeavors, and selling shit that's harder than helion. He still carries the basics, just so he has a wide variety to offer his customers, but the lower levels don't buy from him if they can help it. If I could do this without seeing him, I would. It's not like I'm *afraid* of being here, but Hawk can be difficult to deal with at times. The burly fuck is intimidating as shit. It's not very often you run into a half-Fae turned vampire. Whoever was his sire, is either an idiot, or a genius, but risking killing him doesn't seem like a good option. With how the vampire virus works, Hawk could have very well died if his human half wasn't compatible.

The dilapidated door to his place looks ominous and eerie, the wood door weathered and old, and the steel encasing its edges beginning to rust from lack of magical upkeep. Gripping the cast iron knocker, I cringe at the squeak of it as I tap it against the door. A few minutes pass with no response, so I do it again, hating the feel of the puckered metal under my hand. Swearing comes from the other side of the door, and I step back quickly at the suddenness of the door ripping open.

"Who the fuck is up this early?" He snarls, dragging a hand down his face.

Glancing at my watch, I quirk a brow. "It's not that early, Hawk."

"Oh, it's you. What the fuck do you want?"

"Information."

His eyes narrow, shifting up and down my body before leaning slightly out his door to look at the street. "You're alone?"

I glance behind me, exaggerating my movements in the most obnoxious way possible. "Unless you see someone here that I don't, and if that's the case, you might want to see a doctor about that."

He rolls his eyes, opening the door a bit further, but barely enough for me to squeeze through. My nose crinkles at the overpowering scent of nokweed permeating the room, a lingering cloud of smoke hovering in the air. He closes the door and lumbers his way over to the lounge area, sparking up a smoke the instant he sits down. "Well, let's hear it," he says, motioning to the couch across from him.

"I need all the information you have on Calvin Dean." I grunt when the couch practically sucks my body into it, and I scramble to try and pull myself free of it's obnoxious hold on me.

"Calvin Dean? What the fuck do you want from him? He's a piece of shit, and I wouldn't recommend getting involved with him."

"I'm not looking to get involved, but a bounty has been put out for him, so any information you have about his whereabouts, habits, places he frequents, anything really, would be very much appreciated."

"It'll cost ya," he smirks, settling back into the couch.

"Figured as much." I drop an envelope on the table, and he quickly grabs it, pawing through it. "I think I'm being generous, so I'm expecting *all* the information you have."

"So, someone is finally getting serious about taking him down," he snorts. "With the amount of supernaturals that have been going missing over the years, I thought it would have happened sooner."

I frown. "You knew it was him?"

He shrugs. "There's a few of us that had suspicions, but no one wanted to get involved. Some heavy hitters have gone missing, so at that point, we knew no one was safe from him. Better to not piss him off and disappear."

"Who do you know that's gone missing? I thought only lower levels were being taken."

"Hardly. It's not just lower levels, it's ones most people won't miss. Kurtz and Fennir both went missing about six months ago."

"They're the major nokweed dealers." He nods. "Who gained to benefit from that?"

"All of us. With them out of the picture, suppliers had to find new dealers."

"I wonder if Calvin is being paid to take out the competition specifically."

"Orion barely goes out anymore because of it. He's shaken up enough, and since he's one of the smaller helion dealers, he doesn't want to take any chances, especially closer to this district."

Fuck, why didn't he mention it to me when I went to him a few days ago? He *knows* what I do and the people I deal with, the fucking idiot. "Then it's a good thing I've been hired to deal with him."

"He's got quite a few guys on his payroll, Eris. I don't know if you'll be able to get to him that easily."

"I'll deal with it, just give me everything you have, including their names if you got it."

CHAPTER 20

TAMZIN

"I bought dinner." Nox glances up from his computer, still sitting in the same spot I left him this morning. "Fucking hell, have you moved?"

"I went to the bathroom a few times and made myself a shake," he murmurs, turning his attention back to the computer.

"Come on, take a real break." He glares at me when I drop the greasy bag onto the keyboard. "Seriously, *eat*."

"Fine," he grumbles, grabbing the bag and closing his laptop, probably for the first time today. He opens it, pulling in a deep inhale. "Fuck, that smells good. Jullian's?"

"Yup. Picked up your favourite."

His eyes widen and he tears the bag in his attempt to pull out the massive burger and order of specialty fries. "Oh, man, you got the fries, too!" He says excitedly, opening the container. I quickly grab some forks from the kitchen, plopping down on the couch next to him to hand him one. "Seriously, the best fries ever. How can you go wrong with loaded fries, right?" He laughs, shoveling a huge bite into his mouth.

He seems to be in a better mood now that he's eating at least. I pull out my own fries and get to work eating them. I've got plenty to tell him, but I rather he eats first before we talk shop.

"So how did it go? Did you find anything on Calvin on your end?"

So much for that. "Yeah, a bit." He stops chewing and proceeds to stare at me until I continue. "We can talk after dinner."

"Why? What's wrong with talking about it during dinner? It's not like we're in some fancy restaurant on a date or some shit."

"Maybe I want you to enjoy your food and not talk with your mouth full."

"Does it bother you?" He asks, his mouth loaded with food to prove a point.

"You really enjoy stuffing your face, don't you?" I snort.

"What can I say, I can handle a lot in my mouth." I blink, my eyes drifting to that very mouth. "You just thought something dirty, didn't you?" He laughs. I drop my eyes quickly, hyper-focusing on my own carton of fries. "You got some cheese on your face."

"What?" I glance back at him and freeze. His thumb grazes against the corner of my mouth, lingering longer than should be appropriate for our relationship.

"I got it," he says quietly, slowly pulling his hand back. I swallow around the thickness in my throat when he brings his thumb to his lips and licks it clean.

He at least grants me the courtesy of not asking anymore questions, eating quietly, and letting me stew in my rampant thoughts, mainly about what the fuck *that* just was. I can't actually get a read on him. Is he just fucking with me because I've made inappropriate comments to him in the past? That can't be it. He could still fuck with me without physically touching me and doing shit like that. I'm reading too much into it, but I can't get the thought out of my head, or the feel of his warm skin against mine.

Once we finish, he grabs the trash and goes to the kitchen to toss it. Sitting back onto the couch—closer to me now than he was before, he grabs his laptop and opens it, shifting even closer. "So, I was able to dig up quite a bit of dirt on him. He's got a decent record, even did a few years in prison for some of the minor crimes he wasn't able to cover up. He's got charges ranging from money laundering, fraud, breaking and entering, and a couple of sexual assault charges. Nothing on kidnapping or murder though, so he's not a complete idiot."

He pulls up a bunch of photos, including his mugshots, and shifts the computer closer to me. "He's not what I expected," I mutter, scrolling through the photos.

"I put his face into my facial recognition software. I've gotten some hits on older footage, so I'm hoping I can pinpoint his trail, and once a camera catches sight of him again, I should know exactly where he is."

"What is he?"

"You're never going to believe it, he's human."

"Excuse me? How the fuck did he find out about the dark world then for him to be kidnapping supernaturals. He shouldn't be able to take them down so easily without any power."

"It's gotta be his crew, Tam. He's probably employing supernaturals to help him and paying them a pretty penny to do it. From what I gathered, he used to date a Nephilim, so she probably let it slip about our world. She was one of the first to go missing." He pulls up a photo of a petite blonde. "Savanah Cross, daughter of Emily Russo and Jerimiah Cross. He's also Nephilim, so her bloodline is pretty diluted. I don't know how much of a fight she would have put up." He leans in closer to me, resting his forearm on my thigh as he clicks through a few files until he pulls up multiple video feeds. "He seems to frequent the pit quite a bit, and the Hollow."

He turns to look at me, his face asininely close to mine, close enough that I can see the green flecking his blue eyes and the silver ring around the pupil. I swallow, shifting my eyes away from him to the screen. "I don't think I've ever noticed him in the pit before, but it makes sense. If he's scouting possible marks, the pit would be a cesspool for the depraved."

"The last time he was seen on any of the cameras I've accessed was last week, so we'll see if he ends up popping up before we find him a different way. What did you find out?"

I grab the notepad off the table and hand it to him. "I got the names of some of his crew and a few areas he frequents as well. Apparently, Orion has been avoiding going out because of this prick, so he's well known. Hawk's known about the supernaturals going missing for a while, too, but it's not like they can really make a formal complaint since they're not innocent either. Calvin is basically trapping them and turning them into easy pickings."

"Orion...he's the helion dealer." I nod. "Isn't he Fae? Why the fuck would he be scared of Calvin?"

"The same reason everyone else is." I point to the list of names. "I want to know what I'm dealing with. See if you can find out anything about them, their lineage, abilities, anything, Nox. He's targeting dealers as well, so I think someone is paying him off to take out the competition while still turning a profit on taking supernaturals in general."

"What the fuck is he doing with them? It doesn't make any sense. By the sounds of it, he's not killing them, he's selling them, but for what?"

"Personal bodyguards? If he's human, maybe he has human friends who think they can control dark worlders for their own personal gain. They could have also found a way to siphon abilities, but I would think something of that magnitude would draw more attention, and it's not like they're taking anyone with significant power."

"Alright, I'll get to work on getting the information I can on his goons," he sighs, gripping into his laptop.

I grab it from him, closing it and setting it on the table. "Tomorrow. Tonight, we need a breather." He quirks a brow. "You said you wanted to go to Transcend."

"You *hate* Transcend," he snorts. "I wasn't serious about that."

"It's fine. If it's got booze, I'm happy."

"Tam, we can go somewhere else."

"You like the club though."

"It doesn't matter to me."

"We're going. Go get yourself all pretty so you can find yourself a date for tonight."

He laughs, bouncing up from the couch. "You want me to get dolled up?" He smirks.

"Of course," I smile.

He ruffles my hair on his way to his room, and the gesture makes my heart thump a little faster. Definitely reading too much into it. He's just being his usual playful self, nothing more. He's going to meet a girl tonight and bring her home. Who knows, she might be the one for him. I hate that the thought of that makes my chest tighten and my lungs squeeze with anxiety. I want him to be happy, but the more time that passes, makes me sort of want him to be happy with *me*.

CHAPTER 21

KALIA

There isn't enough alcohol in the world to erase the shitty day I had today. The last thing I wanted to do was meet with *them*, but I had no choice. I was summoned, therefore, I must obey. Fucking Fae bullshit if you ask me. It makes me envious of Tamzin, finding the courage to leave that world behind and live his life the way he wishes to live it.

"Hey, gorgeous. Can I buy you a drink?"

I glance over at the voice, disappointment and disgust rolling through me. I hold up my half empty glass. "I'm good, thanks."

"Oh, come on. Don't be like that," he smiles, the glint of fangs catching in the strobing lights flittering through the room.

"Let me put it simply so you can understand. *No*. You know what that word means, right? I don't think I can dumb it down any further since it's in its most simplistic form at only two letters. Actually, maybe it'll hit home if I say it with more emphasis. *Fuck* no."

"Why are you such a bitch?"

"Why is it that me saying no makes me a bitch? I'm not interested, and I don't appreciate being hounded for the fact I don't want you to buy me a fucking drink."

He flops himself down on the stool next to me, and I can't do anything but gawk at him. "Bartender! Can I get a beer and another drink for the lady."

The bartender looks at me, and I shake my head. "Uh, she doesn't seem to want one," he says, clearly reading my discomfort.

"She's just being shy. She wants to have a drink with me."

"I said no," I snap, moving to shift off the stool. His hand moves so fast I don't even have time to react. "Let go of me," I say through gritted teeth, trying to pull away from him.

"Hey, man. Let her go before I get security."

"One drink," he says, his grip tightening further. Heat builds in my body, simmering under the surface as I glare at him. I open my mouth to yell at him before I do something I may or may not regret, but his grip is suddenly gone. I blink, confused by the situation unfolding in front of me.

"We don't treat females like fucking property," Tam snarls, gripping into the vampire's forearm hard enough that I hear the bone snap before he even reacts to it.

The vamp screams, stumbling back and falling on his ass when Tam shoves him off the stool. "What the fuck!"

"Don't touch her," he growls, his voice loaded with venom, and I swear I notice the shadows curling into the corners of the building pulsing with his anger. They feel heavier—darker than what a normal shadow should be.

"I didn't know the bitch had a boyfriend," the vamp spits, cradling his arm to his chest, but I can already see the bone mending back together. He must be a regular vampire, the slower healing rate showing he's not pureblood like the King that rules over the vampires of this continent.

The vamp grunts, Tam's grip on his jaw puckering his cheeks together. "She's not a bitch. She told you no and you didn't like that, you self-righteous prick." The vamp's eyes dart to the bartender, but he makes no move to help him, if anything, he's happy that he didn't have to get involved himself. “Eye’s here,” Tam hisses. “I’m only going to say this once, if I catch you acting like this again to *anyone*, I’ll fucking kill you.” The vamp’s eyes widen when shadows start to creep across Tam’s shoulders, down his arm towards his face. “Do you understand me?”

“Yesh,” he garbles, unable to speak properly with the grip Tam still has on him.

“Get out.” He shoves him back onto the floor. “I doubt the staff wants to deal with your ass right now, and I rather not see your face again tonight.”

His vampire speed is doing him no favours as he scrambles to get to his feet. He takes off running, shoving people out of the way as he goes. Tam steps up to the bar, not even looking at me. “Can I get a dark lager, please.”

“Sure. It’s on the house.”

“I can pay.”

“Nah, man. I appreciate you stepping in like that. Security has been pretty scarce lately, and I doubt who we have right now would have wanted to deal with that prick.”

“Scarce?”

“Two of our bouncer have been missing for a week now, one Fae, one Nephilim.”

“They don’t happen to live near the Hollow, do they?”

“Yeah, both just on the outskirts, near Navere Boulevard.”

I watch as Tam’s expression darkens, but he says nothing more, letting the bartender move off to get his drink. I settle back into the stool next to him, stealing glances at him from the corner of my eye. He gets his beer, taking a long drink from it before spinning in his stool to face the dance floor. A small smile tugs at his lips, but his eyes seem almost...sad. I glance behind me, following his line of sight to see his roommate, Nox, sitting with a couple of Fae males and females. He’s deep in conversation, but he must sense Tam watching him because he looks up in that moment. He smirks, and then his eyes drift to me.

He seems surprised, tilting his head curiously before shifting his eyes back to Tam. I glance back at him, too, and that's when he turns to look at me.

"You seem to be a magnet for trouble," he sighs, taking another large gulp of beer. "Can't you go anywhere without some type of drama following you?"

"You seem to be at each event, so maybe the drama is following *you* and not me."

So much for playing it cool and not losing my temper with him. He seems to bring out the worst in me, my mouth having a mind of its own in his presence. "Hmm, maybe you're right. Next time, I'll stay away from you." He moves to get up, but I grip into his arm, stopping him. His eyes drift down to where my hand meets his bare skin, the heat from him sending a tingle through me at the contact.

"Thank you," I whisper. "He just wouldn't leave me alone."

"Don't worry, I won't make the same mistake he did," he murmurs, slipping out of my hold.

"You don't have to go," I say quickly when he moves to get up again.

"I'm here with my friend."

I glance back at Nox, who is currently making out with some girl on one of the VIP couches. "He doesn't seem too bothered with the fact you're over here and not there," I point out.

"Yeah," he says, and I swear I catch an edge of disappointment in his voice.

"Is everything alright?" He turns to me again, the corner of his lips tugging downward. "I just mean, you seem a bit off."

"Long day," he sighs, and my heart skips a beat when he settles back into the stool, leaning his back against the counter of the bar. "I don't usually come to places like this, but Nox loves it, and we both needed a few hours to unwind."

"Unwind...as in drinking or..."

He cocks his head partially to glance at me, a small flutter in his cheek forming. "Drinking is part of it, but Nox needs to get laid." His eyes drift down and back up my body in a long sweep, his gaze feeling like a wash of desert air. "Since the last time he tried to hook up with someone, she fell asleep."

My cheeks redden. "I—"

"You don't have to explain. It happens to the best of us," he says, waving his hand dismissively.

"I don't want you pegging me as someone who does that on a regular basis," I say quickly.

"And why is that? It shouldn't matter what I think of you."

Ouch. Well, he's blunt, I'll give him that. "We got off on the wrong foot it seems." He eyes my hand warily when I hold it out to him. "I'm Kalia."

"Eris," he murmurs, turning to face the dance floor again, dismissively, and completely ignoring my hand.

I flex it awkwardly, slowly pulling it back in embarrassment. I hate that he's still hiding who he really is from me. Why can't he be honest? Is it so wrong for him to admit he's a Prince of the Night Court? I shake my head, laughing mentally at the entire situation. Can I really judge him when I'm not being completely honest either? He'll come around in time—he just needs *time.* He'll end up as obsessed with me as I seem to be with him.

"You don't like me," I say quietly, fidgeting with the straw in my glass. When he doesn't say anything, I glance up. He's staring at me with a frown on his face, the line between his brows growing more prominent with each passing second. "I get it," I say quickly, trying to laugh it off, but it comes out hollow and empty. "I've been a pain in the ass."

He rolls his eyes. "At least you can acknowledge that."

My jaw twitches with irritation. Not the answer I was hoping for, but it should have been the one I expected. It would have been nicer if he denied my claim and just acknowledged *me*. "I won't keep you then, since you rather hang out with your friend."

"You seemed adamant about me sitting with you."

"I just wanted to say thank you and I did, so you can go now."

"Fine."

He chugs back the rest of his beer and lifts himself from the stool, his movements holding the preternatural grace beyond that of a supernatural, but definitely one of royal status. He stops, his eyes fixed on Nox once again, and his shoulders slump slightly. His chest heaves like he's taking in a deep, steadying breath, and then he turns towards me. He steps close enough that his thighs graze against my bare knees, the feel of his jeans brushing against my skin sending a fluttering wave through my chest. I glance up at him through my lashes, not sure what to expect from him.

"Do you want to dance?" I blink, lifting my head more to look at him fully. He seems sincere, maybe even a little bit nervous in asking the question. He doesn't seem like the type to struggle with his words or wants, but right now, he's acting shy, more than I ever thought possible from someone like him. "Never mind," he mumbles, taking my prolonged silence as rejecting.

"No! I mean, yes, I want to dance."

He studies me for a moment, his gaze guarded, but he steps back and holds out his hand to me.

CHAPTER 22

TAMZIN

What the fuck am I doing? The last thing I should be doing is getting involved with this girl, and I definitely shouldn't be asking her to dance. My eyes zoned in on her the moment Nox and I walked through the doors, her discomfort palpable even from a distance. That fucking prick vampire had no right to lay hands on her, and I saw red the instant he did it. Nox didn't even attempt to stop me, his soft chuckle the only sound following me while I tore across the room towards them. I had his arm gripped in my hand before I even registered what I was doing, but the moment I saw her face, how upset she was at the whole situation, it's like my body took over.

I grip her hand in mine, soft tingles radiating through my skin the instant our hands made contact. I push down the sensation, ignoring any possibility of what it could mean, and pull her along onto the dance floor. This is so stupid. It's not like this is normal dancing, not with the hoard of bodies bouncing and grinding up against each other. I'm regretting it more and more, not wanting her to think *this* is what I expect from her. I don't even know what the fuck I'm doing.

She steps closer to me, her eyes peeking up at me through her lashes while she tentatively places her hands on my shoulders. She starts bouncing to the beat, while I awkwardly shift my feet, trying not to touch her or get too close to her.

"You don't dance much, do you?" She asks, smiling up at me. I shake my head, glancing around to check on Nox like I have been this entire night so far. My eyes drift back down to her when her hands move down my arms to grip my wrists. She moves my hands, placing them on either side of her hips. I feel like such an idiot, curling my fingers into loose fists so I don't accidently touch her ass, even though I *really* want to touch her ass. It's plump, filling in the sleek dress adorning her small frame. She's not lacking in the curves department, and her red hair glistens in cascading waves down her back. Her amber eyes flick up to meet mine, a smirk tugging at her lips.

"You're not what I expected," she says, tipping her head curiously.

"And what did you expect?"

She shrugs. "I'm not sure exactly, but I didn't think you were so...respectful." I snort, shaking my head. "I'm serious. You're being very sweet tonight." I turn my head away from her, my body moving with hers to the beat. Her hands trail back up, and she settles them on either side of my neck. The heat from her hands has my body shuddering, and she slowly turns my head back to look at her. "Thank you for earlier."

"Anyone would have done it."

She shakes her head. "I highly doubt that. In a place this crowded, you were the only one besides the bartender to notice what was happening. I could have handled it myself, but I appreciate the thought and effort." She steps closer to me, her stomach pressing against mine while she drags her hands down to settle on my chest. Her nostrils flare slightly, and her eyes flutter closed.

Did she just fucking scent me? What do I smell like to her? I'm fighting with my own need to scent her completely, but subtle threads still drift up to me with the close proximity. Her shampoo overpowers her natural smell when I'm not pulling for it directly, the smell of citrus tingling my sinuses. I still catch hints of lavender and honeysuckle, and I catch myself leaning in closer to her hair.

No, Tamzin. We do not sniff random girls that we're actually trying to avoid.

I'm doing such a great fucking job of following that stupid rule I put on myself. Is it so wrong for me to pursue her? If she's up for a random hookup, then what's the problem? Yeah, just a random hookup...I can do that.

Slowly I uncurl my fingers, letting them settle along her hips and the soft swell of her ass. Her eyes drift open again as she tips her head up to look at me, her full lips parting in what seems like surprise.

"What?" I ask.

She shakes her head. "Nothing at all."

Another song starts, this one with a more sensual beat to it, and I glance around to see everyone practically grinding up on each other. I startle when Kalia turns in my grip, my breath hitching when she presses her ass into me. My teeth grind together, my mind flipping through anything it can to distract myself from the feel of her rubbing up against my cock. *Don't get hard. Don't get hard. Don't get fucking hard.* Fuck. She bends forward slightly, shoving that pert ass deeper into my hips, and slowly lifts herself back up, leaning into me. Her hand snakes up behind my neck, and she tips her head enough to look up at me.

"Loosen up," she chirps. "We're just dancing."

I let out a rattling breath, slowly sliding my hands around her waist to settle against her stomach. My heart stutters when she slides her other hand over one of mine and ever so slowly drags both our hands lower—dangerously low. This is dangerous territory, but fuck me, I want it. I press my palm into her pelvis, pulling her tighter against my own body. She sighs, the sound almost like a whimper, and tips her head back to rest against my chest, exposing her long, perfect neck to me. No wonder the vamp was obsessed with her, that flawless expanse of skin is just begging to be sunken into.

Before I realize what I'm doing, my other hand moves, gripping into her throat and pinning her to me. Her eyes snap open, their glittering gold flecks focused on me. Fuck it. I squeeze slightly, tipping her head back further, and my eyes dart to her lips when they part on a small gasp. Slowly, I lower my face down to hers, stopping a mere inch away from her mouth.

"Tell me now if you don't want this," I whisper, my voice low and thick with the desperate need to see where this will end up.

"I—" She gasps again when my grip tightens further, her pulse fluttering heavily beneath my fingertips. "I want it," she says huskily, the tone of her voice making my cock twitch in my pants, pressing into her harder.

Pure heat pulses through me the moment my lips touch hers. Her mouth parts—inviting—welcoming my tongue. One sensual sweep and she moans into my mouth, leaning further into me while her body begins to tremble. Fuck, she tastes better than I imagined, my daydreams about this mouth and what it would be like to kiss her, paling in comparison to the real thing.

I grip further into her throat, tipping her head how I want her so I can plunge my tongue into her mouth fully. By the time I break the kiss, she's panting, her cheeks flush and her eyes glistening with need and desire. "Tam," she whimpers when I let my hand drift between her thighs. I freeze, my body stiffening at her calling me by my real name. She gasps when I pull back from her, bumping into a couple behind me. "What's wrong?" She asks, the look of confusion seeming completely genuine.

"Eris," I say through gritted teeth. "My name is Eris."

Her eyes widen, darting around for a second before locking back onto mine. She steps towards me, and if it weren't for the couple behind me, who have now decided grinded up on my ass is the way to go, I would back away from her again.

"You don't have to hide from me," she says, her voice a hushed tone in comparison to the music thumping through me. "I don't care who you are, I just don't want you lying to me."

"I don't know you, and you don't know me. If you're going to push this...this was a mistake."

"Please!" She grips my wrist, stopping me from stepping around her. "I'm sorry. Please don't walk away. You can't tell me you didn't *feel* something from that kiss."

I *did* feel something from that kiss, and that's a problem as well, but the problem I need to deal with first is the fact she's so hung up on me being Tamzin. "I felt nothing," I lie, my heart cracking a little when her face falls.

"You don't mean that," she chokes out, gripping into my wrist a bit harder. "Why are you saying that? I know you feel something for me. Is it really because I called you Tam? Will you give me a chance if I call you Eris? I'm sorry."

I never expected her personality to change in this way. She's been hot and cold with her attitude, and for a while there, I didn't actually think she was interested in me at all. Her pleading eyes are making me want to see just how far I can push this.

"Are you begging me to take you home?" I ask.

Her throat bobs thickly, her tongue darting out to lick her lips. "Do you want me to beg?" She says, her voice breaking slightly on the words.

"It would be a start."

"You want me on my knees for you?"

Fuck, I would *love* her on her knees for me. That foul mouth parted for me to shove my cock into it. Her luscious lips wrapping around my shaft, and those golden eyes staring up at me while I fuck that pretty little mouth.

Her hand shifts from my wrist to my chest, her fingers dragging gently down the center to the edge of my pants. "Do you want me to suck your cock?"

"Will that be part of your begging?" I ask, my pants getting awfully tight from my cock hardening further.

"Until my throat memorizes every vein."

My body sways at the mental picture she just painted, and fuck me, I want that. I open my mouth to respond, stopping short when I see Nox making his way over to us with his arm slung around a petite Fae's shoulders.

"I'm heading home," he says, a wide grin spreading across his face. Kalia turns to look at him over her shoulder, and his eyes drop down to look at her. He quirks a brow. "Are you sticking around or..."

"I'll head home, too."

"Alone?" Nox asks, his eyes flicking to Kalia again.

She turns to look at me as well, her chest heaving lightly like she's trying to steady her breathing. Her gaze is hopeful, flicking between my eyes, my lips, and back again. I can't stop thinking about that kiss either, and my curiosity is winning the war within my head—the one warning me of the danger this girl will bring my way.

Looping my arm across her low back, I tug her towards me. She gasps, bracing her hand on my chest. "Not alone."

"Excellent," Nox laughs. "Maybe she'll actually stay awake for you."

"That was one time!" She argues, making Nox and me laugh.

I lean down to her ear, finally allowing myself the pleasure of truly scenting her, and fuck me, she's mouthwatering. "You'll be too busy to fall asleep, and that won't happen until I'm done with you." Her body shivers against mine, and she leans back enough to look up at me, her eyes wide. "This is your chance to change your mind." She shakes her head. "Alright, let's go."

CHAPTER 23

TAMZIN

The giggling female latched onto Nox's arm is actually adorable, and he seem happy with his choice for the night. A twinge of jealousy still creeps into my chest, but I squash it down the moment we get into the apartment. The two of them exuberantly run off to Nox's room, while I take my time walking in, closing the door behind me, and turning on one of the side lamp lights. Kalia is a bit more hesitant, her eyes lingering on Nox's closed door for a moment before drifting over to mine, which is slightly ajar.

"Your room?" She asks, pointing to it. I nod, tossing my keys into the bowl on the table next to the door. She makes her way towards it, and I slowly follow her, keeping a few feet distance between us. I hover by the door, leaning into the frame as I watch her take in my bedroom. "It's cute. Plain, but cute."

She turns, settling into the edge of the bed and giving it a little bounce. "It's for sleeping. I don't exactly need to decorate it." Her eyes drift to the ceiling, a smile playing at her lips. "Nox thought it would be funny to put them up. Neither of us really grew up with shit like that since it didn't exist at the time. It's novelty at this point."

"I think it's cute," she says quietly. "I wish I had something like this in my room."

"What part of town do you live in? You just moved here, right?"

She flops back on the bed, settling her hands over her stomach. Her fingers drift across the silken material of her dress, drawing small patterns. "I'm near the pier, over on Glasgow. It's just a small duplex apartment, nothing like this one. I don't exactly have a ton of money to use right now, but I don't mind. Once I get my inheritance I might move, but I sort of like the place. It's an older building with a lot of history to it. I can *feel* the stories within its walls. It reminds me a lot of home."

"Autumn territory."

"Yeah."

"What are the royals like in your district?"

She shrugs, pulling herself up to sit again. "Archaic. They're still all about the old rule and arranged marriages. They just sent off their youngest daughter to get married to Camden."

"I heard." Her brows shoot up in surprise. "I mean, I know he's getting married, but I don't know any of the details. Don't even know her name or what she looks like, but the Night Court likes to keep their business pretty private."

She gets up from the bed, reaching behind her to slowly draw the zipper down on her dress. My breath hitches when it slips off her shoulders, revealing her bare chest, the thin, lacy material of her thong the only piece of clothing on her body. She steps closer to me, curling her fingers into the edge of my shirt. Her eyes drift up, her hand pausing on my stomach. I give her a small nod, and she takes the invitation to push my shirt up over my head, where I have to finish pulling it off because of her small stature.

She licks her lips, her fingers exploring every inch of my bare chest in front of her, tracing ever ridge of muscle and every scar. She pauses on the bigger one just above my hip bone, her brows dipping in confusion. "What happened here?"

"I have a lot of scars, Kalia, I don't remember what each one is from." It's a lie, I know every scar on every inch of my body, and I know exactly who delt them and with what. Anxiety claws at my chest at the fact she might notice the ones on my back, too, and ask questions about those. I tried to have them covered up with tattoos, but there's only so much you can do to hide blemished flesh to that degree.

She traces the tattoo over my heart, my stupid attempt at trying to protect the fragile organ hidden beneath the surface. "A caged heart?" She asks, following the lines of metal bars hiding the black heart behind it. She leans forward, pressing her lips over the ink. "A cage works both ways," she says quietly. "It contains and protects the prisoner, but it also protects those on the outside from the darkness within that cage." Her eyes flick up to mine, and I try to tamper down the erratic pace of that very dark heart beating behind the cage. "You're afraid to get hurt, aren't you?"

"Why do you insist on asking personal questions?"

"Is it wrong of me to try and get to know you? I didn't know questions were such a burden to you."

"I didn't bring you here to talk," I grit out, hating the way my heart aches to do just that, but I can't, not with this random girl that I know nothing about. I can't risk telling her something that may give away the truth about *everything*. It's bad enough she's seeing my scars and probably judging me for them.

She sighs, stepping back to trail her fingers down to the edge of my jeans. She makes quick work of unbuckling my belt, snapping the button in one smooth motion. She lifts her eyes back to mine as she slowly drags the zipper down, hooking her fingers into the waistband to push them off my hips. They drop to the floor with a soft thump, and a small hum slips through her lips when she glances down at my boxer briefs.

"Exactly what I expected from what I felt on the dance floor," she murmurs quietly, palming my cock through the material. She kisses my chest, trailing her lips down to my stomach as she slowly lowers herself down to her knees in front of me. Hooking her fingers into the edge of my underwear, she drags them down, my cock springing free. "Is this how you want me?" She asks, her voice low and seductive, and fuck me if she isn't *exactly* how I want her.

"Yes."

"What do you want me to do, *Eris*," she says, a bite to her tone when she says my name.

"Suck my cock like the vicious little fox that you are, and then...then I want you to beg me to make you come."

Her eyes rim with light for a moment, the amber hue overtaken by a brilliant gold that's absolutely mesmerizing. "Are you going to call me a good girl?" She smirks.

I fight back my own smile. "Only if you *are* one. Good girls get praise; bad girls get punished."

She squirms a bit, settling onto her heels, and slowly drags her hands up my thighs. "You have a beautiful body," she whispers, her tone holding a bit of awe in the words. "I wouldn't have guessed you had as much muscle as you do, so it's a nice surprise." She grips the base of my cock, giving it a firm stroke and swirling her thumb around the tip of it.

I let out a shuddering breath, settling my hand on her hair. It's so soft, like pure silk beneath my palm, and I can't stop myself from running my fingers through the strands. She licks her lips, then teases her tongue on the head of my cock, and that small touch of heat almost sends me into oblivion. Fuck, I needed this. I didn't even realize how pent up I was until her tongue touched me. I haven't even rubbed one out myself—I haven't done anything since Catia. She wasn't exactly stellar, but she provided me with what I needed, little did I know she was already attached. Didn't find out that little tidbit until *after* I fucked her. She conveniently forgot to mention that fact, and I was beyond pissed about it, kicking her the fuck out as soon as the words left her mouth.

I don't want drama, and boyfriends bring drama. I had to fucking kill the guy because of her and her big mouth. Come to think of it, I should have just killed her, too—ended her suffering. A two for one deal if you will. I shake my head.

No, stop thinking about it, you fucking idiot.

I *need* to forget about it and move on. It's in the past and there's nothing I can do to change that outcome.

I grip into her hair, tangling the strands around my fingers, and step closer to her. "Open." She does as I ask, dropping her jaw and sticking her tongue out enough to cradle my cock. The desire to shove into her mouth is pretty strong, but she *is* being a good girl, and good girls get rewarded. I slowly untangle my fingers from her hair and her brows furrow. I brush her cheek with my thumb and smile down at her. "Good girl, Kalia."

She visibly shivers at the sound of her name on my lips, though, I'm sure the praise helps, too. She seems surprised that I'm not taking what I want from her, and slowly she pumps her hand at my base and slides my length into her mouth. My head tips back at the sensation of pure bliss, her warm mouth perfectly cradling every inch it can. She takes me in deep, swallows, then slowly drags her head back until a small pop sounds as her lips leave my shaft.

"Fuck, that's good. Again."

She smiles, repeating the motion again. The sensation ripples through my body, a thick tingling heat building at the base of my spine with every suck, every lick, and every sensual taste.

"Are you memorizing the feel of my cock like you said you would?" Her tongue swirls around the tip and she hums out a breath, giving me a subtle nod. "Good girl. I want it permanently etched into your memory, Kalia." She squirms again, her hand inching closer between her thighs. "No," I snap, and she pauses. "You're not allowed to touch yourself. *I'm* the one that's going to make you come, not you. Do you understand me?" She nods again. I grip into her hair and pull her head away from me. She lets out a sharp gasp, her eyes going wide. "Say it."

"I—I understand," she says breathlessly, her cheeks turning a flushed rosy, red, almost blending in with her hair.

Looking at her this closely, I notice the small smattering of freckles trying to peek through her makeup. They're a bit more concentrated over her nose, fading out over her high cheekbones. I highly doubt she needs the makeup, and I have no idea why she would want to hide something that makes her even more beautiful.

CHAPTER 24

KALIA

Fuck, he's sexier than I expected him to be. I knew he was pretty tightly wound, but I didn't expect him to be this feral and dirty in the bedroom. I couldn't help but squirm while my own arousal built up inside of me. Sucking him off is definitely doing things to my body, and I just want to touch myself, or better yet, have *him* touch me.

He said he wanted to make me come, so I just need to be patient, be the good girl he said I was, and do as I'm told. Fuck, I'm fucked up. I shouldn't be this turned on, but I love a male who takes control and tells me what he wants. I knew from the comments he made at the club that he wouldn't disappoint me, and I'm so glad I'm being proven right. I had zero issue dropping to my knees for him, especially after feeling the thickness and length of his cock. I can feel my insides pulsing just at the thought of it being in me, thrusting into me, moulding my pussy into submission.

"Fuck, yeah, that's good," he groans, tipping his head back when I take him into my mouth again. My jaw aches trying to accommodate his girth, and I can barely take his length. It hits the back of my throat, and I gag, trying to swallow around it. He brushes his thumb against my cheek, the gentle touch a heavy contrast to the feral gaze smoldering in his eyes. "Can I come in your mouth?"

Why is he actually sweet? The fact he's asking if it's okay instead of just doing it like I know he wants to, just goes to show that Tamzin is *good*. I hate that I have to call him Eris. I want to call him Tam, I want to moan and cry out his actual name when he makes me come, but after his reaction at the club, I can't risk upsetting him. I don't want him to kick me out, not until I've had my way with him and buried my very essence into his core.

I nod and his blue eyes rim with light, the colour shift making his irises seem almost grey in the dim light of the room. Thick heat coats my tongue, the salty tang lacing itself into my tastebuds. He pulls back and I swallow him down, licking my lips of every last drop of him.

Surprise radiates through me when he grips my jaw and bends down, pressing his lips to mine. His tongue nudges at my lips and I part for him, moaning at the sensual swipe against my own. That's a first for me. Normally, a guy wouldn't want to kiss after I've had their dick in my mouth, and definitely not after they've come. I know I can still taste him, which means he just tasted himself. Fuck, that's so hot. My breaths are panting and slightly laboured when he pulls back from me. Holding out his hand, I slowly place mine in his, and he helps me to my feet.

I squeak out in surprise when he hoists me onto his hips, carrying me over to the bed. I can't fight the urge to run my fingers through his hair, the blonde strands soft against my fingertips. My hands trail over his shoulders and across his back, the roughness of scars there, too, surprising me. His body stiffens against mine, and the next second, I'm bouncing on the mattress with Tam looming over me.

He doesn't seem to like when I focus in on them like that, but I can't help it, I want to know more about him and what he's been through. I know the tattoo over his heart has a darker meaning than what most people might assume. I gasp when he literally rips my underwear off. *Damn it, I liked that pair.* My eyes watch the fluttering piece of fabric falling uselessly to the floor before locking back on *him*.

"Safe words?" He murmurs, trailing his lips across my thigh. My chest heaves, my body bowing at the sensual swipe of his tongue against my skin, the small nips of his teeth, and the heat of his lips moving further and further until—he stops. My voice whines out in frustration, my lust-filled gaze turning into a glare. "Safe words," he says again, his voice almost a growl, feral and deep.

"I—I don't need them."

I whine again when he pulls back, settling onto his heels. "I rather you have them and not need to use them, than not have them and then we run into a problem."

"Are you planning to maim me while you fuck me?" I smirk.

He rolls his eyes. "Maim, no. Turn you into a puddle, absolutely, which is why I want you to have a safe word in place in case you want me to slow down or stop and actually mean it. I'm not going to stop if you tell me stop, since you might say that anyways in the heat of the moment."

My body practically vibrates in anticipation. I didn't actually expect him to be the full-blown kinky type, but he keeps surprising me. "Uh, the regular ones are fine."

Green, yellow, red?" I nod. "Okay. Say them back to me. Keep going."

"Green."

"I'm okay but getting a bit uncomfortable."

"Yellow," I whisper, my voice trembling.

"It's too much, I need to stop."

"Red."

"Good girl."

He trails his mouth along my skin once again, moving excruciatingly slowly until—

"Oh, fuck," I whimper. My hands lurching down to grip into his hair, the longer strands tangling between my fingers. I tug when he flicks his tongue again, and he groans against me, delving into me before dragging that wicked tongue back up to my clit. My breath is wheezing through my lungs, the ability to pull in a proper breath completely escaping me while he frenzies and ravishes my clit.

I jolt, my hips bucking into him when he slips a finger into me, pulsing it hard and fast, right up to the knuckle. A second one slides in, and I can't stop my legs from shaking now, my grip on his hair tightening. Every thrust and every flick and luscious press of his tongue has me unraveling further and further, pushing me right to the edge. He slides his fingers out a bit, and I feel a third, but he doesn't thrust in.

"Colour," he mutters.

"Green," I gasp, and I swear I can feel him smiling between my legs before he plunges the third one into me. My hips ache, his fingers pulsing and swirling, curling and spreading inside of me, making me feel so fucking full. "Fuck. Oh, Fuck!" I cry out, no longer being able to control my body.

My orgasm hits me like a tidal wave, and I try to squirm away from him, but he presses his other hand into my stomach, pinning me down while he pushes me further, ramming into me with heavy strokes of his fingers. His tongue is like a whole other beast, flicking and swirling, his lips sucking and even his teeth nipping at the sensitive area. I bite my lip, stopping myself from calling out his name, and choking on it as it tries to rip through my throat anyways. I take a deep, steadying breath, reminding myself over and over again.

"Eris," I whimper when he finally pulls away, but my body still feels him, a phantom sensation that he's still pulsing into me, and a deep need to feel *more*.

He leans over me, settling one hand near my head while his other one loops around my back. He lifts me with supernatural ease, shifting me closer to the headboard. He reaches behind it, and I hear a soft clinking before I notice what he grabbed. Fuck. My eyes dart to the edges of the board, to the holes carved into the heavy wood and the tail end of chains attached to internal rings.

The cuffs he pulls forward are leather—soft leather by the looks of it. He settles them onto the front side of the bed and shifts back from me. "Colour." My eyes dart between the cuffs and his face. Do I trust him enough to strap me down? Not having the use of my hands is a bit panic-inducing, and it's not something I've tried before. "Kalia," he says, his voice sharp enough to draw my gaze back to his. He points to the cuffs. "Colour."

"Light—light green," I stutter.

He smirks. "That wasn't one of the agreed upon safe words."

"I don't *know* how I feel about this. I'm curious, but...maybe a little nervous."

"Do you think I'll hurt you?"

"I don't know."

"In the time that you've known me and our interactions, have I hurt you?"

"...no," I say meekly.

"What if I start with one? Would that make you more comfortable? You're Fae, you should be able to break out of these easily enough. They're not spelled in any way to actually restrict. They're more of a guideline of the intention behind them."

"Maybe, yeah," I whisper.

He grabs one of the cuffs. "Colour."

"Green," I say with a bit more confidence.

He grips my arm and slowly hooks the cuff around my wrist, doing up the buckle tight enough that I can't slip free, but not tight enough that I feel any pain from it. "How's that?"

I test the restraint, feeling that he's right, there's no magical signature to them, they're just plain cuffs that I could definitely break out of if I wanted to. "Good," I say quietly.

He leans down and kisses me, the soft touch of his lips sending a flutter through my chest. Once again, his way of doing things a complete contrast to the darker nature of his sexual endeavors. He pulls back enough to look down at me again, his eyes searching for something, but I'm not sure what.

He pulls back, his eyes moving over every inch of my naked body. "You're so fucking beautiful," he murmurs, trailing his fingers across my collarbone, and down between my breasts. His thumb grazes against one of my nipples, circling it until it hardens into a taught peak. "Mmm, I love the way your body responds," he purrs, leaning down to pull that nipple into his mouth.

He nips his teeth against it, his tongue swirling around it before he pulls it into his mouth and sucks gently. My body bows into the touch, wanting more contact, more sensual passes of his mouth. "Please," I whimper.

"Please what?" He rasps, moving to the other one to do the same thing.

"Oh, fuck, that feels so good," I choke out.

"This is just the beginning, little fox. I'll have you panting and screaming in a minute." Fuck, that just made me wetter than the fucking ocean. He inhales sharply, a low growl rumbling in his throat as he slowly drags his hand up my thigh to settle between my legs. "You're so fucking wet," he groans. "Your body knows what it wants, doesn't it, fox?"

"Yes," I squeak out.

"What does it want, Kalia?"

"You," I breathe, the word breathy and needy in a way I never thought possible.

He pulls back again and my body aches at the loss of his heat. Leaning over, he grabs one of the pillows, hooks his arm under me, and settles it under my hips. He settles himself between my thighs, my eyes drifting down to his hardened cock. He grips it, giving it a firm stroke before pressing it against me.

"Wait!" I pant out. He pauses, his brows furrowing in confusion. I shakily lift my free hand up towards him. "I trust you."

He grins and nods his head, reaching forward to grab the other cuff to place around my wrist. "You're being such a good girl, Kalia. Do you know what I do for good girls?" I shake my head. "Good girls get rewarded."

He slides into me, the pressure and suddenness of him filling me has my back arching off the bed. My fingers curl around the cuff chains, and I brace against them when he thrusts in deep. Fuck, he's big, each pulse of his hips sending him further into me. I've never felt so stretched and raw, completely exposed and vulnerable to his desires.

He leans over me again, bracing his hands on either side of my head as his face hovers mere inches from mine. "Colour," he pants out, his warm breath fanning against my skin.

"Gr—green," I pant, trying to talk through the brutal thrust of his cock.

He kisses me, deep and sensual, moaning into my mouth when he presses into me further, rolling his hips up to meet mine. "Fuck, you feel so good," he murmurs, nipping at my lip and jaw, trailing kisses over ever inch of my neck. He bites down on the tendon, my pulse fluttering as I cry out. "That's it, let me hear you," he groans, nipping at me again.

My insides flare with heat, pulsing and twitching around his cock as my orgasm builds and builds. My body squirms under him, my toes curling into the sheets, and the chains rattle when I tug on them. I want to touch him. I want to curl my arms around him and bring him closer to me. Fuck, I just want to feel the weight of him pressing into me, drowning out everything around me until it's just *him*.

He grips my jaw, tilting my head to the side to give him better access as his mouth moves, his tongue swirling and dragging in hot strokes. His fingers curl around my throat and my eyes widen when he pulls back enough to look down at me, slowly squeezing. I can still breathe, but the sensation feels strange and airy, like my mind is trying to float away. I can feel my own pulse beating against his fingers, the heavy, quick beats, a staccato within my own ears.

"Colour," he groans, thrusting into me again.

His grip makes me question my sanity. This is insane. I'm strapped to his bed while he rails me into oblivion, and he's in the perfect position to actually kill me if he wanted to. I've pissed him off enough that I wouldn't actually put it past him, and if he knew the truth about me, he wouldn't even entertain the thought of fucking me right now. I have time to explain everything—at least I *will* have time. I told him I trusted him, and I meant it.

"Green," I say, trying to tamper down the feeling of my powers beginning to burn through me. My chest heaves, my breaths coming in sharp bursts as he tightens his hold further. I can't lose control, but fuck me, I want to. I want to let it all go, let it all out, let myself finally be who I want to be and show him who I truly am. I can't...not yet. I squash down the building power. Focusing in on the feel of him moving inside of me. Every thrust, every pulse of his hips, every twitch of his cock as it rocks my insides into eternal bliss. "Fuck!" I cry out.

"That's it," he huffs. "Come for me. I want to feel you come around my cock, Kalia." He squeezes tighter, stars sparking across my vision as my climax slams into me. My mouth gapes on a silent scream, a garbled squeak the only sound escaping through his hold. The sudden loss of his hand has air rushing into my lungs, the influx of oxygen pushing my orgasm further as he rams into me again and again, rutting me harder and harder. I scream, my hands clawing at the air in a desperate attempt to hold onto something, anything, fucking *anything* to tether me to my own body. "Fuck," he grunts, gripping into my hips hard enough to bruise.

"Tam!"

CHAPTER 25

KALIA

My eyes widen in panic when his hand slams over my mouth. "Yellow," he growls, and the look on his face—the way his eyes glow with anger—has my body quaking in fear. I didn't mean to do that. I've been fighting with myself to not slip up, but in my blissful haze I slipped up. He said yellow though and not red, so I should be okay as long as I don't fucking do that again. "Do you know what I do to bad girls, little fox?" I shake my head. "Bad girls get punished. You made *me* say yellow, Kalia. Fucking yellow, do you understand?" A small nod.

He lifts his hand from my mouth, and I suck in air, desperate for it from barely being able to breathe through that encounter. He slams into me again, pinching my nipple hard between his fingers. I cry out, my thighs tightening around his hips in a desperate attempt to squirm away from him. He does it again and my body jolts at the sensation. It's too much—it's too fucking much. My body bucks and bows, twisting within the trap he's put me in with his body and these fucking cuffs.

"Colour," he huffs breathlessly.

I'm so close to saying yellow that I hesitate in speaking. He pinches my nipple again and I try to twist away, but that just makes the sharp sting worse. His hand slips around my throat again, forcing me to look at him. My breath stutters at how brightly his eyes are glowing now, very obviously *not* normal Fae. His chest heaves with every pulse of his hips, his jaw ticking with irritation. He reaches his other hand between us, and I cry out when his thumb begins to frenzy against my clit.

"Please!" I whimper.

"Colour," he says again.

"Yellow!" I cry. "Fuck! Please, stop!"

"No," he snarls. "You know how this works, Kalia."

Another orgasm tears through me, and I can't breathe, can't think, can't fucking function. I can't feel my limbs, my legs falling weakly open around him and my arms hanging limply in the cuffs. A single tear slips down my cheek, a small sob escaping my lips. He slows his movements, and I glance up at him through a shaky breath, a look of concern flittering across his face.

"Colour," he whispers, almost hesitantly now. The traitorous tear must be enough to think he pushed me too far, his own panic settling into his face.

I swallow hard, feeling the movement because of his grip on my throat which is slowly loosening. "Green," I rasp.

He pulls in a shuddering breath, letting it out through pursed lips. He releases my throat, slowly dragging his hand down to settle over my stomach. "Good. Good fucking girl, Kalia. I'm almost there." His fingers curl into my skin, his hips thrusting into me again and again, over and over. I feel like I'm breaking, both mentally and physically. I no longer have control over my body. I lost that control the moment I got into bed with him. It feels like my body is going to give out completely, but the traitorous whore still reacts to him as he forces another orgasm to build and crash like a vicious wave against jagged cliffs.

My chest is literally heaving as he comes, the thick heat of it shooting into me, the air burning through my lungs like living flames hellbent on destroying me from the inside out. He was right about one thing though; he turned me into a puddle. That's what my body feels like right now, a fucking puddle. No matter how much I will my limbs to move, I can't do anything but lie here, unmoving.

He slowly pulls out of me, a whimper slipping through my lips. Shifting off the bed, he moves to one side to undo the cuff, gently placing my arm down on the bed before moving to the other side to do the same thing. I watch him as he makes his way to another door, assuming the bathroom, and he comes back a few minutes later with a couple of towels in hand. He sets one down on the bed and carefully crawls back up onto the mattress. He grips my knee to open my legs, which I shakily fight him on.

"Kalia," he chastises. "Let me clean you up."

A few torturous seconds tick by before I give into his hold and let him shift my legs apart. Everything is so sensitive, every gentle swipe of the warm cloth pulling a whimper from my lips.

CHAPTER 26

TAMZIN

I thought I took it too far. The moment she said my name I just snapped, my mind already amped up from being lost in the feel of her. When I saw that tear streak down her cheek, I thought I broke her. I never used to be this way, but the more time that passed—the more I felt out of control—the more I needed control in any way I could find. Control during sex seemed like the simplest attempt at finding that fragile thread of power.

Guilt washes over me with every whimper that slips through her lips. Cleaning her up is the least I can do, if anything, I should be doing more for her for what I just put her through. Once I finish, I grab the dry towel to use on her as well. She's quiet as I walk back to the bathroom, tossing the towels into the hamper. Glancing at her once I'm back in the room, I notice her watching me, her eyes dazed, her cheeks flushed, and her chest still heaving lightly with each breath. I toss on a pair of sweatpants, grab a t-shirt from one of my drawers, and head back over to her.

"Can you sit up?" She nods, bracing her hands on the bed to try and prop herself up, but they shake under her in protest. "I got you," I murmur, that guilt hitting me again. I help her up, hooking the collar of the shirt over her head and tugging it down. She struggles to put her arms through the holes, but gets it done, letting out a heavy breath.

I pull her hair out from under the collar, brushing the loose strands away from her face. "What's with the shirt?" She asks, fidgeting with the hem of it.

"For you to sleep in."

Her gaze lifts to meet mine, confusion pulling at her brows. "You're not going to make me do the walk of shame?"

"*Can* you walk?" She smirks, shaking her head. "I'm sorry if I pushed you too far," I say quietly.

"I'm okay."

"Do you want some water or anything?"

"Water would be good," she sighs.

"Alright, get comfy and I'll be right back." I settle my hand on her head, pressing my lips to her forehead. When I pull back, she has a look of confusion on her face. "What?"

She presses her lips together, fighting back a smile. "You're being really sweet," she says quietly. "With the aftercare, and offering me water, and then this," she says, touching her fingertips to her forehead.

"Would you rather I be an asshole and tell you to get the fuck out, even if you have to crawl out of here?"

"I wouldn't have blamed you if you did."

What the fuck is this girl on? Is that how guys treat her? I mean, I *did* kick her out the last time, but that was different. Nox wanted her out of here, and it's not like they slept together. I doubt he'll be kicking the Fae girl in his room out tonight once he's done. He's not actually a dick, he just has dick moments.

"Sorry to disappoint you then," I murmur, walking out of the room before she makes me feel like shit for actually caring. Even my hookups still get treated properly, and in the morning, they're off on their merry way.

Nox is in the kitchen, chugging back a bottle himself when I get out there. He hears me coming and turns to look at me, the bottle still tipped against his lips. He pulls it away and gives me a wide grin. "You need to invest in soundproofing," he snorts. "I didn't expect her to be a screamer."

"I don't think she is normally," I smirk, pushing past him to grab two bottles from the fridge. He grabs another two for himself, assuming one is for the girl, too, and shuts the fridge door. "Did yours stay awake this time?"

He shoves me, rolling his eyes. "That was the first and *last* time that'll happen. It's not like I did anything wrong, and she was wide awake and completely coherent when I brought her home. Maybe she just used me as an excuse to get into our house," he snorts, but the comment gets me thinking.

I mulled over that idea myself, since the situation *really* didn't make sense. She wasn't drunk or high or anything of the sort when she walked out of here that night, so *why* would she fall asleep?

A grunt of surprise escapes me when Nox pokes me in the ribs to get my attention. "You don't think that's what happened, do you?"

"If it is, the question is why?"

"Maybe you have a stalker," he laughs. "Have you seen her around before?"

I wasn't planning to tell him anything about her, but he's got my brain going a mile a minute now. I don't want to believe that the girl in my room is up to something sinister. If she *is* stalking me, maybe she just likes me. She seemed surprised to see Dorian and Croh confront me, so I doubt she had any inkling of who I really am. I'll drag out the lie for as long as possible since she doesn't need to become a target as well. It's bad enough they know about Nox, and I'm hoping the little stunt she pulled at the club wasn't enough for Croh to warrant pursuing her out of spite.

"She doesn't really seem like the stalker type."

Nox lifts a brow in question. "No? She seems to show up wherever you are, and she's working at the Hub now, which you frequent quite often."

I sigh, leaning up against the counter. "Yes, I've seen her before. The night you brought her home, she was at the pit." His eyes widen and he steps closer to me, an edge of anger tainting his aura. "She didn't say anything to me, or really acknowledge me, she was just...there. I saw her leave as soon as I was done my fight, apparently going to Transcend and hooking up with you."

"That's...weird," he mutters, glancing towards my bedroom door. "Why didn't you tell me?"

"I didn't think it was a big deal. It's not like she's the only female that goes to the pits *and* to the club."

"Fine, but the fact she's working at the Hub now makes it seem even weirder. Let's not forget the fact she stepped in on that situation with you and your siblings, too, which is a bit weird I might add."

"I was talking to her at the bar that night...while I watched you socializing."

"I already knew you were stalking me, dude," he chuckles.

"She just moved here not that long ago, so it's not like I can tell if this is typical behaviour for her or not. I have nothing to base it off of."

He pats my shoulder and grabs the bottles of water again, slowly backing away. "Just be careful. Not to say she's dangerous or anything, but you never know."

"I don't sense anything from her outside of a typical Fae."

"Croh flinched when she touched him, did you sense anything then?" I shake my head. "Alright. Just don't do anything stupid with that girl."

I laugh, grabbing my own bottles again. "You're assuming I'll see her again after tonight."

"Won't you?" He smirks. "I can tell you like her beyond your usual hook ups."

"Hardly," I lie. "I'll see you in the morning."

Kalia is under the covers, practically on the edge of the bed when I walk back in. She sits up quickly, flinching slight with the movement. "Thank you," she says quietly, taking the bottle I hold out to her.

"Do you need anything else?" She shakes her head, taking a long drink from the bottle. "Okay, but if you change you're mind, just let me know."

She sighs, wiping the back of her hand against her mouth. "I'm okay, Eris. I don't need much."

My jaw ticks at how easily she can say my fake name now. She must be working really hard mentally not to slip up again. I'm sure she *wants* me to be Tamzin—to be the lost Fae Prince of the Night Court. Not that it's anything to brag about, and it's not like anything of that world is really mine. There are plenty of heirs before me, so I know I'll never see the crown on my head, and you know what? I don't fucking want it. I don't want any of it, not the name, not the title, I don't even want the fucking money. If I had any desire to have those things, I would have suffered in silence and accepted my role for what it was, but I don't want any of it, and I don't want to suffer any longer.

I'm happy with my life now, and with the family I've created. Nox is the only family that matters to me, and I know he cares about me without the title or anything. He accepted me as I was before he knew anything, and he still accepted me after the fact.

I drink from my own bottle, watching her carefully for any signs that I might be missing, but I don't see anything. I see a Fae sipping quietly on her water, trying to avoid making eye contact with me now.

Setting my bottle down, I settle into bed and turn off the bedside lamp, plunging the room into darkness. Lying on my back, one arm tucked under my head, I stare at the glowing stars. Kalia shifts in the bed next to me, and when I glance over, I notice her staring up as well, a smile tugging at her lips. The advantage to being shadow born, I can see in the dark pretty well. Not perfectly, but I assume my vision is better than other Fae.

"They're pretty," she says quietly.

"I think so, too."

She shifts in the bed again, turning to face me and tucking her hands under her head. "I had a good time tonight."

"Me, too."

"Listen," she starts, letting out a shaky breath. "I'm sorry for earlier, but I want you to know, it doesn't matter to me who you really are."

I roll away from her, not wanting to get into this conversation. Everyone says that, but it doesn't mean it's true. I don't know Kalia enough to judge whether or not that knowledge will sway her one way or another, but if this is what she wants to focus on, I have no choice but to end things after tonight.

She sniffles behind me, the sound sending a fresh wave of guilt through me. She shifts again, and I glance over my shoulder to see her back to me now, her body curled as close to the edge as possible. I want to reach out to her, rub her back and tell her it's okay, pull her into my chest and hold her for the rest of the night, but I know I can't, and I definitely shouldn't.

As soon as the morning comes around, I need to do what's necessary and send her on her way. This was probably a mistake on its own, but I definitely can't pursue anything further.

CHAPTER 27

TAMZIN

The sound of laughter rips me from sleep. I groan, rolling over and covering my head with the pillow to muffle the sound. Fucking hell, why is he up so early? My eyes snap open at the memory of last night. The bed is empty, Kalia's scent barely noticeable to me. Why is it so faint? Female laughter, followed by a snort, pulls me from the comfort of my bed.

Nox is sitting at the table with the girl from last night, having breakfast. He spots me right away, giving me an apologetic smile. "Did we wake you?" I glare at him. "I made pancakes if you and your girl want some breakfast."

My eyes dart around the apartment at his comment, my heart ramming in my chest. I jog back into the bedroom, beelining it for the bathroom, but it's empty, too. Her dress is gone—*she's* gone. All that's left of her is her lingering scent that's slowly fading with each passing second, and the shirt she wore to sleep in, folded neatly on the dresser.

A mix of emotions rips through me. Anger—because she left without saying a word. Guilt—because I know I'm the reason she left the way she did. Sadness—I completely shut her out last night when she was trying to apologize, and now it's too late to fix it. I thought maybe we could actually talk this morning, once I had a night to cool down, and coffee to tame my nerves, but she left before I even got a chance to do any of that.

I brought this on myself. Mentally, I had resolved myself to cut ties with her after last night, but the longer I laid there awake, listening to her breathing steady with sleep, the more I convinced myself that I might be able to make it work.

I'm dragging my feet by the time I leave my room again. "Hey, are you okay?" Nox says, his voice laced with concern.

"She left," I mumble.

"What do you mean, she left? I didn't hear her leave this morning." I shrug my shoulders, flopping down in one of the empty chairs. I can feel the Fae girl staring at me, but I don't want to talk to her or look at her. "What happened?"

"I'm not exactly sure," I say, and honestly, I don't. I knew I upset her, but I didn't think I upset her enough to leave without saying a word. My eyes finally drift to the girl, quietly eating her breakfast, and then I shift my gaze to Nox. "Don't forget what you have to do today."

"I'll get it done."

"Will you?" I ask, drifting my eyes to her again.

"Celine has to work this morning, so she won't be staying."

"It's nice to meet you, Celine."

"You, too," she chirps, her voice sounding hesitant in speaking to me.

I grab one of the pancakes, shoving half of it in my mouth before getting up from the table. "Is that all you're going to eat?" Nox calls as I make my way to my room again.

"I have shit to do," I grumble, closing the door between us so he's not tempted to pry further.

Fuck. I can't get out of my own head. I need to get out of here and do something before I completely lose it. What the fuck is wrong with me? Why am I so caught up on some random girl? I should be thankful that she left on her own and that I didn't have to have some awkward morning conversation with her, but I *wanted* to have a conversation with her. I toss on a pair of ripped jeans and a black t-shirt, grabbing my wallet from the nightstand.

"Later, man," I call out to Nox, grabbing my key from the bowl and bolting out the door before he can even respond.

I'm so lost in thought that I don't even realize where my body is taking me until I'm standing outside the door to the Hub. Fuck, I really *am* turning into a stalker. I catch sight of her red hair peeking past the customer standing in front of her and take a deep breath, putting myself in line. Kylo is probably going to rip into me again about not messaging ahead for my order, but I wasn't actually planning to come here this morning.

I let out a small sigh of relief when I see Ridley instead of Kylo manning the coffee machine. I wait patiently, shuffling forward a few steps with each helped customer until I'm in front of the counter.

Kalia's eyes meet mine, not a single acknowledgement of recognition. "What can I get you today?" She asks.

"Why'd you leave like that?" I blurt out.

Her eyes drop to the register. "Your order, *sir*," she murmurs.

"A quad espresso. Kalia, look at me."

She punches in my order, refusing to look at me. "You can tap your card," she says, pointing to the scanner.

I practically slam my card against it, making her jump in shock. "So, you're just going to pretend like nothing happened. Is that it?" I hiss out.

"Ridley will have your order ready in a minute," she whispers, her voice breaking slightly. Her throat bobs and she clears it, turning to Ridley and whispering something in her ear. Ridley frowns, a look of concern on her face, but she nods her head. Kalia moves quickly past her, darting into the breakroom at the back.

"Fuck," I mutter. I can't believe it got to this point. Not only do I look like a sociopath right now, but I've also pushed her to not even want to talk to me.

"Hey, Eris," Ridley says, a small smile on her face as she slides my coffee onto the serving counter. "Here's your order." I grab the cup, pausing as I turn away. I glance back to the breakroom once more, a wave of irritation stilling me. "Wait! You can't go back there!" Ridley calls out, but I'm at the door before she can stop me.

I rip it open, Kalia's wide eyes staring back at me as she sits in the corner on a small armchair. Those beautiful eyes are glistening, like she's trying to hold back tears. "Eris," she says shakily. Her gaze darts past me, to Ridley hovering at the door, and she gives her head a small shake.

Ridley sighs. "Call out if you need to," she says, pulling the door closed behind her.

"Why are you ignoring me?" I ask, forcing myself to stay rooted where I stand.

"It's what you wanted, isn't it? That's your routine, isn't it?"

"I wouldn't have let you stay last night if I was following routine."

"You made it pretty clear last night that you didn't want anything more."

I set my coffee down on a side table and step towards her, pausing when she curls back into the chair further, like she's fucking recoiling from me. "How exactly did I make it clear? If it were clear, I would know what the fuck you're talking about right now."

"Why won't you tell me the truth about you?" She snaps. "Why do you keep lying about it? I don't fucking care if you're Eris or Tam, but I want to know—I want to fucking know *you*."

"Why does it matter?!" I roar, anger seething through my body, burning within my veins. "*This* is why you're acting this way? I don't fucking know you, Kalia! I know nothing about you, and yet you want me to tell you about *my* fucking life?!" Her eyes drop to the floor, her body trembling in the wake of my anger. "I don't have to tell you shit. You're so caught up in the *idea* that I'm Tamzin, that you won't fucking acknowledge me as Eris. Sorry to disappoint you, but I'm not who you think I am."

"Eris—"

"Last night was a mistake," I snarl, the shadows in the room pulsing with my agitation. Her eyes dart around, widening when they begin to slither out from the corners. "I was a fucking idiot for ever thinking I could make this work with you. The fact I felt *anything* for you was a fucking mistake."

"So, you regret it. You regret sleeping with me."

"I regret ever *meeting* you," I snap, instantly feeling like shit at saying those words.

The tears she was clearly fighting break through, cascading down her cheeks as a small sob slips through her lips. "Just go," she chokes out. "Fucking go if I'm so awful to be around."

I fucked up. I let my anger get the best of me and reacted impulsively to this whole situation. She curls her knees up to her chest, her feet barely fitting on the small chair, and right now, she just looks so small and so fucking broken. She buries her face against her knees, wrapping her arms around her legs. My mouth opens to apologize, but I can't get the words out, silenced by the sobs that shake her body.

All the fight leaves my body, the blood in my veins feeling like ice. I back away from her, grabbing my coffee before gripping the doorknob with a shaking hand. Closing my eyes, I let my full tracking ability kick in, pulling her scent into my system, committing it to memory before walking out the door. I can still hear her small sobs rattling around in my head, phantom echoes of a pain I caused. There was zero reason for me to act that way or say those things to her. I didn't mean any of it. I don't regret last night, and I don't regret meeting her, but there's just something about her that tears at my defenses and it's like a caged beast inside of me is clawing its way out.

I swear I can hear Ridley talking to me as I walk out, but my mind won't focus, lost in a haze of thoughts as I replay back everything that just happened.

CHAPTER 28

TAMZIN

"What the fuck." Someone shakes me by my shoulder. "Come on, get up."

"Leave me alone," I groan, burying my face further against my forearms.

They grip into my hair and rip my head up. I blink—blink again. The haze around my sight fragments enough for me to sort of make out Nox in front of me. I slap his hand away, nearly toppling off the stool I'm sitting on.

"You over-served him," Nox snarls.

"He hasn't had that much here, and he seemed fine when he walked in."

"How much is not that much?"

"He's only had like three beers."

"Get off of me," I grumble when he grips into my arm, yanking me to my feet.

"Come on, let's get you home," Nox sighs, slinging my arm across his shoulders and gripping into my hip to help me out of the bar.

I glance back at it, confused when I see the sign to Foolish blinking overhead. "How did I get there?"

"What?"

I stumble over my own feet, forcing Nox to grip into me harder. "I was at the Ram's Head."

"So, you've been barhopping and you don't even remember? For fuck's sake, Tam, I was worried sick. I thought you got taken or some shit because of everything that's going on with Calvin's organization." He stops, my stomach roiling at the sudden decrease in momentum. "Come on, get in." He opens the passenger door to my car and helps me inside, closing the door on me before jogging around the front.

"It's dark out."

"Yeah, you've been gone all day, and you haven't responded to any of my messages or calls. I had to fucking track your phone. What the fuck are you doing in the Hollow district at this hour?"

"What time is it?"

"Almost nine."

Fuck, I got wasted. I don't even remember what happened, and I sure as fuck don't remember going to Foolish. I remember wandering around for a couple of hours, sitting down by the pier for a little bit, and then stopping in at Lush for one drink. I don't remember how I got to the Ram's head, but I remember seeing Hawk there, which he frequents the place quite a bit. I felt completely out of body when I left the Hub, and no matter how hard I try to remember what the fuck happened tonight, I can't pull on any real fragment of memory.

"What the fuck happened?" Nox asks, pulling the car onto the road. I stare out the side window, watching the Hollow stream by in a blur of lights and shadows. I feel nauseous as fuck, so I close my eyes, pulling a harsh breath in through my nose. "Tamzin," he snaps. "What the fuck happened? You said you had shit to do. I spent all day researching Calvin's men and inputting their information into the facial recognition software and you were out gallivanting?"

"I wasn't gallivanting," I pout. "I had a shitty morning, and I just sort of lost track of time."

"This isn't like you, so don't lie to me. What the fuck happened?"

"Kalia was at the Hub," I mumble. "She ignored me and then we sort of got into it and I snapped at her. I made her cry."

"You're this upset over some random female?"

"I don't take kindly to people brushing me off without reason."

"You're being ridiculous. It was a random fucking hookup with some chick that you've seen a couple of times. You got your dick wet, which is what you wanted, so what's the problem?"

"I don't know," I say honestly because I *don't* know what the fuck my problem is. I've become obsessed with her without even meaning to and now having her brush me off like that has pushed my anger to the forefront of my mind. It's worse because of how I treated her today. Even *if* it was just a hookup, I had no right to say something as fucking cruel as that to someone who hasn't actually done anything wrong.

I can't even call her or message her to apologize, the one thing I didn't have the balls to do in person since I never got her number. The thought of having to avoid her now is so fucking daunting. I love the Hub, and I hate that I may never be able to go back there because she's there and I don't want to make her more uncomfortable than I already have.

"What did you find out?" I ask, my voice cracking from the dryness in my throat.

Nox pulls into our spot at the apartment, turns off the car, and turns to look at me. Concern and what seems like pity pulls at his features. "We can talk about it tomorrow. You need to sleep, and you need a fucking shower. You smell like a brewery."

"Fine," I grumble, fumbling with the handle to the door. I pull and pull but it won't open. "Fuck," I sigh.

"Fuck, you're a mess. Hang on." He gets out of the car, rounding it quickly to open the door for me. "Fucking hell, Tam," he groans when I roll out of the car, face planting on the pavement. I sigh, closing my eyes at the welcoming feeling of the coolness against my cheek. "I *should* just leave you here," he grumbles, but he doesn't. He grips me under my arms, hoisting me to my feet, and slinging my arm around his shoulders again.

He's right, I'm a fucking mess. I can barely keep my legs moving at an even pace, and Nox is practically dragging me along, swearing and grunting under his breath.

"Fuck this," he mumbles. He turns his body into me, hoisting me up onto his shoulder like a fucking ragdoll. "I'm tired of dragging you."

"Put me down," I hiss out, flailing in his arms. "Ow, fuck! Did you just bite me?!"

"Keep squirming and I'll do more than bite your leg." I elbow him in the back of the head and smack his ass, trying to get myself free. "Tamzin," he growls, the tone of his voice stilling my movements. "I swear to the fucking gods I'm going to hurt you if you keep flailing." I slump against him, my arms hanging limply down his back, bouncing against him with every step. We get into the elevator, and he *still* doesn't put me down.

"I can crawl from here," I sigh.

"I'm not letting you crawl. What the fuck is wrong with you? Does this bother you that much?"

It *should* bother me, but it doesn't. I know I worried him today, ignoring his calls and messages. Fuck, where's my phone? I can't even tell if it's in my pocket because my fucking body feels numb right now. I don't say anything because I don't want to admit to the fact I'm sort of happy with how he's taking care of me. He sighs, walking through the door when the elevator pings open. The sound of his keys jingling tells me we're close to our apartment, and a few seconds later we're through the door. He carries me all the way to my room, and I half expect him to throw me onto the mattress like a sack of potatoes, but he doesn't, he bends down and gently sits me onto the edge of the bed.

I sway, my head spinning in the dim light of the room. He tugs at the edge of my shirt, and I slap his hand away. "I can do it." Fuck, why does my tongue feel so thick in my mouth. I must be plastered because my words feel awful, slurring like a drunken fool.

"Stop being so fucking stubborn. You can't even sit up straight."

"I'm sitting straight right now," I argue.

"Are you?" I'm really not, I'm leaning over so fucking far that I have no idea how I haven't toppled to the side yet. "Come on, let me help you." He straightens me out, tugging at my shirt again, and this time, I don't stop him. "Do you want to talk about it? Or anything for that matter?" He asks quietly, pulling the shirt off and tossing it in the hamper.

"No." He pulls me to my feet, moving my hands to grip into his shoulders while he kneels down in front of me to pull off my pants. "Am I a bad person?" I finally ask.

He stops moving, tipping his head up to look at me with a frown on his face. "What? No. Why would you think that?" I shrug, turning my gaze away from his. "Tam, you're not a bad person."

"Everything I touch turns to shit. I can't fucking get control over my own life, Nox."

"Is your life right now really that shitty?" I glance down at him from the corner of my eye. "What can I do to make it less shitty for you? I don't know what else to do, Tam. I'm trying to help you, I'm trying to be here for you, but you keep putting this wall around you the moment you let your emotions out. You can't keep burying everything that's happened to you deep inside because eventually you're going to explode."

"I know it's my fault."

He sighs, settling back onto his heels. "I didn't say that. I know you still hide shit from me, too."

My jaw clenches hard enough for it to pop, a fruitless effort in me trying to stop tears from falling, but I feel them burning in the back of my throat anyways. "My pain and burdens are not yours, Nox. I don't need you weighed down with my shit."

"Tam," he sighs, lifting himself back to his feet. I can't look at him, can't handle seeing the pity that I know is written all over his face. He grips my jaw, forcing me to look at him. "Have I not proven to you that I'm here for you? I have no one left, all I have is you, and you *mean* something to me. I'm here for the long haul, whether you want me to be or not. I'm not leaving you. I won't abandon you no matter how much darkness is inside of you. When will you finally realize that?"

"You're *good*, Nox, I don't *want* to burden you."

He tucks some of my hair behind my ear, the warmth of his fingers gently touching my skin a comforting sensation. My heart hammers hard against my chest when he tucks his fingers under my chin and tips my head up. His eyes drift down to my chest—no, to the tattoo over my heart. His fingers trail down my neck to the caged heart, gently tapping his fingertips against the design.

"This. This right here, Tam. I fucking see you, and I can see you breaking bit by bit. Caging your heart is only going to end up hurting yourself. You need to let people in. You need to let yourself feel more than pain and heartache. I know you're scared, okay? Everyday I can see the fear in your eyes, even if it's just for a moment." He flattens his palm over the tattoo, and I know he can feel how quickly my heart is thumping from the contact. "I'll never hurt you, Tam, and I'll never leave you."

I want to believe him, but something of that magnitude is impossible to promise. There's no guarantee of a tomorrow, and no guarantee that he won't in fact leave me. The thought of not having him in my life is soul crushing, but it's something I need to come to terms with. We're immortal in a sense, but we can still die so easily, too.

"I want to see you happy, Tam. I want you to live a life of joy, a life where you can laugh and be yourself. There might be people who won't like you for who or what you are, but the ones that come into your life and accept you, they're the only ones that matter. *Those* are the people that deserve to have a place in your heart. I want you to live, and love, and flourish."

I settle my hand overtop of his, pulling in a rattling breath. "I want to keep you forever," I say quietly.

"I know, buddy. Come on, maybe a bath would be better for you so you can just sit and relax."

I let him pull me along behind him, his steps slow enough to accommodate my uneven, sloppy pace. He points to the toilet, and I sit down shakily, watching him as he runs a bath for me, tossing scented Epsom salts into the now steaming water. The smell of lavender permeates the room, settling into my system and calming me down. He holds out his hand, and I take it, letting him help me up. I fumble with my underwear, tripping when I try to step out of them, and end up falling into Nox. His hands grip into my arms, steadying me.

"Easy, I got you," he murmurs, his breath fanning against my forehead. He holds onto me until I get my legs over the lip of the tub, not letting go until I'm sitting in the hot water. I shiver against the heat of it, curling my legs up to my chest.

He grabs my body wash and a cloth, settling onto his knees next to the tub. "What are you doing?" I say, my eyes feeling heavy with the heady scent of lavender. I feel so fucking tired, the hot water relaxing my muscles further. I settle my cheek against my knees, watching him with hooded eyes.

He brushes my hair back from my face, the gentle touch pulling my eyes to close. "I'm going to wash your back, and then your hair. I don't think you're functional enough to do either on your own."

"I can just sit here though."

"You can, yes, but I wasn't kidding about you stinking. You smell like booze and smoke."

"I think I smoked some nokweed."

"You think? Do you not remember much from tonight?"

"I don't know what happened," I admit.

His movements are gentle as he slowly lifts water onto my back with his hands, the soft pressure of the cloth feeling like heaven against my skin. My back is always aching—always itchy. The scars marring my skin a constant reminder of my past. Nox lingers a little longer over the bigger ones, confident in his movements. He doesn't avoid them and I'm thankful for that. As much as I hate showing my body to him, the proof of what was done to me most of my life, he's the one I trust the most.

"That feels nice," I murmur sleepily.

"I'm glad," he whispers, lapping water onto my back once more. "Tip your head back for me." I do what he asks, my eyes fluttering close once again at the feel of his hand cradled against my forehead as he lifts water onto my hair. He grabs my shampoo, lathering it up in his palms a bit before getting to work on my strands. "Your hair is getting pretty long."

"I should cut it," I sigh.

"No, I like it this length." Running his fingers through my hair, he tugs on the strands, and it sends a jolt of electricity down my spine. Fuck, that feels good. The sensation radiates through my hips, right into my cock. My breathing quickens with each passing stroke of his hand as he washes the suds out. "All clean. Just sit here for a bit and I'll go grab you some water."

He tilts my head towards him, kissing my temple before he pulls himself to his feet and walks out. Small gestures like that make me believe that we could have something more, but the fear of ruining my friendship with him haunts me. He comes back in a few minutes later with a pair of sweatpants slung over his arm.

"I put a bottle down on your nightstand. Let's get you in bed first, okay?" I nod, gripping into the tub to lift myself up. Fuck, I feel like shit. I'm panting by the time I get to my feet and glance up to see Nox holding a towel now, his other hand reaching out to me. I take it, letting him help me over the lip of the tub, suddenly very aware of how naked I am with my semi-hard cock jutting out. His eyes drift down to it, but he doesn't say anything, he just steps towards me and starts wiping me down, scrubbing the towel through my hair. He kneels down in front of me again with the sweatpants in hand. "Leg up."

I do as he asks, lifting one and then the other. He slides them up my hips and I can't help staring at his dark hair in front of me. Reaching out, I run my fingers through his hair, and he slowly tips his head back to look up at me. "Thank you," I whisper, brushing through his hair again.

He grips my wrist, slowly pulling my hand away from him and lifts himself to his feet. His eyes burn into mine, like they're searching for something deep down in my soul. My eyes flick to his lips, his perfect mouth that's slightly parted now. He's standing so close to me—too close. I can feel the heat of his body radiating between us, and I just want to touch him. No, I need get a hold of myself, especially in my intoxicated state. I do the one thing that needs to be done, even thought it physically hurts me to do it. I step back, settling my hand against his chest as a physical barrier between us.

"Tam—"

I shake my head, stepping back again and dropping my hand weakly at my side. "I'm going to bed."

I walk past him, holding onto the wall to stop the room from spinning around me. The nokweed must be fucking with my senses more than usual. I can usually get wasted, but it doesn't normally last this long at this level. "Tam." I ignore him, stumbling the couple of open-air steps until I can grip into the edge of the bed. I feel him hovering behind me, close enough he could touch me, but now he won't…of course he won't. "Tam," he says again, his voice now sounding panicked.

"You can go. Thank you for your help."

"Do you want me to stay with you?"

Fuck, I would *love* for him to stay with me, but I can't keep doing this to him or myself. "No."

"Tam, I—"

"Please just go," I murmur, my voice thick with emotion. "I'm not in the mental headspace to deal with this right now."

"Deal with what? Why are you shutting down again?" He says, exasperation and confusion lacing every word.

"*Please,*" I choke out.

"I don't want to leave you when you're like this."

"*Please,* Nox," I beg, my body shaking with the need to just breakdown into tears.

"Fine." He turns on his heels and walks away from me, the door closing quietly behind him.

My body give out, collapsing into the bed as sobs wrack my body. I'm such a fuckup, the biggest fuckup on the planet. In my attempt to not ruin things, I'm doing just that by pushing him away like this.

CHAPTER 29

NOX

I don't understand why he's doing this. I hover outside his door, hearing him breaking down on the other side of it. He tries his best to hide his emotions, but I fucking see him, I see him for what he is. He's broken and trying so hard to piece himself back together, but with every piece he mends, two more fall out of place. I settle my forehead against the cool wood of his door, my hands clawing into my own palms as I fight back the urge to tear back in there and ignore his request. No, not request, he practically begged me to leave him alone, his voice so fucking broken and lost.

I see the way he looks at me. I look at him the same way, but I don't know if he believes that I could ever have feelings for him like that. I love him. I've loved him for a while now, but I never had the balls to do anything about it. I've never loved anyone like I love him, least of all a male. I've only been with one other guy before, a secret I've kept from Tam because I didn't want to freak him out. Little did I know he was into men as well, an interesting surprise the other night. I sleep with random girls because he does, and it's what's expected of me at this point. It's not like I don't enjoy myself, but I don't *feel* anything for them. The one from last night was really nice and sweet, someone any guy would be lucky to end up with...any *other* guy, not me.

I know him, maybe better than he knows himself, and I know what he's thinking. He doesn't want to ruin the relationship we already have by complicating it further. Personally, I rather give it a try and not live with the regret of not seeing where this could end up. I won't push him though—I can't because pushing it might just end up pushing him away.

Anger boils in my blood at the knowledge he went off and got plastered because he was upset about some fucking girl. I'll kill her if she ended up hurting him, but it sounded like he's the one that lost his shit on her. I don't like her or the situation she's creating, but if I tell Tam to let it go, it'll just piss him off and he'll get more obsessed over the whole thing.

I hate his family for what they've done to him, but none more than his fucking father, the piece of shit. What he's done to Tamzin shouldn't go unpunished, and how could a child deserve such atrocities? How can someone as sweet and kind as Tam deserve to suffer so much? He might be brutal and vicious now, but that's not his nature, that's what he feels is necessary to get by in this cruel world. He deserves to be happy, and fuck me, I want to be the one that makes him happy.

I push away from the door, but I can't settle myself enough to even attempt going to bed yet, especially with him in there like that. I settle into the couch, pull off my damp shirt, and push my supernatural senses enough to keep an eye on him. He doesn't seem to be crying anymore, and his breathing eventually steadies into an even pace. Closing my eyes, I let my power leach into my vision, opening them to a white specular haze. Fuck, his aura is so chaotic right now, a mixture of muddled colours, showing me just how fucked up he's feeling right now. At least he resorted to nokweed and booze and didn't feel the need to use any helion. I hate that he uses that fucking drug, especially when it's so addictive. He doesn't seem to be feeling the effects of it in that way, but the way his body suffered from the backlash of it the other night is making me wonder if he's close to losing control of himself when it comes to it.

I wish he would just stop using it, but that's how the drug works. Once it gets its hooks into your brain chemistry, it's hard to break free of it, even *if* it hasn't hit full addiction.

My eyes narrow, focusing in on the fluctuation in his aura. It shifts from a yellowish green to blue with flickers of red seeping into the outer edges. A darkness starts to creep in, swallowing every bit of colour until there's nothing left. His aura flickers, shrinking until it's nothing more than a second skin cradling his body, and then it explodes, completely enveloping his entire room.

I'm on my feet and at his door before his scream rips through the air. I hiss out a breath when his shadows lash out at me, at me invading its territory. I claw at them, tearing my way into the darkness step by step. His nightmares are becoming more frequent, and that's a bit concerning. I can't figure out what's triggering him so badly that his mind wanders to those dark times.

His sobs tear at my heart, pushing me further forward. I can barely make out the shimmer of his aura within the pitch black of the room. He bolts up in bed, screaming at the top of his lungs, triggering his wings to manifest. They snap out around him, a hot wave of air electrified by his other ability...the one he doesn't use often or talks about. This was the power he manifested because of his fucking brothers, because of the pain they caused him in taking the one thing in this world that actually loved him. Lightning crackles through the room, clipping my arms, my shoulders, my face, but I keep pushing through.

His eyes are wide, brimming with tears and glowing brightly enough that not even his pupils are visible. Lightning licks across his teeth, spilling from his parted mouth with every harsh breath. This is the worst one yet. Normally, his lightning doesn't trigger and all I have to deal with are the shadows, but I don't care.

By the time I get my arms around him his entire body is shaking and covered in sweat. His chest heaves against mine, every breath more laboured and choked with sobs. "Shhh, I got you," I coo, brushing my hand over his head and down his back, squeezing him tighter to me. His hands come up, clawing at my back as a choked sob rips through his throat. "Breathe, Tam. It's okay, you're safe. I got you."

His lightning licks out against my skin, the sting of it minimal now, and the shadows slowly recede back into the corners and into his body. His wings drop to the bed, hanging limply from his back. "N—Nox," he pants, pulling in a shuddering, broken breath.

"It's me. You're okay." His hold on me tightens further and he buries his face into my neck, struggling to pull in a proper breath. His body is still shaking viciously, every single inch of him vibrating with panic. "Tamzin," I whisper. "Breathe with me. In." I inhale a slow, deep breath. "Out." I let the air out steadily through my lips, letting him feel my chest expand and contract in the hopes he mimics me. "In." I inhale again, thankful that he's at least trying now when I hear him inhale a shaky breath. "Out," I breathe, my breath fluttering against his still damp hair. "In." I squeeze him tighter. "And out." He keeps breathing, taking long, slow inhales, until his shaking eases. I pull back enough to look at him, cupping both sides of his jaw. He keeps his eyes down, their glassy sheen and red rim still visible to me. "You're okay," I whisper, kissing his forehead and wrapping my arms around him again.

"You came," he croaks out.

"Of course I did."

"I—I thought...because I told you to leave—because I shut you out—"

"Tam, you did nothing wrong. You wanted time to yourself, and I respect that, but I won't leave you alone when you're going through shit like this." His wings dissolve and I rub at his back to try and ease the ache he must be feeling from having them ripped out without control. "Are you okay?" I feel him nod slightly. "Do you want me to leave?" A shake of his head. "Okay, I'll stay." I back away from him and grab the still sealed bottle of water on the nightstand, handing it to him.

He takes a few small sips, his throat bobbing thickly and his eyes twitching as thought flinching in pain. It wouldn't surprise me if he *is* in pain. The scream that tore out of him tonight was visceral and filled with so much hurt. I'm glad I set up a barrier around our apartment to tamper down the noise, something I did after the second time this happened since we moved in here.

He cradles the bottle on his lap, his eyes down and his shoulder slumped in defeat. "Thank you," he whispers hoarsely.

"They've gotten worse."

"Yeah."

I want to pry. I want him to fucking talk to me and tell me what's going on in his head, but if I do that, he'll end up shutting down like he did earlier. When it doesn't seem like he's planning to drink anymore, I take the bottle from him, cap it, and set it back down on the nightstand. His cheeks are flushed, even though his complexion is paler than usual. I settle my hand on his forehead, frowning at how warm he feels right now.

"You're hot."

"Thank you," he says, laughing weakly. I crack a smile, thankful he still has the mental capacity to joke around right now. "It's just a bit of backlash from my power slipping out like that. I can overheat if I don't have full control over my lightning."

"Makes sense." His breathing still seems a bit laboured, and his body shakes as he lowers himself back down to the bed, wincing when he snuggles up against the pillow. "Do you need anything?"

"I just want to sleep."

"Do you still want me to stay with you?"

He nods, and I quickly make my way around the bed, sliding in under the covers. "I should have never asked you to leave," he murmurs, his voice barely a whisper.

"I know why you did." I press my hand between his shoulder blades, and he shudders, his muscles relaxing under my palm. "I want you to talk to me, Tam, but I won't push you to do that. I just want you to know I'm here for you when you're ready. I think you're keeping shit too bottled up and it's coming out in your nightmares."

"I can't. I can't talk about any of it right now."

I shift myself closer to him and loop my arm around his waist, pulling him back against my chest. His hand comes up to rest overtop of mine, and the joy that gives me should be illegal. "When you're ready," I whisper, settling my head against his pillow and squeezing him tightly.

It doesn't take long for his body to relax in my arms, his steady breathing and heartbeat telling me he's finally calmed down and fallen asleep. Hopefully he rests through the night with no incidents because I don't know how much more of this he can handle. Both mentally and physically at this point, both spectrums taking a beating with his vicious memories coming to life within his head. I kiss him on the head, his soft, still damp hair, comforting against my lips. I want every night to be like this. Not the nightmares and him having to suffer but being able to hold him like this. Fuck, I'm in trouble.

CHAPTER 30

TAMZIN

I don't want to move and risk waking him but being here like this doesn't bother me in the slightest. Sometime in the night I turned in his grip to face him. His face is so close to me right now I can see every single dark eyelash spread out over his cheeks. His lips are slightly parted, full and inviting, and I love that his arm is still around me, like he wanted to protect me while we slept.

I could have really hurt him last night, my powers ripping out around me out of control. I usually have a pretty good handle on the electricity, but being intoxicated must have shattered those walls I carefully put up around that part of myself.

I shift a bit closer to him, the temptation to press my lips against his being a constant thrum in my mind. His brows knit together and I freeze, hating that the small movement might have been enough to wake him.

I grunt out a breath when his arm snakes further around me and he yanks me in close to his chest. He inhales, letting it out through a small sigh, and I can feel the steady rhythm of his heart pounding through his hard chest. I can't help myself now, I run my fingers across his pec, tracing it down to his ribs where he got a wolf tattoo for his mother—a tattoo he got with me.

He sighs again, his hold tightening further, pulling me practically flush against his body now. Fuck male anatomy and what happens to most of us in the morning. I can feel *all* of him, every single inch of hardness pressing into me. "You smell good," he murmurs, nuzzling into my hair. His body stiffens, and the next second, he shifts me back, his wide eyes staring down at me. "Sorry," he says quickly, and the space he puts between us feels like a fucking chasm.

"It's fine," I smile, laughing it off. The last thing I want is to make this awkward for him. He's probably a cuddler, his body just naturally reacting to someone being in the same bed as him.

He tucks his hand under his pillow, shifting it to get comfortable. "How are you feeling?"

Fuck, his voice sounds sexy in the morning. It's deep and laced with sleep still, making it sound more sensual than normal. "I feel okay. No hangover at least."

He brushes my hair back and settles his palm on my forehead. "You still feel a little warm."

"I'll be fine, Nox."

He shifts his hand to cup my cheek, his thumb brushing gently against the skin under my eye. He frowns. "The nightmares are taking a toll on you, Tam. Your eyes are bloodshot."

"I'll be fine," I say again, hating the worry on his face. "I'll take a break from hunting after we deal with Calvin, let myself recover a bit."

He stares at me for a few long heartbeats but finally pulls away with a sigh and rolls onto his back. "I'll make some breakfast, and we can go over everything I found out yesterday so we can make a plan." He rolls over, sitting up on the edge of the bed and stretching his arms above his head. His muscle flex and move—mesmerizing to look at—and a small pop resonates from his back. "If you want to stay in bed a bit longer, I can call you when it's ready," he murmurs, getting up and heading to the door.

He doesn't wait for an answer, slipping out without looking back at me. I roll onto my back and stare at the ceiling, replaying everything that happened yesterday in my mind. There are definitely some blank spots in my memory, the areas that I was missing last night. How the fuck did I end up in the Hollow, and what the fuck did I do?

There's no way I can sleep anymore, and resting seems pointless when my brain doesn't want to shut off, so I get up. My body aches with every movement, slowing down my morning routine. Even brushing my teeth hurts at this point, fuck my life. Nox's voice comes in, muffled through the door, but I can tell he sounds irritated.

"He doesn't want to talk to you," he snarls, his phone pressed against his ear in a vicious hold that's turning his knuckles white. His eyes settle on mine, flickering with enough anger that it's threatening a shift.

"Who are you talking to?" I whisper.

"Why don't you go fuck yourself, *Camden*," he hisses, and my eyes widen.

I didn't think Cam was seriously going to take advantage of the fact he had Nox's number to try and get in contact with me. I strain my hearing, trying to make out anything he could be saying.

"I don't understand the harm in talking to him over the phone. You can't keep him away from me, Nox, and if you don't let me talk to him now, I'm going to come in person."

"The fuck you will. I don't give a shit who you are, you're not to come in contact with Tam unless *he* decides it."

"Please," Cam sighs. "Please just let me talk to my brother."

"Your brother? You have the nerve to even use that term when you've been anything *but* a brother to him? You know nothing about him, and I know you don't give a shit about him!"

"Nox," I murmur, shaking my head. I hold out my hand, and he just glares at it. "Give me the phone." He shakes his head. "Give me the phone."

He looks fucking pissed that I'm entertaining the asshole, but I can't let him fight my battles, and I don't need him to. "What do you want?" I say into the phone.

"Tamzin?" Cam asks, surprise clear in his voice.

"What do you want, Cam?"

"How are you doing?"

"Why do you care?"

"Tam—"

"Just tell me what you want or I'm hanging up."

The family is having a small engagement party, and I was hoping you would come."

"Why? It's bad enough you're more than likely going to force me to go to your stupid wedding, so why the fuck would I go to a party? Are you *making* me go?"

"I won't force you to go, but I *want* you there, Tam. You can bring Nox, too. I know he hates me, but I want you to feel comfortable."

"He *does* hate you. He hates all of you."

"And what about you?"

"I hate you less then the others, but it's not by much."

He laughs, a sound I haven't heard in a long time. "That has to count for something though, right? I'm sorry, Tam. I don't know how to make this right between us, but you're my brother and I love you. I want my family together."

"You seem to be the only one who considers me to be family. Croh won't want me there, and the twins even less, Cam."

"Let me deal with them. Helia will be happy to have you there, too. The others won't step out of line if I have any say in it."

"Dad won't want me there," I say quietly, my eyes flicking up to meet Nox's when I see his fists curl tight enough to turn his knuckles white. His entire body is vibrating, his shift bordering on uncontrolled. I step closer to him and rub his arm, trying to calm him down.

"It's my fucking wedding. It's bad enough they arranged it with no say from me, they will not deny me my guest list."

"What's she like? Your fiancé I mean."

"She's pretty quiet when she's at Court, but she refuses to stay here until she has to. She seems like she's a bit sassy, but she hasn't spoken much since she's arrived in our territory."

"I'm surprised you let her off the property," I scoff.

"I have no plans to cage her like an animal, Tam. The Autumn Court was bad enough, so if she wishes to experience the small joys of living in the world, I won't deny her that."

I'm actually floored by his actions and his mentality. I knew he was different from the others and from dad, I just didn't realize *how* different. I mean, I never really gave him a chance to show me, but he was always pretty aloof when shit was being done to me. He would argue, but he wouldn't step in to stop it. I'm sure fear of repercussion had a role in his actions.

"Please just think about it," he sighs.

"If I say yes, will you leave me alone?"

He laughs, and I'm fighting back my own smile at the sound. "I can't guarantee that, but I won't try to ruin your life if I see you. I'll even sweeten the deal if you let me meet up with you before then."

"I'm listening."

"I'll make sure Croh, and the others don't interfere with your daily life."

"Or Nox's. Croh zoned in on him at the club, Cam. I don't want any of them going after him either."

Nox steps towards me, shaking his head. I hold up my hand to ward him off. "Tam," he grits out. "Don't make deals for me."

"Done," Cam agrees, happiness lacing his voice. "I would prefer to not have to go through him to talk to you."

"I'll text you," I murmur, ending the call before I dig myself even deeper into this mess.

"Why would you do that?" Nox asks, confusion and that lingering anger still in his eyes.

"What?"

"You just agreed to more than you should have because of me. Why the fuck would you do that?"

"Do you honestly need to ask?" I hand him his phone back and flop myself down into one of the chairs at the table. Dragging my hands down my face, I let out a heavy sigh. "If this will get them all off our backs, I'll do what I need to, Nox."

"Tam—"

"Where's that breakfast." He snaps his mouth closed, irritation rippling off of him like a vicious wave.

I watch him as he moves about the kitchen, throwing together a massive breakfast with sausages, bacon, eggs, and toast. The entire time he doesn't say a word, but the more time that passes, the more his body seems to relax. He sets down a plate in front of me and moves to pull away, but I grip into his wrist to stop him.

I tip my head up to look at him, his eyes still guarded. "Thank you," I say quietly, giving his wrist a squeeze before grabbing my fork to dig in. He sighs and ruffles my hair playfully before going to grab his own plate of food.

He settles into his seat with his food and his laptop, opening it up. "So, Calvin has four main guards that go with him pretty much everywhere. Sometimes they rotate out, sometimes it's all of them going, depending on the location and situation. Even at home, he's got them fucking living on property." He flips the computer around, showing me a collage of the four of them with all their stats. I lift a brow at him. "What?" He mumbles.

"This is...thorough," I laugh.

"When I'm anxious I hyper focus on shit, and you made me fucking anxious yesterday, Tam."

I drop my eyes from his, focusing in on the laptop in front of me. The photos are clear, like they've been pulled from social profiles, and the stats on them have everything. Height, weight, even tax information and social security, and their breed.

"Marcus Shaw has a rap sheet on him, but he should be easy enough for you to deal with. He's a vampire, not pureblood, and his abilities are convenient for Calvin but not offensive. I'm assuming they use his illusion ability to break into places, and probably how they're kidnapping dark worlders without anyone noticing. He's a big fuck, so his size intimidates most people. Grant Steel is half Fae, half human. His Fae origin is based out of Blossom Court, and his powers are a neurotoxin that paralyzes. He's kept himself clean or least hasn't gotten caught yet. Reef Klinton is full Fae. Night Court crossed with a former Lunar Court resident. He's got shadow powers like you, but from what I gathered on him, nothing close to your level of power. He can control shadows that already exist, but he can't create them."

My eyes focus in on the lone female in the group. "Zenia Tucker?" I ask. "She seems...petite."

Nox snorts, sitting back into his chair. "She's the worst one of the four, if you can believe it. She's a werewolf, turned by Juniper's alpha himself."

"I didn't think that unhinged prick had enough control to turn *anyone*."

"She's got plenty of scars to prove what she went through in the process, but she's just as unhinged as he is. She likes to toy with her victims, drawing out punishment far longer than is necessary. She's Calvin's hound and right hand, and she's *with* Marcus. No idea how the fuck that happened, since vampires and werewolves don't get along, like at all."

"Like calls to like, as the saying goes. The unhinged are drawn to others just like them. Thank fuck werewolves don't have abilities."

"Actually," he says carefully. "She does. She's not just a werewolf. She started off as a witch. Thankfully, she's not elemental based, but she's still vicious to deal with. Gravity manipulation, so basically telekinesis."

"Fuck. Where did he *find* them? Also, why the fuck are they working for a human."

"He's paying them well, and he's got them hooked on helion." I shudder at the comment. "You need to be careful going up against them, Tam. They *could* kill you depending on how much they're using."

"I can handle them."

"You think so?" When I don't respond, he frowns. "You're going to fucking use again, aren't you," he says, not even bothering to word it like a question.

"I can go without, but it's like you said, they *could* kill me. I don't have a choice, Nox."

"What if we reject the request? This is beyond dangerous to deal with."

"Refusing the guard authority will just put a target on my back, too. They need to be taken down, and if we're the ones they've reached out to, it means they've run out of options. We can't keep letting people get taken. Sure, some of them have been bad people, but they've taken innocent fucking people, Nox. People they deem won't be missed by anyone, and that's just not right."

"Fine," he sighs. "I'm not sure where the best place to hit him is. From the surveillance I have on him, he seems to be frequenting the pier the most and of course his home. I would assume he's got magical security at home, but if we can pull him in transit somewhere, that might be our best bet."

"Have you noticed any patterns with the guard? Specific areas where he doesn't have all of them with him. If I can start taking the guards out one by one, it'll make it easier to get to him."

"From what I've seen, he keeps Zenia with him *all* the time. Marcus strays off once in a while, but only if one of the others is with them. Grant and Reef aren't as attached at the hip, so they should be your first targets."

"I want to deal with them tonight then, before they get back to the house. Get your program running and track them down."

His eyes widen. "You want to deal with them in the middle of the day?"

"If that's what's easiest, then yes."

"That seems really risky, Tam."

I turn the laptop back to him. "I know, but I also know you'll keep me safe."

"You're giving me a lot of credit," he smirks, his fingers flying across the keyboard, his breakfast going ignored.

I get up from the table and put my plate in the dishwasher before moving to stand next to him. He drags his eyes away from the screen, numbers and words streaming across it in a blur as he runs his hacking software. He tilts his head in confusion as I just stand staring at him, his eyes flicking around nervously.

"Eat your breakfast," I murmur, pointing to his untouched plate.

The corner of his mouth twitches. "Are you ordering me around?"

"It's a request. You can't take care of me if you don't take care of yourself." He nods, grabbing one of the sausages and popping the whole thing in his mouth. "Good boy," I smirk, ruffling his hair. "I'm going to get changed."

I'm halfway to my room when he finally speaks. "So, you don't want to talk about last night?"

I pause in my doorway. "About what?"

"Why you got plastered."

My shoulders slump in relief. My heart practically stopped at his question because I thought maybe he meant with what happened between us, but it's not like anything *happened* between us. "I was upset with myself for being an asshole and crushing some girl who didn't deserve it. I'll get over it."

"Is that all this is?"

"That's all it is." I walk away from him after that because it's not all it is. Kalia has turned into an obsession at this point, the thought of her rejecting me for something so stupid fueling me. Once I'm changed and ready to go, I head back out, grabbing my car keys from the bowl. “I’m taking the car. As soon as you have locations on Grant or Reef, let me know.”

“Are you just going to drive around all day?”

“I’m going to scope out the pier and probably do a drive by at Calvin’s place. I want to get a feel for it all before I do anything.”

“Okay. Are you going to be back for lunch?”

“Probably not, but I’ll be home for dinner. We can head out after that if you end up finding shit.”

“Okay.”

“I’ll see you later, Nox.”

“Yeah...see ya.”

CHAPTER 31

TAMZIN

My life just seems like it's going to shit. In my need to fix shit with Kalia, I'm fucking shit up with Nox. My stress levels are through the roof because I can't get a hold on my anxiety. This fucking feeling that's been ingrained into me, the need to always please everyone around me for the fear of being left alone. That's it—that's what this is. I'm fucking scared. Scared of being rejected, scared of being hated, and scared of being alone the rest of my life. It's been drilled into me, how much of a piece of shit I am, how no one can love a monster like me, how I'm broken and useless, destined to do nothing and *be* nothing.

I skip grabbing my car for now, wanting to walk off this pent-up energy burning through me. I can't get out of my own head, thoughts and memories playing through my mind like a shitty movie.

A surprised scream followed by a choked grunt rips me from my thoughts. My eyes widen when I notice Kalia scrambling to pull herself to her feet while she reaches for her smoke, which is trying to roll away from her in the gentle breeze. Glancing around, I realize I've walked myself to the one place I had no intention of going to today. I reach out my hand to help her up, but she glares at it, ignoring the gesture and pulling herself to her feet.

She turns away from me, moving towards the side of the building to the alley next to it. I fucking plowed into her on her way out for a break, and now I feel even more like an asshole, if that's even possible. "Kalia!" I call out.

"Leave me alone," she mumbles, disappearing around the corner.

I sigh, resolving myself to grab a coffee while she's not in there. Ridley glares at me the entire time, handing me my order without a word. Fucking great. Even Ridley fucking hates me now, probably from hearing me lose my shit on Kalia yesterday. Walking out of the shop, I hesitate at the door, deciding to turn to the alley instead of heading back to get my car. Kalia glances up right away, a puff of smoke curling from her perfect lips. The glare she's giving me should wither me into a fucking husk. I stop at the edge of the building, leaving a good ten feet between us.

"Are you deaf?" She snaps. "I told you to leave me alone."

"I will, I just...I want to apologize."

"I don't want to hear it."

"Kalia—"

"Go away!"

"Kalia, I'm sorry! I'm sorry I was such an asshole to you because you didn't deserve any of that! I'm sorry I said those things to you. I said them in anger, but I—I didn't mean them. I'm sorry I can't tell you more about myself, but I don't regret meeting you. I don't fucking regret any of it." My chest is heaving with panting breaths when I finally finish ranting like a sociopath, but at least now I can move on with the fact I apologized. "That's all I wanted to do, Kalia. I just wanted to apologize." I give her a small bow of my head and turn away from her.

"I never regretted it," she says quietly. I stop just at the edge of the building and glance back at her. Her eyes are locked on me, pain and sadness bowing her eyes. "Any of it. I don't regret meeting you and I don't regret the other night. Your words hurt me—they cut into me like a fucking knife because I didn't think I did anything wrong. You honestly think an apology means anything to me when you've said something so fucking cruel?"

"I don't blame you for not wanting my apology," I mutter. "I don't even expect you to forgive me, Kalia. All I want is for you to know how I feel and that you *didn't* do anything wrong. I'll let you get back to work. I have some shit to take care of."

"Shit to take care of," she scoffs. "Another murder fight in the pit?"

"No, something far worse." I walk away before she can pry any further, already hating that I said that much to her.

CHAPTER 32

KALIA

"Hey, are you okay?" I glance up at the sound of Ridley's voice, her face contorting into concern. "Did he hurt you?" I shake my head. "You look upset."

"The whole thing with him is just so fucking stupid," I murmur, grabbing my apron from behind the counter to help her prep for the lunch menu. "He apologized for yesterday, but I hate the fact that I know he's hiding shit from me."

"Like what?"

There's no way in hell I'm bringing up the fact he's actually Tamzin, the youngest Prince of the Night Court. She would probably keel over an die at that information, and Tam would never forgive me for spreading rumours, even if they're true.

"What does Eris do for work exactly?"

"Oh, you don't know?" I shake my head. "He's a hunter." I blink, not understanding what she means. "Sort of like a bounty hunter, but I'm sure he does more than just that."

"Does he kill people?"

She shrugs. "I would assume anyone that's on that sort of list would be hauled in dead or alive. He fights in the pits, too. He's pretty popular amongst the locals, and he's never lost a match in the three years he's been fighting. I'm a bit surprised you even got involved with him. He's hot and super sweet, but he's a bit unstable."

I try to tamper down the simmering anger building in my chest at her words. How dare she call him unstable. She has no idea what someone like him has gone through. If she knew who he was, she might even pity him, but I don't want that either. Everyone knows that the Night Court royals are put through extensive trials in order to increase their power and natural abilities. The side effect of such tactics is the loss of their Fae wings, and some lose their humanity. They never normally take it far enough to trigger a darkling manifestation, but they push it pretty fucking close.

The ritual for power is barbaric, especially when implemented on children. Tam could have turned out so much worse than he did, Croh being a prime example. He's still not as bad as Dorian, and the twins—fucking hell they're terrifying.

I still snap, not wanting her to think that Tam is this *monster* that needs to be feared. She should be more afraid of me than him. "He's not unstable. He's had a shitty life, and he doesn't deserve to have people judging him like that. He *is* sweet, and caring, and kind."

"Then why did you push him away?" She snorts. "If he's so fucking perfect, why would you just walk away from that? If he came here and apologized to you for how he treated you yesterday, why wouldn't you just forgive him?"

"It's not that simple, Ridley," I sigh. "There's other shit we still need to talk about, but he's avoiding it like the plague. *That's* why I was upset with him to begin with."

"So, this wasn't just a random hookup? You're actually into him, aren't you?"

I try to fight back the smile trying to push its way through, but I can't. The thought of actually being with *him* brings a grin to my face. I try to hide it by ducking my head down, but Ridley catches it and laughs.

"I see how it is," she giggles. "Well, he seems a bit obsessed with you, too."

That's what I'm hoping for. I want him to be obsessed with me—I *need* him to be. It's the only way any of this is going to work out in my favour. I want Tam to love me, to only care about me. I know he doesn't give a shit about his family, well, most of his family. He seems to have a soft spot for his sister, especially because of how his brothers treat her. None of them will stand between us in the end, not even Nox.

"Do you know if he's working a job right now? He seemed to be more on edge than normal, and he was in a bit of a rush."

"I'm not completely sure. There are always rumours circulating when there's a bounty on someone, but unless that bounty is someone who is liked, no one wants to risk them finding out if Nox and Eris are after someone. They deal with shady people most of the time, ones that could end up risking the community's safety. That's the main reason the guard authority hasn't stopped them, even with the new order going out."

"New order?" I frown.

"Technically, bounty hunting is no longer legal, or I guess, in the grey zone, but I think they did that so random people with too much money weren't just trying to off some random person they don't like. Their targets over the last six months have been criminals."

"Is there anyone who *should* be on that list?" I ask, hoping to narrow down who Tam could be hunting at the moment.

"There are quite a few that should be, but I wish they could take down whoever has been kidnapping the supernaturals lately. They're mainly disappearing from the Hollow district, but it's only a matter of time before that net gets spread out." She narrows her eyes and points at me. "You better be staying out of that area, Kalia, it's not safe in general, but even less right now."

"I will. I live near the pier."

"Maybe you should get yourself some protection. Unless you have abilities?"

"I can take care of myself but thank you for your concern."

"They're taking out pretty powerful supernaturals. I'm not sure how they're doing it, but if they can take out someone like Krane and Donavan, they would be able to grab you no problem."

"Who are they?"

"Two of the bouncers from Transcend."

"Oh, I heard about that the other night when I was there." Maybe that's what Tam is working on right now. He seemed a bit upset when the bartender mentioned it the other night, and he didn't ask any more questions, like he knew what was going on. "Where's Naverre Boulevard?"

Ridley's eyes widen. "That's basically Hollow territory. Why?"

"That's where the two bouncers live."

"So, another reason for you to stay as far away from that district as you can. There's nothing down there but drug dealers and shady shit. The fucking pit should be there, too, but with the amount of traffic they get through the place, it doesn't surprise me that they didn't want to put it somewhere people won't frequent as often."

"What do you know about helion?"

Her nose crinkles in disgust. "The shit is vile. It's super addictive, and it boost abilities in a fucked-up way. It uses the user's life energy, burning through it like gasoline on an already raging flame."

"So, it could kill someone?"

"If it's being regulated when being used it won't kill you right away, but eventually the addiction will push you to use more and more until your body can't handle the influx."

"Usually sold in vials, right? A weird black liquid with a green tinge to it?"

She frowns again, and I'm worried she's going to get supernatural wrinkles because of me. "Yeah," she says carefully. "Do you know someone using it?" I shrug. "Does Eris use?"

"I don't know, I was just curious because I heard someone mentioning it at the club." The lie comes easily, but there's no way in hell I'm telling her I have suspicion Tam *is* using. I saw the vial tucked against the lamp on his nightstand the other night, but it was pretty full. I don't think he's using it frequently, but I'm concerned on how *long* he's been using it for.

"Definitely stay away from that shit, Kalia," she says, her tone serious, and a twinge knicks at my heart. I've only known her for a little while, but it fills my heart with joy that she cares about me enough to warn me of something so dangerous.

I've gotten more care and affection from these perfect strangers of the Hub in the last week, than I ever truly got from my own family. Fuck my family. Fuck them for forcing me to do things I don't want to do. The only good thing about all of this is the fact I get to live on my own for a little while, not that they *know* I'm living on my own.

"Do you want to grab some dinner with me after work?" She asks, completely surprising me.

I smile—a genuine smile that spreads wide across my face. "I'd love that."

CHAPTER 33

TAMZIN

"I wish you would have just stayed at home," I sigh, glancing over to Nox in the passenger seat, laptop propped up on his knees.

He turns to me and rolls his eyes. "Is my being here such an imposition?"

"That's not what I'm getting at. It's safer for you when you're at home doing this shit, or at least far enough away that you're out of the line of fire if something happens."

"I can handle myself," he snorts. "And I promise not to leave the car if that makes you feel better."

I want to rip into him further, but I squash down that urge and glance up at the shitty building across the street. "I expected...more," I mumble, watching as Reef steps into the building with barely a glance around at his surroundings. His overconfidence is a hindrance to his survival, which I'm planning to prove shortly. Sure, there isn't that much foot traffic near the pier at this hour, but he should still feel a little worried on being seen.

"There's no reason for Calvin to thin out his resources to a shit hole like this. The barrier he has around his property sounds pretty intricate, and I'm surprised he was able to get a witch with high level magic to do it for him. You said you saw a rune system, right?"

"Yeah. When I drove the perimeter, he had obelisks set around the corners of the property. They were black adamant like the ones at Court, working as conduits for the runes. They were glowing with a green hue to them, so maybe we're dealing with a warlock and not a witch. The dark magic of a warlock is more unstable though, so I'm hoping that'll be the key to getting in there if we need to. He wouldn't see me coming if I attacked him in his home."

"We'll play it by ear. If we can get him out in the open, it would still take him by surprise. To take him on at home I would have to get the full recent blueprints to the place and hope that he hasn't made any modifications to the building itself, or you could end up warping right into a wall."

"Alright, let's deal with this prick."

"Taking him out is going to raise flags, Tam. You realize that, right? As soon as Calvin can't get a hold of him, he's going to amp up security."

"I have an idea," I murmur, snagging a lighter out of the center console. He frowns, his eyes drifting between it and my face. "If I make it look like an accident in that shithole, he might not think too much of it. Do you know what they're doing with that building?"

Nox turns back to his computer, his fingers tapping out some random lines of code before he turns the screen towards me. "Looks like a drug hub from the magical signature." He narrows his eyes at me when I grab the vial of helion and drip two drops under my tongue. "Two, Tam?" He says angrily.

"It's dark out. He's a shadow user, too, and a building like that is most definitely *not* lit up."

"I told you his powers won't compare to yours."

"You're assuming he's not on helion, too, or something fucking worse. If they're producing necro, I'm done for without this."

His eyes widen and his face pales before he looks away from me. Necro is the worst of the worst, beyond addictive and basically radioactive for powers. One hit and you're hooked on it, and there's no coming back from that. A few guys stroll out of the building, laughing as they head to their cars.

"I'm going in."

"Here." He hands me an earpiece, and I shove it into my ear with an eyeroll. "Don't give me attitude," he snorts.

"This one better not fry my eardrum like last time. I need my conscience to be clear in my head, not screeching bloody murder."

"Conscience?" He laughs. "Am I your Jiminy Cricket?"

"Way hotter and bigger, but yes." His cheeks flame instantly and he looks away. "You know you're hot as shit, right? It's not like I'm trying to stroke your ego, Nox," I laugh.

He clears his throat, shifting awkwardly in his seat. "Get going before I change my mind in being a good boy and staying here."

I grin, staring at the side of his face. He notices I'm not moving to get out and finally glances back at me with a raised brow. "A good boy?" I chirp.

"Am I not being good for listening to you?"

Fuck me, does he have a praise kink? I lean in closer to him and his body stiffens, his eyes darting down to my mouth. Very interesting reaction since I expected him to lean away, but I swear he sways slightly closer to me instead. "Do you want me to call you a good boy?" I purr, letting my voice drop dangerously low.

His throat bobs with a thick swallow, his eyes slowly drifting back up to look me dead in the eyes. "Maybe," he whispers, his voice breathy and oh so fucking sexy.

If it was anyone else I would fucking kiss him right now. It's the perfect moment for it, and I think we *both* know it, but he doesn't make a move either, and that's enough for me to hesitate. I sigh, leaning back enough to ease the tension between us by a small fraction. "Fine. Be a good boy and stay in the car no matter what. I don't want you getting hurt."

"Always my savior," he chuckles. "You can't protect me from everything."

"Watch me."

He stares at me for a few long heartbeats, enough time for an edge of sadness to tug at the corner of his eyes. "You can't, Tam," he says shakily.

I brush my hand through his hair, his eyes closing at the touch. Gripping gently, I bring him closer to me and press my forehead against his. "You're everything to me, Nox. I'll protect you no matter what and there's nothing you can say or do to stop me from doing that."

His hand settles against my chest, and I swear I can feel it trembling slightly as he pushes me back gently. "Go now before Reef takes off and we lose this chance."

It hurts to pull away from him, but I do it reluctantly and slip out of the car. I glance back to see him watching me as I make my way towards the warehouse, the eerie quiet settling into my bones heavily. I can feel the helion pulsing in my veins, nipping at my senses with the desire to be unleashed. Feeling my life energy in this way is so strange to me, but the feeling is intoxicating. Everything is heightened, everything around me coming into full focus, and I can see why people get addicted to it. Feeling this high all the time would be glorious, but so fucking exhausting in the end.

I give Nox one final glance, his eyes gleaming in the night like he's watching me with his shifter sight. Actually, he probably is. His sight is beyond that of normal shifters, his Fae side enhancing it in a way that allows him to see the auras around him in every colour imaginable. I wonder what my aura looks like to him. It feels like it would be pitch black, like the soul my family fought to corrupt.

Allowing the shadows to caress my body, I warp into the warehouse where Nox had pointed out. The metal platform rattles slightly beneath my feet, forcing me to grip into the railing to steady myself. I see Reef right away, glancing up in my direction with narrowed eyes. He stares for what feels like forever as I try to slow my breathing and steady my heart. He shakes his head, walking towards an internal door with an eerie green glow bleeding out from beneath it.

"I'm in," I say quietly.

A small crackle sounds in my ear followed by Nox's concerned voice. "Do you see him?"

"Yeah. I landed in a weird spot that made a bit of noise, but he couldn't see me through the shadow cloak. He went in through a door off the North wall."

I hear the subtle clicking of his keys on the laptop. "The room is about fifteen hundred square feet and I'm getting a magical signature off the room."

"Is it ward magic?"

"I don't think so. The magic seems internal, Tam. Whatever they have in there is a ticking timebomb."

"Perfect."

A beat of silence as Nox processes my comment. "Excuse me?"

"I'm planning to blow the place up once I take care of him."

"Tam—"

"It'll be fine, Nox. I'll make it out before that happens."

"You better or I'll fucking kill you myself."

"How are you supposed to kill me if I die in here," I snort, trying to keep my voice down.

"I'll find a way to bring you back so I can kill you all over again."

"Aw, you would miss me that much?"

"Of course I would," he snaps back.

"Alright, alright, just standby."

A high-pitched ringing starts to resonate from the room, the sound making me flinch back. I warp myself down near the door, gritting my teeth when the sound starts to scrape around my skull. I gasp out a breath when it finally stops, and I creep closer to the door, peering in through the small glass window set into its frame. I see Reef moving around the room, goggles and a mask strapped to his face. The walls are lined with massive glass tanks filled with fluorescent green liquid.

Small metal tanks are scattered around as well, lines hooking one large tank to another. Metal tables are set up in the center of the room, covered in vials, beakers, burners, and stacks of papers.

Reef stiffens, and I shift away from the window the second he starts to turn around. The hair on the back of my neck begins to prickle, so I look back through the window carefully, and blink in confusion. Where the fuck did he go? My eyes scan the entire room, but he's no where to be found, and I don't see another door in there for him to sneak out of.

Taking a deep breath, I slowly open the door, sneaking through the small gap I allow myself. I gag instantly at the smell of antiseptic and sulfur, covering my nose with my arm. My eyes are watering already and I've been in here for a fucking minute.

"Tam, everything okay?" Nox asks when I cough and gag.

"I'm not sure," I choke out, walking around the room and taking in every detail I can. I don't see Reef, but I see a computer with three monitors set in one of the corners. "There's a computer system in here. There are these massive tanks with toxic looking liquid in them. This set up is fucking insane, man."

"I'm going to try and hack into the system inside and see if I can figure out what the fuck they're making in there."

"Nox, I don't see him. It's a fucking sealed room but he's not fucking in here anymore."

"That's not possible," he murmurs, typing away. "The schematics of the building don't show anything but the one door you went through. He has to be in there."

"Can he void warp?"

"Not that I'm aware of. He doesn't have that level of power."

"Nox—"

I grunt in pain when I get slammed into one of the walls, metal canisters scattering across the floor and pipes ripping from the tanks. I blink rapidly, trying to clear my vision and the pounding headache forming in my skull. Reef steps out of the shadows in one of the corners, his eyes glowing viciously with a green tinge to them. Fuck me, he's on helion right now. I struggle to my feet as he stalks towards me, throwing my hand out towards him. Shadows rip up from the ground, clocking him across the neck, ripping the mask completely off his face, and sending him flying through the burners, beakers, and other glassware on the metal table before slamming into one of the tanks.

The sound of glass cracking radiates through the room and the liquid inside starts oozing through the damage. My eyes widen when a green gas begins to hiss out from the cracks as well, my gaze shifting to Reef trying to untangle himself from the mess. The sleeve of his jacket is on fire, and he panics, flailing and smacking at his arm to try and put it out.

"Nox," I whisper with a shaky voice, realizing my mistake. My mind feels hazy, and I'm struggling to blink away the sudden weight pressing into my mind. Reef hits the ground with a loud thump, his body limp and unmoving.

"Tam? What's going on."

"It's...going to...blow," I pant out, stumbling and crashing into the wall. I can't feel my fucking body, the doorway narrowing in my vision. "I'm...not..." I crash to the ground, willing myself to move as I struggle to drag myself across the glass covered floor. The exit seems so far away now, getting further away with every harsh breath as my vision blackens.

"Tam! Get out of there!"

"Neuro...toxin," I slur.

CHAPTER 34

NOX

My boots pound against the ground as I run full tilt towards the warehouse, slamming into the door and practically ripping it off its hinges. My eyes frantically search the facility, locking on the bright green glow in the distance. It's too far—too fucking far for me to reach in time before those ever-growing flames in the background ignite the noxious gas I'm now smelling. It reeks like rotten eggs, the scent of sulfur, a fucking bomb waiting to go off.

"Tam!" I scream out, running towards the last place I know he was. I pull on my shift, my wolf ripping to the surface and tearing up the distance in long strides. *No.* I flatten my ears and push myself faster when I see Tam's limp body just outside the door. I skid to a halt in front of him, taking in the scene unfolding behind him. Thick green gas crawls across the ground, inching its way towards Tam and the open door. I hold my breath, gripping the back of his shirt in my teeth and drag him a further distance from the door.

"Tam!" I scream the moment I shift back, shaking his body, but he doesn't move. I settle my ear near his mouth, choking on a sob of relief when I feel his warm breath tickle against the skin. "Tam, wake up!" I try again, gripping his jaw and giving his head a small shake. His eyes flutter slightly but that's all the reaction I'm going to get out of him.

I need to get him out of here before this place blows. I see Reef's body lying on the floor of the lab, cursing the fucking prick for ever existing and putting Tam in this situation. Gripping his arm, I hoist him onto my shoulder and lift myself back to my feet, running as fast as I can back towards the exit. I need to make it. I need to get us through that door, but I can *feel* the air shift, the subtle crackle of flame meeting gas.

I throw my body through the door with him, calling on my powers just before we hit the ground. I scream, covering his body with my own as the building behind us explodes, burning and writhing with flames that won't stop bombarding the weak shield I've placed around us. I push my power further, begging my body to hold on just a little longer, just enough time to get us through the worst of it. Blood trickles from my nose, dripping down and cradling against my lips, mixing in with the blood starting to ooze from my eyes and mouth as well.

My entire body is shaking with the strain, and tears run down my cheeks, mixing in with the blood leaving my body in hot waves. "Tam," I choke out, hugging his limp body closer to mine as the burn of the building tears into my shield, chipping away at it, piece by brutal piece.

"Oh my god!" I hear someone scream, the faint distant sound of footfalls drawing closer. I weakly glance up, my barrier shimmering and wavering around me. I blink, trying to clear my vision of the blood fucking blinding me right now, but all I see is red. Red hair, red light, red *everything*. "Nox?!" The female voice gasps.

"Help—help him," I sob.

"Him? Nox, your fucking bleeding from every fucking orifice! Hang on."

I don't have the strength to even look at her, my body draping over Tam's, heavy with exhaustion as my shield flickers out. I tried. I tried so fucking hard to save him, but with my barrier disintegrating, my hold slipping right through my fingers, I feel the wash of heat burning into me once more. New heat hits me, and then I feel nothing, like the flames have receded back from their assault.

"Is that your car?" I nod, struggling to lift myself up. "Easy. Let me help you."

"The fire."

"It's staying back, but we need to go." She cups my face in her hands, wiping a cloth across my blood covered eyes until I can blink and finally see who it is. "Can you move?"

"Kalia?" I whisper. "What are you doing here?" Her shirt is covered in blood, and I cringe at the fact she didn't even hesitate to use it to help me.

"I live up the road. I had dinner with Ridley and I'm just getting home. I saw the fire and came running to see what happened, and that's when I saw you." Her eyes drift down to Tam still under me, his head tipped to the side. "Is he..." Her voice trembles with concern.

"No. He got dosed with a neurotoxin."

"What the fuck were you doing here?"

"We need to go. We can't be here when the emergency unit shows up." I stagger to my feet, stumbling to the side as my body screams with pain. Kalia ducks under my arm to steady me. "Thanks," I grit out.

"We can go to my place since it's closer, if you want?"

"Can you drive?" She nods. "Can you help me with him?" She nods again and carefully shifts away from me, making sure I can stay stable on my feet.

With her help, we get Tam slung between us, his feet dragging uselessly against the ground as we shuffle our way to his car. I can already hear the sirens in the distance getting closer with each passing second. I take Tam completely and lay him out in the back seat while Kalia slides into the driver's seat to start fucking around with the controls to shift herself closer to the steering wheel. I'm limping now, holding onto the hood as I make my way to the passenger side and slip in. I shakily grab my laptop off the dash, sliding it into my bag with shaking hands.

She keeps stealing glances at me as she drives, the emergency crew ripping past us when we turn onto Glasgow. "Are you okay?" She finally asks quietly.

"I'll be okay."

"You're still bleeding," she points out, motioning to my ears now.

"I don't doubt that," I snort, wincing as I lean over to look back at Tam. "I need to figure out what he got dosed with."

The sound of leather squeaking pulls my attention to her—to her hands gripping into the steering wheel hard enough to turn her knuckles white. "Will he be okay?"

"I don't know." It's true. I have no idea if he'll be okay. He's got a few cuts and bruises on him, nothing his dark worlder blood can't handle, especially being royal, but who fucking knows if the neurotoxin will leave any permanent damage. Fuck, this was such a bad idea. I never should have let him go in there alone. I should have fucking done a better job in scouting the fucking place. This is my fault—*my fucking fault.*

"Nox?" My head snaps to Kalia, her eyes wide, darting between my hands and my face. I glance down, pulling in a shaky breath at seeing the slight shimmer of power radiating out of my skin. "Breathe. He'll be okay." I nod, curling my hands into fists to try and physically pull my powers back in. "What's your ability?"

"Space manipulation. It's sort of like telekinesis, but I move the space around things or air particles in general."

"You're an elemental?"

"What? No."

"That sounds like an air ability, not space." I stare at the side of her face in shock, and she glances at me from the corner of her eye. "You didn't realize?"

"I—I never pushed my powers beyond simple things to ever really test that."

"How long have you known Eris?"

"About five years now. I've been living with him for almost four."

"You two seem really close."

I glance back at Tam, my heart tightening painfully in my chest. "We are."

"Are you feeling better now?" I glance back at her, and she points to my hands.

I flex them, shaking my head with a smirk pulling at my lips. "You were trying to distract me."

"Partially, but I don't mind getting to know you either." She slows the car in front of a small duplex at the very end of the street. "We're here."

"You live here?" I ask, leaning forward to look up at the shabby building in front of us. The siding is falling off, and the roof is very obviously missing panels. "You fucking walk all the way here every day?"

"I don't mind the walk, it gives me time to think. The place was all I could really afford when I moved here, but it's grown on me." She slips out of the car, and I grab my laptop bag, slinging it across my body before opening the back door to pull Tam out. "Do you need help?" She asks, closing the doors and locking it while I lift him into my arms, cradling him against my chest.

"I'm okay." I nod towards her place. She hands me the keys to the car and heads up ahead of me to open the door. Thank fuck there's only like three steps to get up onto the porch. Rickety as shit, but still functional.

"Sorry for the mess," she says quickly, but confusion washes through me when I look around.

The place is bare. A few trinkets sit on the small side table where she sets her keys down before closing the door behind me. She's got a couple of blankets piled on the couch, and one random pizza box sitting on the stained coffee table, but I wouldn't classify that as messy. The place barely looks lived in. "How long have you lived here?"

"Just a few weeks." A few weeks? This girls doesn't seem to have anything to her name, and now I feel a bit of pity towards her. "You can put him in my room for now," she says, pointing towards a door down a small hallway. "It's not much, but he can rest in there for as long as he needs to." I follow her down the hall, pausing in the doorway to the bedroom—if you can even call it that. "Sorry," she whispers, fidgeting with her bloody shirt and avoiding my gaze.

"Why are you apologizing?"

"I just...my set up is a shithole in comparison to your place."

"A home is whatever you make of it, Kalia. I'm not judging you for what you have or don't have." I settle Tam down on the mattress, unhooking my bag, and settling it on the floor. "Do you have any tweezers? Maybe a bowl with some warm water? I need to get the glass out of his wounds for him to heal properly."

"Oh, yeah, of course." She takes off out of the room, and I hear her rummaging through the cupboards and drawers while I lift Tam's shirt to make sure his body isn't as bad as his arms and hands. Fuck me, even his face has shards embedded under the skin, and the large gash ripping through his eyebrow and eye is a bit concerning. "Thank you," I say to her once she shows back up with everything I need. "I'll clean him up really quick and then try to find any info on the neurotoxin."

"Do you want me to clean him up while you do that?" I frown at her. "I just mean, it'll be quicker and better if you know right away what you're dealing with."

"Okay," I sigh, hating that I'm letting her fucking do it, but she's right. I need to pull up the information I got off of the internal system to see what was inside those tanks. I settle myself into the small armchair in the corner, pulling the laptop onto my lap while Kalia gets to work dealing with the glass in Tam.

There's so much fucking data and it's not even close to being organized. It takes me at least twenty minutes to scan through the basic information before I get access to the chemical composition they used to develop the shit. Fuck me. This must be what they're using to kidnap the supernaturals. Some of them have abilities, and there's no way they would just go down easily without something causing their submission.

My hands freeze over the keys, bile rising in my throat as I scan the composition. "Fuck," I murmur.

"What's wrong?"

"I thought the angelic council put a squash on this shit years ago, but somehow these fuckers got their hands on the formula and modified it further. It's got ghoul toxin, vampire venom, and it's laced with Fae magic to force an integration into the bloodstream." I type another line of code into the system, scanning through the lines of information ripping across the screen. "There's an antidote. Without it he's not waking up."

"What? Where can we get it?"

"They had some stored in the warehouse, but they've got a storage supply in another building closer to the pier. It looks like they're using that as one of their product bases."

"I'll go," she says, getting up from where she was kneeling on the floor next to Tam.

"Like hell you will. Eris almost died tonight, Kalia. These people are fucking dangerous."

"You going would draw more suspicion. I mean, just look at you." I glance at myself, covered in blood and probably a bit intimidating right now. "I'll be quick. In and out, and they won't even know I'm there."

"I don't like this."

"Do they have security systems?"

"More than likely, yeah."

"Can you deal with it?"

"Yes," I sigh. I get up from the chair and pull the earbud out of Tam's ear, handing it to her. "When he wakes up, I'm going to tell him that I told you no."

She smirks. "He's well the fuck aware that I'm impulsive and don't listen." She takes the bud, slipping it into her ear and moving towards the small dresser to pull out a clean shirt. My eyes widen and I turn around quickly when she rips the dirty one off. "It's not like you haven't seen me half-naked before," she laughs.

I don't fucking care if I've seen her half-naked or not, the last thing I need is to be making things even weirder between all of us. She brushes her hand down my arm, and I turn to look at her, now fully dressed. "I'll get it, Nox," she says quietly, giving me a small smile.

I clear my throat and step back from her. "You'll be looking for glass syringes. The liquid is amber in colour. Don't dawdle, you got it? If someone sees you, you fucking run."

"I'm not an idiot," she scoffs. "I know what I'm doing."

"Do you?" I ask, lifting a brow. "This isn't the typical situation someone like you would be put into."

"Someone like me?"

I wave my hand up and down her body. "I'm not saying it to be a dick, but all you got going for you is the fact you're a hottie."

She presses her lips together, the corners twitching as she fights back a smile. "Compliments will get you no where."

I roll my eyes. "It's not like you can fight your way out of there."

"You know nothing about me. I told you before, I can handle myself."

"Fine, but if you die, I won't be grieving your stupidity. I should be the one going."

"I highly doubt you want to leave him here with me when he's in that condition."

"You're right, I don't." *Because I don't trust you*. I want to say it, but I bite my tongue and keep the comment buried. She helped us tonight, and she's doing something really fucking dangerous to help us again.

"Can I take the car?"

I toss her the keys, and she catches them easily. I study her a bit closer, surprised by her quick reflexes. "Make sure you park a ways away though. We don't need them flagging the car. Walking makes it seem like you're just out for a stroll down by the pier." I unclip the switchblade from my hip and hold it out to her. She glares at it for a second, tipping her head up in question. "In case you run into problems."

"I don't need that."

"Kalia, you should have something on you in case you get cornered."

"I'll be fine. I'm not good with knives anyways, so I would end up losing it and giving my attacker another weapon."

"Fuck, you're stubborn."

"It's my personality." She pats me on the arm and makes her way towards the door. "I'll let you know when I'm close."

"Alright, I'll let you know what I see on the surveillance system."

CHAPTER 35

NOX

I'm glued to the monitor, watching Tam's car on every single camera I can access as Kalia drives down towards the pier. The security on the building isn't nearly as heavy as the one on the warehouse, which is a bit surprising considering what's inside. I thought for sure they would have at least the same level, but I'm proved wrong when I easily slip in through the system and take control of it. I catch the car pulling off one street over from the pier, and seconds later, Kalia's in my ear.

"I'm here."

"I'm looping the camera feeds right now, so you'll be invisible to anyone else watching. The building itself is empty, and the magical system will be offline in about two minutes. You'll have fifteen seconds to get through before the barrier snaps back into place."

"How am I supposed to get back out?" She asks, her voice breathy like she's running now.

"I'll drop the barrier again when you're ready to leave. Signal me on the camera by the back entrance, which is where I want you to go in. You'll lose signal on the earbud because of the magical signature interference."

"Okay, I'm at the back door now." She glances up at the camera, giving it a small nod.

"Barrier down in three...two...one. Be careful, Kalia."

She smirks at the camera and steps through the door I've just unlocked, closing it behind her. I let out a long breath, lacing my fingers behind my head as I watch her cautiously make her way through the small building, moving from door to door until she stops at one. She glances at the camera in the hall and steps inside of the room where no cameras exist for me to keep an eye on her.

The minutes tick by so fucking slowly, my leg bouncing with anxiety. I sigh in relief when she finally steps out of the room with a small duffle bag slung across her chest. Her cheeks seem flushed in comparison to earlier, and I lean in closer to the monitor as I watch her walk back out into the back area of the building. I start the countdown to the barrier once again, watching her as she shifts from foot to foot in front of the door, glancing at the camera every few seconds. I could easily leave her there, the thought so fucking tempting if it weren't for the fact she now holds the key to Tam's survival.

She jumps slightly when the barrier flickers out of existence, wasting no time pushing through the door and taking off in a sprint back to the car. "I got it," she laughs.

"Good job, Kalia." I can't help smiling as I see her wide grin through the cameras. She hops into the car, blocking my view of her once more. "I'll see you in a bit. Don't speed back or you might draw attention."

"See you soon."

I keep the monitor up with the street cams showing her progress, but once she gets out of the lower pier district and turns onto Glasgow, I feel confident she's not going to fuck this up somehow. I make my way over to Tam, dropping to my knees beside the bed. My chest aches seeing him like this, so fucking vulnerable in a completely different way. At least with the nightmares I feel useful when I help him through it and comfort him, where now...now I can't fucking do anything but wait and hope that the antidote works for him.

"You'll be okay," I whisper, brushing his blond strands from his face. His wounds are all healed for the most part, pink skin where the cuts were the only sign that something happened tonight. "You have to be." Leaning towards him, I do something I've wanted to do for so fucking long. I kiss him. Just a soft press of my lips to his, but the touch is something I won't soon forget. It's something I'll hold onto and cherish because I know this will never happen between us.

He had every opportunity tonight to make his feelings known and take the leap, but he didn't. instead, he pulled away. Sure, I could have made the first move, but I don't want to be the one to take control of this building tension between us.

"You said you would be fine," I whisper against his lips, fighting back tears. "You fucking lied to me, Tam. This isn't okay, not even close." I cradle his head, pressing my lips to his temple. "I fucking love you." A small sob slips through my hold, quiet tears streaming down my cheeks as my emotions break through the dam I've created.

"I'm back," Kalia calls from the entrance. I quickly wipe my eyes, clearing my throat as her soft footfalls lead into the bedroom. "Hand me one of the syringes," I murmur, holding my hand out to her without looking at her.

She settles one of the tubes into my hand, and I try to steady my nerves as I twist his arm to expose the veins near his elbow. "Are you okay?" She asks quietly.

"No," I say honestly. There's no point in lying right now. My emotions are pretty clear, and I just don't fucking care if she sees me like this. Once the needle is nestled into his vein I press the plunger, watching the glow of the amber liquid as it spreads up his arm to disperse through his system.

"I grabbed a few syringes just in case," she says, settling the duffle bag next to me. I settle his arm over his stomach and push myself to my feet. I startle at how close Kalia is standing to me, a deep frown line forming between her brows. "You need some sleep." I shake my head. "Nox, you look exhausted."

"I'm fine. I rather stay up until he wakes."

"Suit yourself." She shrugs, moving to her closet to grab a few pillows. "I'm going to crash on the couch for now. Wake me if you need anything."

"Thank you for helping, Kalia."

She smiles. "I owed him at least this much."

She quietly makes her way out of the room, closing the door behind her. I grab the blanket off the end of the bed and tuck it in around Tam before moving to the other side and crawling into the tiny ass bed next to him. I try not to jostle him too much, but for me to fit on here with him, I need to shift myself practically flush with his side. I sigh, lacing my fingers with his and settling both our hands against his stomach. I know I need to get some sleep. I can feel my body slowly shutting down as the adrenaline from tonight wears off, my eyes fluttering closed with exhaustion.

CHAPTER 36

TAMZIN

Everything hurts and my body feels like lead. There's warmth at my side and a soft pressure around one of my hands. I struggle to pry my eyes open, my vision blurry and painful as I try to blink. I have no fucking clue where I am or how I even got here. I wince at the throbbing pain ramming against my head, threatening to split my scalp open from the pressure building. My tongue feels like sandpaper in my mouth, my throat so fucking dry I can barely swallow.

I don't recognize this room, and definitely not this fucking bed. My head tips to the side, my heart ramming in my chest at the sight of Nox sleeping curled up next to me, his hand tightly gripped in mine. His eyes are red and puffy, his face caked in dirt and blood with streaks trailing down his cheeks. He's a mess, and the memories of what happened slams into me like a freight train. He got me out. I thought I would die after being dosed with that toxin and seeing the flames lick and spread through that room.

As though sensing me, Nox slowly opens his eyes. His gaze is unfocused for a moment, but he blinks a few times, his eyes going wide before bowing in sadness. "You're awake," he croaks out, his voice strained and raw. He pulls his hand from mine and hovers it awkwardly over me, like he's afraid touching me will break me.

"What happened?" I say thickly, the strain of talking scraping my throat further.

His face morphs into one of anger. "You promised you would be careful. You said you would be okay," he hisses, pulling away from me, and fuck me, the feeling of him pulling away like that has me whimpering. He gets up from the bed and stalks out of the room without another word, leaving me confused and gaping at the empty space.

Hushed voices carry from the other room, and a few moments later, I hear a door slam shut. I stare at the ceiling, processing Nox's reaction in my mind. I glance over to the door when soft footfalls draw my attention, my eyes widening at the sight of Kalia in the doorway, a bottle of water in her hand.

"Nox," I croak.

She steps into the room, walking right up to the bed to stand next to me. "He...needed some air. Come on." She cradles my head, helping me sit up enough to drink some of the water. I greedily gulp it, coughing a bit when she finally pulls it away from my lips. "I'll leave it here. You can have more after, but don't drink it too fast."

My body feels so fucking heavy, my limbs trembling at just the thought of moving them. "Where are we? What happened?"

She glances back at the door for a second before crouching down next to me, brushing her fingers against my cheek. "We're at my place. I was on my way home from dinner with Ridley when I saw the fire at the warehouse. I went to check it out, and that's when I saw Nox on the ground, shielding you from the blast."

"Shielding me?"

"You were out cold. We had to get the antidote to the toxin to wake you. Nox was in pretty rough shape, Eris."

"Idiot," I murmur, and she frowns. "I told him not to get involved."

She pushes to her feet, anger pulling her features into harsh lines. “He saved you. You think he would have just sat back and watched you die? You better not pull that fucking attitude with him when he comes back, Eris, he can’t handle that right now.” She moves to her dresser and starts pulling out some clothes, proceeding to strip down and change into them right in front of me. “I have to go, or I’ll be late for work,” she murmurs, throwing her hair up into a ponytail. “Stay as long as you need to and lock up when you leave.”

I’m so confused by this entire situation, that I don’t get any words out before she walks out of the room again. Quiet voices carry again, but my brain is so fogged up that I can’t even begin to make out what they’re saying, and soon the click of the door closing again hits me.

The back of my neck prickles and I glance over to see Nox leaning against the doorframe with his arms crossed. Kalia was partially right. Nox wasn’t in rough shape, he *still* is. Now that he’s standing, I can see the damage done to him. His clothes are ripped and covered in dirt and blood, some of it plastering his hair in sticky clumps. Trails of dried blood line his skin down from his ears and even his eyes, his upper lip showing his nose was bleeding at some point, too. I turn back to stare at the ceiling, hating the feeling of guilt and pain gripping at my chest. He was hurt because of me. He put himself at risk *because of me*.

“I thought I lost you,” he says quietly, and I swallow back the tears burning in my throat. “Tam, look at me.” I shake my head. I can’t handle looking at him right now, not when I know what I’ll see there. “So, it’s like that then, eh? Fine,” he mumbles, walking into the room to pack up his laptop. Grabbing a duffle off the floor next to the bed, I can feel his piercing gaze staring at me. “When you’re ready to go home, let me know.”

“Where are you going?” I ask when he reaches the doorway.

His shoulders slump, but he doesn’t turn to look at me now. “Outside,” he says sharply, all traces of kindness gone from his tone.

He should have just let me die. Death would be a mercy in comparison to having to live with him resenting me for what happened, and I just can't handle him hating me. I'm not trying to be rude or dismissive, but I hate the fact he put himself on the line to save my ass when he fucking promised he would stay in the car. I would have never forgiven myself if something happened to him because of my mistakes.

It's a struggle, but I sit myself up in bed, feeling drained and exhausted just from the small movement. My legs tremble under me, my arms unable to hold my own weight as I try to lift myself to my feet. "Fuck," I grit out. Whatever that neurotoxin was, it seems to be affecting my healing right now, and I fucking hate that I feel like shit. I grab the water bottle with a shaking hand, gulping down the rest of it like I'm dying of thirst.

Everything hurts. Every single step I take is a struggle, my hand braced on the wall as I shuffle my way out of the bedroom into the small apartment. This wasn't how I thought I would end up seeing where Kalia lived, and I sure as fuck didn't expect to see *this*. She has nothing to her name, barely anything in the small space that she can even call her own. I feel like even more of an asshole for treating her the way I have, knowing that she's struggling like this. At least she *has* a home though. I take a few deep breaths, judging the distance to the door and hating that it seems to narrow and get further away from me, bringing back the harsh memory of last night. I never thought I would make it through that door at the warehouse, the distance seeming too great and so fucking daunting as my body ceased to function.

My breathing turns harsh, my chest tightening at the memory and panic that I felt in thinking I was going to die in there. I grip into my chest, trying to ease the pain, but I can't calm myself down, and stars start to spark across my vision. My legs shake under me, and I just fucking can't. I can't do anything but let my body slide down against the wall, crumpling to the floor in a pathetic heap. I can't stop the tears from bubbling up and spilling out over my cheeks in hot tracks, and I don't want to. I'm so fucking tired. Tired of trying to be strong and resilient when all I want to do is fucking crawl into a corner and let myself break.

The front door creeks open, but I don't have the mental strength to even look up at him and the look of disappointment on his face. I'm fucking pathetic, nothing like the person he pegs me to be. "Tam," he says quietly, his booted feet coming into my line of sight in a blurry haze. "Tam," he says again, his tone sharper. My head shakes as I slowly lift my gaze up to meet his. I don't see disappointment. I don't even see pity, which would be just as bad.

"I'm sorry," I whisper.

He crouches down in front of me, balancing on his toes as he rests his forearms on his thighs. My eyes get drawn to his hands hanging loosely, the hand that held mine all night. "Why are you apologizing?"

"I'm sorry I fucked up. I'm sorry I put your life at risk. I'm fucking sorry that I'm such a fuck up, Nox. Your life would be so much better if I weren't in it, and you wouldn't—" I choke on my words, slamming my eyes closed against the pain ripping through my chest. "You wouldn't be living such a shitty life."

"Who said my life was shitty? The way I see it, my life is filled with excitement and entertainment because of you. I have no one, Tam. There's no one left for me, but you. I have no family or loved ones. I have no one in this world that gives a shit about me, only you. Without you I would have nothing, I would *be* nothing."

"You said you would stay in the car."

"I did, but I rather suffer the consequences of breaking that promise and still have you in my life, than to have kept that promise and lose you. I would do anything for you, don't you realize that?"

"I don't deserve you," I choke out, hating that I'm a blubbering idiot right now.

"Maybe, maybe not, but you're stuck with me either way. One of these days you're going to have to let yourself be open, Tam. You're going to truly accept yourself, and the people who really love you will stand by you no matter what. You'll love, and whoever is lucky enough to be on the receiving end of that will see how great of a person you are." He cups my cheek, wiping the tears still streaming down. "They won't care where you came from, they'll only care about who you are. Anyone would be lucky to have you, Tam."

"I want to go home."

"Okay, I'll get you home."

He pushes himself back to his feet and holds out his hand to me. I take it, letting him pull me up and tucking me in against his side as he steadies me the entire way out. He locks the door, and as I settle into the passenger seat, I take in the small duplex in front of me. "I can't believe she lives here," I murmur as Nox slides into the car. I watch him as he fidgets with the controls, pushing the seat back into its usual spot.

He glances over at me, and I lift a brow in question. "Kalia drove us here last night. I wasn't really in any condition to be driving, and I didn't know where we were going."

He backs out of the small driveway, pulling out onto the road, and I settle myself back into the seat. I keep stealing glances at Nox, his posture a bit stiff, his focus on the road, and his hand gripping the gearshift harshly. I settle my hand overtop of his, trying to get him to calm down since he's clearly still on edge. He startles at the sudden contact, but instead of pulling away like I expect him to, he flips his hand palm up and gently squeezes my hand.

I stare at our intertwined fingers, trying to understand what the fuck is actually happening right now. "Kalia seems to really like you," he says, pulling me out of my thoughts.

"She didn't seem to like me very much yesterday. I stopped in at the Hub in the morning to apologize to her and it didn't go well."

"It must have gone well enough for her to have done as much for you last night as she did. She's the one that went to the warehouse to get the antidote...alone."

"What?"

He spares me a quick glance, like he's trying to judge my reaction. "I took care of the barrier and the security cameras while she went in. I told her I would go, but she insisted, saying that she would draw less attention. I couldn't really argue with her reasoning, since she lives in the area, so no one would question seeing her just roaming the streets."

"I don't understand why she would do that."

"I told you, she likes you. I had to talk to her this morning and warn her of the dangers in this area. I gave her a rundown on Calvin and showed her the pictures of him and his crew so she can avoid them. I figured after what she did for us last night you would want to protect her."

He's right in the sense I don't want her getting hurt, especially living in that part of town, but the last thing I wanted was him giving her any information about any of it. "Does she know *why* I was there?"

"I told her what we do and that Calvin has a bounty." He glances at me. "She didn't seem concerned or even surprised."

"We need to deal with this quickly. Calvin's going to be pissed off about his warehouse, but with shit going missing from where you got the antidote, he's not going to think it was some freak accident."

"The shit they're making is bad, Tam. That neurotoxin has to be what they're using to kidnap supernaturals."

"Did you figure out what it was?"

"Ghoul toxin, vampire venom, and Fae magic. Everything is bound together in a way that laces itself into the system. Without the antidote, the ghoul toxin would have destroyed your body from the inside out." He glances at me again just as we pull onto our street. "Are you feeling any side effects?"

"A few, but I don't know if they'll linger or go away eventually. It feels like my healing isn't working right."

“The cuts and bruises on you healed at least, but I think you should take it easy for the rest of the day.”

“Ugh,” I groan, thumping my head against the seat.

He squeezes my hand, and the motion sends a flutter through my chest. “No arguing. If you want to get back out there, you need to do it at full strength.”

“This sucks,” I pout, shamelessly milking the pity party Nox is entertaining me with.

He pulls the car to a stop in our parking spot, killing the engine, and turning to look at me. “It doesn’t have to,” he smirks.

I grin. “What did you have in mind?”

CHAPTER 37

TAMZIN

This is *not* what I had in mind. After taking a hot shower and scrubbing every inch of my skin with Nox checking in on me enough that he should have just sat in the corner to watch me, I got tucked into bed in my comfiest pair of sweats. I slept for a few hours, waking up to a massive spread for lunch, delivered right to my lap. Nox is way too fucking good to me, but I *really* hoped that the comment earlier would have led to something different. Of course it didn't. Not only is Nox not interested in me in that way, he's also way too stubborn and caring to even suggest I do anything but rest and let him take care of me.

"Nox," I sigh as he strolls into my room again, this time with dinner. "I'm feeling better. You don't need to keep coddling me."

The withering look he gives me shuts me up, and I accept the tray without another complaint. He opens his mouth to say something, but snaps his mouth shut, whipping his head towards the door. Seconds later, a small knock sounds. "Who the fuck is here?" He snarls quietly. He storms out of the room, pissed at being interrupted of whatever the fuck he thinks *this* is. "What are you doing here?" I hear him say, his voice dripping with anger.

Fuck me. Did one of my siblings actually find out where I live, too? They're usually the only ones that could pull that level of anger from Nox.

"I just wanted to make sure he was doing okay. I—I don't have either of your numbers or else I would call."

I sit up straighter in bed, surprised to hear Kalia's voice drifting through the apartment, and I'm even more concerned now as to why Nox is treating her so harshly. "He's better, but he's still resting," he says, his tone easing a bit.

"Can I see him?"

A long pause weighs through the apartment, but soon I hear footsteps, and Nox is opening the door. Kalia stands next to him, her eyes downcast as she fidgets with the edge of her shirt. She slowly lifts her gaze, locking her eyes on mine. "Hi," she says quietly.

"Hi," I whisper back.

She glances up at Nox, to all six-foot-two of brooding mass in front of her. "I'll give you a minute," he mumbles, closing the door behind him and leaving Kalia and I alone.

"How are you doing?" She asks, taking a tentative step into the room.

"Better. Nox is keeping me well fed and rested," I smirk, rolling my eyes and pointing to the massive plate loaded with fries and a greasy cheeseburger.

"I interrupted your dinner."

"Not at all." I pat the bed next to me, and she hesitantly walks towards me, crawling up onto the bed, but leaving a good distance between us. "Relax, I won't bite." Her lip twitches. "Not hard anyways."

She rolls her eyes. "Is your defense mechanism snarky and flirtatious comments?"

"Better to laugh than cry." Her face falls in understanding. She brushes her hand through my hair and leans in closer to me, my breath hitching in my throat. "What are you doing?"

"Can I kiss it better?" I swallow, giving my head a small nod. She smiles, her eyes drifting down to my lips before she leans in further, pressing hers lightly against mine. "Eris," she pants, breaking the kiss for a moment before forcing her tongue through my lips to press against my own.

A deep moan rips through my throat, and I lace my hand into her ponytail, gripping it hard and holding her face against mine.

"I want you," she gasps, sliding her hand across my chest and down my stomach.

"Nox is in the other room."

"So? It's not like he cares."

A twinge of hurt grips at my heart at the comment. Of course he doesn't care, why would he? It's not like he's been celibate, and he's made no real acknowledgement that he wants anything with me himself. She slips off the bed, grabbing my tray of food and setting it down on the dresser. She slowly pulls her shirt off over her head, her eyes never leaving mine as I stare at her. I should tell her to stop. I should end this like I had planned to, not drag her along in thinking that anything can really happen between us beyond just this, but I can't. I'm really starting to like the girl, and she's proving herself and her loyalty more and more, chipping away at my shields and making it hard *not* to trust her. She drops her pants and the air in my lungs whooshes out of me in a hot wave, my eyes raking over every inch of her. She smirks, shimmying her underwear down and finally undoing her bra, dropping it to the floor before climbing back up onto the bed.

"Kalia—"

"Shhh, let me take care of you," she purrs, gripping the waistband of my pants and tugging them down. Her eyes drift to my cock as it springs out, a smirk on her face. "You work fast."

"What can I say, you're a very attractive female."

Her cheeks flame and she licks her lips, bending down to kiss my stomach, slowly working her way down...down...*fuck*. My stomach tenses instantly at the feel of her warm mouth cradling my cock, her tongue swirling and caressing every inch of me. My head tips back against the headboard, my eyes rolling into the back of my head at the pure pleasure building inside of me. It burns and tingles, settling into my spine. Fuck me, I just about come when she turns her attention to the base of my dick and balls, pulling each one into her mouth and releasing them with a soft pop.

She takes me into her mouth again, sucking and bobbing, pulling me closer and closer to release. "Are you done with your dinner?" Nox's voice streams into the room as the door swings open. My head snaps to him, his eyes wide and darting between me and Kalia just as I come. His eyes darken, morphing into something I haven't seen before as he stares at me panting and half-naked with a very naked Kalia straddling my knees. "What are you doing?" He asks, his voice sharp and measured as his eyes snap back to Kalia.

She licks her lips and smirks at him, the little shit. "Did you want to join?"

He swallows hard, his jaw ticking and flexing. His eyes shift to me again. "I want nothing to do with you, Kalia," he says viciously, the tone sending a shiver raking up my spine.

"Do you want to touch, Eris?" She croons, snapping his attention back to her. "He seems like the type that would be into something like that, if that's what you prefer." He clucks his tongue, glares at me, and rips out of the room without another word. A few seconds later the front door slams shut. "He's so sensitive," she snorts.

"I should go check on him."

"No. I'm not done with you yet."

"Kalia," I sigh, but she ignores me and crawls her way up onto me, settling in against my hips. I grip into her shoulders to stop her from pressing her lips against mine. "Kalia," I say again.

"Why are you so obsessed with him?" She snaps. "He gets mad at you for the stupidest shit, including you hooking up with me. Is it so wrong for you to be intimate with someone?"

"He's just worried."

"About what? I'm not going to hurt you." She touches my cheek gently. "I would never hurt you, Eris."

Fuck it. That would have been the perfect opportunity to test the waters with him, but if anything, he seemed disgusted with the idea. I pull her down, slamming my mouth against hers and devouring the moan that slips through her lips. She reaches between us, gripping my cock and slipping it between her thighs. I groan, biting her lip at the feel of her heat wrapping around my length. Fuck, she feels so good. Her hips shift blissfully, her inner walls fluttering around my cock with every stroke.

"Fuck, that's good," she breathes, tipping her head back and bracing her hands against my chest, giving me a perfect view of her tits bouncing in front of me.

I reach up and cup them, rolling her nipples between my thumb and fingers. My cock hardens further as I watch it slide in and out of her, enamoured with the way our bodies join together. This girl went above and beyond for me last night, too, risking herself by going into enemy territory to find the only thing that could wake me. She didn't have to do that. Fuck, she didn't have to help us to begin with, but she helped Nox and took us to her home, keeping us off the radar of the authorities.

I grip her throat and pull her face towards me, slipping my tongue through her parted lips. She hums, the sound vibrating through her like a purr, and her pussy tightens around me as she gasps into my mouth.

"Come with me," she whispers, tugging my bottom lip with her teeth.

I claw at her back, pulling her body flush against mine and letting the pure pleasure course through me and explode out of me. "Fuck," I grunt, and she buries her face in the crook of my neck with a small whimpering breath.

CHAPTER 38

NOX

"I must be either drunk or dreaming to have *you* here wanting to fight." I glare at Kaliem, flexing my hands at my sides in agitation. "Who pissed *you* off enough to come to the pits?"

"Does it fucking matter?"

"I've never seen you fight, kid." My wolf snarls in my head and Kaliem's eyes widen when my hold slips enough that I feel my eyes shift in agitation. "The fights are no powers and no weapons."

I scoff. "You just keep changing the rules to your own advantage, don't you." He lifts a brow in question. "You allowed weapons just a few nights ago."

He frowns, shifting awkwardly in his seat. "This is a death battle. Do you understand what that means?"

"Yeah, only one of us is coming out of that ring alive."

He smirks. "Alright, I'll allow it. If you win, I'll give you four grand."

No wonder Tam fights down here. If he's pulling in cash like that for fights, it would just motivate him further. Being able to take out his aggression to its full potential and getting paid to do it. I fucking need a bit of that right now because I'm fucking furious. Fuck Kalia and her manipulation because that's what all of that was. She's taking advantage of him, and Tam being Tam, he doesn't see it. It's like she feels as though she's entitled to his time now because of the fact she helped us, but I fucking see right through her.

How the fuck can *she* see what Tam can't? Unless he just refuses to see it...he can't be that stupid not to notice, but I could be wrong. The fucking bitch, flaunting what they were doing, and then trying to egg me on by asking me to join in. The *audacity* to throw my feelings towards him in my face, taunting me by trying to get me to admit that, yes, I want to fucking touch him. I want to do more than touch him just so *she* won't go near him again.

Kaliem dismisses me, having one of his men escort me down to the locker rooms. I have no idea how long I sit on this rickety-ass bench alone, my leg bouncing with my growing agitation and anxiety. I can hear the screams and cheers of the crowd above me, clearly entertained by the fight currently going on. Kaliem said tonight was set up as a rotation fight, going easy on me by putting me as the last fight of the night to go up against whoever wins until the end. A pity fight. The fighter up top will probably be exhausted by the time I get to them if they're good enough to take on opponent after opponent.

"You're up on deck." I startle at the voice, seeing Kaliem's bodyguard standing in the doorway. He motions for me to follow, and I take a deep breath, pulling myself to my feet and walking with him to the cacophony of cheers. "Good luck," he snickers when we hit the main level, pointing to the cage, where they drag out a body.

My adrenaline spikes, my shift vibrating beneath my skin. I step up to the cage once it's clear, feeling the ripple of power radiating out of the metal. The barrier slams down the moment I'm through the doorway. My opponent doesn't have a scratch on him from what I can tell, but his back is to me while he tries to rile up the crowd.

He finally turns and my blood turns to ice in my veins. Fuck me, this is just my luck. Tam has never mentioned running into him down here, so what are the chances he's fighting in the pits after a fire breaks out at the warehouse. Grant fucking Steel grins at me, the bloodlust oozing out of him in a heavy wave. He shifts closer to the middle of the ring, bouncing on his toes and rolling his neck. His knuckles are bloody, but I doubt that blood is his.

I fucking hate this. What the fuck was I thinking in coming down here? My anger at Tam and Kalia shouldn't have bothered me enough to sign up for a fucking death match, but here I am, lining myself up to die. No, I can't die here. I need to make it out because if I'm not there to protect Tam, no one else will. I need to make it out of here alive, and to do that, I need to take out a fucking criminal.

That's fine by me, one less asshole on the streets to kidnap supernaturals. I use that knowledge and wrap it around me like a cloak, allowing my anger for him and all the innocent people he's taken to wash over me. That anger pushes my shift to just below the surface, allowing my power to simmer in every pore, every muscle, and every vein. We're not allowed to use powers, but Kaliem never said anything about hiding those powers. As long as I don't shift or trigger my actual power, I should be fine.

My eyes widen, my body moving on instinct alone because of my wolf's heightened senses just as his fist comes flying right for my face. I dodge, hiss out a breath, pressing my hand to my cheek and pulling it away to see a streak of blood on my palm.

Mother fuck, he's actually using powers, but this isn't anything that was on record. He should just have neurotoxin, one that causes temporary paralysis if I'm not mistaken. Could he be using a direct link to his life force, a loophole to Kaliem's rules?

"I'm impressed that a mutt like you can move like that," he sneers.

I wipe my hand on my pants and glare at him. "You of all people are calling *me* a mutt? At least I'm all supernatural, unlike you."

He bares his teeth, throwing another fist my way, and once again clipping me with whatever the fuck *that* is. "That'll change soon enough," he spits out.

What the fuck is that supposed to mean? The only way he could change that is by either getting turned by a vamp or a werewolf, and the former isn't a guarantee with the way the venom works on the system. If his human half doesn't have the genetic makeup for the venom to take hold, he'll end up dying in the process. Is Zenia planning to turn him? Fuck, that could be a real problem if that's what Calvin's plan is. Recruiting a vampire and a werewolf into his inner circle gives him access to try and turn humans for his own personal gain.

My mind is distracted enough that he lands a heavy blow to my torso, launching me back into the cage. Searing pain rips through me as the burn of the magic tears at my skin. I grit my teeth, fighting the scream trying to tear its way up my throat, and force my eyes open to see the fucker coming straight for me. My wolf is *raging* inside of me, snarling and begging for release to tear into this fucker and his cheating ways. Fucking Kaliem. No wonder Tam was so pissed off at him when he came home the other night.

Grant sputters and staggers back seconds after my hand makes contact with his throat, the crunch of his trachea like music to my ears. He retches, earning himself a chorus of laughter and screams from the crowd he was working over before. I glance up to the suite above the pit, locking eyes with Kaliem. He smirks, lifting a brow and nodding his head in approval. Fuck him, fuck Grant, fuck Kalia, and you know what? Fuck Tam. Fuck him and the feelings I have for him. Fuck him for being so god damn perfect and kind and caring that I fucking fell in love with him. Fuck him for not seeing it...for not seeing *me*.

I'm slamming into Grant before I even realize my body is moving, pinning him between my legs as I pummel my fists into him, blow after blow, blood spurting, bones cracking as he tries to defend himself. Rage burns through my chest, my shift rippling through my skin like a swarm of locust trying to break out. In his panic, his toxin seeps out of his pores, leaching into me like a thick blanket. I shake my head, my limbs going numb. Big fucking mistake. My wolf is so far in his rage state, at all my emotions swirling inside of me like a vortex, that the toxin barely touches him, but my hold on him crumbles.

I snarl, feeling the shift overtake me and Grant's eyes widen in horror. Spit drips in thick globs from my mouth onto his chest and face, and he thrashes under me, trying to get free, but my wolf isn't some small thing that can be easily thrown around. I'm bigger than this fuck, and screams erupt around me when the crowd realizes what's happening. A shifter pushed into a frenzy is beyond dangerous, and there's no way to stop me from tearing into his throat when we're both caged behind magical walls.

His screams turn into breathy gurgles, his blood pouring into my mouth in thick, hot waves, and then, a hushed silence coats the entire pit. I snarl, backing away from his now limp body, darting my eyes around the cage. They land on Kaliem standing on the other side of the door, his expression wary as he looks between me and the now dead half-Fae behind me.

"What am I going to do with you," he sighs. I growl at him, shaking my head, trying to pull my shift back, but I can't—I can't fucking shift back right now. He tilts his head curiously. "You can't shift back?" I shake my head again, huffing and panting. "I see...his powers didn't work in his favour then." I glare at him, and he rolls his eyes. "I had a feeling he was doing something during his other fights, but he was being pretty subtle about it. With a shifter, his toxin numbed your control." I lunge towards him, snapping my teeth in agitation, my mind frantic and overwhelmed enough that I know I've lost all sense of reason. "Do it." One of his guards steps up to the door, opening it. I launch myself at him, crying out when something slams into my neck. Darkness overtakes my vision, my body limp and heavy, until there's nothing left to feel.

CHAPTER 39

TAMZIN

Kalia doesn't stick around, claiming she has other plans for the night that she can't exactly get out of. I'm not upset exactly, more disappointed since I'm by myself in the apartment. Nox still hasn't come back and it's starting to get a bit late. Maybe he ended up going to Transcend to blow off some steam, upset not even beginning to cover the anger I felt coming off of him when he left here.

My phone is vibrating on the nightstand when I walk back into my room, and I quickly grab it, frowning at the display. "Yeah?" I snap, not wanting to deal with the drama that is Kaliem.

"You need to get down to the pit, right now."

"I have no desire to step foot in your establishment for a while. I'm still pissed off at you."

"It's Nox," he says, hanging up before I can ask him what the fuck he means.

I'm tearing through the apartment and out the door within seconds, running full out towards my car. The tires squeal in protest as I tear out of the parking spot and speed down the road towards the pit.

"Where is he?!" I snarl the moment I burst into Kaliem's office, completely bypassing his guards.

He glances past me to the two idiots groaning on the ground behind me. "That really wasn't necessary," he sighs, getting up from his chair. "Come with me."

I grit my teeth, my knuckles cracking at the force of my hands fisting at my sides. "Where the fuck is Nox, Kaliem? What the fuck happened?"

He motions with his head, and I have no choice but to follow him out the door and down the hall. "He came looking to fight. He seemed pretty agitated, but he agreed to the rules, and I put him in at the very end of a round robin." He stops outside a metal door, where I hear snarling and snapping of teeth. "His opponent was Grant Steel." I sway on the spot, bracing a hand against the wall as every fucking scenario possible flicks through my head. "I didn't notice Grant using his ability until he went up against Nox. The toxin affected his control, and he's still sort of...wrong. He couldn't shift back and was in a frenzy. We had to sedate him, but as you can imagine, that didn't hold for long. We barely got him into containment before he woke up."

I sag in relief, knowing that Nox survived one of Calvin's men in the fucking pit of all places. Why the fuck would he come *here*? "Open it." He hesitates a moment, flinching at the loud bang of something slamming into the door. "Open the fucking door and back away."

His eyes widen when I let my power slip, the shadows around me pulsing and vibrating. He nods his head, gripping the door handle and glancing at me one more time. I nod, and he rips the door open just as I slam a wall of shadow in the frame like a barrier. A whimpering howl pierces through my chest, the sound of him hitting my barrier filling me with guilt. I step into the room, watching a still shifted Nox drag himself to his feet, his hackles rising at the feel of a threat in front of him. He growls, snapping his teeth.

"Nox," I say quietly, shifting into the room with my hands up in placation.

He snaps his mouth shut, eyes narrowing, and head tipping at the sound of my voice. His skin ripples, like he's trying to pull on his shift but failing miserably. He whimpers again, slamming his eyes closed when a vicious tremor takes over his body.

"Easy, buddy. Just breathe." I move closer to him, and he snaps his jaws, a visceral snarl radiating out of him in a way that rattles my bones. "I know you're angry with me," I say, dropping to my knees in front of him. "I don't know why exactly because you won't talk to me, but I'm sure I deserve it if it's coming from you." A low growl vibrates in his throat, and I drop my eyes to the ground, bowing my head to him. "I'm sorry if I hurt you, Nox, and I'm sorry this happened to you, but I just want to take you home. You need to try and get a handle on your shift. Try to remember who you are. You're my best friend, and I hate that you thought this," I say, motioning behind me to the pit. "That this was the only solution for you."

I settle onto my heels, resting my hands palm up on my thighs, a complete show of submission to him. Tilting my head to the side, I expose my neck to him, a sign other shifters give when they're surrendering their will to an alpha. If I have any hope in truly getting through to Nox when he's in this state, this is my best option. Letting myself be exposed like this is a bit nerve-wracking. He whines again and my eyes dart up to glance at him when I feel his presence shift closer. His skin ripples again, the fur across his body shifting with the tremors moving along his flesh. I don't know much about Grant's neurotoxin, only what Nox was able to find out in the short amount of time we've been on this hunt.

His sharp pants are hot against my skin, his eyes burning with a brightness that has my own breath hitching in my throat. His eyes show me everything. His pain, his sadness, his anger, his fucking soul, and I just want to hug him to me and try to fix the pain I've caused him.

"Nox," I whisper, his eyes burning into mine, forcing me to stay focused on him, even though all my instincts are telling me to look away. He steps closer to me, settling his head on my shoulder, the softness of his fur caressing the skin of my neck. Slowly I lift my arms, wrapping them around his massive body and squeezing him to me. "Let's go home. Hopefully you can sleep this off."

He snorts out a breath, backing up when I finally release him. I drop the shadow barrier on the door, Nox following close to my heels. Kaliem looks down at him and Nox growls, baring his teeth completely. "He still can't shift?" He asks.

"He's calmed down, so I'm going to take him home for now. Where are his winnings?" Kaliem lifts a brow, a smirk playing at his lips. "Kaliem, I'm not fucking around. He won the fight so give me his fucking winnings before I bury you and this whole pit."

"Fine," he grumbles. We follow him back to his office, Nox's nails clacking against the shitty concrete floors. "Here," he says, tossing an envelope towards me. I peek into it, doing a quick count, finally looking at him again. "What now?" He sighs, clearly not liking the glare I'm giving him.

"You know exactly what. Where's the rest because I know for a fact a fight like that was worth more than two grand." Nox snarls next to me, proving the fact that this wasn't the agreed upon total.

"Fuck, you're both infuriating. He must learn that attitude from you," he snarls, tossing me another envelope.

"Be grateful I'm not kicking your ass for more than what you promised him." I point to Nox, my shadows curling around my hand in irritation. "You are *never* to allow him to fight here again. Do you understand me? I don't fucking care what he says or does, Nox is not to set foot in the pit ever again."

"Fine. You should know, it was a pretty good fight though. The kid is savage with all that pent-up rage."

"Noted," I grumble. "Nox, let's go." He follows me through the building, Kaliem's guards giving us a surprisingly wide berth. I get to the car, opening the door to get in when I hear him bark. "Right, fuck. Sorry, man." I jog around to the passenger side and open the door for him, smirking at the fact he's sitting in the seat now with his tongue lolling out the side. I stare at the side of his face once I sit down, and he eventually glances at me. "Want me to open the window for you?" Would you look at that, canines *can* glare. The look he gives me makes me think he wishes me dead right now, but I just laugh because his reaction at least tells me he's starting to settle into himself and falling out of the shifter frenzy.

I drive the speed limit back to the apartment, stealing glances at Nox the entire time. At one point he licks the window, much to my disgust, but he huffs a breath of thanks when I do in fact open the window for him. He stays pretty quiet the entire elevator ride up, and then just trots off to his room. Me being me, I follow him, leaning against the doorframe as I watch him circle on his bed, trying to get comfortable, until he finally curls himself into a ball and closes his eyes.

"Do you want me to stay with you?" He opens one eye and lets out a short growl. "Nox, don't be like that." I step further into the room, pausing when he lifts his head and bares his teeth. "So, you're just going to stay mad at me?" A huff and an eyeroll from him before he drops his head against his paws. Kicking off my shoes, I ignore his next growl and climb up onto the bed. His body stiffens when I settle my hand on his back, petting the length of him. "I'm sorry. Whatever I did to upset you, it wasn't my intention. I don't even know why you're mad, Nox, but being mad at me shouldn't warrant you going off and almost getting yourself killed." He huffs again, scooting his body further away from me, and the clear rejection fucking hurts. "Alright, I get it, but I'm not leaving you." I settle into the bed, staring at the ceiling and its matching glowing star stickers to my own until I hear his breathing steady and finally succumb to my own exhaustion.

CHAPTER 40

NOX

I groan at the noise, rolling over onto my back. My eyes snap open, my hands clapping across my body in shock. A nervous laugh slips at the relief I feel at finally being back in my non-shifted form, distracted momentarily from the absolute racket coming from the kitchen. I swear to god if he's destroying the kitchen I'm going to lose it. My body aches as I pull myself from the bed, protesting at the fact I spent so many fucking hours in my wolf form. I pause in the doorway when I see Tam starting the blender of all things, stacks of pancakes already on the table.

I cringe, my head pounding at the sound of the stupid thing whipping the ice around against the blades. I stalk up behind him, unplugging it from the wall. He startles, turning around with wide eyes as he's met with me looming over him.

"Too. Fucking. Loud," I say slowly.

His lips twitch, fighting a smile. "It is, isn't it?" I roll my eyes and step back from him, noticing his chest heaving a bit more rapidly than normal. "What the fuck are you doing?"

He frowns. "Making you breakfast," he murmurs, pointing to the plate of pancakes set up for me, the syrup ready and waiting. "I was making a shake for you too since I know you like having one in the morning no matter if you eat or not."

"Why are you doing this?" He looks away sheepishly, grabbing the blender and a glass. He doesn't answer me, just walks past me to set the glass down on the table. "Tam—"

"Just eat, please."

I sigh, and he steps back to give me room to move to my seat. I notice the envelopes from last night sitting in the middle of the table, still sealed. He stands awkwardly, watching me with a worried expression until I grab the glass and take a big gulp of it. His eyes follow the motion of me putting it down, and the silence is starting to get to me. "It's good, thank you," I say, my heart twinging a bit at the small smile that finally graces his face.

"I know you're mad at me," he starts, backing up a couple of steps from me. "So, I won't blame you if you don't want to go with me tonight." I frown, confused on what the fuck he's talking about. "The engagement dinner. I—I can handle going alone, sorry."

He moves to walk away from me, but I get up quickly and grip his arm to stop him. His entire body is shaking, and I don't know if it's from what happened last night, or if it's because of the dinner tonight getting to his nerves. "You're not going alone."

"I don't want you going if it's just going to upset you. I shouldn't have brought it up."

"Tam." He shakes his head, trying to pull out of my grip but it's half-hearted. I grip the back of his neck, forcing him to look at me. His eyes widen, surprised by my sudden aggression, and fuck me, it's turning *me* on. "I'm going with you," I say carefully.

He swallows, his eyes drifting to my lips for a second before darting up to my eyes. "Okay," he croaks, clearing his throat quickly.

The silence stretches between us, the seconds ticking by, and just when I finally get it in my head to just do it already, my phone buzzes in my pocket loud enough to snap Tam out of his stupor. "Fuck," I grumble, releasing the grip on his neck, but I'm not in a rush to let go of his arm. I dig through my pocket to pull out the phone, frowning at the bank notification that pops up. "What the fuck."

"What's wrong?"

"We just got paid for the Calvin bounty. This doesn't make any sense." My phone buzzes again with a text message from the contact. I'm so fucking lost, showing him the message.

He frowns, shaking his head. "Something like that would be on the local news." I let him pull away from me, and he quickly moves into the living room to turn on the TV, scrolling through the channels until he lands on the local news station, where sure enough, the story is unfolding.

"The home of Calvin Dean went up in flames last night. The cause of the fire is still under investigation, as well as the number of victims found within the home. Emergency crews responded quickly, but the fire was not easy to subdue. There seems to be some speculation as to what type of fire it was as it strangely didn't spread beyond the borders of the home. The bodies, which were recovered from inside once the fire was extinguished, were burned beyond recognition and will take time to notify next of kin. At least three bodies were found, most likely the residents of the home."

"We need to get down to the coroner and find out what the fuck happened, Nox."

"It was definitely done in a way that our contact thinks it was a legitimate hit. It sort of feels wrong for taking their money when we didn't even do the job."

"Fuck that. We both almost died taking out two of them. If whoever did this isn't going to claim the hit, I'm not turning my nose at the money."

"It had to be someone with a personal vendetta against him."

"For them to take them out at his house with all that warding, they had to have been pretty strong. Do you think it could have been an elemental?"

"Fire maybe, yeah. I don't know anyone with power to that level though. If they tore through the wards, they would have had to be pretty supercharged."

"Finish your breakfast and then we'll head out."

"So demanding," I snort. He rolls his eyes and heads off to his room while I do what he asks and finish the breakfast he made for me. He comes back out in clean clothes, looking fucking good as hell, and he catches me gawking at him. He tilts his head in confusion, but I shake my head and jog off to my own room to take a quick shower and change as well.

"Ready?" He asks, tossing a leather jacket over his frame.

"Yeah, let's go."

The ride to the coroner's is quiet, but it doesn't feel overly awkward like I expected it to be. Tam lets me drive, too, which normally isn't like him. He loves his car, just as much as he loves the control of it. He's always about control over every part of his life, no matter how big or how small. He sits quietly in his seat, staring out the window with his brows slightly furrowed like he's lost in thought.

"What should I wear tonight?" I say quietly, trying to get him to at least talk to me a little bit.

"Oh, uh, one of your suits is probably the best call."

"Which one do *you* want me to wear?"

He glances over with a quirked brow. "You want me to pick what you're going to wear?"

I shrug. "Sure. I rather be presentable for your snobby family."

He grins. "At least I'll have you there as a distraction."

"You mean a buffer," I laugh.

"Whatever you want to call it, but you're my date tonight."

"I'm surprised you didn't ask Kalia to go instead."

The smile on his face falters and I'm kicking myself mentally for fucking ruining this small banter. "Nox," he sighs. "I like Kalia, but I don't know her like I know you, and I'm not going to bring some random girl that knows nothing about me to the fucking Court. I'm not ever planning to tell her who I am either, so it's not like this fling is going anywhere."

"Does she know that?"

"No, not yet, but I'll end it. I like her, Nox, but I just can't drag anyone else into my family bullshit."

I know I should feel bad for him, but I'm fucking ecstatic. All I want is for him to get rid of her, to finally give me the chance to work up the courage to tell him how I feel. The moment he officially breaks things off with her, I'm going to do it—I fucking need to. I need to do it or I'm risking him finding someone else that he might not be as hesitant about telling the truth to.

"I'm sorry your life is so complicated," I whisper, and it's true, I *am* sorry. He doesn't deserve all this stress and heartache.

"It's less complicated when you're not mad at me." He sheepishly glances over at me, nervously rubbing his palms on his thighs. "Are you still mad at me?"

"I'm slowly forgiving you."

"Are you going to tell me *why* you're mad at me?"

"Maybe someday, but not right now." His shoulders slump and he turns to stare back out the window. "It's not just on you, Tam. I'm angry at myself for a lot of reasons, too, but I'm not in the headspace to talk about it."

"Whatever I did to upset you, I'm sorry. I don't want you being upset with me."

He says it without looking at me, and my heart thrums with the need to reach out to him and comfort him. I don't want him being upset at the fact I'm upset with him, but I honestly can't tell him right now that I was pissed at him for hooking up with Kalia last night. After everything we went through, that was his solution—his escape.

We pull up to the coroner, and I open my mouth to say something to him, but he's out of the car before I get the chance. I sigh, getting out and following him in. The receptionist up front seems panicked when she sees Tam and I walk in, glancing around nervously.

"Eris," she whispers, gripping into the small charm around her neck and running it along its chain.

"Delilah," Tam croons, trying to tamper down her anxiety. "We need to talk to Colby."

"He's busy at the moment."

"We figured. That's what we're here about. Please call him." She hesitates for longer than Tam likes, and his shadows begin to creep out from his body. She pales, jolting to her feet so fast I fear she'll trip over herself as she runs down the hall. Tam sighs, turning to look at me as he casually leans back against the counter. The position draws my attention to his entire body. The dark jeans hugging his thighs, the white henley stretching perfectly across his chest and abs, and that fucking jacket. Fuck, I've always loved that jacket on him, perfectly worn and loved.

I rip my gaze away from Tam when Delilah and Colby walk in. Tam follows my line of sight, smirking at the nervousness on Colby's face as well. "Eris, what can I do for you?"

"We need to see the bodies."

"Excuse me? It's still an open investigation."

"We were hired by the guard authority to deal with Calvin, and someone went ahead and did our job for us, so do us the favour of letting us see who the fuck we're dealing with."

"Fine," he sighs. "It's not like I can really win against you, can I?"

Nope," Tam laughs, pushing away from the counter and motioning for me to follow them down into the cold abyss. "What's your take so far?"

Colby holds the door open for us to walk in, where eight tables are draped with white sheets. "I have no doubt that Calvin is in here, and one is female, based on build and structure. They're unrecognizable and we're going to have to run dentals to confirm."

"You don't think it was a typical house fire, do you?" I ask, moving to one of the tables, where he pulls back the sheet to reveal a very dead, very destroyed body.

"Not even close. Whoever did this is beyond powerful. I would say they're royal bloodlines level or close to it. This was most definitely a targeted attack. Calvin might be human, but her..." He pulls back the sheet. "Taking out a direct underling to a werewolf alpha is pretty impressive, and it's not like she didn't have powers to defend herself. I think that's Marcus," he says, pointing to the table next to Zenia. "They either knew the attacker, or they didn't see whoever it was coming."

I pull on my power, letting the sight take over my senses to try and get a read on any residual aura fragments. "Do you see anything?" Tam asks quietly.

"It's chaotic as fuck but weirdly feels familiar." I lean in towards Zenia's body, inhaling and cringing instantly. I rub at my nose, which just makes Tam laugh.

"Why would you think that's a good idea?" He snorts. "They smell bad enough without your wolf nose butting in, especially a werewolf."

"I was trying to see if I could isolate what smells so familiar about this magic. I know I've smelled it before, but I can't figure out where."

He comes up beside me, bumping into my shoulder. "It'll be a while before you get that smell out of your sinuses," he chirps.

I lean down towards him, nuzzling my nose right up against his neck, and inhale his scent deep into my body. "All better," I growl, and he shivers but doesn't pull away from me.

I'm definitely not regretting doing that, and if I don't push the boundaries now, how the fuck am I supposed to know if he would ever entertain the idea of us becoming a thing? I take one more deep breath of him, committing his smell to memory, and letting it overtake all the awful scents trying to overwhelm me in here.

"So, my scent helps you?" He asks, his voice low in a way I haven't heard before.

I pull back enough to look at him, his irises rimming with faint light. "You smell like home." His eyes widen at my honesty. Hell, *I'm* surprised by my honesty. It's like my brain is suddenly getting scrambled with him so close to me.

He drops his eyes and takes a small step back, but I swear I notice a faint blush scatter across his cheeks. He clears his throat and turns his attention back to Colby, who is watching the two of us with a curious expression. "If you end up picking up on the magical signature, I want you to call me. I don't know if whoever did this is friendly or someone we need to worry about."

"Alright, I will," Colby says, nodding his head, and Tam motions for me to follow him back out.

He gives Delilah a smug grin when we make our way past her, glancing back at me the moment we're through the door. "Do you want to grab some lunch?" He asks, waiting for me to unlock the car.

"Like go out for lunch?"

"Yeah. If you don't want to, we can order something instead."

"Lunch sounds great."

He smiles—a genuine smile that lights up his entire face. Fuck, I need to get my emotions under control or I'm going to end up in real fucking trouble.

CHAPTER 41

TAMZIN

He's acting so fucking weird. Not in a bad way by any means, but he's being more possessive around me. I'm sure the fact of me almost dying rattled him quite a bit, but I've been in dangerous situations before, and he's never been *this* clingy. He literally growled at a guy that bumped into me on our way into the restaurant for lunch. The poor dude scampered off like he was about to shit himself. I'll admit, it's sort of hot seeing him like that, warding off any possible threats, but his face softening the moment his attention turns back to me.

The words he said earlier keep playing over and over in my head. *'You smell like home.'* That comment *did* something to me. He's my home, too, I just don't have the balls to admit that to him like he did. I'm actually a bit nervous about tonight, but I hope that it just goes off without a hitch, and I don't have to stick around longer than is necessary.

Cam calls me on our way back to the apartment, pulling me out of my head. Nox glances over when I pull my phone out, frowning when I roll my eyes. "What?" I snap into the phone.

"I don't know why I thought I could expect a normal greeting from you, but at least you answered."

"What do you want, Cam." Nox's grip on the steering wheel tightens, the leather creaking under the strain.

"Just checking to see if you're still coming tonight."

"Yes. Nox and I will be there."

"Awesome," he says, my chest tightening at the genuine happiness in his voice. "Dinner will be at seven, but you're welcome to come earlier to have some drinks with us."

"I rather not."

"Please? I want to be able to hang out with you and talk to you, Tamzin."

"That's what dinner is for, is it not?"

He sighs, clearly frustrated with my sass. "Mom and dad won't be there until closer to dinner."

"Sure, but the nightmare twins, Croh, and Dorian will be."

"I've talked to them, and they know not to start anything. You're my brother, Tam, and I'm getting married. I want you there."

"Why can't I just go to the wedding? Why the fuck do I have to go tonight, Cam? Just because you talked to them doesn't mean they won't start shit."

He sighs again, his voice sounding sadder than I've heard in a long time. "You don't have to come. I'm trying to make things right, but I'm not going to force you to do anything. I'm sorry for bothering you." He hangs up before I can say anything else, and I throw my phone onto the dash.

"What's wrong?" Nox asks.

"I feel like I'm being an asshole by talking to him like that. He said I don't have to go tonight if I don't want to, but he just sounded so fucking upset saying it."

"He's right though, you don't. If you're not comfortable going, then we won't go."

"He's trying to make things right," I sigh.

"You believe him?"

"I don't know what to believe anymore, Nox. I don't know what's real and what's not, and I feel like my very reality is slipping away from me. I want nothing to do with that life, and I do hate my family, but can I keep going the way I'm going and not have to pay for it later? I can't handle losing more of myself to all of this."

I don't even realize my leg is bouncing like a jackhammer until Nox settles his hand on my thigh, stilling me. "Whatever you decide to do, I'll support you."

Fuck, why does he have to be so good? "I think I'll go," I say quietly, like I'm waiting for him to judge me on the decision. I don't really want to see my parents or half my siblings, but I want to make sure Helia is okay, and I sort of feel bad for Cam that he's being married off to some recluse Princess from the Autumn Court of all places.

"Okay. What time do we have to be there?"

"Dinner is at seven, but Cam would like us there earlier."

"Do you *want* to go earlier?"

"No," I sigh. "But I should."

He pats my thigh and puts the car in park. Fuck, I completely lost track of everything around me and didn't even notice him pulling up to the apartment.

CHAPTER 42

TAMZIN

I choke on my beer when Nox walks out of his bedroom looking like a fucking god. He quirks a brow, doing up the buttons on his sleeves. "You good?" He asks.

"Yeah," I croak out, clearing my throat and feeling the heat of my embarrassment creeping into my face.

He comes to stand in front of me, my breath hitching when he leans down towards me. "How many beers have you had already?" His minty breath wafts across my face, and I swear I can taste him on my tongue.

"F—five."

"Hmm. I think you're cut off for now." He grabs my beer, pressing it to his lips and swinging back the rest of its contents. He glances down at me, his eyes roaming over my own outfit. "The suit looks good on you."

"You, too." He smirks, setting down the now empty beer and grabbing his jacket off the back of the couch. Fuck me, his ass looks *so* fucking good in dress pants. The man has a dump truck for an ass, and I just want to bite it. I shake my head. *No, you horny fuck, we do not fantasize about biting your best friend's ass.* Fuck, I'd probably chip a tooth on the thing, but it would be so worth it.

"Ready to go?"

"Yeah." I try to subtly adjust my pants to hide the traitorous appendage between my thighs and follow him out. I drive this time, not wanting any issues when we pull up to the Court boundary. He's staying pretty relaxed as we wind our way through the city, pushing into the outer boundaries where the monstrosity of a mansion comes into view. I can feel the ripple of power from here, the barrier pressing hard enough that it makes my car shudder. I'm panting by the time we pull up to the gates, the security guard stepping out right away.

"Name?"

I roll my eyes. "Seriously, Nolan? It hasn't been *that* long."

He stiffens, nostrils flaring in agitation. "Name," he snarls.

"Tamzin, Prince of the Night Court. Now open the fucking gates before Camden comes out here personally and runs a blade through you for keeping his brother waiting."

I can see he wants to fight me on this, but the threat that Camden will end up killing him for delaying me is enough for him to push the button to the gate to let us through. I give him the most sinister grin I can muster and a little finger wave as I accelerate fast enough that the tires squeal and smoke. I glance back through the rearview mirror and turn to Nox.

He's grinning from ear to ear. "He's so mad," he laughs, glancing back to see Nolan coughing and waving his hand to try and clear the rubber-scented toxic cloud I left for him. I take in everything around me, a twinge of nostalgia settling into my chest. My eyes focus in on one of my favourite trees in the distance, the one where I buried my precious dog under. "You okay?"

"Yeah," I say quickly, blinking a few times to try and clear the burn of tears from them.

"Don't lie to me."

I sigh, ripping my eyes away from the tree. "That's where I buried Harbinger."

"Do you want to go visit him?"

"No. I rather not be a blubbering mess at dinner." He doesn't say anything more and I'm so fucking thankful for that. "Nope," I say the moment I get out of the car and see the valet step up to it. I lock it, shoving the keys in my pocket.

"You can't leave that here."

"I can do whatever the fuck I want. I want my car in sight so I can get the fuck out of here when I want. Touch it and I'll kill you."

That shuts him up, and he pales at my threat, scrambling back when Nox comes up to stand next to me like a dark, brooding guardian. The door opens before we even get up the stairs, Cam smiling when he sees us.

"You came," he says happily.

"Don't make a big deal out of it," I grumble. I grunt in surprise, squirming in his grip when he bear-hugs me and lifts me up off my feet, cracking my back in the process. "Put me down, you barbarian."

He sets me down, the smile still stretched across his face as he turns to Nox. "Thank you for coming," he says, holding out his hand to him. Nox stares at it, then glances at me with a quirked brow. I shrug, leaving it up to him. Cam's smile falters, his hand slowly dropping back to his side, but Nox sighs and steps closer, gripping into it.

"Don't make me regret this reunion," he growls, tightening his hold on Cam's hand.

"I'm not the bad guy here, Nox."

"No, but you turn a blind eye to those who are. Tam might be willing to give you a chance, but I'm not so easily swayed. You weren't the one there to pick up the pieces after your family *broke* him, and I swear to the fucking gods if you hurt him, you'll be dealing with me."

"Noted," Cam grumbles, shaking out his hand once Nox releases him. "If you'll follow me."

Nox walks in behind me, his eyes flicking around when I glance back to look at him, like he's trying to take in every detail as we make our way through the front entrance towards the parlour. Yes, this fucking house has a parlour—so pretentious. Helia spots us first, her eyes widening in surprise. She jumps up, quickly moving towards me before Croh and Dorian even notice.

"You came," she smiles, pausing a few feet away from me and smoothing her dress out.

"You look lovely, Helia." She blushes, her eyes darting to Nox when he steps up beside me. "Helia, this is Nox. You haven't officially met, but he's my best friend."

She steps towards him, and he eyes her warily. "Thank you for taking care of my brother."

"It's my pleasure. He's an amazing person."

She smiles and turns back to look at me. "I didn't think you would come. Cam mentioned it to us—that he invited you—but we all thought you would just tell him to fuck off. Lex and Flinn made bets with Croh that you would chicken out."

"Croh bet that I would come?"

"He did," she smirks. "He knows how stubborn you are, but he also knows you're a shit disturber."

"I'm not here to start anything. I'm here to support Cam on this stupid move by our parents."

She sighs. "Yeah, he doesn't seem too happy about it, but he's taking it all in stride."

"What's she like?"

She shrugs. "She's pretty quiet. She doesn't stay at Court, much to the King's dismay. He doesn't like the fact that a Princess of another Court is out and about in society. Cam wants to grant her the small freedom while it's still available. She doesn't seem too happy when she's called back here, but father insists she comes to Court at least twice a week until the wedding."

"Come have a drink, *brother*," Croh calls out.

Helia gives me a sad smile and heads back over to the chair she was sitting in by the fireplace. "Fuck me," I grumble, rolling my neck in irritation.

"Maybe later," Nox whispers, walking over to Croh before I can respond to that, my mouth gaping slightly.

What the actual fuck is going on with him? I'm usually the one that makes sexual innuendos, highly inappropriate comments to someone who is very clearly straight, but Nox...Nox has been pushing my comments further instead of recoiling or brushing them off, and now it's making me question everything. I clear my throat and walk over to them just as Cam hands Nox a glass of whisky. He holds one out to me as well, and I try my best not to flinch at the burn of it. It's not that I hate hard liquor, but I prefer beer when I'm actually drinking and not doing shots.

"Fuck me. I fucking told you not to make that bet with Croh." I stiffen at the sound of Flinn's voice, and Nox takes a step closer to me. "Look what the fucking cat dragged in," he sneers. "You lost me money."

"It's not my fault you still haven't learned not to make bets for stupid shit."

"You shouldn't be here," Lex hisses.

"Enough," Cam snaps. "There will be no petty bullshit during *my* night."

"Your night," he scoffs. "Your own betrothed isn't even here."

"She will be. She promised not to miss tonight."

"Inviting the reject probably scared her away," Flinn cackles.

"She doesn't know Tam was invited. I didn't want to overwhelm her with it, especially if he decided he couldn't make it."

"Can we stop talking about me like I'm not here?" I snap.

"We wish you weren't," Lex snaps back.

"You're just mad that you lost the bet," Croh laughs. "Now pay up before I kick your asses."

Flinn and Lex swear under their breath and hand Croh a couple of bills each. Nox steps closer to me again when Flinn locks eyes with me, a vicious sneer on his face. His gaze shifts to Nox, and my shadows strain against my hold, wanting to protect him from the psychopath.

"Who are you?" He asks, disgust dripping from his voice.

"Tam's friend."

"Tam doesn't have any friends."

"Funny, since I'm standing right here."

"Is he paying you to be here? There's no other reason a mutt like you would be in our home."

Nox growls, his skin rippling with the threat of a shift. "Nox," I say quietly, gripping into his wrist when he threatens a step towards Flinn.

"That's a good dog, stay on your leash," Lex cackles. The next second, he's sprawled on the ground, blood spurting from his nose.

I blink, trying to process what the fuck just happened. Cam looms over Lex, his wings unfurling behind him and his shadows rippling around his body in undulating waves. "I fucking warned you. If you ruin tonight, I will lock you in the fucking pit."

"You hit me," Lex spits out, wiping at his nose.

"Get over it. You will not speak to Tamzin or Nox in that way."

"Prince Camden." Cam gives Lex one final glare before turning around to acknowledge the slightly panicked staff standing in the doorway. "The Princess has arrived."

"Thank you, Megwin." She bows her head and steps away from the door. My mouth drops in shock and confusion, Nox swearing next to me, while Lex pulls himself to his feet. Cam jogs over to her, holding out his hand for her to take. "Tamzin, this is Princess Kalia of the Autumn Court. Kalia, this is my youngest brother, Tamzin, and his friend Nox."

What the *actual* fuck.

CHAPTER 43

KALIA

Fuck. Fuck! What is he doing here? Why the fuck didn't Cam tell me that Tam was coming tonight? I didn't think they were friendly at all, especially to be inviting him to Court when he's been practically shunned for the last five years. If I wasn't panicking internally, I would find his reaction comical. I didn't want him to find out like this, and definitely not yet. Cam's actions are forcing my hand, and I am *livid*.

"It's a pleasure to meet you," I say quietly.

He blinks, shaking his head of his shock. He strides towards me, and it takes everything in me not to cower at the absolute rage seething from him. "Tam?" Cam murmurs.

"*Princess* Kalia," he says with barely restrained anger. "So, you're engaged to my brother."

"I am."

"Interesting." My eyes dart up quickly when I notice Nox stalking forward as well. The fucker looks pissed, but at the same time, he looks absolutely thrilled. Of course he would be happy with this, thinking that I'm tied down to this male laying claim to me. I mean, it's not Cam's fault, it's my father's. In another life, I might have actually fallen for him, but I don't do well in being forced into situations against my will, and Tam was the key to getting me out of this. It's fine—everything will be fine. I can still make this work. I know Tam feels something for me, I felt it last night, and I can feel the tension between us, even now.

"I was under the impression that you no longer associated with Court," I murmur, glancing at Cam when he settles his hand at the small of my back.

"It would have been very convenient if I didn't, wouldn't it?" Tam snaps. I shoot him a glare, gritting my teeth to stop myself from snapping back at him. I didn't *lie* to him, I just omitted the reason as to why I'm really here.

I don't want to get married to Cam. I don't want to be tied to this Court and its ways, going from one prison to another. Tam knows all too well what awaits anyone who lives by the Night Court rules, and I wish he would just fucking do something about it. He's stronger than them—strong enough to take out his father, the fucker. I shiver at the thought of having to deal with him tonight. Every time he speaks or comes near me, I have to fight down the bile that threatens to rise up my throat.

"Would you like a drink, Kalia?" Cam asks, pulling my attention back to him.

I smile, nodding my head. "Please."

"I'll get it," Tam interrupts when Cam moves to pull away. "Enjoy your future *wife's* company." I flinch at the bite in his tone, wanting to reach out to him when he turns away. Nox lingers a moment longer, his eyes practically burning a hole into me. He wasn't shy about his distrust of me before, but now? Now the situation has just completely solidified everything for him. He's going to be a problem. I can still make this work, but not if Nox is in his ear.

"Nox—"

"*Princess*," he snaps back, bristling with agitation. Fuck, I can't push him, or he might actually lose his shit and shift right here. I *would* let him do that if he meant he went rabid on everyone here, but I can't risk him coming after me as well, and he might hurt Tam without meaning to.

"Your drink," Tam murmurs, handing me a vodka soda.

Cam lifts a brow in question, turning to his brother with an air of suspicion. "How did you know what she drinks?"

"She seems like the type," Tam murmurs, chugging back his own drink, which he filled almost to the brim. I don't think I've ever seen him drink hard liquor. He always goes for beer when he's out at the bar.

"Dinner is ready," Megwin calls through the door, and everyone shuffles out of the room, unaware of the insane tension building between Tam and me.

I want to reach out to him and haul him back so I can talk to him, try to explain my side of things, but I can't with Cam at my side and Nox planting himself between me and Tam.

"Where are the King and Queen?" I ask as Cam pulls my chair out for me to sit. I can feel Tam watching me as I adjust the skirt of my dress around me, the frilly material caressing his pants. It's a tense situation being sandwiched between Cam and Tam, but it makes sense. Tam is the least likely to do anything to me in Cam's eyes. Little does he know, the rage burning in him is already searing at my nerves, flaying at my control.

"They'll be here later. I'm not sure if they'll make it for dinner."

The wait staff sets out the first round of plates in front of us, a weird silence radiating through the room. I hate it. I can feel the animosity oozing from every single one of them, though Cam and Helia seem to be sort of happy at the fact Tam is here.

"So, Tam. Does your visit today mean you'll be frequenting Court again?"

"No. I'm only here because Camden asked me to come. It's not every day my eldest brother gets engaged, and I wanted to show my support." His tone is clipped, and he's not really eating any of the food, just sort of pushing it around to make it look like he is. I glance at him, noticing how he leans further away from me into Nox, who is whispering something in his ear. Tam shakes his head, and Nox's eyes lock on mine, seething with anger.

"I see. Well, your presences is both a surprise and an honour. I'm glad to finally know who you really are, *Tamzin*."

If he wants to play the game, I'll fucking play. He lied to me, too. Mind you, I knew he was lying because I knew who he way from the first moment I saw him. I came here for *him*, not Cam, not the Night Court, but for Tam. Him and I are a lot alike, something I'm planning to prove to him. We're both rejects to our house, outcasts that don't want to fit the mould, forced to do things we may not want to, just to hold onto the small piece of ourselves that still exists.

Flinn and Lex throw in jabs at Tam through dinner, quickly being squashed by Cam with more threats of violence. Fucking barbarians, the lot of them. Nox doesn't say a word the entire time, only whispering quietly to Tam every so often. I'm impressed that he's able to keep his shift in check even with the amount of anger still coursing through him. Lex throws some harsh comments at him as well, slowly progressing his line of torture to his making.

"So, how do you feel being the bastard to a Prince that wanted nothing to do with you? I knew your father got around, but I didn't think he subjected himself to shifter whores." Nox stiffens at the insult, but says nothing, which just pisses Lex off more. "I heard your bastard half-sister killed him. Was her whore mother and yours, friends?"

"Lexington, that's enough," Cam snarls just as Tam slams his hand down on the table.

"Fine, I'll stop ripping on the mutt, but I'm not done with the reject. I still don't understand why you thought you would be welcome back here. There's nothing for you here anymore. *Nothing*. We burned everything that belonged to you."

Tam's chair drags back harshly. "Tam!" Nox calls out.

“I need some air,” he snaps, ripping through the doors. Moments later, the front door slams hard enough to rattle the entire house.

“Excuse me,” Nox mutters. Lex and Flinn cackle like sociopaths, and surprisingly, Croh looks a bit concerned.

“I can come with you,” Cam says, shifting his chair back.

“No. I’ll handle it. Thank you for dinner, but I think it’s best if we go. We’re not welcome here.”

“Damn straight,” Lex snickers, leaning back on his chair.

“You’re not proving anything,” Croh snaps, yanking on his chair and sending Lex toppling over. Croh gives Nox a small nod, an inkling of acknowledgment at the pain they’re causing Tam.

Once Nox is through the door, I excuse myself to use the washroom, but bolt towards the front door. “This was stupid!” Tam screams, throwing his hand towards the door just as I open it. Nox glances at me and shifts towards me. “And you! You’re a fucking liar!” He snarls, storming towards me.

“You lied, too.”

“It’s not the same and you know it. I liked you, Kalia. I fucking trusted you after you helped us, meanwhile, you’re fucking engaged to my brother! You’re a fucking Princess, and you’re living in that shitty house. Why? Tell me why?!”

“I was going to tell you. I don’t want to marry him. I want a life, Tam, not a prison.”

“Too fucking bad, you don’t have a choice. You can’t just slip out of this marriage, Kalia. This is fucking serious.”

“I want to be with *you*.”

He huffs out a humourless laugh. “That’ll never happen.”

I step closer to him, but Nox throws his hand up, stopping me. “Don’t say that!”

“The fact you attempted to start a relationship when you knew it wasn’t going to go anywhere at all is asinine. You cheated on my fucking brother. How do you expect me to react?”

“You don’t even like him! You hate your family and so do I!”

He moves so quickly I don't even have time to react. His hand tightens around my throat, his face mere inches from mine. His eyes glow viciously, the promise of pain and death within their depths. "How I feel about my family is *my* business, but it doesn't give you the right to manipulate them like this. Cam has been good to you, trying to make you feel welcome, and you've just thrown it in his face." I stumble when he shoves me back. "I never want to see you again. I don't know you, and you better act like you don't know me. You're a fox through and through. Manipulative and conniving."

And then he's gone, vanishing in a cloud of shadow, leaving me gaping and floundering with Nox looming over me. "Stay the fuck away from him."

"Nox, I never wanted to hurt him. I fucking helped you both! You have no idea what I've done for you."

"I don't fucking care what you've done. All his life he's been lied to and used, and I won't allow him to suffer the same fate with you in his life. Stay the fuck away from him or I'll fucking kill you."

I swallow, dropping my eyes to the ground to try and stop myself from crying. His boots crunch on the gravel of the driveway, and the next moment, I see him shift, taking off across the vast expanse of grass on the property. I know I fucked up, but I can still fix this. I *will* fix this.

CHAPTER 44

NOX

Fuck. This went worse than I thought possible. The last thing either of us expected was to see fucking Kalia in there, the fucking Princess of the Autumn Court—Camden's *fiancé*. It's so hard to track him like this, the trail of scent barely noticeable when he uses his void warping, but I had a general idea of where he might go after all of that, and thankfully I was right. I catch his scent downwind, tearing across the property, and slowing my pace as I get closer to the tree he mentioned earlier.

I shift back, quietly making my way over to him kneeling on the ground in front of a small gravestone. "Hey," I say quietly.

"Leave me alone," he mumbles, his voice thick with tears.

"I won't do that."

"Please, Nox. I can't do this right now."

"Do what? There's nothing you need to do, Tam. You're frustrated and hurting, and I just want to be here for you. Is that so wrong?"

He sobs, curling over to rest his forehead against the grass. "I'm cursed. Nothing in my life goes right, and I swear it's like the universe is out to get me. The one time I feel like I'm getting a hold of my shit and even consider letting someone into my life, it all bursts into flames."

"You liked her."

"Yeah," he sniffles. "I really did, and now if it comes out what happened between us, Cam will hate me all over again."

"It's not your fault, Tam. You didn't know."

"Lex and Flinn are right, I'm a fucking failure. I shouldn't be here. Fuck, I shouldn't even exist."

I grip his arm and rip him to his feet. He stumbles, but it's like all the fight has just melted out of him. "Don't fucking say that," I snarl. "You deserve to be here, and I don't just mean here at Court, I mean *here*, Tam, on this earth." He swallows and turns away from me, and I grip into his arms harder. "Look at me. Tell me you don't believe the lies you're telling yourself."

"Why do you care? I'm fucking poison, Nox. You would do well to just slink out of my life before I actually get you killed."

"I *want* to be here. If I die, at least I can be happy with the fact I had you in my life."

"I don't want you getting hurt."

I press my lips to his, completely silencing him and shocking him and myself. This wasn't what I had planned, not even close, but I can't just stand by and listen to him bashing himself and tearing himself down. I dart my tongue out, playing against the seam of his lips, and groan when he parts his mouth for me. The kiss is pure bliss, filled with every emotion I've kept bottled up for years now, wanting and waiting for the right time.

He's panting when I pull back and rest my forehead against his, his hands resting against my chest. "Why?" He whispers.

"I love you, Tam. I'm *in* love with you, and I have been since the night I saw you stumbling out of Court. I may not have truly understood the emotions I felt then but watching you every day has just solidified what I feel for you. I hated seeing you with Kalia, and that's why I was angry with you. *I* wanted to be the one that you went to for comfort, and I thought that we were progressing to that moment, but then Kalia showed up and you just...you picked *her*, not me."

"I thought you were straight."

I laugh, pulling back to look at his still shocked face. His eyes are red and glassy, showing me just how much all of tonight broke him. "I can't control who I fall in love with."

"Why didn't you just tell me? Why did you just let me keep fucking around with random girls? Hell, *you* fucked around with random girls."

I didn't want to put that pressure on you, and honestly, I didn't understand what I was really feeling towards you."

"So, all those comments you made—"

"I wasn't joking, I was testing the waters. I didn't think you were actually interested in me, but you made comments, and then the way you acted when I stayed with you...I was scared, Tam."

He cups my cheek, my heart thrumming in my chest at the look of pure love on his face. "You love me."

"Yes," I whisper shakily.

"Say it again."

I smile, placing my hands on either side of his neck. "I love you." Fuck it feels surreal to say it, but damn it, it feels good.

"Again."

I laugh, pressing my lips to his once more. "I love you," I murmur against them.

"I love you, too."

His words hit me like a truck, spreading through me like wildfire, completely warming me from the inside out. I don't think I've ever been this happy in my entire life. All my fears and reservations about telling him the truth were for nothing. I wasted so much fucking time playing through scenarios in my head, doubting the feelings he felt for me in return. Never again. I'll never hesitate to tell him how I feel, and I won't waste a single second more. This is real. He loves me and I love him, and my life finally feels complete. Nothing else fucking matters anymore. Not who he is, what he's done, his fucking family and their opinion of him, and sure as fuck not Kalia. I *won*.

CHAPTER 45

TAMZIN

Nox completely blocks me from Cam when he comes out to try and get me to stay. Lex being Lex, runs his mouth again, but this time, Nox doesn't take it lying down, and Lex ends up sprawled out on the front lawn with a broken nose and a black eye. I watch from the car as he completely lays into Cam about the behaviour of my family and for him to get his shit together before hell gets brought down on him by his own creation.

He slams the car door once he gets in, letting out a long puff of frustrated air. "You didn't have to go that far," I sigh.

His eyes drift up through the windshield, to Kalia standing in the doorway, looking concerned with her hands curled up against her chest as she watches Lex try to start a fight with Cam now. Croh steps in though, cupping Lex around the throat and dragging him into the house, kicking and screaming like a fucking child.

"I should have done that right from the start," he mumbles, starting the car. He glances at me, frowning. "I'll stop and grab you a burger. I noticed you didn't actually eat any of the food."

Of course he noticed. He notices *everything* about me, meanwhile I'm fucking blind as a bat when it comes to him. No, that's not exactly true. I'm blind to the things that involve me and him since

I didn't actually see his declaration of love coming. Love. He fucking loves me. My heart swells with joy at the thought because I honestly never thought I could be the type of person that could be loved. I didn't think I was someone who *deserved* to be loved, especially from someone as great as Nox.

Is this really happening? Am I seriously falling into a relationship with fucking Nox? Fuck me, I hope so. He orders me a burger and fries, and an ice cream cup to cheer me up. I laugh at him when he puts in the order, and he just smiles, like it's the most normal thing in the world. Needless to say, I demolish the burger and half the fries, Nox snagging some while he drives. The ice cream was definitely a nice addition, and he glances at me when we stop at the light because of the small hum of pleasure I let out. He quirks a brow, watching me lick at the spoon.

"It's good. Did you want some?" I ask, shoving the spoon in my mouth again. He nods his head, and I quickly pull some onto the spoon again, holding it out to him. I swallow hard as he sensually wraps his lips around it, pulling it into his mouth easily while his eyes stay fixed on mine. "How is it?"

"Good," he whispers. He grips into the back of my neck, pressing his lips against mine. His tongue slips in, swiping against my own, and my heart threatens to beat right out of my chest. "This taste better, though," he purrs. He rolls his eyes and clucks his tongue when a horn honks behind us.

Fuck me, I'm in trouble. If he's being this flirty and open now, what's going to happen once we get home? Fuck, am I ready to have *sex* with him? Gods I would love to have sex with him, touch every inch of him and drag my tongue over every fucking muscle on that man's body. He's seen me naked plenty of time, but I've only seen him a few times, and each one was fleeting.

My nerves start getting to me the closer we get to the apartment, and my leg starts bouncing without me realizing it. Nox's warm hand settles on my thigh, gripping into it to get me to stop. "What's wrong?"

"Nothing!" I squeak out at an abnormally high pitch.

"It's clearly not nothing. Your leg is going like a fucking jackhammer."

"I'm fine."

He clucks his tongue, gives my leg one final squeeze, and drives the rest of the way in silence. He's quiet when we pull up to the apartment, and the walk to the elevator, and the longer he goes without saying anything, the more nervous I get. He hits the button to our floor, and I watch as the numbers flash painfully slow. He steps towards the panel and hits the stop button, the elevator jolting at the sudden lack of momentum.

"Nox, what are you—"

He's in front of me in a second, pinning my body between his and the cold steel wall behind me. "Tell me why you were so agitated in the car."

"I told you it was nothing," I say breathlessly, because fucking hell, he's too close. Every inhale pulls his scent into my system, so heady it makes my eyes flutter closed.

They snap open when his hand slides up the side of my neck to grip into my hair, forcing my eyes to his. "Don't lie to me."

Way too fucking close. His lips are barely an inch from mine, and his warm breath caresses my skin. "I—" I swallow, trying to slow my racing heart when he moves his face to my neck, his nose dragging up the length of it on an inhale. "I can't think when you do that," I choke out.

"Hmm, is that so?" I shiver at the feel of his tongue on my skin, then his lips, my knees almost buckling when he bites down at the tendon in my neck. "Fuck, you smell good," he moans.

"So—so do you." Fuck, he's turned me into a bumbling idiot. Why the fuck can't I even speak properly? I can't move with the way he has me pinned, I can barely fucking breathe. His grip on my hair tightens, tugging my head back to completely expose the column of my neck to him. My cock hardens, throbbing against the dress pants painfully with every second that passes.

"Now, tell me, Tam...what was on your mind in the car ride over? If you answer honestly, I'll give you a reward."

"A reward?"

He kisses my throat, and I swear to the fucking gods if I come in my pants, I may as well die right here from sheer embarrassment. I slam my eyes shut when his other hand settles on my belt, his palm pressing against my stomach.

"Tamzin," he whispers, and his voice saying my name in that deliciously sensual way has me whimpering for him. Fuck, I thought *I* had game when it came to seduction and shit. I feel like an amateur in comparison to him, or maybe it's just because I've thought about him in that way for longer than I want to admit.

"I was thinking about us having sex," I blurt out, clearly brainwashed by the feel of his mouth on me. I'd probably tell him anything at this point if he asked.

He pulls back to look at me, and it's like my body is magnetized to him, leaning into him on instinct alone. "Do you *want* to have sex with me?"

"No. Yes. I don't know, fuck. I do, but I don't want to ruin it. I don't want to disappoint you and have you realizing that this isn't what you want. That *I'm* not what you really want. You've never been with a guy before, Nox. I don't want sex to be the thing that ruins what we already have."

He frowns, pulling away from me and pushing the button on the elevator once more. Fuck. I think I fucked up. I stare at his back the entire ride up, my breathing harsh while my heart thumps erratically. He steps out, and I send up a silent prayer of thanks that my legs still work so I can walk after him. He pulls off his jacket the second he opens the door, and I just can't take it anymore.

"Are you upset?"

He tosses the jacket onto the back of the couch, glancing at me over his shoulder while his fingers move to the buttons on his shirt, undoing the top two. He turns to look at me fully, untucking the shirt from his pants. Fuck, why is that hotter than him completely put together? There's only one thing that could make this better and that's—Fuck. The way his forearms flex as he rolls up the sleeves of his shirt is one of the hottest moves on the planet. What the fuck is it about forearms? It's so much worse for my self-control because of the way his tattoos sneak up under the material. I love the full sleeve look, but I didn't have the balls to go that far with my rebellious phase.

"I'm not mad. You're entitled to your opinion, but do you want to know what I think?" I nod, and he takes a step closer to me. "I don't want to live with the regret of not seeing where this could go. I've waited long enough, letting myself stew in my emotions and just choking it down when all I wanted to do was taste you. If you don't want this to go any further, then you need to tell me right now because if you don't..." He steps towards me again and undoes the one button I have done up on my jacket. "I'm going to push this *and* you as far as you'll allow me to." He hooks his fingers into my jacket, slowly sliding it off my shoulders until it's thumping to the floor behind me. "Do you want me to stop?" I swallow, his fingers shifting to the buttons on my shirt now. "If you want me to stop, you need to say it, Tamzin."

"Nox." My eyes slam shut when he flicks one of the buttons on my shirt open.

"Tell me to stop," he whispers, snapping another one.

"Don't." He pauses and I slowly open my eyes to see his glowing softly, his lips parted. "Don't stop."

My heart pounds so viciously I can hear and feel my own blood pumping in my ears. The look on his face turns from hesitant to feral in the blink of an eye, and his hands move like fucking machines, getting every single button undone within seconds. He rips my shirt open, trailing his mouth in hot kisses across my skin, settling on the tattoo over my heart.

Slowly, he lowers himself down to his knees in front of me, his gaze fixed on mine while his fingers move flawlessly to undo my belt, then the button on my pants. The sound of the zipper sliding against its teeth resonates in the silence of the room.

"Your reward," he smirks, slowly sliding my pants down my hips to settle on the floor. His eyes shift to the very obvious bulge in my underwear, a small hum slipping through his lips. "I don't actually know what I'm doing here, so let me know if I fuck this up."

"You can't fuck this up. Unless you bite it off...please don't bite it off."

He grins, showing off all his perfect teeth. "No teeth, got it," he snorts.

CHAPTER 46

NOX

Fuck, I'm so nervous. He must be, too, since he's shaking like a leaf. His stomach flexes with each hard inhale, stuttering when I finally grip into his underwear to pull them down as well. I didn't know what to expect, but it wasn't *that*. I've seen him naked plenty, but I'll admit, I've never seen him hard. Fucking hell, he's bigger than me, and here I am about to put it in my mouth...well, try to anyways.

I swallow hard, gripping into the base of his cock and giving it a firm stroke. My eyes drift back up to him when his breathing quickens. Shifting closer to him, I keep my eyes on him and let my tongue explore the length of him, taking my time around the tip. I know what I like, and I'm hoping I can recreate it for him—hoping he likes the same things. It's different than what I expected, but the soft moan that slips through his lips sends a flutter through me, a joy that I'm the one pulling that sound from him.

He sets his shaking hand down on my head, his fingers digging into my scalp and hair, and sending a shiver raking up my spine. "Nox," he pants, and fuck me, the way my name on his lips sounds so breathless and filled with lust has my own cock hardening in my pants.

I don't know what's going to happen after this, but I'll take it one step at a time. I know how obsessed with control he is, and a twinge of fear skitters through me at the thought he's going to want to fuck me, and not the other way around. The one guy I've been with just wanted sex, not foreplay on his end, and he just wanted me to rail him like it was the most obvious choice in the world. Neither of us really act like the submissive type, so the relationship dynamics might get a bit complicated. If that's what he needs for this to work, then I'll do that for him. I'm already on my knees for him, and seeing how he looks at me, just makes me want to fucking *bend*.

I can taste him already, his precum coating my tongue, and fuck me, why does it taste *good*. This is for me. Mine. He's all fucking mine. I take him into my mouth and his grip on my hair tightens, a heavy groan radiating out from him. I'll admit it, his cock is perfect. The soft, velvety feel of him, smooth against my tongue. I can feel it throb with every dip of my head, taking him deeper and further into my mouth. I try to relax my jaw, keeping my teeth covered with my lips because I will not be the one that ends up fucking up his dick with my inexperience.

"Fuck, Nox. That feels so good." I hum against him, my cock straining painfully against the restriction of my pants. He rips my head back and I gasp in surprise. "Touch yourself. I want you to make yourself come while you suck my cock." Fuck me, his controlling behaviour is hot as fuck. He doesn't take my hesitation too well, and his eyes rim with light. "Now," he growls. He doesn't release his hold on my hair, and I can't even look away from him as I reach for my belt. "Shirt first. I want to see all of you, Nox."

I smirk at him and undo the rest of the buttons, shrugging out of the dress shirt. His gaze devours me, roaming over every inch of skin, tattooed and not. He's had a heavy obsession with my tattoos, and he's come with me plenty of times to add new ink.

"You like what you see?" I ask.

His eyes darken. "I love what I see, but I want to see more—all of you, Nox." His hand slowly slides out of my hair, and he motions for me to get up. I do what he asks, slowly undoing the belt, the sound of the buckle clicking against itself seeming so loud. His eyes drift down to my fingers as they undo the button and the zipper. Hooking them into both the pants and my underwear, I slide them over my hips, letting everything fall to the ground. He licks his lips, his eyes slowly drifting back up to mine. "You're perfect," he whispers.

I step towards him, cupping his face in my palms. "*You're* perfect," I whisper back, pressing my lips gently against his. "Now let me take care of you like you deserve."

"Nox," he says breathlessly, my name hitching in his throat as I lower myself back down in front of him. Having my cock free is pure bliss, and my hand itches to stroke it as I take him back into my mouth. "Touch yourself."

My body slumps in relief at the permission from him, like it was waiting for him to acknowledge my own need. I moan around him on the first stroke of my palm, my mind picturing his mouth on me. I won't ask that of him because this is about him right now and making him feel wanted and needed. I swear his cock gets bigger in my mouth, and I take him as far as I can, feeling him hit the back of my throat. I swallow around him, trying to tamper down the gag reflex that's clawing at me from the invasion, and slowly slide him back out of my mouth with an audible pop.

"Fuck, that's good," he pants, settling his hand on my head again. "Do you like sucking my cock?" I nod, licking around his crown before plunging him back into my mouth. Fuck, I'm so turned on, my own release burning in my spine, ready to erupt out of me. "Nox," he grunts. "I'm coming." He tries to pull my head away from him, but I growl and grip into his balls, massaging into them and tipping him over. Thick heat coats my tongue, but I swallow him all down, slowly pulling him out of my mouth and swallowing again. His eyes are wide as he stares at me, like what I just did was a completely surprise. "Why did you do that?"

"I told you I wanted to taste you. All of you, Tam." My own cum spurts out, coating my hand and the floor in thick ropes. Slowly I lift to my feet, grunting in surprise when he grips my cock and coats his own hand in it. He pulls away, the remnants of myself lingering on his fingers, and he takes each one into his mouth, sucking them clean. "Fuck," I groan. "Don't do shit like that."

He smirks. "Why?"

I slam my lips against his, diving my tongue into his mouth with a feral moan. I smile against his mouth when he grips into my ass and squeezes, laughing when he does it again. "You like my ass?"

"I just want to bite it," he says easily, nipping at my lip.

"Hmm, kinky."

He laughs, giving it one more squeeze, and takes a small step back from me. "You're good with your mouth," he smirks.

"So, I did okay?"

"Yes, Nox, definitely better than okay."

New nerves start to settle into me on where we go from here. I don't want to put pressure on him for more, but I also don't want this night to end just yet. I take a deep breath, steeling myself for the awkwardness this might create. "What now?"

CHAPTER 47

TAMZIN

I'm still riding the high from finally being intimate with Nox that I don't understand the question. "What?"

He sighs, taking a step back to put a bit of distance between us, the motion feeling brutal, but I understand the need for it. We're both in a haze still from what just happened, and neither of us can think straight standing too close to each other.

"What do you want, Tam? I don't want tonight to end, but I don't want you to feel pressured into actually having sex. We can just spend the night together and let it all sink in. Plus, how do we even do this? You like your control, but I don't know if I'm mentally prepared to have you fuck me. I'm actually nervous at the idea of it, but that's not on you." He steps back towards me and grips my hips, ducking his head to look at my downcast eyes. "I want you. I want to *be* with you, so I don't want you thinking that's what's causing my hesitation."

My heart beats frantically in my chest because I haven't thought about the mechanics behind it. He's right, I have an obsession with control, and the thought of allowing someone else to take that control from me is terrifying. Even with Kalia riding me, I had to tamper down my anxiety and remind myself that I was still in control of that situation. The thought of completely submitting myself to him has my lungs tightening in my chest.

"Hey," he coos, tucking his knuckles under my chin to tip my head up to him. "Let's just go to bed, okay? I'm not going to force you into anything. I don't want you to feel panicked in our relationship."

"Relationship," I say quietly. "This is real."

He smiles. "This is real, Tam," he whispers, pressing his lips to mine so gently that my heart swells with joy. "Do you want to go to your room or mine?"

"Mine, please."

"Okay." He kisses my forehead and weaves his fingers through mine, pulling me along behind him. I am *so* glad I'm behind him because I can clearly see that perfect ass of his, and yup, I still want to bite it. It's like he senses my thoughts, pausing in the doorway and looking over his shoulder at me with a quirked brow. "You were checking out my ass, weren't you?" He smirks.

"Guilty," I laugh. "I can't help it. How is it so fucking perfect? Do you do squats or some shit?"

"What can I say, I've been blessed by the ass gods."

I climb into bed, Nox settling in behind me and pulling me tight against his chest. His lips press against the sensitive skin behind my ear, and he inhales deeply, kissing me again. Lacing my fingers through his, I curl back into him, relishing the feel of his body pressed against mine. We've spent nights together before, but it feels so different now having both our feelings out in the open. I wish I would have seen it sooner, and I wish I would have done more.

"Are you okay with us just being like this?"

His arms tighten around me further, and I swear he can feel my heart beating viciously in my chest from the contact. "I told you I was. Nothing needs to change, Tam, but it's nice to know that my feelings for you aren't one-sided. That's enough for me, even if we never do more than just this."

But I want to give him so much more. I want to give him everything. He's been my rock, my pillar of stability every single time I was on the verge of losing every piece of myself. While my own soul kept getting blown away, he was collecting the pieces to help put me back together. He's everything to me, my best friend, my brother, my fucking soulmate. He's been the one person in this world that has seen every dark part of me and not once has he turned away.

"I love you," I whisper.

He hums low in his throat and buries his face into my neck. "I love you, too. Now, get some sleep."

I'm tired but I can't sleep right now, my mind too filled with thoughts and memories, playing back every possible action from him that could have been a sign that led to this moment. I feel his grip on me loosen a little bit, his breathing steadying behind me, and I smile to myself at how easily he passed out. I'm sure he's tired, and probably pretty happy because I am, too. He's been through a lot the last few days, and I'm sure sleeping in his wolf form last night wasn't very restful.

I awkwardly turn in his arms to face him, his face scrunching in protest. I smirk, pressing my lips between his brows to smooth the lines out, and brush his hair back from his face. I can't help but stare at him, taking in every detail that I've seen every single day and appreciating him even more. His dark lashes—enviously long—fanning out against his cheeks. His gorgeous tawny skin, naturally sun kissed and perfect. I love his hair, raven black and soft beyond belief. I just want to lay here and pet him, running my fingers through the silken strands. He seems to enjoy it at least, nuzzling further into the pillow with a soft smile pulling at his lips, even in sleep.

I press my lips to his forehead, closing my eyes and shifting myself closer to be on the same pillow as him. Who would have thought that Kalia would be the reason this happened? I thought that maybe giving her a chance would make me happy. That thought being the reason that I became infatuated with her, close to the point of obsession, but it wasn't. I should thank her for bringing Nox and I closer together, but I don't want to speak to her again. I wish I could get out of going to the wedding, but I know Cam will be really upset, especially after everything that happened tonight.

He tried. I have to give him credit for that. He punched Lex for fuck's sake, which he's never done. Even Croh seemed to be getting upset with their antics. I'm used to it, hating that it still got to me, but it was worse when they started going after Nox. They can say what they want about me, but I can't handle them judging him for anything. I wanted to rip into them, destroy them on the spot, but I knew if I started anything at Court of all places, I wouldn't be the only one they locked away and tortured. I won't risk Nox falling victim to their ways, to the pain they can so easily create.

CHAPTER 48

TAMZIN

My eyes snap open at the soft moan behind me, my body reacting instantly to the feel of his hard cock pressing into my back. Fuck, I'm just as hard as he is right now, fucking male hormones and the lack of control we have over them in our sleep. I bite back my own moan when his fingers dig into my hips, grinding me back against him. The skin-on-skin contact sends heat skittering through my veins, lighting up my insides in a way that makes me want more.

I reach behind me, wedging my hand between our bodies, and rub the length of him. He whimpers, rocking his hips into me again, his warm panting breaths skating across my skin. "Tam," he groans, and then his hips pause. "What are you doing? Fuck, I'm sorry."

"Don't be. If I hated it, I wouldn't have started rubbing on you."

He loops his arm around me, dragging his nails across my chest. "You like me molesting you in your sleep?"

"Maybe."

He bites at my shoulder and my body bows into his at the sting of it. "Don't tease me."

"I'm not. I want you."

"Tam—"

"Fuck me, Nox."

"Tam," he sighs.

"I know you won't hurt me. My need for control is because I'm afraid of getting hurt, Nox. I'm not afraid with you."

"I would never hurt you, Tam. You mean everything to me, but I don't want you to feel pressured into this."

He grunts out a breath when I stroke his cock again, and his hand slides up to gently grip at my throat. He nips and sucks at the skin on my neck, shifting his hips into my hand. His other hand creeps under me, shifting around to grip at my cock. My hips buck into his hand, my breaths panting out harshly through my lips. He dips three fingers into my mouth, surprising me enough that my body stiffens.

"Lick them," he growls. "Get them nice and wet for me." I do as he says, swirling my tongue around his fingers. He pulls them out and slowly teases one of them at my ass. Fuck. Panic hits me, and he must sense it because he presses his lips against my neck again. "If I can't get my fingers in you, I won't get my cock in there, Tam." I nod, whimpering slightly when he presses a second one into me, splaying them to spread me. He thrusts them in slowly, his other hand palming my cock, stroking me right to the edge.

"I—I have lube in the nightstand."

He pulls away from me so fucking fast that I can't help but laugh at his exuberance. He grunts out in surprise, and I roll over to see him bounce up from the ground, like he *didn't* just fall off my bed. My eyes dart down to his cock, sticking straight out like an arrow, and way bigger than I remember just last night. I startle at the sound of the lube cap popping open, glancing back at his face.

"What?" He asks.

"Uh, I don't think you'll fit."

He grins, full of mischief and sensual promise. "Oh, baby, I'll make it fit."

Damn it, I'm definitely in trouble. How am I supposed to argue with him when he looks at me like that? He crawls back onto the bed, rolling me over onto my back, and I can't stop the embarrassment I feel right now. I try to look away from him as his eyes roam over every inch of my naked body, but he grips my jaw and forces me to look at him. He doesn't need to say anything, the look is enough to pin me to the bed and watch him. He squirts some lube onto his fingers rubbing them together and pressing them to me again. I can't help but bow at the pressure, and I just about lose it when his mouth is suddenly on me, kissing and licking and swirling, tasting my entire cock before pulling it into his mouth.

He works his fingers slowly, thrusting and spreading with every sensual dip of his mouth on my cock. He hums when he's able to get a third one in, working me up all over again until I'm a fucking whimpering and moaning mess under him.

"Fuck, Tam," he groans, pulling away from me.

He grips his own cock and gives it a firm stroke, licking his lips as he stares at me. He shifts himself closer, laying his length right up against mine, and then grips them both and starts rubbing them together. Fuck, that's so hot, and it feels fucking amazing. Feeling his length, the heat of it and the firmness pressing against mine while he works both of us to the edge is fucking amazing.

I whine when he pulls away, but he smirks, leaning over me to hover his face right above mine. "I'll go slow. If you want me to stop, just tell me to stop and I will."

No safe words. He doesn't know that side of me, and I'm hesitant to tell him about it because it is one hundred percent part of my control trauma. He'll stop, even if I don't really mean it, and that thought has me loving him so much more. He's not here to play games or push me to the point where I might break.

"Tell me you understand," he whispers.

"I do. I trust you."

He smiles, pressing his lips to mine softly, and pulling back again. Grabbing the lube, he slathers his cock in it, rubbing a bit more over his fingers again and rubbing it against me. He lines himself up and my breath hitches at the pressure. He frowns, leaning over me again to claim my mouth, dipping his tongue in sensually. He nips at my lip and sucks on my tongue, slowly thrusting his hips into me, inching himself in little by little.

"Are you okay?" he murmurs, moving his mouth down along my jaw and biting into it when I moan.

"Yes." The word rattles out of me, and my hands claw at his back, pulling him in closer to me.

His tongue drags up the length of my neck, his breaths panting while he tries to control himself and his rhythm, taking it slower than I thought possible. It must be torture for him—the desire to just thrust into me but pacing himself so he doesn't hurt me and make me spiral. I claw at his back again when he wraps one of his hands around my cock and start pumping it in the same rhythm as his hips. The weight of him on top of me *should* make me panic, but it doesn't, I feel *safe*. For the first time in my life, I fucking feel safe and wanted in a way that no one ever has made me feel.

My head tips back at the pressure of his cock finally filling me, his hips flush against mine. He pauses, letting me adjust to his size. Gripping my jaw, he holds me still, his mouth like pure bliss against my own.

"I told you I would make it fit," he purrs, nipping at my lip and tugging it into his mouth.

I laugh, smiling against his mouth. "You did."

"This feels so good, Tam."

"Better than the girls you've been with?"

"Yes, because it's you." He drags out of me slowly, thrusting into me, hard and deep. "This is so much more than some random hookup, Tam," he pants, kissing me again. His hand tightens on my cock, pumping and swirling his thumb across the head of it. "I want to *be* with you."

Fuck me and my traitorous emotions. I can physically feel my barrier cracking with every word, my emotions slowly slipping out of my hands like a silk ribbon. I hook him around his neck, pulling his face down so he can't see how close I am to breaking. Relief washes through me when he doesn't question my actions, he just kisses my skin, sucking and nipping in a way that would definitely leave marks if I didn't have supernatural healing.

With every thrust my pleasure builds, my breathing turning harsh, my body breaking out in a cold sweat. "Nox," I moan, gripping into his thick hair as my body lifts into his with toe-curling pleasure. Fuck, this is one of the best orgasms of my life, but he doesn't let me come down from it. He slams into me again and again, his hips stuttering, and our body slick with the cum spreading across my stomach from my own release.

His mouth crashes against mine, a muffled growl ripping through his throat with his own release. He moves to shift off of me, but I grip into him, pulling him against my body. He tries to fight me, clucking his tongue at the death grip I have on him.

"Tam—"

"Please. I'm okay, Nox. Just give me a few minutes."

"You're okay? My weight isn't panicking you?"

I shake my head, and he finally relaxes, settling his full weight into me like a weighted blanket. His face is buried in my neck, his panting breaths caressing my sweat-dampened skin. He hums out a cute little breath when I start to drag my fingers up and down his back in soothing strokes.

"Next time," he sighs. "I'll let *you* fuck *me*."

"Really?"

"Of course. Who knows, I might enjoy it more than fucking you. You seemed pretty into that."

"I've been with guys before, I just...I've never been on the receiving end of it."

"How was it?"

"Really fucking good," I laugh.

"I really should get you cleaned up." He tries to shift again, grunting when I squeeze him tighter to me.

"A little more."
"You're very needy," he chuckles.

CHAPTER 49

NOX

I've seen bits and pieces of Tam's emotions, but he's always kept that wall up around him, only letting fragments break off when he just can't hold them together anymore. His reaction to people getting too close to him and the feeling of being trapped is very much like an animal being cornered. I never expected him to want any of this, and I had resolved myself to be the one to submit to him so that he wouldn't have to give up his need for control. That's what it is, a need. It's not a want, and I can see that now. He *wants* to feel a connection to something—to anything—but the fear of being hurt keeps holding him back.

I promised him I wouldn't hurt him, but I'm still scared that I'll end up doing it without meaning to. I know I won't purposefully break him, but promising something like that, borders on dangerous territory.

Being with him like this, with his arms wrapped tightly around me and the way our bodies press together, feels fucking amazing, and I never want it to end. Even my wolf is satisfied with this turn of events, finally feeling subdued within my mind.

I have a need in my chest, a desperation to take care of him, and I hope he'll let me do just that. "Come on, we should be functional today."

"You suck," he groans, his arms falling away limply when I pull back from him.

He's a mess, but so am I. we're both covered in his cum, and I definitely need to clean his ass up from unloading everything into him. I grip his arm, laughing at his protesting mumbles, and drag him to his feet to lead him into the bathroom. He watches me with a smile on his face while I get the shower running and set some towels out.

"So, you're going to shower with me?" He asks, pointing to the two towels.

"That was the plan. I made the mess, so it's my job to clean it up."

He hums out a breath and smirks, walking into the shower before me. I watch him, completely enamoured by every part of him, though seeing him getting himself dripping wet is definitely a bonus point. He glances over at me, quirking a brow in question. "You're staring."

"I am. I can't help it, you're fucking gorgeous."

He drops his eyes to the ground, but I swear I see his cheeks flush. He steps further into the shower when I walk towards him, giving me room to get in. I grab the body wash from him, earning a glare, but I just smile and grab the washcloth to lather it up.

"Turn around," I murmur. He sighs but does what I ask, staring at my chest as I slowly clean him off. I love watching the way the soap clings to his muscles, gathering around the dips in his abs before running down his hips. "Now your back." He glances up at me and rolls his eyes. "The attitude," I chuckle.

"I can clean myself off," he murmurs, but turns around again.

I settle my hands on his shoulders to rub at them, loving the way his body relaxes instantly, his head tipping forward on his chest. "I know you can." I lean in towards him, kissing him behind the ear. "But I want to do it." Slowly my hands drift lower, down his back and over his perfect ass.

"Nox," he whispers.

"As much as I would love to have you walking around with my cum inside of you, reminding you of what I did to you this morning, I'm not cruel." I dip a finger into him gently and he lets out a rattling breath. "I'm sure the memory is burned into you though, isn't it? The feel of me inside you, thrusting into you," I whisper, curling my finger into him. He settles his hands on the shower wall and nods his head subtly. I step closer to him and nip at his shoulder. "You're mine, Tam, all of you. Do you understand me?"

"Yes," he sighs.

"Say it. Say you're mine."

"I'm yours, Nox."

I can't help preening at the lack of hesitation in his response. "And I'm yours, always have been, and always will be. The only way I would ever leave you now is in death."

He stiffens in front of me, glancing back at me over his shoulder. The lines between his brows are just begging to be smoothed out, so I kiss them, trying to ease the sudden shift in him. "Don't fucking say that."

"Isn't that a good thing? I'm telling you that no matter what you say or do, I'll never leave you willingly."

"I don't even want to think about you dying, so don't ever bring that up again."

I wrap my arms around him, hugging him tightly to my chest. I kiss his neck, his cheek, wanting to ease the sudden panic I set off in him. "I'm sorry. I didn't mean to upset you, I thought I was being adorable and shit, professing my love for you."

"You don't need to profess anything. I know how much you care about me." I grip his jaw and turn his head enough to be able to press my lips to his. He hums in his throat, groaning when I pull back. "A little more," he murmurs. I smile and kiss him again.

We really need to set some ground rules because we're never going to get anything done if we keep ourselves in this little bubble of bliss we've created. I would love nothing more than to stay in this apartment for the next week, just getting lost in the feel of each other, but I know we can't. Between trying to figure out who the fuck took out Calvin before us, and then the wedding, Tam is definitely going to feel he still needs to go to. We have a lot of shit to take care of.

"What do you want to do today?" I sigh, hesitantly releasing him and stepping back before my body betrays me.

"I would love nothing more than to stay in bed all day, but by your tone, I figured you don't think that's a good idea."

"I think it's a great idea, but we both know we can't do that. We need to figure out what happened with Calvin. Someone else had it out for him, and it's clear it's someone strong enough to take them all out in one go."

I step away from him and slip out of the shower, wrapping one of the towels around my waist. He follows me out after a few minutes, glancing down at the towel. "You need to put clothes on. There's no way in hell I can concentrate if you're even partially dressed."

I laugh and head out of the bathroom to get changed in my own room. Just because I'm getting dressed, doesn't mean anything. I throw on my favourite pair of sweats, foregoing the underwear for now, and a snug white t-shirt. "I'm going to make breakfast!" I call out once I get in the kitchen. Coffee first though. Tam doesn't function well without a strong coffee in the morning, and I doubt he'll be going to the Hub anytime soon. Once Kalia is married, I don't think she'll be working there anymore. I mean, why would she? A princess shouldn't be hiding like that and working a normal job, but I can't blame her for wanting that for herself.

I shouldn't feel pity for her, but I do. She's like Tam in a lot of ways, hating her family, hating the life she was born into, and hating the expectations that come from it. I startle when Tam touches my back, jumping slightly.

"Fuck, did you not hear me?" He laughs.

"Sorry, I was lost in thought." I glance over his outfit as he makes his way over to the coffee machine to grab himself a mug. "Damn," I mumble.

He turns and leans back against the counter with a smug grin on his face. "What?"

"Breakfast is almost ready, so have a seat."

He doesn't pry, thank fuck, but he *must* be thinking the same shit as me. He's wearing sweats, too, hanging low on his hips with a way too tight tank top clinging to his frame. His hair is still wet, hanging in soft waves down to his chin, and fuck me, he looks so good when he glides his fingers through it to push it back. He looks happy—like genuinely happy. His blue eyes seem brighter, filled with life, and not the darkness that has been trying to strangle the light from them.

I settle a plate of bacon, eggs, and toast in front of him, grip his hair and tug his head back. He stares up at me, a smile playing across his face. I smirk, bending down to press my lips to his, ruffling his hair on my way back to the kitchen to grab my own plate.

I'm about to sit down when I notice Tam's line of sight. "What?"

"I should grab my phone," he sighs.

"I got it. Mine's there, too." I head over to the pile of our closes from last night in the entrance, proof that neither of us could wait to jump right into this new relationship. I dig through his pockets, grabbing his when I hear my own vibrating against the floor.

"Who is it?"

"Kaliem." Tam's eyes widen, but I shake my head and answer the phone. "Yeah?"

"Nice to see you shifted back," he chuckles.

"What do you want, Kaliem."

"Word on the street is you were hired to take out Calvin and his crew and now they're all dead."

"And?"

He laughs, the sound sending a shiver up my spine. "We both know neither you nor Eris actually killed them."

"Is that so."

"They were taken out by an elemental. The coroner you hassled yesterday is my cousin, and he gets a bit loose-lipped when he's had a few drinks."

"Why are you *actually* calling me, Kaliem?"

"An elemental went to Orion's the night you came to the pit...looking for necro."

"Necro?" Tam shifts in his chair to look at me fully, his face shifting into confusion at the once sided conversation. I sigh, pulling my phone away from my ear to put it on speaker.

"Yes, necro. He doesn't carry the shit, so they ended up getting some helion instead."

"What did they look like?"

"Female, dark hair, petite, a fucking attitude on her by the sounds of it. She threatened him, accusing him of lying to her about not having the shit, but he said what everyone else already knows. Calvin was the one monopolizing the necro, so most dealers won't actually touch the stuff. She let a bit of her power slip then. Orion almost shit himself, put word out right away to warn others about her. She's definitely not a regular, and I'm not sure how she even found out about Orion."

"Do you have anything else on her? Anything that might help identify her?"

Kaliem sighs at Tam being the one to ask the question, clearly pissed that I put him on speaker. "Hello to you, too, Eris."

"Cut the bullshit. Is this chick going to be a problem?"

"I'm not sure, maybe? Anyone specifically looking for necro isn't up to anything good. The shit is super addictive, and the power enhancement is asinine. If an elemental gets a hold of the shit, it could be an issue."

"We'll look into it. Thanks for the call, Kaliem."

"Are you planning to come back to the pit?"

Tam rolls his eyes, turning back to his plate of food. "I think it's time I settle down. I got myself a new lover who is amazing in bed, cooks, cleans, and takes care of all my needs. The last thing I want to do is risk ruining that. Consider this my official retirement."

Kaliem chuckles. "Fair enough, enjoy your temporary retirement." He hangs up before either of us can bitch at him for that comment.

"Asshole," Tam grumbles.

I set his phone down on the table next to him, ruffling his hair again because I'm obsessed with doing that. I can't help it, it's so soft, and he doesn't seem to mind. He glances at it, touching the screen to light it up. I catch sight of the multiple message notifications and the missed calls before sitting down next to him. He makes no effort to call back whoever was blowing up his phone, but his mood has shifted to bitter.

"It's not important."

"Tam."

He sighs, shoving his phone over for me to look at. "It's mainly Cam, a few from Helia, and one from Croh of all people. There's an unknown number in there, too, but I have a feeling I know who it's from without even checking."

"Kalia." He nods. "How the fuck did they get your number?"

"Cam has a big mouth," he grumbles. "Now I need to get a new number, which is *beyond* annoying."

"Do you want to go talk to Orion yourself?"

"I think I should. I wish the fucker had cameras on property, but no one wants proof of shady dealings. Who the fuck is this girl?"

"Do you know any hunters that fit her description?" He shakes his head. "What about Phoenix?"

"She's not petite, she's almost as tall as me, and I'm pretty sure she's not an elemental."

"I'm going to call Flannery at the organization to see if they got any new hires."

"Fine. We need to send in our payment to them anyways before they get pissed off that we're working off the books." I'm fighting back a smile as I watch him angrily shovel food into his mouth. Resting my elbow on the table, I settle my chin on my palm. He glances up at me, pausing his chewing. "What?" He mumbles around the mouthful.

"You're cute when you're broody." He rolls his eyes, shoving another forkful of eggs into his mouth. I laugh. "You are."

"I'm not brooding."

"Pretty sure your face doesn't normally have those adorable wrinkles between your brows." He rubs at his face and drags his hands through his hair with a heavy sigh. "I don't think that's how it works," I snort.

"I'm just pissed off at all of it. Between the Calvin disaster and my family now trying to pry into my life, I'm just feeling a bit overwhelmed."

"Hmm. Throw in a new relationship with an absolute hottie and you really have the trifecta of problems."

"You're not a problem, you're the solution to my stress." He grins, showing me a perfectly straight row of white teeth. "And I would love nothing more than to fall into that stress relief right now, but we really should get a handle on all of this. If we have some random hunter moving in on our marks completely unsanctioned, what's to say they won't come after us directly. The organization won't take kindly to someone doing that either, but what I still don't understand is why. Why do that and not get paid for it? Was it a personal vendetta? If she's looking for necro, was she trying to get it directly from the source? She must not have all the information because Calvin wouldn't keep that shit at the house."

"We should check out the storage unit Kalia went to for the antidote. I didn't see any necro registered in stock from the files I pulled from the warehouse, but they might just be keeping it under the radar."

"Fine. We'll hit it on the way to Orion's. I rather talk to him in person.

CHAPTER 50

TAMZIN

I shouldn't be as happy about this situation as I am. I definitely rather be at home with Nox, rolling around in bed with him for the foreseeable future, but driving down to the pier with him holding my hand is really fucking nice. We decided I was driving just to give him an easier time to use his laptop to bring down the barrier around the place so I can get in and check it out, not that either of us is complaining.

He's still on edge that we even have to do this, that protective side of him kicking in at full force. I can't really blame him, we've both been through some shit the last few days. I sort of hate that we're doing this during the day—more chances of being seen—but with the authorities focusing in on the mass murder that happened at Calvin's, I doubt they'll even think to check this storage unit that wasn't even under his name but an alias that Nox was able to dig up.

"It doesn't look like much. I sort of expected more," I say, glancing out at the unit through the windshield.

"The barrier isn't as heavy as it was at the warehouse either. I really think they were just overconfident that no one would figure out this was holding shit like drugs." He holds out an earbud to me, and I set it in, instinctively reaching for the bottle of helion I put in the cupholder. He grips my wrist, stopping me. "No. You don't need it. There's no guards or anything inside. The place is empty, Tam. *Please*."

My heart tightens in my chest at the pleading look in his eyes. "It's a force of habit," I murmur, regretting it instantly when his gaze hardens. "I'm not addicted," I say quickly. "I've just had to use it every time I've gone into this type of situation."

"I don't want you using it anymore. At all, Tam." My heartrate spikes at his tone, demanding, but still filled with concern.

"You're so bossy," I laugh, trying to lighten the mood.

"This isn't a joke and it's not a game. I'm fucking serious, Tamzin. Get off the helion." My defenses go up now, the fear of being controlled overwhelming me enough that I start shaking slightly. I try to slip out of the car, but he grabs my arm to stop me. I don't want him to notice how much this is bothering me now, but it's too late. His grip loosens. "Tam—"

"Let me go, Nox."

His hand drops away, and I'm hit with guilt instantly. I glance at him, but he won't meet my eyes, instead grabbing his laptop to boot it up. His throat bobs a few times, the muscles in his jaw working like he's trying to bite back words that are fighting to come out.

"Nox—"

"Barrier will be down in sixty seconds." His tone is dull, methodical, a clear sign that I fucked up. "It'll be down for ten. No coms inside, but I'll watch you through the cameras that are in there and drop it again once you're at the back door."

"Okay." There's no point in arguing with him right now, but I don't want to argue with him at all. This is something we're going to have to sit down and discuss like mature adults. I know he's concerned, but I'm getting worried with how he's reacting to it. I didn't do it on purpose today. It really was just a force of habit.

"Three...two...one."

I take a deep breath and picture the layout of the building Nox showed me before we left, popping in just inside the back door. I feel the ripple of power blanket the building again seconds later and slowly start making my way through the hallway towards the room he had Kalia infiltrate. It's like a trove for drugs, including the shit I got dosed with at the warehouse. Fucking bullshit drug that should have never been created. Why couldn't the rogue hunter take out this place instead of going after Calvin himself? I would have *loved* to torture him and make him beg for his life, make him feel the panic and pain he's inflicted on every single dark worlder he's kidnapped. With him and his crew gone, we have no leads as to where those missing people are and who they ended up with. Probably brainwashed and working for corrupt assholes that will just use them until they're no longer needed.

I can't focus on that, and I hate that there's nothing I can do now to help them. I have to leave that investigation up to the authorities and hope that they'll be able to find them and find a way to free their minds. I'm assuming one of the liquid vials in here is how they've been able to manipulate them so easily as well. If they used dark worlder powers to create it, then it could be a combination of anything. The vials in here that I know nothing about need to be turned into the authorities so they can break up the chemical composition and hopefully reverse the effects of it.

I shove what I can into one of the nylon bag on one of the shelves and sling it across my body. I inventory what I can as I make my way through the building, taking note of the random bare shelves that seem to have housed something recently. I stop outside the back door and glance up at the camera, hoping Nox isn't pissed off enough that he leaves my ass in here. I mean, I *could* get out. It would suck and hurt like a mother fucker, but I wouldn't *actually* be trapped in here.

The seconds tick by and then minutes, anxiety and worry boiling inside of me. I glance at the camera again. "Nox?" I say, wishing he could hear me through the damn earpiece, but no response comes through. I shift my weight from foot to foot, preparing myself to just bite the bullet and void warp through the wards. The barrier shimmers in front of me just as I start pulling on my shadows, snuffing out of existence right in front of me. I sigh, opening the door and prepping myself for the argument that is waiting for me once I get back to the car.

"Tam!" Nox screams.

I glance up, seeing him bolting from the car and running towards me just as I get sent flying, slamming into the outer wall of the unit. I blink, trying to get my bearings as I struggle to my feet. Fuck, it feels like I get hit by a fucking train. What the fuck just happened?

"Where's my daughter?!" A male voice booms, and then a shadow blocks out the sun. Dark wings flare out behind him, his face filled with murderous rage. Flickers of flame skate across his wings, the feathers a deep red tone. He's an elemental Nephilim, but not very strong. He's probably never really had a need to develop his abilities. A deep, rumbling growl vibrates into my bones, and the Nephilim turns to see Nox in his shifter form, snarling at him. "Back off!" He yells, turning himself enough to keep us both in his line of sight. He seems panicked now, not anticipating someone to be with me.

"I don't even know who your daughter is," I groan, pulling myself to my feet.

"Savanah. You work for Calvin! You have to know who she is."

Nox's growl cuts short, his eyes fixed on the male in front of us. "You're Jerimiah. We don't work for Calvin. We were hired to take him down."

"Lies!"

"It's not a lie." I try to keep my voice placating, holding my hands up to show him I don't mean him any harm. His eyes dart to Nox when he shifts back, his hulking form unnerving. "I promise you, we hate him just as much as you do, and we're happy he's dead."

Jerimiah breathes heavily, his wings flaring out for a moment before he tucks them in tightly against his back. He narrows his eyes, focusing in on me. "You're Eris. I've seen you in the pits."

"Yes, so you should know what I do for a living. I'm sorry, I don't know where Savanah is."

"Why are you here?"

"Why are *you* here," Nox snaps.

"I've been keeping an eye on the place for a while. I've seen some of Calvin's men frequent it, but with the news of what happened to him and his compound, I needed to do something, or I would lose my chance of finding my daughter."

"If you *actually* came in contact with one of his men, you wouldn't be breathing right now. What the fuck were you thinking?"

"Nox, he's desperate." Nox's eyes drift to me. "Can you blame him for wanting his daughter back after all these years."

Nox walks towards him, holding out our business card. "Call me in an hour and I'll see what I can dig up. I can't guarantee anything, but I'll do my best."

Jerimiah looks about ready to break down in tears, but he takes the card and nods his head. He glances towards me, dropping his eyes to the ground sheepishly. "I'm sorry I attacked you."

"No worries. I've had worse happen to me over the last few days."

"I appreciate the help," he murmurs, pulling his wings back into himself. "I'll call you for sure."

We watch him head out, getting into a black SUV. Nox is suddenly in front of me, his hands gripping at my face, turning it from side to side. "Are you hurt?"

"Nox—"

"Are you hurt?!"

I grip his wrists and hold his gaze. "I'm fine, okay? I'm not hurt."

He lets out a rattling breath and steps back from me, digging his hands through his hair in frustration. "I should have noticed him sooner. That should have never happened, I'm so sorry."

"Nox, stop. Nothing bad happened so stop blaming yourself." He turns away and starts walking back towards the car, and I have to jog to catch up to him. "Nox."

"We need to get going. I want to make sure I'm home by the time Jerimiah calls, and we don't know how long it'll take to talk to Orion."

"We? You're not going in with me."

He glares at me over the top of the car while I toss the bag into the backseat. "Excuse me?"

"He's a helion dealer. I'm not letting you anywhere near him and risk you blowing a fucking gasket."

"After what just happened there's no way in hell I'm letting you go in there alone."

I open my mouth to argue, but he's already in the car, slamming the door closed. I cringe at the sound, trying not to let my anger take over at the fact he just hurt my baby like that. He fucking knows I love this car, and she does *not* deserve that kind of treatment. I take a deep breath, reining in the mental picture of punching him in the face as justice for her, and slide into the car. He's pouting—fucking pouting with his arms crossed; his face turned away from me to stare at absolutely nothing outside the window.

I can't do anything but sigh and throw the car in drive. He says nothing the entire ride to the edge of the Hollow, grumbling under his breath when I stop in front of Orion's shop.

"Do you want to talk?" I finally ask, hating the way he's acting right now.

"Just go."

I shake my head, hating the flashbacks I'm getting from his words and hating the word vomit that rips out of my throat in anger. "You're just like *them*. Trying to control me and then brushing me off when I have even an inkling of self worth and the need to do things on my own. I'm trying to fucking protect you, and you're acting like an asshole."

His eyes widen. "Tam—" I slam the door closed between us before he can even start on his excuses, and head into the shop. I expect him to follow me and go against my request for him to stay in the car, but he doesn't. After a few seconds, I make my way down into Orion's entrance.

He glances up when he hears my footsteps, tilting his head curiously. "I didn't expect to see you. Are you running low on your supply already?"

"I'm here about the girl. The elemental that was looking for necro."

He frowns. "Kaliem called you." I nod. "I told him everything I knew already just so he could warn everyone to keep an eye out."

"I want to hear it from you. You know how Kaliem is, especially with me, and I wouldn't put it past him to withhold some details just to fuck with me. Do you have cameras?"

"Surprisingly, I do, but they glitched the second she walked in. I'm going to assume it has something to do with her power. Sort of like the sun letting off a solar storm flare and fucking with electronics."

"She was *that* powerful?"

"I could feel it from the moment she walked in through the door. She didn't let off any power until I told her I didn't carry the stuff, but she seemed agitated enough to not have a full handle on her power. She had dark hair, like almost black, about five-foot, maybe five-foot-two, and she was arrogant as fuck."

"What colour were her eyes?"

"I don't know, she wore shades in here, so I would assume she was riding a high already and glowing like crazy."

"Fuck, okay. How much helion did she buy?"

"Three vials."

"Let me know right away if she shows up again."

"Do you think she's the one that went after Calvin?"

"It seems that way, but I still can't figure out why. Listen, I have to go. Nox needs to get home soon, but I'll talk to you."

"Nox is with you?" I nod. "How's he doing?" I frown at him, and he throws his hands up. "I knew his mom."

"You're the one who sold her helion?"

"I'm not proud of it, but yeah. I didn't see the signs of addiction on her. She was only buying a vial a week from me."

"Be thankful I told Nox to stay in the car then. If he came in here, he would kill you. I would steer clear of him if you can help it."

He swallows, his complexion draining of colour, but nods his head. I turn from him before my own anger at that knowledge takes root and overwhelms my sense of reason. I can feel my shadows pulsing beneath my skin, begging to be released, desperate for blood. I'm a vibrating ball of fury by the time I sit back in the car, Nox's stare burning into the side of my head.

"What?" I snap, whipping my head around to look at him.

His jaw ticks, but his voice is calm when he speaks. "I'm sorry if I've made you feel like I'm trying to control you."

"I can't do this right now. I'm on edge, and you speaking is grating on my nerves."

"Wow," he huffs. "Fine."

Fuck, I'm just piling it on, digging myself into a hole I'm getting really close to not being able to climb out of. I always end up doing this, finding reasons to push the people I actually end up caring for away. I can't even blame anyone else but myself for it, it's all on me. It's not his fault his words and actions trigger me, and I know I need to find a way to calm myself and work through it. I can't keep letting my mind wander to my darkest moments and drag me down away from the light. Nox is that light, but my past keeps creeping in, clawing at me and pulling me under until he's barely a spec in the distance I so desperately want to reach.

He sulks the entire drive back to the apartment, bolting out of the car the second it comes to a stop. I barely make it to the elevator before it closes on me, glaring at him when I slide my hand between the doors to stop it. He shifts the strap of his laptop bag, putting the thing between us as we ride it up, and it all literally feels like torture. I can't blame him for giving me the silent treatment, but I just can't handle it. I open my mouth to speak, snapping it closed when his phone rings in his pocket.

"Hello? Hi, Jerimiah. Yeah, just give me a couple of minutes, I'm just getting home."

The elevator opens and he breezes past me, leaving me alone and in shock at how cold he's now being towards me. Breathe. I need to breathe and give him time to calm down—fuck, I need to give *myself* time to calm down. If I hadn't let my emotions run free like they did, I wouldn't have snapped at him. He's setting himself up at the table when I finally walk in, his phone pinched between his shoulder and ear, and his fingers flying quickly across the keyboard. I don't even bother grabbing myself any lunch, not wanting him to think I'm hovering around him while he works. Instead, I head into my room, changing back into my sweats, and flopping down on the bed to wallow in my self-hatred.

CHAPTER 51

TAMZIN

I slip in and out of sleep, snapping awake at the sudden silence and falling back into the darkness when Nox's voice carries softly through the apartment. I don't know how long it's been, how long I've been riding this line of oblivion and vicious reality.

Footfalls on the tile drag me back to the surface again but knowing he's standing in my doorway is making me wish I could just slip back into the darkness of sleep. I can *feel* him staring at me, but I can't look at him...I'm too afraid to deal with any of this right now.

"I want you to listen to me," he says, his voice quiet. "I chose you, and you accepted me. Choosing you means saying yes to all your trauma, darkness, scars, your fucking family, all of it, Tam. Your pain is my own, my burden to bear as well, so you don't have to do it alone, and that means I'll love you forever. I know you lash out in anger, and you don't mean it, not when it comes to me. I can see the guilt written all over you, but I don't...I *won't* ever hold that against you. I'm upset at the fact you accused me of trying to control you, but that was never my intention. I'm worried about you...I'm *always* worried about you, and I just want to protect you. If I could take away all your pain, I would without question. I would shoulder that burden without complaint because you deserve to be happy. I *want* you to be happy,

Tam, whether that's with me or with someone else, nothing else matters."

I feel the bed shift under his weight as he sits down at the end of it, his hand settling gently on my leg. My heart thumps loudly in my chest, loud enough that I can hear my blood pumping in my ears. He gives my leg a squeeze after a few minutes of silence and lets out a sigh.

"Okay," he mumbles, taking my heavy silence as a dismissal, but I just don't know what to say.

How the fuck do you respond to a declaration like that? I haven't been good with my words for a long time. Nox has tried to coax that side of me back out over the years—the fun loving, carefree me, that could throw jokes left and right. It was different then. My memories safely locked away in my head—a defense mechanism I created to not have to actually deal with my issues. There's only so long you can hold up those unstable walls yourself, and eventually my past came back to nip and chew at my psyche, clawing at the cracking walls until they began to crumble faster than I could shove the pieces back into place.

The bed shifts again. "How did it go with Jerimiah," I ask, not wanting him to leave yet, but too much of a coward to actually admit that to him.

"There's a small hope he'll find Savanah. It took some time, but I think I got a few solid leads. I sent him everything I found, so it's up to him how he uses that information. I pulled the feed from Orion's system, too, and isolated when the cameras went down, cross referencing it with the street cams in the area. I got some footage of the girl, but nothing good enough to get a positive I.D. on her."

"You've been busy."

"I had no choice, not with you in here ignoring me."

I sit up quickly and glare at him. "*Me?* You're the one who stayed quiet the entire car ride and elevator ride up."

"You made it pretty clear you couldn't *deal with me*. How else did you expect me to react? I was waiting for *you* to make the decision to finally fucking talk to me, since me talking grates on your nerves. Your words, Tam."

He's throwing it back in my face but he's right. I said that to him and I never should have, but it's a bit hard to take that back now. "I'm sorry."

"Words spoken in anger, still hold fractions of truth," he snaps.

"You want to know the truth? The truth is I fucking hate myself and I hate that I'm fucking poison to you. I'm not *good* for you, Nox. Don't you fucking see that? I'm trying so fucking hard to get out of my own head and to just finally feel something other than this stupid hatred, but I can't! I can't just let it go and move on like my past wasn't the worst thing to happen in my life. I'm broken—beyond broken—and there's no fixing me, no matter how much you believe you can. You say you love all of me no matter what, but I'll just end up ruining you."

"You don't want to be with me then, is that it?"

"No! I *want* to be with you, but I want a normal fucking life with you. The reality is, that'll never happen, and you don't deserve that."

"I should deserve whatever I want, and what I want is you. I don't care about normal, we're both too fucked up to even think that's a possibility. Stop pushing me away because you believe it's the right thing to do. It's *my* choice."

"And what about *my* choices?" I argue.

"Your choices should be based on your actual wants and needs and not manipulating yourself into believing you don't have a right to try and be happy. If you truly don't want this or me, then just say it, but if there's even an inkling inside you that *wants* me, then stop fucking fighting it."

I do want him and everything he's offering, but it's selfish to fucking want it, knowing it'll ruin him.

"Tell me what you want." I shake my head. "Tell me, Tam." I shake my head again, and suddenly he's on top of me, pinning my arms down against the bed, his knees straddling my thighs. "Tell me," he growls, his lips within kissing distance, teasing me with the exact thing I want. "Use that pretty mouth of yours and tell me what the fuck you *want*."

My breath stutters, the heat of his body washing over me like a comforting wave. I try to steady my heartbeat, but it's not having it, and my entire body betrays me with how close he is. He notices because of *course* he does, and he rolls his hips against mine, showing me he's as hard as I am right now. I choke back the moan trying to tear its way up my throat, unable to look away from his piercing gaze. His eyes flicker between his shifter glow and his natural light, and that's when it clicks. This *is* real. Up until this moment, even with all his words proving otherwise, I felt like it was all a ruse or some sick trick to fuck with me.

"This," I whisper, fighting his hold and lifting myself up to press my lips to his. He groans into my mouth, parting it without hesitation, and I truly allow myself to get lost in it and taste him.

His hands shift from my wrists to the bed, giving me the freedom to wrap my arms around him and pull him to me. I dive my hands under his shirt, digging my nails into his back. He groans, deepening the kiss further and pressing his full weight into me. I tug at his shirt, and he pulls away long enough to rip it off himself before his mouth finds mine again.

Suddenly, I'm on top of him. He flawlessly rolled us over, his legs braced on either side of my hips as he grips my hair and pulls me down to his face again. My hands roam over every inch of his chest, reveling in the hard muscle straining beneath the surface. Don't get me wrong, I *love* women and their bodies, how soft and pliable the tissue is when I grip into it, but I love Nox more. He doesn't fight me when I pull away from his mouth to trail my lips across his jaw, nipping at the skin playfully. His grip on my hair is still there, his fingers digging into my scalp deliciously. His breaths pant out harshly as I move my mouth down his throat, and I smile when he tips his head back, completely exposing his neck to me.

The act of submission, especially from a shifter, has my cock hardening in my pants. It presses achingly against the material of my sweats, but I try to focus on him, on the heat of his skin against mine, the taste of him as my mouth devours every inch of exposed flesh. My fingers move to his belt, making quick work of it. I can feel his cock begging to be released, and he groans when he lifts his hips enough for me to tug his pants down. I need them off completely, not wanting anything between me and his perfect body. He watches me as I shift off the bed to tug them down his legs, his eyes darkening seductively.

"Stop," he says when I move to climb back on. "I want you naked, too." I smirk and grip the base of my shirt, moving slowly as I pull it off. He hums out a breath, his eyes now rimming with iridescent light as he watches me shift my attention to my pants. They drop with a small thud in the quiet room, and I stand here, letting him drink in the sight of me. His eyes shift to a whiter hue as they travel over my entire body.

"What do you see when you look at me?" I whisper, his eyes snapping up to meet mine. "My aura," I explain.

His gaze softens, his eyes shifting back to the iridescence of his shift. "I see good. I see light and kindness bleeding through the darkness that plagues you. I see a pure soul, Tamzin." My heart thumps loudly in my ears, my throat feeling suddenly dry at his words. "Seeing an aura lets me see what's inside a person, even if they've been made to believe they're bad," he adds, knowing exactly where my mind went. He smirks. "I can see how much you want me, too."

I roll my eyes. "I didn't think you needed your sight to see that."

"Even with the sight, I've been blind. I didn't understand what I was seeing until now. You love me, like *really* love me."

My chest tightens, but I nod. "More than you could ever know."

"Grab the lube." I hesitate, but he nods towards the nightstand. I grab it and place it in his outstretched hand. He settles it next to him and curls his fingers. "Come here." I swallow and crawl back up onto the bed. "What do you want, Tam?"

I glance down to his cock, licking my lips. "I want to taste you," I whisper. He says nothing more, just smiles and leaves me to touch him again. I start at his mouth, diving my tongue against his until we're clashing—lips, tongues, and teeth. He moans, chasing my face as I pull away, and letting out a disgruntled breath. "You like kissing me?" I tease, dragging my tongue across his chest and nipping at one of his nipples.

"I love kissing you," he says breathlessly. I work my way down his stomach, gripping into his cock while my lips and tongue move across his hips and thighs. His stomach flexes, dipping down in the sexiest way and tightening every muscle beneath the surface. "Tam," he pants when I move my attention to his balls, sucking each one into my mouth while I move my hand up and down his length. He fumbles with the lube, trying to shove at me. I glance at him, furrowing my brows, and I see his throat bob before he nods his head.

I take it, watching him carefully as I squirt some onto my fingers. He swallows again and lets out a shaky breath. He's nervous about all of this, that's clear on his face as he watches me carefully without saying anything. "We don't have to do that, Nox." I don't want him to end up regretting it if he's not a hundred percent sure.

He shakes his head. "I want to. You submitted to me, and I don't want you to think I wouldn't do the same for you."

"I don't care. I just want you happy."

He smiles, his eyes softening in the sweetest way. "I already am."

I nod, slathering my cock in lube as well and adding a bit more to my fingers before I grip his cock with my other hand and plunge him deep into my mouth. His head tips back on a moan, his fingers gripping into the sheets around him. I work his length, swirling my tongue around his tip before sucking back on him hard. Slowly, I slide my fingers down to his ass, teasing one gently around the rim. He tenses instantly, but I won't force my way in, slowly playing and softening him up with every stroke of my mouth.

It takes a bit of time, but I get one finger into him, slowly thrusting it in and out with every dip of my head. "Tam," he pants, his hips bucking into me. I sneak a second one in and it's like he doesn't know what to do with his body. His hips swivel slightly, like he wants to grind into my hand, and fuck, if that isn't hot as shit. I hum against him, pleased with his reaction, and slowly work my fingers in deeper, thrusting and twisting, spreading and curling them into him. "Fuck," he gasps.

I pop him out of my mouth and give him a few firm strokes with my fist. "Does that feel good?"

"Yeah," he breathes, his eyelids fluttering like he doesn't know how to actually react to it.

"You're being such a good boy, Nox. Letting me suck your cock and play with your ass." I slip a third finger in and his back arches off the bed. "Look how well you're handling my fingers. I'm going to make you come and then I'm going to fuck you. Is that what you want? Do you want me to fuck you with my cock?"

"Fuck, you have a dirty mouth," he laughs, the sound breathless.

"Tell me you want my cock inside of you." I need him to say it. I need him to fucking say the words before I explode.

"I want you to fuck me," he says shakily, gasping when I take him back into my mouth and work him into an absolute frenzy.

He comes, the feel of it hot and thick down my throat, but I drink him all down, licking and sucking until there's not a trace of him left. His ass tries to suck my fingers back in when I pull them out, and my chest heaves with my own building pressure. "Turn over."

"What?"

"On your knees. I want to look at that perfect ass of yours while I fuck you." He snorts out a laugh but does what I ask, shakily rolling over until that *very* perfect ass is presented in front of me. I can't help it, I bend down and bite into it, *hard*.

"Fucking hell," he squeaks out. "You bit me!"

I drag my tongue on his skin and bite him again, smirking when he lets out a little squeal. "So fucking perfect," I mutter, kissing the area I just bit. I grip into his ass with both hands, massaging the tissue and just about coming myself at the pure perfection of it. I drag my thumb against his hole and grip my cock, cradling the tip of it against him. His body begins to tremble, and guilt settles into me. "If you want me to stop, just tell me."

He presses back into me, and I grip into his hips to stop him from shoving my cock into him. "Don't stop," he whispers.

"You're shaking."

"Don't fucking stop."

I reach around him and grip into his cock, giving it a firm stroke as I press a bit further into him. His body sinks further into the bed, his face turning on the mattress to look back at me. His eyes are hooded with need—not fear—and my heart thrums heavily in my chest at the sight of him like that.

CHAPTER 52

NOX

I'm struggling to keep my breathing steady, my skyrocketing heartrate a lost cause at this point. Fuck, he's feral as hell and can suck a mean dick. That was probably the best blowjob I've ever had, and I've had a lot. I'm nervous as shit about this, but he's given me every opportunity to refuse. I don't *want* to say no to him, I want to experience him completely, in all his forms. He's hot as hell when he's the submissive, but way hotter when he's talking dirty and telling me what to do. I know that's what he needs, and after everything that happened today, I want to make him happy. I don't want him thinking I want to control him, the comment earlier still eating away at me like a persistent gnat.

I can't stop the small whimper that slips through my lips when he pushes a bit further into me, my body caving in at the pressure, just to be met with his hand palming my cock. It's a lot of sensation, and I have no idea how the hell he kept it together when I did this to him. I shudder when he leans over me and drags his tongue up my spine, moaning softly while his hips pulse into me.

"You're almost there. You're being so good," he sighs, thrusting into me a little more. "One of these days I'm going to strap you down and completely have my way with you."

Wait...what? What the fuck does he mean, strap me down? Does he have a bondage kink that I know nothing about? "What?" I choke out, needing to know what he means because *what?!*

"Hmm, I guess you never noticed my headboard modifications." I glance up at said headboard, my eyes widening when I see the holes in the corners with rings in them, the faint glint of metal hanging behind them. How the *fuck* did I never notice that? "Now you know all my secrets," he chuckles, the sound both amused and dark as hell. His freehand slides up my back to dig aggressively into my hair. I shiver at the feel of his nails against my scalp, his cock shifting further into me. He lets out a heavy breath, and I feel his hips sitting flush against mine. "Are you okay?" He asks, his body preternaturally still behind me.

I can't believe I just took all of him into me. I honestly didn't think it would be possible, especially with his size and my inexperience, but he did a fantastic job in getting me ready for it. The sensation is oddly nice—the feeling of fullness and stretch radiating through my hips.

"Nox?" He whispers, his fingers moving gently through my hair now.

"Yeah. Yeah, I'm okay."

"Can I move?" I nod, groaning when he slowly drags his cock back, thrusting forward again just as slow. "Fuck, you feel good," he murmurs, curling his body around mine and stroking my cock again.

My entire body feels like a live wire, current rippling through me with every deep thrust. I hiss out a breath that turns into a moan when he drags his teeth against my shoulder blade and bites down, his hand shifting from my hair around the front of my throat. Fucking hell, he *is* kinky as fuck, but why is it so *hot*? He grips into my throat, squeezing as he pulls back, lifting me onto my knees until my back is pressed against his chest. He bites down on my shoulder, his whimpering breaths making my cock harden further. The stroke of his hand is blissful, my orgasm building heavily along my spine. He's winding me up tighter and tighter until I break, coming in his hand while he pumps his hips into me harder and deeper, pushing me even further over the edge.

"Tam," I grunt, feeling lightheaded and weak, both from my orgasm that doesn't seem to want to come down, and the hold he has on my throat.

"Mmm, fuck," he moans, nipping and sucking at the skin on my neck as the thick heat of his cum explodes inside of me. His hips stutter, and both his hands move until he's hugging me tightly around my chest and waist, squeezing me against him. "Are you okay?"

"Yeah," I pant, even though it felt like my soul just left my body for a minute. I grip into his arms and lean back into him. "Your bed's a mess."

He laughs breathlessly, nuzzling into my neck with a deep inhale. "You're a mess, too." He inhales deeply at my neck, squeezing my body tighter against his. "Fuck, I love your smell."

"You're scenting me?" I chuckle.

"Always. I don't think there's ever been a day where I haven't scented you. Your smell keeps me grounded, and I could literally drown in it. I never want to have a moment where I can't find you, Nox, and this..." He inhales again, letting out a happy little sigh. "This is my path to you, no matter where you are."

I don't know whether to be honoured or horrified at the fact he actually scents me every day. No, I *should* be horrified, but I really *do* find it endearing. If I had his tracking ability, I would probably do the same thing, but as I shifter, I'll admit, I've taken it upon myself to pull in his scent more than what would be deemed normal. I was being honest with him the other day, he smells like home. Tam is my home, forever and always.

"Let's take a shower again," he murmurs as he trails kisses down my neck to the tip of my shoulder. The feel of his warm lips on my skin sends a shiver creeping up my spine in the most delicious of ways.

"With the way your mouth is, I would think you would *want* to keep me dirty."

"Oh, I want you filthy, but I want the pleasure of making you filthy once you're clean."

"I don't think I'll ever have a clean day again with you in my life," I snort, and he laughs along with me, slowly releasing his hold on me. I whimper slightly when he finally pulls out of me, and he presses his hand between my shoulder blades.

"Are you okay? Did I hurt you at all?"

I shake my head. "No, you were perfect. Kinkier than I expected you to be, but still perfect. Were you serious when you said you wanted to strap me down?"

When he doesn't respond right away, I glance back at him over my shoulder. The guarded expression on his face has me shifting around on my knees to face him. "Not if you don't want me to," he says quietly, his eyes drifting to the side away from me, like he's embarrassed now for even bringing it up. He may have said it in the heat of the moment, but there's always some truth in his words.

"Do you usually tie up your hookups?" He nods, his shoulders drooping slightly, like he's ashamed for admitting it. "Is that part of your control thing?"

"Yes," he whispers, settling onto his heels.

I feel like I'm walking a fine line that's bordering on a topic he's really not comfortable with, but I want him to be completely honest with me about every aspect of his life. The fact he's kept this hidden from me for as long as I've known him is impressive, but also a bit concerning. The fact he thought that I would judge him for something like this breaks my heart a bit. "Hey," I say quietly, cupping his cheek to turn his face back towards me. "You know you can tell me these things, right?" He nods his head, his eyes focusing on my chest and not my face. "Tam, look at me." He closes his eyes and shakes his head, trying to pull away from me, but I grip into the back of his neck to stop him. "Tam," I snap. "I'm not judging you. I'm trying to see you and trying to understand everything about you because I love you."

"I'm a fuck up," he chokes out. "It just slipped out. I—I didn't mean to say it."

"Don't regret it, even for a second. That's who you are, and if that's what you want from me at any point, then I'll do it, Tam. I'll do it for you."

"I don't *want* that to be me. I don't want to feel like I need to restrain people because I need control."

"Tam, you've already proved to me and to yourself that you're capable of relinquishing that control." His eyes flutter closed when I lean into him and press my lips softly against his. "You're everything to me," I whisper against his mouth, and he lets out a shuddering breath, leaning his forehead in against mine.

"I'm...not ready to talk about all of that."

"Okay. Just know that I'm here when you are."

"Come on, it's my turn to clean you up."

I smile and kiss him again before releasing my hold on him and letting him pull away. "We should probably change the sheets, too."

CHAPTER 53

TAMZIN

I glance back at Nox on my way to the bathroom, watching him pull the sheets from my bed and tossing them into my hamper. He must sense me watching him and glances back at me as he pulls out a clean set from one of my drawers. His smile completely lights up his face, the joy there causing my heart to stutter and skip. Heat creeps across my cheeks and I quickly turn away from him to get the shower heating.

I'm setting the towels out for us when his arms creep around me from behind, his hands lacing against my stomach as he leans into my neck, breathing in deeply. I can't help but lean back into him, loving the feel of his body pressed against mine.

"Is it selfish of me to want to just lock ourselves away for the foreseeable future? I just want to drown in these moments with you."

I smile and tilt my head to try and look at him, but he buries his face into my neck to avoid my gaze. "I would love nothing more, but you know we can't—not yet. We have time, Nox, and after all of this is over and done with, we can just enjoy our time together. After the wedding, we can take some time away from hunting, and if you want to travel for a bit, we can. Whatever you want, we'll do it."

"I would love that. I would love to do everything with you, Tam."

He kisses my neck and steps back from me, moving around me to get in the shower. He hisses out a breath when the heat of the water hits his skin, and turns to look at me with such a serene smile, that my heart feels like it'll explode in my chest. He jerks his head, summoning me towards him, and I return the smile, stepping into the stream as well. Before he can grab the bodywash, I reach past him to grab it myself. He huffs out a laugh and nods his head, settling his hands on the wall while I drag the cloth over his shoulders and back.

Everything about these small moments is just too perfect. Perfect enough that I fear they're a dream, or that they'll slip away, even though I'm latching onto them with a vicious hold. He moans softly when I drift down to clean him out, his fingers curling against the glass on a heavy breath.

"All clean," I whisper, kissing his back. He spins around, stepping into me until my back presses against the opposite wall. His hands shift up my neck to cup my cheeks, holding my face still as he stares down at me with so much emotion rolling around within his eyes. "Nox?" I say, my voice breathless.

"I love you," he says, each word ringing through me like a celestial gong. Heat spread through my entire body when his lips press gently against mine.

His tongue slips out, teasing and prodding until I open myself up to him. He groans, stepping into me and deepening the kiss further. I could get lost in moments like this. There are no expectations, but complete proof of his want and need, his love for me clear with the care and passion behind something so simple as a kiss. No, that's wrong to think. A kiss is never simple. There's always some intention behind it, no matter how small and fleeting. A kiss can convey everything you can't say with words, the action a different language for what you truly mean.

I grip into his ass, pulling him flush against my body, and I shiver at the feral moan that vibrates through him right into me. It sinks into my core, rattling through my bones like a tuning fork. He groans when the sound of his phone ringing in the other room radiates through the apartment, and he tries to pull away, but I grip into him harder.

"Tam," he sighs.

"A little more," I groan, pinning his bottom lip between my teeth.

"You're insatiable," he laughs, but he plunges his tongue into my mouth again, ignoring the phone call. The phone starts ringing again, and I mentally curse whoever the fuck is calling him right now. "It could be important."

"Fine." He pulls back and smiles a devious smile at my pouting face.

"Come on," he snorts, turning off the shower and tugging me along behind him. I take the towel from him and quickly dry myself off, watching as he saunters out of the bathroom with the towel slung low around his hips.

A few minutes later, I hear him talking quietly on his phone while I throw on another pair of sweats, saying fuck it to a shirt. I thought I was being clever in being topless as I walk out into the living room, but Nox hasn't even attempted to get dressed yet, his hands adjust the towel again while his phone stays pinned between his shoulder and ear. The frown on his face has me pausing, and I tip my head in question. He grips the phone again, shaking his head at me.

"What do you mean?" He murmurs, walking himself into the kitchen to pull out some leftovers to heat up. He points to the table, and I settle into the chair, watching him as he heats up some food. "So, no one knows who the fuck this girl is?" he says, sliding a bowl of pasta in front of me before heating some up for himself.

I smile at how easily he falls into the caretaker roll, and dig into my meal, not realizing how fucking hungry I actually was until the thick creamy sauce hits my tongue. I demolish half the bowl before his is even heated, and he smirks at me as he settles into the chair across from me.

"Alright, keep me posted. I don't understand how an elemental hunter was able to just slip in here unnoticed." He hangs up the phone, tosses it on the table, and lets out a heavy sigh.

"Everything okay?" I ask around a mouthful of noodles.

"This chick is a ghost. No one at the organization has any clue who the fuck she is or where she came from. There's already a bounty out on her, directly from the organization. They don't take kindly to hunters taking bounties, less so when they're not paying their cut."

"Who's taking the bounty on her?"

He shakes his head. "It's an open bounty. Whoever finds her first and brings her in gets the cut."

"That's stupid and dangerous. That's basically pitting hunters against each other."

"No kidding. It's worse because they'll also wave the next month's fee to whoever brings her in." I quirk a brow at that, and he shakes his head. "No. We're not getting involved in this hunt, Tam. It's going to be a shitshow."

"One month of not having to pay the organization a percentage of our wages is huge, Nox. If we take on as many hunts as we can in that month, we're fucking set. We could take off an entire year without having to worry about finances."

He sighs, leaning back in his chair and draping one of his arms off the back of it. My eyes drift down to the tensing muscles in his stomach, to all the tattoos caressing his skin and rippling with every small movement. "Eyes up here," he chirps, and my head snaps up to see him watching me, a smirk pulling at his lips.

"You need to put some clothes on."

His eyebrow creeps up in the most adorable way, and the dimples in his cheeks trigger from the feral smile he gives me. "You're one to talk," he scoffs. "I'm not the only one proving to be a distraction here. Mind you, you're a *very* sexy distraction, but a distraction none the less."

"At least I have pants on," I mumble, shoving another forkful of pasta into my mouth.

"Do you want me to put pants on?" He asks, shifting himself lower in the seat and spreading his thighs, the poor towel struggling to stay hugging his frame.

I swallow thickly. "No, but I know you should." He laughs at my honesty and nods his head, lifting himself up to his feet, the movement graceful in that supernatural way. He stands there until my eyes finally roam over his entire body to settle on his face again, where that dimply smile makes my heart stutter at an abnormal pace. He turns, my jaw dropping when he rips the towel from his body to walk away from me completely naked. "That's cheating," I choke out.

He laughs, my eyes trained on that beautiful ass of his as it flexes with every torturous step away from me. I shake my head of the indecent thoughts the moment he steps through the door into his room, officially out of my view, and focus back on the food in front of me. He takes a few minute to come back, but when he does, the shit eating grin on his face has my cheeks heating. His sweats hang low, his damp hair disheveled across his forehead in the sexiest way imaginable, and the asshole didn't put a shirt on.

"Nox," I groan.

"I'll put one on when you do," he chirps, flopping back into his seat to finish the now room temperature meal in front of him. "What do you want to do for the rest of the night?"

"Is there something we *should* be doing?"

"I would like to inventory the shit you got from the warehouse before we end up handing it over to the authorities. I still have a few syringes of the antidote from Kalia." I flinch at the sound of her name and quickly drop my eyes to my plate. He sighs. "We're going to have to talk about her eventually."

"Why?" I grumble.

"Unless you decide to not go to the wedding, you're going to end up seeing her again. Kylo's going to be sad if you just stop going to the Hub, too."

"I don't need to go there while she's still working there. Once she's married, she'll get locked down to that house."

"So, you don't want to talk about her?"

"What is there to talk about?" I snap, feeling the betrayal and anger slowly coiling inside of me. He shrugs, and his silence is purposeful, like he's pushing me to talk about it without saying it. "She lied, Nox. She lied to me about everything about her."

"You lied to her, too, though. You lied to her about who you are."

"She fucking cheated on Camden. She lied about more than her identity, and I can't just let that go. She's living in shambles, meanwhile, she's a Princess in good standing with her Court."

"She obviously wanted to *have* a life, Tam. Can you blame her for wanting to experience what a normal life would be?"

"Why are you defending her? I thought you fucking hated her?"

"I do, but I can see where she's coming from as well. My dislike of her doesn't stop me from feeling bad for her. I won't say I'm not glad she fucked this up because her fucking up just paved the way for me to be with you. Because of her, I get to *be* with you, Tam."

"It never would have worked out between me and her anyways," I mumble.

"You liked her. You thought you could be honest with her eventually, and I get it. We all fell for her lies and tricks, but it doesn't mean I can't see it for what it is. She's broken just like you. She wants more for herself than the royal name following her like a burden, just like you. There's no shame in admitting you felt something for her because of your similarities, even if you didn't realize the extent of it."

"So, what do you think I should do? Do you think I should just forgive her? Do you think I should just let it go and not tell Cam about her infidelity? Am I just supposed to let all of this go and not feel anger or betrayal?"

"It's up to you if you want to forgive her or not. She never hurt you, Tam, she was just trying to find herself some semblance of normalcy in her fucked-up life. As for Cam, I don't think you should tell him. It's not like they were in a relationship prior to this engagement. Is it really cheating when she has no emotional ties to him? I can't blame her for wanting to experience things on her own terms, including sexual encounters and relationships. I can't tell you how to feel about any of this but letting this fester and eat away at you isn't going to do you any good. I think you need to let it go for yourself, no one else."

His phone rings again, but his eyes stay fixed on mine while it rings and vibrates its way along the table. "Are you going to get that?" The longer he stares at me, the more anxious I get, the pressure from him pushing me to look away from him.

He sighs and finally answers it. "Hello?" He sits up straighter in the chair and sets the phone down on the table, switching it over to speaker. "Say that again."

A sigh filters through the speaker and then Kaliem is speaking, his voice sounding exhausted. "I got a hit on your mystery girl. She just got spotted deep in the Hollow. She went to Merrick's this time."

"Merrick? He deals in nokweed and Helion. What the fuck was she doing down there?"

"Merrick is dead."

Ice trickles through my veins at the words, my mind trying to process what the fuck happened down there. "Did she kill him?" I say quietly.

"Emergency crews are still trying to put out the fire. I don't know what happened, but clearly this chick is unhinged."

"She attacked him so early in the day. I can't fucking believe it."

"What the fuck have you been doing all day?" Kaliem laughs. "It's not that early, Eris. It's like nine."

I grab my phone and check the time. How the fuck did it get so late without me realizing it? I know he was on the phone with Jerimiah for a while, but I didn't realize so much time had passed between then and us fucking. Time seems to move differently when I'm with him, like everything around us just melts away until there's nothing but us.

"I'll have you know I did something *very* important today," I chirp, smirking when Nox lifts a mocking brow.

"More like *someone*, not something," Kaliem laughs, and I can't help but laugh along with him.

Nox rolls his eyes and leans forward, bracing his elbows on the table to interlock his fingers under his chin. "Eris's sex life is none of your concern, but if you must know, it was the best lay of his life—like ground shattering. I swear I heard the heavens weep in jealousy."

Kaliem snorts and cackles, meanwhile my face heats up to the point it's probably the shade of a tomato. I mean, he's not wrong, but Kaliem would be one of the last people I would ever talk about my sex life to. Nox grins widely, clearly enjoying my discomfort as he crosses those perfectly tattooed arms across his bare chest.

"Anyways," Kaliem chuckles. "I'll leave you with that information to do with as you see fit."

"Thanks for the call, Kaliem," Nox says, tapping the call to end. "What do you want to do?"

"I'm not sure. I sort of want to go to Merrick's to see for ourselves what the fuck happened, but I think we might have to call the guard authority first so we can have a bit more freedom to do what we need to. We should probably warn them about this girl, especially if she's going to make it a point of blowing shit up and killing people."

"You're right. Let's get some proper clothes on and head out. We'll call the authority on the way."

"Fine," I grumble, lifting from my seat to put my plate in the dishwasher. "But when we get home, I want you naked again."

"Deal," he laughs.

CHAPTER 54

TAMZIN

The entire building is a skeleton of what it was. Some flames are still licking their way across the scorched bricks and ground, the foundation a pile of rubble with barely a skeleton left of the steel beams jutting out from the ground. I shift nervously in my seat as Nox drives up to the blocked off area, pulling the car over into an open spot next to one of the authority vehicles.

"Let's go," Nox murmurs, turning the car off and stepping out of it without waiting for me.

I'm slower to get out, trying to take in the destruction around me without the prying eyes of the judgmental people in our midst. Nox is already talking to Benjamin by the time I get out, and he glances back at me questioningly. I give my head a small shake, and he shifts over so I can stand next to him.

"Eris," Ben murmurs, dragging his hand down his face in a clear sign of exhaustion and frustration.

"You look like you've seen better days."

"No kidding. If I would have known all the shit that was going to happen after putting that bounty out for Calvin, I would have planned everything a bit better."

"It's not like you anticipated a rogue hunter going after everyone for random shit. I don't even know what's happening. Like sure, these guys are criminals, but Merrick...even with his shady dealings, he didn't deserve any of this."

"Definitely one of the better criminals on the market. The guy was just trying to make a living wage in this shitty city."

Ben holds out some badges to us on lanyards. "You guys can have access to any of the blocked off areas with this. You can have access to anything if you can figure out who's doing this so we can put a stop to it before the next person this chick takes out is someone completely innocent."

"I'll see if I can get an aura signature on whatever is left. I doubt either of us can pull a scent from anything to deem it useful, but we'll do what we can. How are you managing keeping the human authorities out of this?" Nox murmurs, glancing at one of the emergency vehicles driving by us at an excruciatingly slow pace.

"We're okay for now since we classify ourselves as specialty authorities. It helps that the captain of their police force is actually Nephilim, though. Infiltrating their unit was simple enough, and it's easier to get dark worlders integrated into their society, than to let it slip to the humans on what the fuck is actually going on around them."

"Fair enough," Nox snorts.

"Listen, I know we don't see eye to eye on your line of work, but if I didn't have faith in you two, I would have never reached out to you to begin with. You guys do a lot of good, keeping the streets clean in your own way, even if I don't condone vigilante work."

"Vigilantes don't get paid," I point out, earning a glare from Ben and a snicker from Nox.

"Would you rather me call you mercenaries?"

"I rather you call me Batman," I smirk.

"If you start wearing a cape and jumping off of buildings, I will," Ben snaps back.

I glance over at Nox, a devilish smile playing across his lips. "I would look really good in a cape, don't you think?"

"Most definitely. Why stop at the cape? I think you should get the full getup. Though, I think leather would look the best on you instead of spandex."

"Really?" I ask, turning my back to him. "I think my ass would look stellar in spandex though."

We both burst out laughing at the absolutely horrified look on Ben's face. "You two are so fucking weird," he mumbles.

"Don't be jealous. If you want a cape, too, I'm sure we can make that happen."

"I'm good, thanks." He smiles and shakes his head, motioning towards the destroyed building. "Go, before I change my mind and take those passes back from you."

I grin, backing away from him while I give him an exaggerated bow. "We'll be keeping these for the foreseeable future." Ben rolls his eyes, clearly done with my antics, and heads over to his car. I turn, jogging to catch up to Nox. I bump into his shoulder playfully and glance up at him. "So, you want to see me in leather?" I muse.

"I think you would look sexy as fuck in leather, but I still prefer you with minimal clothing on."

"Touché." He brushes his fingers against the back of my hand, and that small contact sends heat rippling through my body. "Do you think you'll be able to pull anything from the residual aura?" I ask, slipping my hand into his.

I smile when he gives my fingers a gentle squeeze, and he leans in closer—close enough that I feel his warm breath fan across my ear. "I'm not sure, but I'll try to pull on whatever I can. Will you be able to filter through any of the scents to try and pull a tracking note?"

I shrug. "Maybe. It'll be difficult to isolate it when I don't even know what I'm looking for. With the smells all melding together, it might be a bit hard, even for me."

"Alright, let's get started. Hopefully Ben's unit doesn't try to give us a hard time."

"They can try," I snort. "It won't end well for them if they try to start shit."

"You know we don't belong here. We're everything they hate, so you can't expect them to accept us and what we can do."

"I still rather be a hunter than ever work for the authority. All their rules and regulations, I would never be able to conform to that type of collar."

"Hmm, but a collar would look so *good* on you." I glance up at him, to the smirk pulling at his lips. "A pretty little necklace, like this one." My heart rams against my chest when he pushes me against one of the brick walls out of view, pinning me to it by my throat. His large, tattooed hand, circles my neck and gently squeezes. "Perfect fit," he purrs, pressing his body flush against mine.

"You're being bold," I choke out, my throat bobbing heavily against his hand.

"You're going to learn very quickly that I will have what I want, when I want it, and there isn't a single person on this planet that can stop me. I have everything I want now, and I'll never let it go." He grips into my throat harder, tipping my head up in the process, and presses his lips to mine. The groan he lets out pulses through my body, and there's no way I could ever deny him. I part my lips for him, that groan turning visceral, radiating through my body in a way that makes it feel like it's my own. "I love kissing you," he murmurs, resting his forehead against mine and slowly releasing his hold on me.

I grip into his hips, holding him close to me when I feel him wanting to shift back. "I love kissing you, too, and I love that you pick the most inappropriate times to do it," I laugh.

"There is no right or wrong time for me to show you how much I like you, Tam, only regrets if I don't do it. I've gone too long in holding back my feelings for you, and there have been so many moments that I wanted to pin you up against a wall and show you, but I...I was scared. I'm not scared anymore, and I don't fucking care what anyone thinks about our relationship. I hope you don't care either." He pulls back enough to look at me fully, his brows dipping in a way that shows concern now. “Do you...want to hide our relationship.”

My eyes widen. “No! I don’t care who knows either. I’m not ashamed of who I like, and anyone who tries to fucking start shit is going to get punched.”

He smiles, presses his lips to mine again quickly, and officially steps back. My hands slide away from his body, falling against my sides weakly. “That makes me unbelievably happy.”

“Come on, let’s get this over with so we can go home.”

CHAPTER 55

NOX

He seems happy enough. I was a bit concerned in bringing up how we would go about portraying our relationship in a public setting. If he wanted to keep it a secret for a while longer, I would have agreed with him, not wanting to make him feel uncomfortable. I'm glad he's so confident in his sexuality and doesn't feel shame in being with a male in the public eye. I *want* to be able to show him affection at any moment, being able to touch him and kiss him when I feel like it and not having him pull back or recoil out of fear of what others might think.

We get a few dirty looks from Ben's team, but they don't say anything, giving us room to work. Tam glances back at me once we get into the center of the destruction, and I close my eyes, pulling on my sight. I feel it burn through me as I open my eyes again, the familiar whiteness creeping into the edges of my vision. I glance back at Tam, my heart thumping faster in my chest at the look on his face. My sight doesn't scare him, if anything, he seems enamoured when it takes over.

Carefully and slowly, I trail my eyes across every section within my reach, pushing my senses as far as they'll go to try and see what the fuck happened here. The taint of fear and panic is still in the air, fragments of anger creeping into the auras.

"What do you see?" Tam asks quietly.

"Pain, fear, anger. Everything I expected but I hate to see. This wasn't quick by any means, but I'm not getting the sense that this was planned. Something happened here to make the elemental snap." I close my eyes and pull on my shifter senses, drawing in a long breath. "I'm getting that familiar scent again. Fuck, why can't I place it."

I open my eyes again to see Tam with his closed, his nostril flaring as he pulls on his tracking. His brows furrow, his lips pressing into a thin line. "Are you catching hints of honeysuckle?"

I frown, and when I don't respond, he opens his eyes again. I sniff the air, my nose crinkling at the heavy scent of smoke and burning flesh, with hints of nokweed. "I don't. I'm catching smoke, burned flesh, and nokweed." I sniff again, my frown deepening. "Mint, too, though. It's faint, but I can smell traces of it." Tam clucks his tongue, moving through the rubble carefully. "What?"

He shakes his head. "I'm not sure yet." I can't shake this feeling that he's hiding something from me, but I stand and watch him as he moves through the broken building. He bends down and pulls up a broken vial, bringing it to his nose. "Merrick had some secrets," he murmurs, turning to show me the vial. "This is Necro."

"Fuck. So, this chick got what she wanted."

"Seems like it, but I doubt it was willingly given to her. This wasn't a drug deal...this was a robbery and execution."

"If this hunter is on necro, we're fucked. She's strong enough without it."

"Necro will end up killing her. That shit isn't meant for long term use."

"There's not much more we can do here, and we got everything we could from the place. Let's go home."

He sighs, pushing himself back to his feet and tossing the vial back down on the ground, the glass shattering against the broken concrete. "I'm so done with all of this," he grumbles.

"Come on." I hold out my hand to him, and his face softens as he slips his hand into mine. I give it a small squeeze, tugging him along behind me as we make out way out of the danger zone. "We'll have fresh eyes on this in the morning."

"I really want to have this dealt with before the fucking wedding, but I feel like that's wishful thinking at this point."

"I can't believe it's this weekend."

"Royal weddings don't work the same as normal ones for us. They want it done and over with as quickly as possible so there's no room for error."

"I want ours to be quick, too." His hand slips from mine when he suddenly stops, and I turn to look at him, his eyes wide and his mouth gaped open. I smile and walk back towards him, rubbing at his arms. "Is that so surprising?" I chuckle.

"I...you want to get married?"

"Eventually, yes." I wrap my arms around him, hugging him tightly against my chest. "I want to spend my life with you, and I hope you feel the same way."

His fingers grip into my shirt and he inhales deeply against my neck. "I do. I can't picture my life without you, so of course I would want to spend it with you."

Joy blooms in my chest at hearing him say that. It was bold of me to throw that out there and presume he would want to officially tie himself to me, but having him want the same thing, makes me so fucking happy. A throat clears behind me, and Tam laughs when I let out a low growl.

"Easy," he chuckles, slowly dropping his arms from around me. He glances past me and takes a small step back. "What is it, Ben?"

I turn to face him, and his brow goes up in question when Tam slides his hand into mine. "How did it go?" He asks.

"As well as we thought it would. We didn't get much, but enough to know this wasn't a planned hit. This was a crime of sudden anger, so whoever this chick is, she's beyond dangerous when backed into a corner or pushed too far."

"Did you pull anything to be able to track her?"

"I've scented her a few times now and she seems familiar, so whoever it is, she's someone I've come across in passing at least," I admit, glancing down at Tam when his hand tightens in mine. His brows are drawn, and that feeling of him hiding something from me nags against my chest again.

"Alright. Let me know if you find anything that we can help with. Our resources are at your disposal."

I roll my eyes. "We don't need your resources. I could easily render everything under you completely useless with a few strokes of my fingers." Tam chokes out a laugh, and I glance down at him from the corner of my eye, amusement playing across his lips. "I'm good with my hands," I add.

"Okay," Ben sighs. "I don't know if you're talking about your hacking skills or your sex life, neither of which I want to be privy to, since one is illegal and the other is just too much fucking information."

"Fair enough," I snort. "We're heading out."

I pull Tam along behind me, but I hear Ben clear his throat again. "Are you two..."

I turn to glare at him, his eyes widening when I let out a small pulse of power. "Is there a problem?"

"No," he says quickly. "Just curious, that's all."

I pull Tam up against my side hard enough that the breath grunts out of him when he slams into me. "I thought you didn't want to know about my sex life."

"I overstepped."

"Yes, we're together," Tam says, and I glance at him to see him staring at me with furrowed brows.

"I wish my husband and I had the confidence you two have out in public." That pulls my attention, my head snapping back to look at

Ben. I never would have pegged him as someone to like men, but I guess Tam and I don't really make it known either. Fuck, I hid my attraction to him for years, and not once did Tam assume I was into him. "Good luck with everything," he murmurs, giving us a kind smile.

"Wow, I didn't expect that," Tam says the moment we get into the car.

"What?"

"I didn't know Ben was married, and I definitely didn't know he was with a guy."

"Maybe he'll be more open about his personal life now that he's seen us interacting." He reaches over and grips my hand, bringing it to his mouth to press his lips to my knuckles. "Let's go home."

I pull out onto the street, my eyes constantly drifting over to look at him while he stares out the window with a faint smile on his face. "What are you thinking about?" I say quietly.

"You," he laughs. He turns to look at me. "Us."

"Are those thoughts happy thoughts?" He nods. "Do I get to know any of those thoughts?"

"I can show you one of them," he smiles.

My eyes widen when he undoes his seat belt and moves closer to me, his hands moving to my pants. "Tam, what are you—" I choke out a breath when he pulls my cock from my pants and strokes his hand down the length of it. "Tam, I'm driving."

"I know. Keep your eyes on the road," he chirps, smirking up at me as he swirls his wicked tongue around the tip.

"Fuck," I groan, settling my hand on his hair to grip into the strands. He hums out a breath and dives down on it, plunging it deep into his throat. My eyes practically roll back in my head at the sensual strokes of his tongue, the way it swirls and licks at my entire length before his lips stretch around me again. "Fuck, that's good. Fuck, you're so good, Tam." He hums again and that just about sends me over the edge. I don't want to come yet. I want to drag out this blissful haze for as long as I can, never wanting to lose the feel of him against me. "Good boy, Tam. Suck that cock. Fucking make me come, and I want you to swallow down every last drop."

He gasps, pulling back and licking his lips. He smirks up at me, rubbing his thumb across the head of my cock. "You're dirty," he snorts.

"Not as filthy as you. I want you to choke on it. Take me as far as you can and fucking gag on my length."

"Call me a good boy again," he whispers.

I grin, gripping into his hair to pull his face up to mine. I press my lips to his, loving the small whimper he lets out when I yank his head back away from me and shove him back down. He doesn't fight it, taking my cock back into his mouth like it's the only thing he *wants* to do. "You're a good fucking boy, Tam," I growl, moaning when his throat tightens on my crown.

How the fuck is he so good with his mouth? It's fucking sinful. Tam *is* pure sin. Everything I thought I wanted and needed pales in comparison to what I want when I'm with him. I want all of him, his lust, his needs, his fucking desires, and I want to make all his dreams and fantasies a reality. There is nothing better than these moments with him, filled with longing and need. Being with him is like living in a world where heaven and hell have merged into a symbiotic entity. The joys and light of heaven, the darkness and depravity of hell. I feel like tipping the scales a bit and plunging headfirst into the side of darkness, where Tam can flourish with that tongue and body of his.

I can't stop my hips from rocking up into him, my stomach tightening while tingles radiate up my spine. I'm so close—so fucking close—but I'm holding myself back on the precipice of release. I don't want this to end just yet, but my vision is beginning to blur from the pain I'm causing myself from holding back. He'll be pissed off if I crash his car. He might laugh at the reason behind it, but he'll still be pissed at the end of it.

"Fuck, Tam, I'm coming." He sucks back hard, diving down further with his mouth, and I feel my cock hit the solid wall of his throat.

"Fuck," I whimper, my fingers digging in harshly on his hair while my body convulses and curls in around him. "Fuck," I say again, this time in relief as my cum explodes out of me straight down his throat. He swallows, swallows again, slowing his sucking and licking until I'm completely spent.

My entire body is shaking, my skin clammy from the insane orgasm he just ripped from my body. He pulls back just as I slow roll the car into our space at the apartment, my hand trembling on the key to turn the ignition off. My breath shudders out of me, my head tipping back against the headrest with a dull thud. I can feel his eyes burning into me and slowly tip my head to the side to look at him.

"Come here," I whisper, my throat dry from the panting breaths tearing through my throat. He smiles and leans in closer to me. Slowly, I lift my hand to cup his cheek, guiding it back to grip into the back of his neck. "Mine," I growl, pulling him towards me to crash my lips against his. He slants his mouth, parting his lips in desperate need, and I plunge my tongue into his mouth until he whimpers and moans, the sounds greedy and desperate in a way that has my heart clenching and my stomach tightening.

"I love how possessive you are," he says breathlessly against my lips.

"I love that you let me be." I quickly tuck myself back into my pants, much to Tam's dismay if the huff of irritation is any indication. "Let's go," I laugh.

The second the elevator doors close, I pin him to the back wall and grip into his ass. A feral grin spreads across his face, and he laces his hands through my hair, pulling me down to kiss me. We're a tangled mess of limbs, tongues, and teeth, stumbling out of the elevator once it reaches our floor. Tam laughs at my struggling to get the keys out, smacking my ass when I end up dropping them to the floor.

"Come on," he whines.

"What's the rush?" I snort, finally getting the key in the lock and shoving the door open.

"I want to cuddle." I quirk a brow and he rolls his eyes. "I like being in bed with you," he admits quietly.

"I'll be there in a minute. I'm just going to brush my teeth, and I'll grab us some water, too."

I head towards my room, but my eyes stay lock on his retreating form as he makes his way to his own room. I can't help but smile at the smile on his face. I haven't seen him smile as much as he has these last few days in a very long time, his darkness always overtaking any sense of happiness he's been granted. Each moment has been fleeting for him, slowly chipping away at his soul. I want to protect it—protect *him*. I *need* to protect everything that makes him good.

I throw on a pair of sweats, not wanting to go in there in a way that makes him think I expect anything to happen. Honestly, I would love to just spend time with him, not that the sex hasn't been great, but we've been going at it pretty consistently. As much as I love fucking around with him, I fell in love with him for the simple fact that he exists. Everything about him just made me fall in deeper, loving every minute of our time spent together, even if we just do mundane things.

I grab a couple of bottles of water and head into his room, smiling when I see him tucked in under the covers, his eyes hooded with exhaustion. It's been a long day, and we've both been pretty emotional, our tempers running hotter than normal.

"Have some water before you fall asleep. You haven't drunk enough today."

"Yes, dad," he grumbles, pulling himself up to sit when I hold out a bottle to him.

"Daddy," I smirk.

He tries to hide his own smile behind the lip of the bottle, but I can see it clear as day. He can't hide a genuine smile, not when it crinkles his eyes adorably. He holds out the half-drained bottle to me, a devilish grin pulling at those perfect lips. "Thank you, daddy," he purrs. It actually sounds ridiculous when he says it like that, and I burst out laughing. "Why are you laughing?" He huffs.

"Daddy coming out of your mouth doesn't suit you."

"Hmm." His eyes drift down my bare chest. "What do you want me to call you then?"

I crawl up onto the bed, pushing myself to hover my face inches away from his. "I like it when you say my name," I whisper. "Every time you say it, it makes me feel special."

"Nox," he whispers, his warm, minty breath, fanning across my lips.

"Hmm, yeah, just like that." I press my lips against his, smiling as I pull away and roll in next to him. I can feel him staring at me as I tuck my arms under my head and stare at the ceiling, the glowing star stickers muted with the light of the bedside lamp still on. I press my lips together at the sound of his breath huffing out, and then the room is plunged into darkness from him flicking the light off. I glance over at him, watching him tuck in under the covers with his back to me. I roll over towards him, looping my arm around his body. "I thought you wanted to cuddle," I whisper, loving the way he shivers when my breath caresses against his ear.

"I do," he admits, pressing himself further into me.

I tighten my hold on him and kiss his neck, loving the happy sigh he lets out as he snuggles further into the pillow. I've held him like this a few times in the last few years, posing as his anchor after his nightmares. The fact he associates my embrace with comfort fills my heart with joy, and it was the least I could do for him.

I always felt so useless when he experienced those terrifying nightmares. Memories that haunt him and claw their way into the waking world. I fucking hate his father for what he did to Tam, and I hate his entire family for allowing it. I know I should feel a shred of pity, knowing they all went through similar experiences, but I know Tam got the worst of it because he fought what his father was trying to do to him tooth and nail.

They tried to corrupt him, break him, *ruin* him, but he held on. He gripped his soul with desperate hands and clung to it like his life depended on it, and it did. Without that pure soul of his, he would have turned out like Croh or the stupid twins, pure darkness and deception.

Tam goes limp and heavy in my arms, finally being pulled into the blissful world of sleep. I squeeze him closer to me, nuzzling my face into the crook of his neck to breathe in his scent. Fuck, I love his smell. I could drown in it and die, and I would be the happiest I've ever been. I trail my lips down his shoulder and back up to his neck before tucking his head under my chin. I just want to stay like this forever, him in my arms, us living a life together and finally being happy and free.

CHAPTER 56

TAMZIN

I grunt in surprise, my eyes snapping open when I feel a hand smack down on my ass through the comforter. I groan, curling into my pillow and pulling the sheets up over my head.

"I made you breakfast," Nox says, pulling the sheets back down and pressing a kiss to my temple.

"What time is it?" I grumble.

"Nine. I figured you would want to go with me to check out Calvin's place. Ben messaged me this morning and said we would have access to the property. I know what I scented at the morgue, but maybe we could get a better sense for what the fuck happened out there."

"Ugh," I groan, making no move to get up.

"It's going to get cold."

"What did you make me?" I mumble. I hear a small thud and open my eyes to see him setting down a massive mug of steaming coffee on my nightstand. "That's not breakfast."

"Sit up and you'll see it," he snorts. I grumble incoherently and drag myself up to sit, rubbing at my eyes. "You're adorable," he laughs, ruffling my already disheveled hair, and setting a tray down on my lap. My eyes widen at the spread, and I turn to him in surprise. "Eat up," he smiles.

"This looks so good."

He really outdid himself this time. The tray is loaded with pancakes, bacon, sausages, eggs benedict of all things, half a grapefruit, and toast. "Eat as much as you like."

"Are you not eating?"

"I already had a shake." He climbs up onto the bed next to me with a smile on his face. I feel a bit of guilt at the fact he made me this extravagant, gluttonous breakfast, meanwhile, he's had a shake. I poke around at the food, taking one of the pieces of bacon into my mouth. "What's wrong?"

"I don't understand you," I murmur.

"What do you mean?"

I point at the tray. "You do all of this for me, but you don't spoil yourself in the same way."

His eyes soften, that kind smile still laced across his lips. "I like spoiling you. I like seeing you happy, and I know how much you love your food. I promise I'm okay, and when I get hungry, I'll make something for myself." He brushes his hand over my head, leaning in closer to me. "I like taking care of you, Tam. You deserve it—all of it."

"Will you at least eat a sausage?" I ask, spearing one with my fork and holding it out to him.

"Fine, I'll eat a sausage," he laughs, opening his mouth for me. He hums out a cute breath, chewing it with that fucking smile still gracing his lips. I love that smile. It makes him look younger, and so carefree. He's genuinely happy right now, and it's crazy to think that it's because of me.

I can feel him watching me as I keep eating, and I glance over at him when I feel the bed shift. "What are you doing?" I ask when he shifts himself to sit behind me. I shudder the moment his hands rub at my shoulders, his fingers and thumbs digging in blissfully. Fuck, this isn't fair. We could have had this for so much longer if we weren't both fucking idiots, too scared to tell each other how we really felt.

His lips press against the back of my neck, the heat of his mouth on me as he trails kisses up to my ear feeling absolutely amazing. "Mmm," he moans, nipping at my ear.

"Nox," I whisper, tipping my head forward when he drags his thumbs up the back of my neck. He kisses my shoulder, and I whine when he pulls away, shifting off the bed. "Where are you going?"

"I need to put distance between us, or we'll never get anything done today. Finish your breakfast while I get changed, okay?"

"Fine," I pout.

He grips my jaw, tipping my head up towards him to press his lips against mine. I whimper into his mouth when his tongue delves through my lips with a sensual stroke. "Stop making sounds like that or I'll have to lock us in here," he growls against my lips.

"You say that like it's a bad thing."

"It is when we have shit to do."

I roll my eyes, watching him as he walks slowly out of my bedroom, each step exaggerated, like he's trying to torture me by flaunting that perfect ass and the way the sweatpants hug every curve. I want to burn all these moments in my memories, making them easily accessible at a moment's notice so that I can relive it and replay it at my leisure. Memories are great, and I'll cherish them for all of eternity, but nothing beats the real thing. Being able to experience it in the moment, to feel and hold him, to touch every inch of him and witness all these moments in real time. *That's* the true beauty of life and being able to actually live in these pleasurable moments, no matter how small or insignificant they may seem to anyone else from the outside looking in.

I quickly polish off the massive meal he made for me, setting the tray off to the side so I can get ready for the day. As much as I hate having to go to that asshole's house to try and figure out what the fuck happened, I'm glad I get to go with Nox. If I had to deal with all this on my own, I think I would break mentally. I'm actually impressed I haven't spiralled into oblivion with the weight of everything that happened. Kalia still infiltrates my thoughts, but the feeling of anger and betrayal keeps the feelings I had for her at bay. I liked her. I hate that I liked her and fell for her, but she did her best to weasel her way into my life.

I shake my head, trying to knock the thoughts of her out of my mind so I can focus on what's important right now. Nox is all that matters. Nox is the key to my happiness, and he's my future.

He's sitting at the kitchen table with his laptop open in front of him. He glances up, smiling as his eyes travel across my body. "I love those jeans on you."

"Oh, thanks," I say, glancing down and rubbing my hands down my thighs. They're one of my favourite pairs, perfectly warn and butter soft. "What are you doing?" I set the tray on the counter and quickly put the dishes in the dishwasher before settling into the chair next to him.

He turns the laptop enough for me to see and points at the screen. "I was just checking the traffic cams near the place to see if there was a lot of foot traffic hanging around. You know, like gawkers and shit, or people that like solving their own crimes like some sort of fetish. It seems clear for the most part, and the cops have a decent permitter set up as a barrier."

"We should probably take the passes Ben gave us, just in case."

"Yeah, for sure. There's at least one officer hanging around," he murmurs, pointing to a black vehicle parked a block down the road. "That car has been there for a few days, so it's probably an undercover officer."

"They're going to love us showing up there," I snort.

"I'll send Ben a message to let him know we're heading over, so hopefully he gives the guy a heads-up, so he doesn't give us a hard time."

"Alright, I'm ready to go whenever you are."

He snaps the laptop closed and leans down a bit further in his seat, his legs flaring out enough for his knee to bump against mine. My eyes drift down, right between his legs—because *of course they do*—and stay transfixed on his crotch. Fuck, those jeans are snug, hugging him in all the right places and leaving very little to the imagination. Not like I need to imagine anything since I've seen his cock up close and personal a few times now, but there's just something about clothing hiding treasures like that one, just out of reach.

"Tam," He laughs.

"Huh?" I snap my eyes back up to his face, to the Cheshire grin spreading across his face.

"Do I need to throw on a snow suit to keep your head in the game?"

I shake my head. "It won't help," I mumble, earning a hearty laugh from deep within his chest.

"You're ridiculous."

"I can't help it. Now that I've been with you, it's like it's all I can think about."

"My cock?"

I shake my head again. "Just *being* with you. Obviously, your body helps, and knowing how good that fucking cock is, gives you some brownie points, but just knowing that all of it is mine now...I can't stop looking at you and appreciating you."

He gets up from his chair, dragging mine back a bit so he can settle himself into my lap. My eyes flutter closed when his fingers brush through my hair. He cups my jaw on either side and tips my head up to look at him fully. "I appreciate you, too," he whispers. "I'm angry at myself for waiting as long as I did to tell you the truth about how I felt, but I hope we can make up for lost time." He kisses my forehead before resting his head against mine. "I love you, and I'll love you forever."

"I love you, too, Nox." I curl my arms around him, pulling him into me. He settles his face into the crook of my neck, hugging me tightly on a deep inhale. The feel of him pressed against me is pure bliss, and his scent swirls around me like a comforting blanket. "We should go."

"Just a few more seconds," he mumbles, inhaling again. I smile, gripping into his back and loving the feel of his firm muscles through the silky t-shirt. "Alright, I'm good," he sighs, pulling back and shifting off me.

CHAPTER 57

TAMZIN

"It's a fucking wasteland," Nox murmurs from the passenger seat, his eyes trailing across the property as we drive by it to the main entrance—or where it *used* to be. The obelisks that rimmed the property when I scouted it just a few nights ago are complete obliterated and crumbling to the ground. I feel no magic here anymore, the runes protecting the area shattered out of existence.

"I can't believe the damage."

"Eh, I've seen worse." He points to the foundation of the house. "At least it's still standing." The walls crumble, crashing to the ground the moment he finishes the sentence. "Never mind," he snorts.

I pull up next to the unmarked vehicle, rolling down my window. The guy inside drops his window, too, and the glare he gives us has me grinning like an asshole. "You must be Nate."

"And you two must be the hunters playing dress-up as cops."

"It's not our fault your superior thinks we can do a better job than you lot," Nox snaps.

Nate rolls his eyes and waves us off, rolling up his window to officially cut off the conversation, if you can even call it that. "What an asshole," I cackle, pulling up to the house and down the driveway.

"I fucking hate that shit. We put ourselves at risk with what we do, yet we get shit on for doing the dirty work they don't want to do."

We get out of the car and carefully make out way towards what's left of the house. One of the stones rolls under my foot, throwing me off balance. Nox is there instantly, gripping into my arms to steady me.

"Thanks," I sigh, kicking the offending rock away from me.

"This is bad, Tam. It's like she went off like a nuke. This isn't just fire magic..." He closes his eyes and inhales, his chest expanding heavily with the effort. "Volatile. I don't think this is someone we can just capture and bring in. If we come in contact with her, she could go off like this again and take out innocent people with her."

"Do you think she's more than an elemental then?"

"I'm not sure. If she was looking for necro, and already has her hands on helion, she's going to be trouble to deal with, even as just an elemental."

I already know what's going to end up happening, but I don't want to bring it up to him because I know that's going to end with us getting into an argument again. If she's drugged up and boosting her power, the only way to even come close to handling her would be to dose myself as well. The last thing Nox will want me doing is using helion again, but what choice will I have? If it's between him or me dying or having to use the drug to save our asses and have a chance standing against this psycho, I'm going to choose the drugs. I would drown myself in the shit if it meant protecting him. I would let myself burnout if it meant Nox got to live.

I think we both know it's going to come down to some type of fight because I doubt this girl is just going to come quietly. The more time we spend on this case, the more I want to just pack up everything and get the fuck out of here. I can't shake this deep dread that's been gnawing at my senses for the last few days.

The scent I thought I picked up at Merrick's reminded me so much of Kalia. I know she's glamoured herself with dark hair once before, but I haven't gotten any type of magical signature from her in any of the interactions I've had with her. We've been together, even in the intimate sense, and it's really difficult to hide magic when you're in a mental state of euphoria. I can't actually convince myself that it's her because it doesn't make any sense. She wouldn't have any reason to go after Merrick, or even to visit Orion. I can see her getting pissed at Calvin since he's tied to me, and if she's that fucking obsessed with me, a psycho *would* go after another psycho that threatens what they deem belongs to them.

I shake my head. There's no reason for her to be that obsessed with me, but the way she acted at the engagement party is scratching at my mind. I grunt out a breath, backing away from Nox to rub at my nose. I was so lost in thought that I ran right into his brick wall of a back.

"You good?" He chuckles.

"Yeah, sorry. I got distracted." He quirks a brow and I sigh. "Just trying to mentally piece everything together. I'm trying to figure out how all of this ties together and for what reason. It's one thing to go after Calvin, he was a prick, but to go to Orion and then Merrick and end up killing him, I don't get it. Is her goal in all of this to obtain drugs? If that were the case, why wouldn't she go after the warehouse?"

"Maybe she doesn't know about it. The place was under a completely different name, and you would have to have my level of hacking to find out that information."

I gnaw at my lip. What he's saying is true, and if it's true, it should clear Kalia completely since she *knows* about the warehouse. She was there and saw everything that was inside, including the helion and neurotoxin. I frown when the memory of the empty shelves come to mind.

"What if they've already hit the warehouse and got what they wanted? There would be no reason to destroy it if there was no one to stand in her way."

"She would have had to get past the warding. Whether that was with a program like I use or just by sheer force sure, but even *you* would struggle to get across that without a backlash."

"Not so much if I had helion in my system." His eyes darken, his brows dipping down, warning me of the danger of this conversation.

"I'm just saying. If she already had helion, she could have forced her way through the wards."

"The doors were still locked when we went back. If she had forced her way in, she would have had to break the door down or at least bypass the lock system."

"Unless you let her in..."

His frown deepens. "What the fuck are you getting at? Do you know something I don't know?"

I shake my head. "I don't know for sure, but I'm trying to piece things together. It doesn't make sense, but I have one person I can't stop thinking about."

"Who?"

"Kalia."

His eyes widen. "That doesn't make sense."

"She can use glamours. At the club, it was her that stood up to Croh."

"The dark-haired chick was Kalia...fuck, I...do you think she stole necro when I let her in to get you the antidote?"

"There was an entire shelf that was empty when I went in, Nox."

"We should break into her house. We need to fucking know, Tam. If she's got a massive stash of necro, we have no idea what she might have planned. Why didn't you mention it sooner?"

"I couldn't think of any reason for it to be her. I never scented magic on her, and she wouldn't have any reason to stockpile drugs."

"You still should have said something."

"I don't want to think about her!" I snap. I didn't mean to snap, and I'm regretting it more because I hate the look of pity that crosses his face. "I just...I'm trying to move on from her, so the last thing I want is all of this to be tied to her."

"Well, unfortunately, she's here to stay, and she's now going to be a part of your family."

"Just another reason for me to avoid them like the plague," I grumble.

"I hate to say this, but we really should check out her place."

"Fine."

"But...we need to make sure she's not home, so..." He pats me on the shoulder, and I do *not* like the look he's giving me. "We need to stop at the Hub."

"No. Nuh uh, no fucking way."

"Tam, that's the best way to know if she's not at home."

"I'm not fucking doing it."

"Fine. I'll go in, but you owe me big time for this."

I smirk. "Want me to blow you in the car again?"

He laughs loudly, his eyes crinkling at the edges. "I'll admit, that was beyond hot, but I don't know if I have it in me not to crash the car if we go another round like that."

I grin. "It was that good?"

"Mind altering," he snorts.

"Hmm, good to know. I told you I was good with my mouth."

"That you did."

CHAPTER 58

KALIA

"Girl, what is going on with you?"

Ridley bumps me in the shoulder, almost knocking the tray of buns out of my hands. I glare at her, setting it down before she actually makes me drop them.

"Nothing," I mumble.

"You've been spaced out and miserable the last few days. Is everything okay? Boy trouble? Is it Eris?"

I actually flinch at the sound of his name, quickly turning away from her to stand in front of one of the cutting board counters to work on some tomatoes. "It's complicated. I can't really talk about it, but I think I'm going to have to quit working here soon."

"What?! Why?!" She screeches, gripping into my arm to turn me around, the knife in my hand clattering to the counter with a loud clank. "Do you not like working here anymore?"

"That's not it. It was always going to be temporary, but I had hoped I could work things out and at least keep working here a few days a week. Unfortunately, I'm going to be moving again soon, and I won't be frequenting this part of town."

"Ugh, that sucks! I really like working with you, and it's been fun to hang out."

I smile at her, trying to tamper down the sadness creeping into my heart. Ridley has been a good friend—a genuine friend. She's never pried into my life or judged me on any of my choices or comments, and she's just been the perfect person to hang out with. It makes me hate the Night Court more. Everything about this is bullshit. I wouldn't have to give up this job, this friend, or this life if Tam would just see reason and take me away from this mess. I don't *want* to marry Cam. I don't want to go from one prison to another. I refuse to go through with this wedding, and I will do everything within my power to get away from that hell so I can finally live my life. Tam will understand. He'll see that everything I've done and plan to do will end up benefitting the both of us.

I tried to give him time, and I thought he would calm down enough to finally come and talk to me, but he's been avoiding the Hub, so I haven't had the chance to explain myself better. He doesn't see it yet, but he will, and I won't let anyone stand in our way. No one will hurt him ever again, no one will care for him the way I do because I see and understand him better than anyone in this world. We're exactly the same. Born into families we despise and forced to do things that end up breaking us piece by piece.

"I'll cherish your friendship more than you know, Ridley."

She grips my wrist, tugging me towards her, and wraps her arms around me. "If there's anything you need, you can always talk to me, Kalia. I don't know a ton about you, but I can tell you have some darkness in your past that is still eating away at you."

If she only knew that the darkness isn't in my past, it's lingering just below the surface of my psyche, lying in wait to pounce the moment I break completely. "Thanks, Ridley," I murmur, pulling away from her when the bell at the door rings.

I swear I feel the blood in my veins completely turn to ice, all heat draining from my face at the sight of Nox walking through the door. He keeps his expression neutral, but I catch the slight flicker of light in his irises when his gaze settles on me. It's barely a glance, his face morphing into a wide grin as his eyes shift to Ridley.

"Hey, Ridley." His voice is sweet and light, and I fidget with the knife on the counter, not sure what I should do in this situation. I want to ask him how Tam is doing, but I know if I bring him up at all, he'll fucking explode on me. I can feel the animosity seeping out of him. "Can I get a matcha latte, and a quad espresso, please."

"For sure, Nox," she smiles, taking over the register for me since I'm being completely useless right now. She turns towards me, her eyes going wide as she mouths. "Are you okay?"

I shake my head, dropping my eyes the second I feel Nox's gaze turn to me again. I can't stop my hands from shaking as I cut through the tomatoes carefully. I sneak a peek towards the window, seeing Tam's car parked along the sidewalk, the hint of movement catching my eye through the dark tinted windows. He's here. He's within reach, but still so far away from me. I want to tear out of this building, stomp my way to stand next to the car and bang on the glass, demanding that he speak to me, that he listens to what I have to say. I want him to know my story, my feelings, all the wrongs I've done in the name of *him*. I was burdened before, but nothing like the burdens I've taken on the moment I knew I needed to *know* him.

I want him. No, I *need* him. I need him in my life like needing air and water and food in order to survive. I can't breathe. The air in my lungs thins, my chest tightening with the fear that he won't fucking see me for *me*. I want to scream and cry and just let every bit of fragile control loose. He *will* see me. I will be all that's left standing, and I won't give him the option to see anything else.

"Here's your order," Ridley says, ripping me from my mental warzone.

"Thanks, Ridley."

He turns to leave, my mouth opening and closing like a fish out of water, with barely a squeak of breath coming out. "Nox," I croak. He pauses, his back stiffening, and I catch the ripple across his skin, a clear sign that his shift is threatening to be released. He hates me, and I know his poisonous words will just taint Tam's idea of me. I know Tam felt something for me, and that connection between us doesn't just go away. He turns his head slowly to look at me over his shoulder, his glare a promise of pain. His eyes rim with light, a low growl rumbling deep in his throat. "I'm—I'm sorry."

"Save it," he snaps. "He doesn't need you, he never did, and guess what? He never will. He's *mine*."

My knees buckle under me, forcing me to grip into the counter to stop myself from crumpling to the ground at his harsh words. He can't mean that. Tam just needs time, that's all. Time that even *I* don't have right now. I'm running out of precious time myself, the wedding date drawing nearer, looming over me like a fucking blade on a guillotine. His. Nox said Tam is his...what does that mean? Nox is his best friend, so I know he wants to protect Tam, but he doesn't need to protect him from me. I would never hurt him—I can't even dream of ever hurting him. I *helped* him for fuck's sake. I helped them *both*.

The moment the door closes behind him my legs give out. "Kalia!" Ridley gasps, crouching down next to me and rubbing soothing circles against my back.

"He hates me," I whisper.

"Nox can be hard to deal with sometimes, and he's very protective of Eris."

Tears burn at the back of my throat. I need to fix this before it's too late. I would go to his apartment after work to confront him there, but I've been summoned to that hellhole Court again for dinner. Fuck, I wish there were a way to get out of it, but no matter how many excuses and scenarios I play out in my head, none of them are good enough to get out of a direct order from the King. My family is no help either, sacrificing me to the devils we know so well.

"I need a minute," I murmur, shakily getting to my feet with her help, her warm hand cradling my elbow.

"Okay, take a break. I'll finish prepping for lunch."

I nod, slowly moving to the breakroom to grab my smokes. I give her a weak smile before I slink out the back door into the alley. I know what I need to do. I've been preparing myself for it, but I had hoped it wouldn't resort to such drastic measures. I had hoped that I could just convince Tam to run away with me, to leave this world behind and start over with me somewhere far from this place, and as far away from the Fae districts as possible. He won't leave willingly though, and I know he won't just abandon Nox, much to my dismay. It would be easier if they just didn't exist...obliterated from this world so that all that was left, is us. Me and him against the world.

CHAPTER 59

NOX

I can barely keep my anger contained as we drive towards Kalia's duplex. Seeing her sent a spark through me, a need to fucking end her where she stood. Just laying eyes on someone like that shouldn't elicit such a visceral response, but she brings out the worst in me. I think it's worse because I know she was actually able to get under Tam's skin, able to manipulate him and take advantage of him. Tam is too fucking good, giving the benefit of the doubt to those who don't deserve even an inkling of his attention.

I know I'm partially to blame. I let her into our home, and that gave her the in she needed to sink her claws into him. The damage she did to him once he was able to pull away from her hold will take time to heal, leaving scars that may never go away, but I will do what I can, being the salve that he needs in order to make those wounds disappear into nothing.

"How did she look?" Tam asks quietly, ripping me from my mental battle.

"She looked about ready to pass out when she saw me."

"If Kalia was this rogue girl, wouldn't she have been more...I don't know, hardheaded I guess?"

"She's good at playing games, Tam. She's lied and manipulated you at every turn."

"I lied to her, too."

"You lied about your name. You didn't pretend to be someone you're not. She is not the victim here, you are."

I stare at the side of his face, his eyes trained on the road ahead of us while his jaw ticks and clenches. "I don't want to be classified as a fucking victim, Nox," he says through clenched teeth. He glances at me quickly, his irises glowing brightly with his barely contained emotions.

"You may not want to hear it, but you are. You've been a victim your entire life, suffering in silence, but deserving nothing but love and understanding." He clucks his tongue and rips his eyes away from me to stare back out at the road. His foot presses on the gas a bit more, causing the car to lurch forward, forcing me back into my seat. "Tam."

He eases off the gas, but his grip on the steering wheel is vicious, like he's fighting not to rip it apart with his bare hands. "Run away with me," he whispers.

"What?"

He pulls up down the road from Kalia's duplex and shuts off the car, turning in his seat to face me fully. "Right now. We can pack up our shit and just go somewhere, anywhere as far away from here as possible."

"You're serious?"

"Yes. Fuck all of this shit. I don't care about any of it, Nox."

"I would love to run away with you, Tam...but we can't. Not yet at least. People are dying and we're deep in the middle of it. Can you live with yourself, knowing that someone is killing anyone within their warpath?"

"I have a bad feeling about all of this, Nox, and I just want to fucking get out of here."

"Let's see what Kalia is hiding. If it's not her, then we'll revisit the idea of leaving. Though, I don't think you should bail on Cam's wedding. I rather witness that girl get locked down so she never comes near you again."

"Is it weird that I feel bad for Cam? I think that if he knew what Kalia has been up to, he would just cancel the wedding and send her back home."

"Not at all. He has no idea who he's getting involved with, and as much as I hate him and the rest of your family, they shouldn't have to deal with someone like her."

"Let's go," he grumbles, bolting out of the car before I have a chance to say anything else to him. I hate where his mind is at right now. He's on the cliff's edge, and I don't know if he's anticipating that edge crumbling, or if he's planning to launch himself from it to dive down to the jagged edges below. It's like I'm reaching out to him, but every time I think I'm close to bringing him from the brink, he gets further and further away.

He waits for me at the door, which I half expected him to kick it down the moment he got up to it, but he just stands there, staring at it with furrowed brows. "What is it?" I ask, settling my hand along his lower back.

He turns his head quickly to look at me, his lips slightly parted in surprise. Was he that caught up in his own thoughts that he didn't actually hear me walk up to him? If he's this distracted, that could end up being a problem. Being in this mindset leaves room for a lot of errors, and we can't afford to make any mistakes when it comes to this.

"Tell me you're okay." He clears his throat, dropping his eyes from mine. "Tam," I snap.

"I'm fine." He grips the doorknob, the distinct clink of the lock snapping audible to the both of us. He pushes the door open, and we both quickly get inside, closing the door behind us. Tam closes his eyes, his nostrils flaring as he scents the air, and I keep myself as still as possible, practically holding my breath so I don't distract him further. "There's definitely something here," he mumbles.

"What do you mean?" He doesn't answer me, he just heads off towards the bedroom. "Tam," I hiss out, jogging after him. He doesn't hesitate in his steps, walking right up to the closet and ripping the doors open. His eyes scan everything, all the clothes as he shifts them from side to side, his gaze moving to the floor and then to the upper shelf inside. "Tam, there's nothing here."

"You don't smell it?"

I close my eyes and open my sense to what lingers in the room, my nose crinkling at the subtle hint of helion. "It's faint, but I smell helion."

He nods, his eyes fixed on the closet like he's dead set on it being in here. "Not just helion," he murmurs, dropping into a crouch on the floor. He raps his knuckles on the flood, the thunk, thunk of the wood rattling through the quiet room. He keeps doing it, moving his knuckles along, inch by inch until a hollower thunk sounds. He glances up at me with a quirked brow, motioning to a panel of the floorboard.

"I got it." I drop down next to him, pulling a partial shift to extend my claws. I dig them into the edge of the wood, trying to get some purchase in the crack, finally getting enough to be able to lift it up. Tam reaches into the secret compartment, pulling out a small duffel and setting it on the ground between us. "What is that?" I grumble, rubbing at my nose.

He unzips the bag, revealing vial upon vial inside. "Necro. It's her, Nox. She has to be the one that took out Calvin and Merrick."

"You said she didn't smell like she had powers though, and I didn't catch anything when I saw her today either. Do you think maybe she's just working with someone?"

"I don't know, but either way, I think it's time we talk to Cam. He needs to know about this because if she *uses* this, she's fucking dangerous."

"Alright, grab the bag and let's get out of here."

Tam moves to zip up the bag, but freezes suddenly, his head whipping towards the door. I hear it, too, the sound of feet on the gravel, coming towards this house.

"Maybe it's the unit next to her?" He shakes his head, his eyes widening. "It's her?" He nods. "Fuck."

"I can get us out of here, but I can't take the bag."

"You can't warp the both of us without going down," I hiss out. His eyes drift to the bag. "No," I growl. "You're not fucking using helion."

"Then you need to let me do it without."

"Tam—"

"We don't have time!" He shoves the bag back in the hole and quickly slides the floorboard back over it, gripping into my arm. I open my mouth to argue, but the next second, I feel myself getting pulled into a vortex of power, my stomach roiling and my head spinning.

I stagger a few steps, Tam stumbling away from me and falling to the ground on hands and knees, his chest heaving with harsh breaths. His arms tremble with the weight of his own body, and I fight back the bile rising in my throat, stumbling towards him to help him to his feet. He popped us out right by his car, the gleaming black paint a welcoming sight in this situation. I grip into him, helping him towards the passenger seat while his feet drag against the ground with each step.

He's pale—too fucking pale. His head lolls to the side the moment he collapses down into the seat, and I have to brace myself on the hood as I make my way to the driver's side. I shouldn't be driving either, but we can't risk staying here any longer. Kalia is already going to realize someone broke into her house just because of the broken lock. I have no idea how good her nose is, but our scents are fresh in that house now, no lingering scent from the other night, but I'm hoping she doesn't actually notice.

Tam groans in the seat, slumping further towards me. "Hey, stay with me," I murmur, gripping into his shoulder to push him back into his seat. I reach across him, strapping the seatbelt over his chest to secure him.

He can handle warping himself, but it's way harder on him when he has passengers to drag along through the void. It's not something he uses often, so there's never been a need for him to practice it. He's gotten better in being able to warp himself without too much of a lag on his power, but he still has a sort of cooldown period before he can do it again. Warping both of us like that will have him incapacitated for at least a few hours, and all I can think of right now is getting him home and into bed so he can recover.

"You'll be okay. I'll get you home so you can rest."

"I need to message Cam," he murmurs, fumbling to try and pry his phone from his pocket.

"I'll message him when we get home." I grip his arm to stop his struggling, and he lets out a heavy sigh. He still looks like shit, his forehead now gleaming with sweat. I settle my hand on his forehead and his eyes flutter closed at the contact. "You're getting too warm, Tam."

"I'll be fine," he grumbles.

I'm fighting an internal battle seeing him like this. I didn't want him to have to resort to using helion to get us out of there but seeing him like this—weakened—he pushed himself because he didn't want to upset me, and I need to live with that.

"I'm sorry, Tam." I don't know what else to say to him because I *am* sorry. I'm sorry he had to push himself like that, I'm sorry I didn't find out when the fuck Kalia was getting done work, I'm fucking sorry that I somehow still keep fucking everything up.

"You didn't do anything wrong."

I glance over at him as I pull off of Glasgow onto the main road, but his eyes are still closed, his head tipped back against the headrest. "You pushed too hard."

"I'll be fine."

"You...didn't use the helion, and I—"

"I didn't want you to be upset with me. I know how much you hate the shit, but I can't deny that it helps me have better control of my powers." He opens his eyes and slowly tips his head to look at me. The light in his eyes seems dull, like the darkness inside of him is trying to claw its way out right in front of me. "I'm weak, Nox."

"You are not weak," I snap. "You are the strongest person that I know." He rolls his eyes, turning away from me again. "Tam, tell me you don't believe that. Tell me you don't believe the lies you're telling yourself."

"They're not lies."

"They are. You are strong, caring, beautiful, and a force to be reckoned with. You have so much to give, but sometimes you give too much, Tam. That's why you feel that you're weak. Anyone who pushes themselves as much as you do would strain themselves to the point they believe they're weak. It's not weakness, not even close. You may not be able to see it, but I can see how much of yourself you're still holding back. Why? Are you seriously afraid of showing people who you are? You're stronger than this, and you're stronger than the person you're trying so hard to cling to."

He physically turns away from me, curling himself against the side of the seat, his head thudding against the glass. I don't know what else I can say to him to finally have him understand what I see. I see all of him. All his flaws and imperfections, all of which make him perfect in my eyes. You don't have to be afraid of the darkness. Embracing it and understanding that there is no light without darkness is the way to truly live. No one is perfect, and holding onto the want and need of being perfect will bring you nothing but pain and disappointment.

CHAPTER 60

TAMZIN

He always has a way of stirring up the worst of my emotions. I'm not trying to be a dick, but I know that ignoring him, especially when he's being open and honest like this, is just going to upset him. He's trying to bring me out of the pit of my own despair, but I'm so used to being in this dark chasm, that it's difficult to fully climb out of it. I always have one leg in the damn thing, easily slipping back into it with the smallest of shoves.

The car stops, the engine turning off with the small click of the key. Neither of us move to get out, and I hear Nox shifting in his seat. I don't look at him—I can't. I don't want to see the emotions battling it out on his face. He sighs, and then the door opens. I unclick my seatbelt when I hear his door close, startling when mine opens. I stare at the ground—at his feet just outside my door. His hand comes into view, his palm welcoming and inviting. Slowly I slide mine into his, letting him help me out of the car.

My body still feels weighed down, my limbs shaking as I steady myself against the side of the car while Nox closes the door. He holds out his hand again, tugging me closer to him as we walk. The silence between us is heavy, with every step it feels like I'm being dragged further back from him. I cling to him, gripping into his arm, desperate to hold onto him like the anchor he's been the last few years.

He curls his arm around me, squeezing me against his side as we step onto the elevator. My eyes feel heavy, but I blink away the haze, desperate to keep myself standing and prove to him that he's right, that I'm not as weak as I think I am. My eyes close, each passing second beckoning me to just drop to the floor and fall asleep right here. I lean in a bit further to Nox, resting my head against his chest. His fingers curl into my arm possessively, the sound of the doors dinging open ripping me from my thoughts.

"Almost there," he says quietly, leading me out of the elevator. "Do you want some lunch?"

"I—I just want to lie down."

"Okay." He leads me to my room, and I stumble forward, gripping into the edge of the bed with a heavy sigh. "Do you want to change into something more comfortable?"

"I need to call Cam."

I can't just let myself succumb to the desire to sleep. There's too much at stake right now with that psycho hording some of the most dangerous drugs on the planet. We have no idea what she's planning, or what she's going to do with that stash. For all I know, we're all in danger, but Cam more than anyone. She doesn't want to marry him, claiming that she wants to be with me, and that makes me wonder on how much she actually knows about me and my family. Maybe I was right all along, and the girl has been stalking me right from the beginning. I'm an idiot for falling for her innocent act, giving into that small fragment of desire, and the idea that she could be someone I could actually be with.

"I told you, I'll call him."

"He's my problem," I huff, flopping down on the bed. I glance down when Nox starts to undo the belt on my pants. "What are you doing?"

"You'll be more comfortable without a belt on, or pants for that matter."

"I can do it."

"Will you fucking stop?! Why are you acting like this?" He rips the belt from the loops in one smooth motion. Impressive, but I shouldn't be surprised. I want to argue with him when he undoes the button on my pants, but quickly snap my mouth closed at the absolutely vicious glare he gives me. "That's right, keep your mouth fucking closed. I don't want you fighting me on everything when I'm trying to help you." He rips my pants from my legs, letting out a soft hum when he notices me not wearing any underwear. "Sit up." I shakily do as he asks, staring at his chest as he pulls my shirt off over my head. I watch as he walks over to my drawers, grabbing me a pair of sweats to put on. I hold out my hand to them, but he just glares. "Up."

"So bossy," I grumble, shakily getting up to my feet.

I sway on the spot as he kneels down in front of me. He glances up and quirks a brow. "Well?" I sigh and move my hands to grip into his shoulders to balance myself while he tugs each leg on. He's slow to pull up the pants, but he finally settles the band around my hips and presses his lips to my stomach. "You're a good boy when you listen. Was that so hard?" He murmurs, slowly kissing his way up to my chest as he lifts himself to his feet. He cups my jaw, pulling my gaze up to look at him. "Answer me."

"No, Sir," I whisper, my heart thrumming viciously in my chest. I swear he can probably hear the damn thing pounding frantically against my ribcage as it threatens to beat right out of my chest.

He leans down, stopping a breath away from my lips. "Good," he whispers. He doesn't move any closer or further away, just hovers right at the edge of me. I want him to kiss me, to press those full lips against mine to prove to me that I've been good in doing what he asks of me. Fuck, when did I turn into this person? This desperate being in need of attention and reassurance. No, I didn't turn into this, I've *always* been like this because I never got the attention I so desperately craved from my family. I never felt loved or needed, and I sure as fuck never felt wanted. "Do you want lunch, or do you want to go to sleep for a bit?"

"I—I want you to kiss me."

"Hmm, that wasn't one of the options I gave you."

"Please." I sound desperate as fuck, but I don't even care anymore. I need this, all of it. I need his attention and love—I crave it.

His lips move a fraction closer and my heart kicks up to a painful rhythm. They ghost over my own, but it's not enough, I need more. "Lunch or sleep," he whispers, the tone playful and coy. The asshole is fucking with me now, and the blood in my veins burns with the need to just take what I want like I've always done.

"Lunch," I say breathlessly because I can't deny the hunger I feel right now, and not just for food, but we'll start there.

"Lunch it is." I fucking whimper when he pulls back from me, and a devilish smirk tugs at his lips. He brushes his thumbs against my cheeks while he stares right at me, locking my gaze to his. "Beg for it again," he sighs.

Fuck, he's such an asshole, but the need inside of me that wants him to do as I ask, too, is too great. "Please, kiss me," I say quietly with no hesitation. If he wants me to beg, I'll fucking beg. "Please, Nox."

"Fuck," he groans, closing his eyes through a deep inhale.

I melt into him when his mouth finally presses against mine. I part my lips for him, coaxing his tongue into my mouth with sensual teases with my own. I moan, loving how possessive the kiss gets when he grips into my hair, holding my face against his, and positioning it in the way he wants me. He backs me up, the edge of the bed hitting me knees and crumpling my legs beneath me. I fall back onto the bed with Nox looming over me, his arms braced on either side of my head to stop him from crushing me. The look of surprise on his face is comical, and I smirk up at him.

"Sorry," he chuckles.

I shake my head. "I'm fine, just sort of got a bit of sea legs right now. I'll be fine, I promise."

"Hmm." He bends down and quickly presses his lips to mine again before standing up between my legs, which are hanging off the bed awkwardly. "I'll make you a sandwich. I won't be long."

"Okay."

I settle my hands on my stomach and watch him walk out of my room, smiling when he glances back at me over his shoulder. I can't keep the smile off my face as I stare up at the ceiling. It takes me a few minutes to get enough motivation to move from this position, but eventually, I get myself properly in bed, partially under the covers. It doesn't take him all that long to make me a sandwich, and it looks fucking amazing as he sets it down on my lap.

He sets down a can of pop on the nightstand and brushes my hair back from my face as I take a massive bite. His hand hovers a second longer on my forehead, and I glance up at him, at the look of concern on his face. "What?"

"You still feel really warm," he murmurs, bending down to press a kiss to my temple while he ruffles my hair.

"I feel okay, just a bit sluggish. I should be good to go in a few hours. Did you call Cam?"

He moves around the bed and hops up onto it on my other side, settling back into the pillows with his hands tucked up his head. "I figured you would want to be in the conversation."

"But you said—"

"I know what I said, but I don't want you to think I'm brushing you off by doing things for you. I wanted to call him because you're in no mental headspace to be doing it on your own, Tam. I'm not trying to undermine you."

I polish off the sandwich and chug back the pop before setting the plate down on the nightstand. I shift towards him, curling myself up against his side, and sighing when he drapes his arm down to settle against my back. "Thank you."

"For what?"

"Everything," I snort. "For lunch, and for being so caring."

"I'll call him now before you officially pass out." He shifts closer to me to dig for his phone in his back pocket. I watch as he dials Cam's number and shifts the phone to speaker. It rings and rings, and just when I think it'll end up on voicemail, Cam's voice filters through the speaker.

"Nox?" Cam says, confusion clear in his voice. "What's going on? Is everything okay? Is something wrong with Tam?"

I bury my face in his chest to hide my laughter. I never thought I would see the day that Cam would be this worried about me, and it sends a small flutter through my chest. "I'll answer those in order for you," Nox snorts. "A lot is going on, everything is not okay, and there's always something wrong with Tam."

I smack him on the chest and glare at him, but he just smirks, sets the phone down on his stomach, and rubs at the area I hit him for a second before settling his hand on my head to brush through my hair. "What's going on?"

"We need to talk...in person. This isn't something we should be discussing over the phone."

"Does Tam know you're calling me? Is this about him?"

"I'm here, Cam," I sigh. "There's a lot to go over, so I'm hoping we can meet up with you tonight if you have time."

"You can come to Court. We're just having dinner tonight, so you're welcome to join us."

"I rather not, but I can meet you before dinner. Is...Kalia going to be there?"

"Yeah. Dad calls on her a few times a week. He's not a fan of the fact she's staying off property, so he's trying to make her life hell by pulling these stupid forced dinners. Does this have something to do with her?"

Nox gives me a look and shakes his head. I sigh. "We'll talk about it later. We'll be there around five."

"Okay, I'll see you then." Nox grabs his phone to hang up but pauses when Cam clears his throat. "I'm sorry about what happened last time you were here. I told them not to start shit, and they completely ignored me. I—I just want you to be happy, Tam, and I'm sorry we've made your life miserable."

"I'm happy now. I finally realized what I had right in front of me, and I'm not giving it up without a fight."

Cam chuckles. "Take care of him, Nox." He hangs up on his end before I have a chance to say anything to that comment.

"It's pretty fucked up that he was able to see what neither of us would acknowledge," Nox snorts.

"He just took the way you were protecting me as something more, that's all."

"But it *was* something more. I protect you the way I do because I love you." He leans down and kisses my forehead.

I laugh, glancing up at him. "You love forehead kisses, eh?"

"When I do that, I'm not just kissing you, I'm kissing the voices, too."

I literally snort at the audacity, prop myself up, and punch him in the gut. "Rude."

He laughs and yanks me back down on top of him with no resistance from me. "Shhh, let the voices sleep. Actually, you should be sleeping, too. We have a few hours, but I want you rested to deal with your family and all this bullshit."

"Are you going to stay with me until I fall asleep?"

"Do you want me to?" I nod, gripping into his shirt as I pull myself further onto his chest. My eyes close, feeling heavier and heavier with each gentle stroke of his hand through my hair. "I'll stay for as long as you need me to, Tam," he whispers.

"Forever then."

He laughs, the motion making me jiggle against his chest. "Forever."

CHAPTER 61

KALIA

Someone was in my fucking house. I looked everywhere, trying to find some sign as to who it could have been, finally ending up in my room. I frown when I notice my closet door slightly ajar and rip it open. Nothing seems to be out of place, but I drop to the ground and pry up the floorboard. I sigh in relief when I see the bag still tucked in there, pausing when I notice the scratches on the edge of the board. Closing my eyes, I inhale, frowning when I catch hints of very familiar smells. Nox and Tam. I can't tell if it's a lingering scent from the other night or not, my sense of smell nothing compared to some of the dark worlders, but I swear it smells more potent compared to before.

Did they seriously break into my house? What the fuck were they even looking for? It's not like I have much to my name in here, and they shouldn't have any reason to suspect me of the things going on in the Hollow. The scratches make me think that I'm wrong in that thought, but if they found the bag, why would they leave it behind? If they know what I've been doing and what I'm hiding, wouldn't taking it be the first reaction—the smarter reaction?

They made a grave error in leaving me with my haul, but I doubt they know what I have planned. I'll make good use of it, putting the cogs in motion to finally have everything I want. Once I'm free of the Night Court I'll only have Nox standing in my way. All that will be left standing is me and Tam, and at that point, he won't have any other choice but to trust me. I'm doing this for him, for the life we both deserve, one free of all rules and restrictions.

My phone buzzes in my pocket and I pull it out, rolling my eyes before answering it. "Yes?"

"Kalia," Cam says, and I can hear the hint of a smile in his voice. I shouldn't be as irritated as I am when he speaks since he's done nothing to me to make me actually hate him. It's not his fault our families are both fucked. "I'm just confirming that you'll be joining us for dinner tonight and whether or not you need a car to escort you."

"Yes, I'll be attending, and no, I don't need an escort."

"I'm sorry that you have to keep doing this," he says quietly, and a twinge of guilt settles behind my ribs. "I wish we would have met under different circumstances, one where our parents didn't find it necessary to push us on each other."

"It's not your fault." It's true, it's not. Cam doesn't deserve this type of treatment either, but he's collateral damage in my end goal. I can't let any of them stand in my way, not when I'm so close to having what I deserve.

"It feels like it is, but I know you're right. I'll see you in a few hours, and please be safe getting here."

"Goodbye Camden."

"Goodbye, Kalia."

I toss my phone on the ground and grab the bag from the hole. Setting it down on my bed, I grab the helion, dripping a drop under my tongue. The effects are instantaneous, the drug coursing through my veins like liquid fire. I smile, holding out my palm to see the flames shift from orange to blue. It's been a chore trying to suppress my abilities, trying not to let them slip even a fraction. The last thing I needed was someone realizing the type of power I have, but suppressing it for as long as I have, has created a bit of a lag on my ability. The helion helps—more than helps. I can see why people are obsessed with it, using it to their advantage. I mean, how dangerous can it really be if Tam is using it? He seems fine...a little unstable, but fine.

The necro was harder to come by, and the three vials I got from Calvin's warehouse weren't nearly enough for what I need to do. That dealer didn't have to die, but him refusing me the drug, even after showing him I had the money to buy it, just made me snap. I wouldn't use necro myself, not when the side effects are so volatile. The thought of burning out completely because I used too much of it is the only reason I haven't even tried it. It's for one purpose, and one purpose only.

I grab one of my purses and shove a bunch of the vials into it before heading to the bathroom to take a shower. The least I can do is make myself presentable for this stupid dinner. The King better be there tonight, not like some of the other nights he's requested my presence just to completely disappear for day with his Queen on supposed Court business. Such a ruse. He's just flexing his power, proving that he can force people to bend to his will. He'll be the first to go, him and his wretched Queen.

CHAPTER 62

TAMZIN

"We need to go if you want to be there before they start their dinner!" Nox calls out from the kitchen.

"Fuck, okay. I'm coming." I grab my phone off the nightstand, pausing when my eyes land on the bottle of helion. I glance back at the door, palming it quickly, and throwing it into my pocket as well. I'm hoping I don't need to use it, but with where we're going, I want to be able to get me and Nox out of there as quickly and easily as possible if the need presents itself. "Alright, I'm good to go," I mutter, grabbing my keys off the side table.

He pulls himself from the couch and follows me out. The elevator ride down is quiet, and I keep glancing at him, expecting him to ask me questions about how this is all going to go down, but he doesn't. He gets off the elevator first, his steps determined as he heads for my car.

"Do you want me to drive?" He asks, turning to look at me with a frown on his face. "You're moving slower than normal."

"I'll admit, I really don't want to do this."

"Then don't," he shrugs. "You hate your family anyways, so is there really any reason to warn them? Do you honestly think she has it in her to off your entire family? They're Night Court, Tam."

"She's obviously accustomed to murdering already so I wouldn't put it past her to do something that stupid. She doesn't want to marry Cam, and someone as dangerous as her will do stupid shit when backed into a corner. If she feels like she has no other way out of this...yeah, she'll go that far."

"So, you're going."

"I have to, and I'm driving," I add.

He rolls his eyes and hops into the car before me. I settle into my seat, knowing very well that I'm literally moving as slow as molasses. I know that I need to do this, but I *really* don't want to fucking deal with my family if it comes to it. Sure, I may have set the meeting up with Cam, but if they're all there for dinner, I'm dreading the fact I might run into my parents.

"Today, or..."

"Shut up," I grumble.

He laughs and pats at my thigh. "It'll be okay. You've got me with you."

"I know you think that should make me feel better, but it doesn't. My parents aren't very...open about non-traditional relationships."

"We don't have to tell them anything. It's none of their fucking business."

"I'm not hiding you," I snap. He lifts a brow in question. "I mean, I'm not planning to walk in there and flaunt you, even if that's what I want to do just to stick it to them, but I'm not fucking hiding the fact we're together. I know Cam and Helia won't care. If anything, they'll be happy about it. Croh, I have no idea how he'll react to it, but the twins...they'll make it difficult."

I pull out onto the road, forcing myself to just fucking get it over with. Once I tell Cam what's going on, he can deal with it as he sees fit. I don't want to be the one that has to confront her about any of this, and I definitely don't want to be the one that has to take her down. I'm sure Nox would have no qualms in putting her in her place.

He would end her where she stands if I gave him the word since he seems to hate her more than I do with everything that happened.

"I'll do whatever you want me to do, Tam, *be* whoever you need me to be."

I reach over and he takes my hand without question, settling both our hands against his thigh. "I just want you to be you, no one else, Nox."

***

We still had a bit of trouble getting through the gate, but I shouldn't be surprised by that. Cam is sitting on the steps up front when we pull up, and he quickly bounces to his feet with a smile on his face. I let out a long breath and Nox squeezes my hand, trying to reassure me that it'll be okay. "Just tell him everything," he says, leaning over to place a kiss on my cheek. I watch Cam watching us, his eyes widening slightly, but the smile doesn't fade, if anything, it gets bigger.

"Looks like Cam is team Nox," I chuckle.

"Hmm, maybe I shouldn't hate him then," Nox snorts, pulling away from me and opening his door.

I watch him walk right up to Cam without hesitation, like he *isn't* the fucking next in line to rule the Night Court. I can't hear what Cam says to him, but Nox slaps him hard on the back, making Cam stumble forward in surprise while he laughs. "Fuck me, they're getting too buddy, buddy." I shouldn't be upset about that. I rather Cam like him so he'll leave us the fuck alone, but at the same time, I don't want the backlash that I know will end up coming from all of this.

"Tamzin," Cam smiles, holding out his hand to me. "It's nice to see that you finally made it official with your beefcake here."

I roll my eyes. "You're going to tell me you expected us to get together?"

"Absolutely. You could cut the sexual tension between you two with a butter knife." He motions towards the house. "Do you want to come in for a drink?"

"I rather not run into anyone else," I mumble.

"Tam, you don't need to avoid this place. This is your home, and I *want* you here. One drink. We can talk about whatever you need to talk about over one drink."

I glance over to Nox, pleading with my eyes for him to save me from this, but he just shrugs and quirks a brow, daring me to give in. "Fine. One drink, and then we're out of here."

"Awesome!" Cam says excitedly, bounding up the stairs like a fucking kid.

I let out a ragged breath, and Nox comes closer to me, draping his arm across my shoulders. "It'll be fine. One drink, we tell him everything we know, then we're out of here. It'll be over before you know it."

I lean into him, letting him lead my up the stairs. Cam waits for us, holding the door open with a goofy grin on his face. "You two are cute as shit together."

"You're making this weird," I sigh.

He tilts his head in confusion. "What? Why?"

"It's weird that you're so okay with all of this when we both know the rest of the family won't be."

"Who gives a fuck what they think? Are you happy?" I blink but nod my head. "Then that's all that matters. Our opinions don't matter, Tam, they never did. I want you to be a part of my family, but I'm not going to force you to be here unless you want to be."

"Where's everyone else?" I ask, squeezing Nox's hand when he slips his into mine.

"They're around. The twins are pissed off we're holding *another* dinner. They're getting pretty fed up with dad's shit and the way he's trying to control all of us."

"And Kalia?" Just saying her name has my heart pounding viciously in my chest. Nox must sense my unease because he tugs me closer to him and presses a simple kiss to my head.

"Kalia isn't looking forward to tonight either, but I can't blame her. I'm not sure exactly when she'll be here."

"Do you not send a car for her?"

He shakes his head and leads us into the parlour. "She refuses every time. She's probably going to take a cab or something."

Nox clucks his tongue, and I know why. Not knowing when she'll show up is a bit of a problem. We need to get as much information out as possible before that happens.

"What are you drinking?"

"Uh, just a beer is fine," I say awkwardly, following Nox over to the chairs. I grunt in surprise when he tugs me down to sit on his lap, leaving the other chair open for Cam.

"And for you, Nox?"

"I'll take a beer, too, if you have it."

Cam comes over with two bottles, and we both take one, giving him a small smile. "So, what do you need to talk to me about?" He asks, flopping himself down in the chair across from us. He doesn't seem bothered in the slightest by Nox's actions, and guilt starts to flutter around inside of me at the fact I've been so short with Cam these last few years. I open my mouth, but snap it closed quickly when Croh waltzes in.

"Tamzin. I didn't expect you to be here," he says, walking himself over to the bar. His tone is casual, maybe even a bit kind, which is throwing me the fuck off.

"Uh, yeah. I needed to talk to Cam about some things."

"Mind if I sit in?" He stands next to Cam's chair, eyeing the position Nox and I are in. "Huh, I didn't think this would ever end up happening," he snorts.

"Excuse me?"

He waves his hand towards us. "I figured something was going on between you two with the way Nox was acting when you guys were here."

"Fucking hell, did *everyone* know what the fuck was going on, when *I* didn't?" He tips his head and frowns. "Nox and I didn't get together until after we left here."

His eyes widen, a grin spreading across his face. "Seriously? So, you're stupid *and* blind." His eyes shift to Nox, who has stiffened under me from Croh's gaze. "I'm sorry my brother is such an idiot."

Nox chokes on his beer, spitting part of it onto my neck as he coughs. "I never would have thought I would ever hear *you* of all people apologize," he snorts. "Least of all for Tam not seeing I wanted to bone him."

Cam spews his whisky out through his nose, all of us laughing when tears spring to his eyes from the burn of it. This is the weirdest, most fucked up conversation I've ever had with my siblings. I never expected it to go as well as it is, never expecting Croh to be so accepting of the fact I like guys, too.

"Alright, fuck. I can't handle any more of this," Cam laughs. "What did you want to talk about?"

I glance at Croh, contemplating if it's the best idea to be talking about it all in front of him, but I don't really have a choice. "It's about Kalia."

"What's about me?" All our heads snap towards the door, to where Kalia is standing, dressed in dark slacks and a deep green blouse. Her eyes drift from Cam to Croh, a frown forming on her face when her eyes fall to me sitting in Nox's lap. "What's going on? What is this?" She says, pointing at me and Nox.

"Kalia, you're early," Cam laughs awkwardly, lifting to his feet to go over to her. Croh takes his place in the chair, lifting a brow in question at me. I shake my head, fixing my gaze back on her. A low growl starts to rumble in Nox's chest, and I quickly squeeze his thigh to try and calm him. "I wasn't expecting you until closer to dinner."

"I figured I may as well come over and hang out a bit, but I didn't expect your rogue brother to be here...with Nox." Her frown deepens. "What's going on?"

I shiver when I feel Nox's face drift closer to my neck. He pulls a deep inhale, pressing his lips to my skin. I can feel the smirk on his face, and I mentally picture myself kicking him in the shin for antagonizing her. She's a fucking sociopath, so pushing her is *not* the best course of action.

"We were just having a little chat with your betrothed," Nox purrs, nipping at my ear.

"Will you stop that," I hiss out.

"No," he says bluntly, curling his arm around my waist and squeezing me against his chest possessively.

"I see," she says carefully, and I catch a flicker of light caressing her irises. Fuck me, she's so pissed right now. This was the one situation I didn't want to be put into because with her here, I can't fucking say or do anything.

"We should go," I murmur.

"Wait, you don't have to go yet. You said you needed to talk, so we can just go out back or something. I'm sure Helia wouldn't mind keeping Kalia entertained for a little while."

"Will you be staying for dinner?" Kalia asks, and I notice her shift in posture, the way she tugs her purse closer to herself, like she's trying to protect it.

"I wasn't planning on it. I came here to talk to Camden, not to socialize."

"Sure seems like a social gathering to me," she snaps. "I think you should stay for dinner. It should prove to be *very* entertaining."

Something is wrong. I don't know exactly why I'm getting this feeling, but the way she said that has the hairs at the nape of my neck standing on end. Nox's grip tightens around me at my sudden stillness. "What's wrong?" He whispers against my ear.

"Something isn't right. She's up to something."

"What do you want to do?"

"I don't think we have a choice. We'll have to stay and see what happens." I clear my throat and give Kalia the fakest smile I can muster. "Sure, we'll stay for dinner."

"Really?" Cam says in surprise. "That's amazing!" He grips into Kalia's hip, hugging her to him. "Why don't you head up to Helia's room for now. We're going to finish chatting."

"Why can't I stay with you?" She bats her eyelashes and drags her fingernails down his chest. The fucking manipulative bitch must know. I close my eyes and pull with my senses, snapping them open when I catch the hint of drugs.

"Tam wants to talk in private, and I want to respect his wishes," Cam argues.

"Nox," I whisper. "She has necro on her."

Nox stiffens, slowly shifting his hold on me. "Why the fuck would she bring it here."

"I don't know."

"Fine," she huffs, pulling away from him and turning quickly. She breezes through the door without a glance back at us.

"Cam, you have to listen to me very carefully," I say, trying to keep my voice as calm and quiet as I can. "Kalia is dangerous."

"Dangerous?" Croh snorts. "Have you *seen* her. She's a fucking sheltered princess—"

"She's unhinged. I don't exactly know what her goal is, but we have proof that she's the one that burned down Calvin's estate, and she attacked and killed a Hollow drug dealer to get her hands on necro."

"Necro?" Cam whispers harshly. "What the fuck do you mean?"

"She has it on her right now. I fucking scented it." Confusion and anger overtake Cam's features. I can't blame him for having mixed emotions about this, since I didn't think the girl was capable of anything like that either, but the more I think about, the more the signs seem to light up. I said it before, I'm attracted to every shade of red.

"What am I supposed to do with this information?"

"I don't know. She's killing people unsanctioned, Cam. I'm just presenting you with the information, but it's up to you on how you want to deal with it."

"She's Autumn Court, Tam. It's not like I can just lock her away when she's a fucking Princess."

I shrug. "Princess or not, she's going down a fucked-up path. I'm telling you this because I don't want you getting hurt if you're caught up in whatever plan she's got going. She doesn't want to get married to you."

"How do you know all of this."

I hesitate in answering, not wanting to rub salt into the wound that's already open and bleeding. "Tell him," Nox murmurs. "You have no reason to defend her. You did nothing wrong."

"I slept with her," I blurt out, and Cam's eyes widen while Croh laughs. "I didn't know who she was, and she showed interest in me. She was at the pit the night you showed up, and she's the one that stepped between me and Croh at the club."

"Wait, that chick had black hair."

"A glamour. She's been playing all of us this entire time, but I don't fucking know why."

A scream resonates through the house, all of us jumping into motion. "What are you doing?!"

"Helia? Helia!" I scream, tearing away from Nox while he yells at me to stop. I come to a screeching halt when a body slams to the ground in front of me, completely engulfed in flames.

CHAPTER 63

TAMZIN

"Mom," I whisper, recognizing her even through the flames licking across her limp body.

"You dare attack us?!" I glance up to the balcony above us, my father storming towards Kalia with a vicious look on his face. Helia stands a few feet behind her, her eyes wide and her hands covering her mouth as she stifles her sobs.

"What the fuck is going on?" Lex comes running up from the basement, stopping short at the sight of our mother lying dead on the floor. "You!" He snarls when he notices me, but Croh steps in front of me with his hand up.

"It wasn't him. Back off." Flynn comes up behind him, his eyes darting around the room, trying to understand what the fuck is happening right now.

"You will not control me," Kalia snarls, her hair lifting around her as flames skate across her body. My eyes narrow on the hint of green glow around her irises. "This Court will fall by my hand."

"Was this the Autumn Court's plans all along? Were you sent here to try and destroy us?" My father spits out, taking another step towards her.

She throws her head back and cackles maniacally. "Hardly. My family doesn't care about me, they just wanted to marry me off, but

I don't want *Cam*." Her eyes drift down to look at me, her gaze softening a fraction. "I want *him*."

My father looks over at that comment, a mix of emotions playing across his face before finally settling on disgust. "You," he snaps. "I should have known. You bring nothing but chaos in your wake, you insolent child."

"He's here to save your asses!" Nox snaps, coming up to stand next to me, which is a mistake. Kalia's expression contorts into rage when her eyes fall on him.

"He's *mine!*" She snarls. My father takes advantage of the distraction, lurching towards her, but he can't stop her as he is, not when she's using. I don't think she's on necro, the familiar glow of helion flickering in her eyes. Helia jumps in shock when Kalia nails my father with a blast of fire, launching him off the balcony. His shadows whip out around him, trying to grab onto anything on his descent, but her fire burns too brightly to give him any form of an advantage. He screams, groaning when his body slams into the ground right next to my mother.

My first instinct is dig for the bottle of helion in my pocket. "No!" Nox snaps when I unscrew the dropper.

"I have no choice. She's hopped up on helion herself, and no one else here has anything but shadows to use. The way she's burning right now, no one will be able to gain any ground with her."

"Tam, you can't. It'll kill you."

"I'm sorry." His eyes widen when I drain the entire contents of the dropper under my tongue. I have no idea how much I just took, but it burns through my system instantly. I stumble away from him, gripping at my chest. My heart feels like it's going to beat right out from under the confines of my ribcage, and I grit my teeth against the pain.

"Tam," Nox says in a hushed whisper, moving towards me again and rubbing at my back.

"Get away from him! He's mine!" Kalia scream, launching off the balcony and manifesting her wings the moment she hits open air.

I grip the front of Nox's shirt, pulling him closer to me. "I love you," I whisper, slamming my lips against his for a few precious seconds before shoving him towards Cam. "Keep him safe!"

"Tam, no!" Nox screams, thrashing against Cam's hold on him. He breaks away, clawing at Cam's other arm, but Croh steps towards him as well to restrain him. "Tam! Let me go, you fucking pricks! He's going to get himself killed!"

Kalia grabs a vial from her purse, slamming the entire thing back in one gulp. Fuck, I'm so fucked, but I can't let her hurt the rest of them. My eyes drift back to my parent. As much as I despised them and wanted my dad dead, I never wanted it to end like this. With him gone, Cam will take the crown, and hopefully he'll be able to finally make the Night Court something better.

"Tamzin," Kalia purrs. "Stand by my side and help me finally rid this world of those who hurt you. Nox is just using you because you're convenient, he doesn't actually care about you."

I stare up at her hovering above us and let my wings unfurl around me. The shadows in the room pulse weakly, trying to fight the effects of her ever-growing light. The amount she just took might end up killing her, but not before she takes some of us down with her. "You're wrong. Nox has been with me through some of my darkest moments. He cares about me more than you ever could."

"But I love you! We're perfect for each other. Why can't you see that?! I've been watching you, too, and I know that you and I are the same. We're meant to be together. Me and you, Tam. Not me and Cam."

"Kalia, why are you doing this?" Cam murmurs, pain lacing his voice as he struggles with Croh to keep Nox contained. I can see the shift rippling across his skin, threatening to break free in his growing anger and agitation at being restrained. Lex and Flynn hover at the edges, slowly stepping closer to me while their eyes stay trained on Kalia.

"You don't deserve happiness. Not when you and your family have created nothing but pain and heartache." She points towards me. "You broke him. He is smarter and stronger than all of you, and you fucking broke him for your own sick pleasure. You don't deserve to call him a brother. You don't deserve to breathe the same air as him. None of you do!" She screams.

Helia tries to sneak down the stairs, seeking the protection of the others, but her movement draws Kalia's attention. She's burning brighter than any elemental I've ever seen, and it's wishful thinking that she self destructs before she ends up killing someone else.

"Helia!" I cry out when a stream of fire careens towards her. I launch into the air, slamming into Kalia, but her attack has already gone off and is headed straight for Helia.

Grunts of pain radiate through the room, and the next second, Nox leaps into the air, shifting mid-stride, and slams into Helia. He whimpers when the flames clip his back, singeing his fur. He snarls, snapping his teeth in Kalia's direction while he stays planted in front of Helia's cowering form.

"I told you to protect him!" I snarl, turning my attention to Cam, but he and Croh are sprawled on the ground and slow to rise to their feet.

"If you hadn't noticed, your boyfriend is massive and vicious," Croh grumbles.

Kalia spins towards me, absolute fury on her face. "Why are you attacking me?! I'm doing this for you!"

"For me? I don't fucking want this, Kalia, and I sure as fuck don't want you."

Her face contorts into confusion and pain at my words. "You don't mean that. You hate them!" She swings her arm out towards my brothers, flames erupting from her palm with the movement.

"Fuck," Croh grunts. I glance over in time to see Lex slam into Croh and Cam to knock them out of the way while Flynn tries to put up a shield of shadow around them all, planting himself in front of Dorian.

He grits his teeth against the assault, the shield breaking apart from the intensity of the flames ripping through the darkness.

I summon my shadows, their form lurching from my body to wrap around her, but I can't keep a firm hold on them or her. My eyes are burning from her light and the proximity to her internal heat. I pull in a rattling breath, drawing on the power I've kept restrained my entire life. Lightning begins to crackle around me, forks of it skittering across my body.

"You can't take me down," she laughs. "You think your power compares to mine? I have the advantage here, Tamzin, this is why it's so easy to take all of them out. Darkness can't survive in the light, and your electrical ability will do nothing against a flame."

She's right, but I have no choice but to try. Holding my palm towards her, I let the current flow through me, snapping it out against her body. She screams in pain, but it really can't take her down. A fire elemental can progress their power to the level of lightning if they're strong enough, and I'm learning the hard way that my powers really won't touch her. The lightning curls around her body, her teeth gritting together as she tries to absorb the attack.

"You're in my way. You'll understand once this is all over."

My eyes widen when she's suddenly in front of me, her fist colliding with my sternum, launching me back to slam against the wall. It cracks to the ceiling from the force of her blow, my body crumpling to the ground below.

"Tam!" Nox screams. I struggle to lift my head to look at his reverted form, his eyes wide in panic as Kalia turns her attention back to him. "Don't do this!" He pleads.

"You don't deserve him!" She screams. "This is *your* fault. You poisoned him with lies about me. He loves me. He fucking loves *me*!" She grips her purse, lifting the strap from across her chest to hold it out in front of her. "You all deserve to suffer."

He launches himself off the stairs towards her, his wings manifesting into deep emerald hues just as her body lights up with flames. My eyes widen when I realize what she's doing. The necro is liquid form, but with flames they'll turn into a gas that could infect us all.

"Nox! The necro!" His eyes dart to the bag going up in flames just as he slams into her, dragging her to the ground with him. "Nox! Get away from her!"

CHAPTER 64

TAMZIN

I scramble and claw at the ground, trying to get my body to move, but it's still numb from the vicious hit she blasted me with. Cam and Croh are running towards them as they plummet to the ground, but it's like they're running in slow motion. The cracking of glass seems so loud in my ears, red vapour pouring out from the bag gripped tightly against Kalia's chest. The effects are instantaneous on Nox, and my heart shatters. His eyes shift into black voids the moment the drug hits him. That level of necro...another crack through my heart.

"Nox!" I cry out, but it's too late, he's inhaled so much of it already, and the cloud of it is slowly creeping out towards Croh and Cam. Lex, Dorian, and Flynn run towards Helia, trying to move her away from the threat poisoning the air.

Nox blinks rapidly, his chest heaving in heavy pants while Kalia sneers at him. Her eyes have shifted to black as well, the necro coursing through her system. What was the point of all of this? She must not have planned to have it affect her. The drug is volatile, and in heavy doses like this, it's deadly. It's *deadly*, and Nox just got nailed with her entire stash.

Croh and Cam grunt out in pain, slamming into an invisible barrier. They bang their fists against it, trying to get to Nox, trying to get him the fuck away from Kalia. The vapor hits the barrier as well, curling up the side of it like an undulating wave.

"Nox, no!" I stumble to my feet, slamming into the barrier myself, pounding my hand against it.

He tips his head towards me, a sad smile pulling at his lips. His entire body is twitching and convulsing, his life energy pushed into overdrive. He's never formed a barrier of this magnitude in the years I've known him, but he's being pushed well beyond his limits now as the drug burns through his life energy at an asinine pace.

"Nox! Please!"

"I'm going to kill you!" Kalia snarls, launching a stream of fire towards him.

It hits a wall in front of him, and he doesn't even flinch, his eyes still locked on mine. No, this can't be happening. Those black voids stare back at me, but I can feel his emotion, I can feel what he's planning to do, and I can't even stop him. I'm fucking weak and useless, and tears spring into my eyes.

"I love you, Tam. I'll always love you," he says quietly, his voice breaking on the words.

"Please don't do this! We'll find a way to help you, please! *Please*!" My voice is thick with tears, and his face blurs in front of me.

A slow shake of his head. "You know there's no coming back from this. It's necro, Tam, and not a small amount."

"*Please!*" I plead again, screaming and clawing at his barrier. I hit it with everything I have, physical blows, shadows, lightning, *everything,* but he's too strong right now, and nothing is getting through. Even Kalia can't break through the internal barrier he's put around himself, trapping her between two with no way to attack and no way to escape. My nails snap and bleed at the desperation within me to get to him, to stop him, to fucking *save* him, and with each futile attack, sobs wrack my body. "Nox! I love you! Please don't!"

"It's already done," he whispers.

He rips his gaze away from me, Kalia screaming and clawing at the barrier between them like a savage beast hellbent on destruction. He throws his hand up and I see the barrier shimmer and pulse, launching her back to slam against the barrier behind her. A loud hum begins to resonate within, debris whipping around Nox with every step he takes towards her. The necro swirls above him, slamming into Kalia's gaping mouth on every inhale. She's pinned three feet off the ground, her hands clenching into fists while her arms are spread out beside her.

"You can't be this strong, even *with* necro in your system," she spits out, coughing as every fragment of gas dives into her.

"You're the one that said I was an elemental as well, Kalia. Let's see which one is stronger, your fire...or my wind."

My eyes widen at his words. He was an elemental all this time and I never realized it. Kalia screams, a blast of energy erupting from her. It radiates through the house, the ground shaking at the force of it, but Nox's barrier holds. Each step he takes is methodical and torturous, her eyes darting around as panic settles on her face.

She turns her head to me, tears welling in her eyes. "Tam," she croaks.

She did this. Because of her, everything was torn from me. She killed my parents, tried to kill my siblings, and almost killed me in the process, but that's nothing compared to what she's done to Nox. I can't steady my breathing, my chest heaving in panic when I see him sway in front of her, sweat beading on his brow as black tears begin to track down his cheeks.

I look away from her, closing my eyes, and resting my forehead against the barrier as Nox shifts his hand into claws and plunges it into her chest. She screams, and then her voice turns into a gurgled moan, finally falling silent. I stumble forward when the barrier breaks, and glance up to see Nox fall to his knees. I rush towards him, skidding across the blood-soaked floor to cradle him in my arms. I hear the crackle of debris as my siblings walk towards us, but they don't try to interfere.

"Nox," I whimper, brushing his hair from his eyes. They're slowly reverting to his usual colour, the necro bleeding out across his cheeks.

His throat bobs, each inhale of his seeming more and more shallow. He shakily tries to lift his hand up towards my face, and I cup the back of it, pressing his palm into my cheek. "I'm...sorry," he whispers, and another sob rips from my chest. "I wanted...forever," he says weakly.

"You can't," I cry, burying my face into his neck and squeezing him to me, like my hold on him can keep him tethered here. He's burning out. That fucking bitch took the one person that ever truly gave a shit about me away from me. Without him, I have nothing—I *am* nothing.

"Tam," he whimpers, and I pull back to see him shaking, his teeth clenching in pain.

"Shhh, we'll find a way to help you."

He shakes his head, his smile pained and strained. "I'm dying," he chokes out, tears streaming freely down his face, and I can hear the sobs of my own family at his words.

He saved us today. Every single one of us should have succumbed to the effects of the necro, but he kept it contained at the expense of his own life. He always hated the drugs, always pushed me to stop using because his mother died from it, and here he is, falling to same fate as her. He doesn't deserve this. It should have been *me*, not him. He's everything that's good in this world, while I'm nothing but a tragedy.

"I—I want you to live, Tam," he whispers. "Please don't cry." He shakily wipes at my cheeks, but the tears won't stop coming.

"I can't do this without you," I whimper, leaning my forehead against his.

"You can...and you...will." He swallows thickly and coughs, a choked gasp slipping from his lips. "I'll always be...with...you. I...I love...you."

"Stay," I sniffle. *"Please,* stay with me."

He grips into the back of my neck, his hand shaking with the effort. "I want to," he cries. "I...don't want to...die. Laugh...love...be...happy, even without...me."

I press my lips to his. "I love you," I whisper, kissing him again. He whimpers out in pain, the kiss feeling feverish and desperate, which just breaks me completely. His hand falls away from me, and I pull back. "Nox?" I can't breathe. His eyes are closes, his lips slightly parted. "Nox?!" I give his body a small shake and his head lolls in my grip. "No," I whimper. "Please. *Please stay*." I'm hyperventilating now, each breath choked and burning in my lungs as his face blurs from my vision completely. "Nox," I cry. "Nox!"

I scream, my throat going raw as my powers whip out around me in my pain. I did nothing. With all my power, even with helion, I was fucking useless. All this time, I thought it made me stronger, but it didn't. It did nothing for me when it really mattered, and because of these fucking drugs, Nox was taken from me.

"I'm so sorry, Tam," Cam murmurs, settling his hand on my shoulder.

I lash out, slapping him away. "Don't fucking touch me," I snarl, pulling Nox's limp body closer to me. "He died protecting you fuckers. I should have never come back here. I should have let her fucking kill you if it meant keeping him! He didn't deserve this!"

"He was good, Tam," Helia says quietly. "He didn't have to protect me, but he did because he was good."

"None of you deserved his kindness, not when you called him a mutt right to his face. I didn't deserve it either, but he loved me. For once in my life, I had someone who loved me as I am and now, he's gone."

"Tam—"

"Leave me alone," I mumble, pressing my lips to Nox's forehead, the same way he always did to me. My own tears fall against his face, mixing with the ones now drying on his cooling skin and the dark tracks of necro bleeding from his eyes.

"No. We're not leaving you right now," Cam argues.

"For once in your life, can you just respect me? I don't want to hear you, let alone look at you."

"I understand that, but we have a lot of shit to deal with. Our parents are dead, Tam. The fucking Princess of another Court just got murdered in our territory—"

"I don't fucking care. That's your problem to deal with, not mine. I don't even want to be here. I'm not a part of your Court, Cam." I lurch to my feet, cradling Nox's body against my chest as I turn to glare at him, my body trembling as the side effects of the helion I ingested hit me like a brick.

"But you *are* a part of this Court."

"Excommunicate me then. I don't want anything to do with you. I never want to see any of you, ever again."

"You're family—"

"Nox was my family. He was the only thing keeping me here. You are *nothing* to me. I hate you more now than I did before, and that's saying something."

"You're angry, I get it, but you don't mean that."

I turn to look at Lex and Flynn, neither of which will meet my gaze. "You've tormented me my entire life. Anything I had that brought me joy was taken from me because of you. I'm done, Cam. I'm so fucking tired of all of this."

"Do you...want to bury him by Harbinger?"

"No. He's going next to his mother."

"We'll take care of the funeral arrangements at least."

"I want nothing from you!"

"Tam, please. I'm trying to make things right. I've been trying this whole time to make things right with you, but you keep rejecting me at every turn."

"That worked so well, didn't it? Those two fuckers had nothing but amazing things to say about me and about Nox," I snap, nodding my head to the twins. They flinch at my tone, tucking themselves further behind Croh and Dorian. "We're done here."

"Tam!" Cam calls out, but I walk away from them towards the door. I expect them to follow me out, but I'm thankful they don't.

I can't handle anymore of this bullshit. With every step towards my car, I feel pieces of myself breaking away, fragmenting and turning into powder to be blown away in the wind. The glue that held me together is gone, and I can't find my own way of keeping myself intact. I can't stop my tears from falling, sobs wracking my body as I lay Nox down on the backseat. I need to make arrangements for him, get the plot ready next to his mother. I'm not sure if he would want an actual funeral or not, but he has no family, and only a few friends. I can't handle seeing them at this point though, not wanting to stand there and hear them give condolences over and over again, and asking me what happened.

The Night Court happened. The one thing I wanted to keep him as far away from, ended up being the reason for his death. He should have lived for centuries, smiling and happy and mine, but now he's gone, and I'm alone once again. His final words were his love for me and for me to be happy, but how am I supposed to be happy without him? We should have ran away from here when we had the chance, but I let my head get in the way—let my emotions and need to finish things get in the fucking way.

This is *my* fault. It's always been my fault. I want to take him home, but I know that's just going to prolong what I know I need to do, and it'll just make it worse for me in the end. If I take him home, I won't be able to bring myself to act and take him to the funeral home. I pull in a rattling breath, shift my car into drive, and pull away from the house that has ruined my entire life.

CHAPTER 65

TAMZIN

Julia at the funeral home did a wonderful job. The plot was surprisingly easy to purchase, and she cleaned Nox up beautifully. I didn't tell anyone when he was being buried, but I catch movement out of the corner of my eye, noticing my family standing off by one of the large willow trees, huddled together as they watch me say my final goodbyes.

I open the casket one last time, choking back a harsh sob at seeing him lying there. I brush my fingers through his hair, trying to commit every detail about him to my memory, including the feeling of his soft strands slipping through my fingers. I blink rapidly, but I can't stop the tears that are building along my lashes from falling. I press my lips to his forehead, sobbing as I press them to his lips one final time. "I'll always love you, Nox," I whisper.

Closing the casket hurts, my heart feeling like it's being squeezed in a vice as I cut him from view. He gets slowly lowered into the ground, and I crouch down beside the hole, gripping a handful of loamy dirt in my hand. I kiss my fist, slamming my eyes closed as I release the dirt down, hearing it thunk against the mahogany wood.

I feel exhausted mentally and physically, these last few days feeling like an eternity as I tried to get everything in order. He left everything to me, which I never expected. I packed up his room, putting everything in storage until I would be ready to go through his things again. I wasn't getting rid of anything, so everything got neatly packed away like I've been doing with the memories of him. I took down the stars, too, in his room and in mine. I couldn't handle that painful reminder of him. What once brought me joy, now it brings me nothing but sadness and pain. I found his will tucked away in an envelope under some of his clothes in a drawer. I never made one myself, and I had no idea that he had one made up. I transferred all the funds he had saved into my account, but I have no idea what to even do with that money. He earned every penny and it's his. We should have left this place and bought ourselves a real home. I hate myself for not following through with the idea, if I had, he would still be here.

I hear the cracking of stone behind me and let out a sigh. "I told you to leave me alone," I grumble, wiping my palm against my pants as I watch Nox get covered with dirt.

"We wanted to see if you were doing okay. You haven't returned any of my texts or calls, Tam. We were worried about you."

I let out a heartless, dark laugh, finally turning to look at Cam. "Why would I respond when I said I never wanted to see or speak to you again."

The twins step forward, bowing their heads. "We're sorry for the way we treated you and Nox."

"I don't want to hear it. If you're hoping for forgiveness, you'll be waiting your entire lives because I won't give it to you. You can take your apologies and shove them up your ass—fucking choke on them. You're assholes, and you're the ones that deserve to be in that hole."

"Tam," Helia whispers, stepping in front of them. "We're you're family. We understand what you're going through, we lost our parents, and you didn't...why didn't you come to their funeral?"

"They birthed me, but they were not parents to me. They got what they deserved." I glance at Cam and give him a mirthless grin. "*King Camden*," I snarl.

"I *am* your King," he says simply. "And as your King, I'm granting you what you want...an escape." He holds out an envelope to me, and I stare at it with disgust clear on my face. "Take it, Tam. You can do what you want. We want you to stay, but we understand you don't want that. There's nothing left for you here."

I open the envelope, reading over the scrawling print quickly, a frown drawing my brows down. "Solar Court wants Night Court warriors?"

"They're pulling in people from every Court they can. We're not sending anyone ourselves, but I thought you might want to consider that option. You can find a new purpose if you so wish it, free from the confines of this Court."

"Typical," I snort. "Trying to make it out like you're the ones deciding to get rid of me. I wasn't planning to stay here longer than I needed to. Even if you didn't release me from my so-called duty to this Court, I would have fucking ran. I want to be as far away from this place as I can."

"I release you from your duties, Tamzin. You'll always be a Prince of the Night Court, and you'll always be my brother. I hope some day you'll give us the chance to truly make it right."

"You think I want to go to another Court? Solar of all places?"

A small smile tugs at his lips as he nods at the sheet of paper in my hands. "Nox has a half-sister," he says, and I swallow the lump in my throat, glancing down at the paper again. The memory of him telling me that himself pulses through my mind. "She's the Queen's right hand. Who knows, you two might have a lot in common, just as you did with Nox."

His sister. Can I handle being in the presence of someone that will bring up memories of him? The thought of doing that feels like torture, but do I deserve anything less? Maybe I can do for her the one thing I couldn't do for him...protect. It's all I ever wanted to do. I wanted to protect him and keep him safe, even when the safest option was to just stay away from me. He loved me for me, and I loved all of him. Can I allow myself to feel something for her to?

"Try and live your life, Tam. It's what Nox would have wanted, you know that. He wouldn't want you to break again just because he's no longer here." I hate that he's right in saying that. Nox *would* want me to live my life. I just never thought it would also mean that I needed to move on from *him*. Fuck, I miss him so much already. I miss his laugh, his smile, his smell, and his touch. I miss his presence and very essence. Maybe his sister can fill that small void that's reopened in my heart. "Goodbye, Tam, and if you need anything at all, please don't hesitate to reach out."

I don't respond—I barely acknowledge them walking away from me but catch them all glancing back over their shoulders at me. I glance back down at the paper, reading it over and over again, trying to convince myself that this is a really bad idea, but I can't. There's a piece of Nox still out there in the form of a half-sister, and my curiosity is getting the better of me. I don't need to talk to her or have her acknowledge me. I just want to see her and see what she's like. I'll go there and embrace who and what I am, since it's not like I'm not used to people hating the Night Court name already. I'm not locked down to a Court any longer, and I can leave whenever I wish to. Solar Court...fuck it.

EPILOGUE

TAMZIN

One Month Later

Fuck, these people are assholes. Mind you, their animosity isn't as bad towards me as I thought it would be. They're mostly ignoring me or trying to steer clear of me when I walk by. I thought I would be closer to the inner sanctum, but I've been stationed at the outer Court, doing mundane duties and protecting the towns within the territory. I still haven't seen Jacqueline, Nox's half-sister, but there shouldn't be any reason for her to come this far out.

I've been here an entire month already, and not a single person has even tried to hold a conversation outside of duties. Most of the negative attention has been focused on one person, someone I didn't expect to see in any Court, let alone Solar. Atlas, the corrupted Fae Prince of the Lunar Court. Well, technically he's the King of the Lunar Court, but since it no longer exists, Prince seems like an appropriate title. A dark Prince with a dark past, just like me. He wiped out his entire family, plus a few extras along the way in his fall. He's not what I expected. Looks wise, I can see it. He has a presence about him that shows how capable he can be, but he walks around like he's trying to make himself smaller and unassuming.

I grit my teeth in anger when I see him getting jostles and pushed as he makes his way through the cafeteria, sitting himself down at a table in the far corner, alone. No one goes near him, and they definitely don't make eye contact with him, but they have no problem talking about him behind his back.

"I don't understand how they let him back into Court after he was banished," one of the guards at the table behind me murmurs.

"It has to be some kind of joke, or maybe he's here waiting to be executed for his crimes," his friend snickers.

I sigh, poking around at the food on my tray when a shadow overtakes my table. I glance up to see Captain Henley standing in front of me, his brow quirking up curiously. "Not hungry?" He asks. I shrug. "You'll be working the town today," he murmurs.

"Alone?"

He shakes his head. "I'm putting you with Atlas."

I perk up at that, straightening myself up taller on the bench. "Okay."

He gives me a small smile. "You're okay with that?"

"Why wouldn't I be?" His expression turns exasperated. "I don't care what he is or what he's done. Does he look like someone that would go on a rampage for no reason?"

I nod towards Atlas, looking lonely as fuck over there with literally no one even sitting near him at other tables either. "You're right. He's actually really kind, and he does everything he's asked to do without question. I'm going to let him know he'll be working the town today."

He heads off towards Atlas, and the douchebags behind me pipe up right away. "You're going to end up getting killed if you work with him," the one laughs.

"He's a fucking darkling. Even a Night Court reject like you should know how dangerous they are."

I stand up and turn to glare at them, my shadows pulsing out to wrap around my wrists and throat. "I'll guarantee you I'm more vicious than he is," I snap, grabbing my tray to head toward Atlas's table. Henley is walking away, giving me an eyeroll as he walks by, and I notice Atlas picking at his food with his fork. "Chin up," I murmur, climbing over the bench to sit next to him. He glances around with a frown on his face. "What?"

"Do you not have anywhere else to sit?" He asks.

I frown and gnaw on my lip. "Is there a problem with me sitting next to you? Do you smell funny or something?" He seems genuinely thrown off at the fact I'm willingly sitting next to him, and I feel awful for how everyone has been treating him. He's a lot like me, judged for no reason and treated harshly for something we have no control over.

He smiles shyly, his eyes drifting across my face as he takes me in. "Do you know who I am?" He asks hesitantly.

Poor guy, he really seems to be struggling, like he's waiting for me to snap or lash out. "You're Atlas."

"Yes," he says simply, his expression turning guarded.

"You killed your family fifty years ago." His smile falters. "I don't care what you did in the past. I'm not innocent either. We all have our own traumas that we have to live with, but if you did something like that, you must have had a good reason."

His eyes widen, and I know what he's thinking right now. He can't understand how I can just be so casual about something like that, but I can't judge someone just because of what they've done in the past. That doesn't define a person in the slightest, and I don't know the reason, but I'm sure it had to be something important.

"I'm Tamzin." I hold out my hand to him, and he takes it, smiling at me again. My stomach growls, the appetite I haven't truly felt in a while finally coming out to play. I grab my fork and start shoveling food into my mouth.

"What are your lines?" He asks.

"Night Court."

"Night Court? How did you end up here?"

I don't really want to tell him the whole truth about why, the pain of it still too fresh and too new. I shrug and chug back my orange juice. "I'm not sure, exactly. By the look of things, they've been trying to bring in Fae from every sector. I don't know if they're trying to unify us in a way, or if there's something else going on."

"The Night Court doesn't socialize with anyone, though, so why?"

"It's not that we don't socialize, it's just that everyone is sort of afraid of us...sort of like they are around you. They fear that which they don't understand." I shovel more food into my mouth, trying to throw back as much as I can while I still feel like eating. I can feel his eyes on me, taking in every detail available to him. "Anyways, it looks like the two of us are working the town today, so chin up."

A huge grin spreads across his face, changing his features into something so much softer and less guarded. "That actually makes me unbelievably happy. I appreciate you actually giving me a chance."

Henley was right, he seems super kind and sweet, and with what I've witnessed surrounding him, I want to be his friend and help him any way I can. "Have you not made any friends?" I ask.

"None. They all avoid me as much as possible. They're civil, but there's no familiarity between me and them."

"How long have you been here now?"

"About a month," he murmurs.

"Same as me then. I'm surprised we haven't been paired together sooner, especially since we're both outcasts," I snort. "I'll meet you out front when you're done, and we can walk to town together. Sound good?"

"Yes, that sounds great."

I grab my tray, tossing the trash out, and feeling not only Atlas's gaze on me, but the glares of a few of the other guards as I walk out. They already don't like me, but they'll like me even less now for befriending him. He's been rejected by the Court, and everyone knows what he's done, even if they don't know the reason. I had my doubts once I came here, fighting off the regret I was feeling and forcing myself to believe that this was the right thing to do.

Seeing Atlas of all people and being able to talk to him, solidified my decision to be here. I haven't seen Jacqueline yet, and I might never get to meet her, but if I can build a true friendship with Atlas, I can do for him what Nox did for me. Caring for someone that others have rejected and being there for them in any way I can be. This was the right thing to do, and all I can hope for now is that I try to allow myself to be happy with what life has thrown my way.

Atlas didn't reject me or shy away from me because he's a lot like me. A flutter of excitement courses through me at knowing I made a friend here, in a world that knows what I am, a world that has always rejected me. I might actually find some solace in the company of someone others deem dangerous and underserving of living, but everyone deserves the chance at happiness, whether fleeting or eternal.

I lost my eternal happiness when I lost Nox, but I hope he's smiling and happy with my decision now as he watches me live the life he granted me with his sacrifice. I'll never forget him, I mean, how could I? He was everything to me, and I'll always love him, that will never change. I slip into my small apartment and flop down on my bed, staring up at the ceiling with a smile on my face. Sadness and happiness swirl in my chest as I focus in on the stars above me, the stickers my gentle reminder from him. "I'm trying to do what you wanted, Nox," I whisper. "I'm trying to be happy without you. It's hard—so fucking hard—but I know you're watching over me. I hope you're proud, and I miss you so fucking much." I swallow around the tears building in my throat. "I don't know if I'll ever love someone like I loved you, but you've been right about a lot of things, and I have faith in the fact you've never lied to me, in life, or in death. I love you."

I roll over onto my side and close my eyes, wanting to just lie here for a few minutes. I shudder, convinced that I feel his arms wrapping around me, pulling me in against his chest while his scent completely consumes me. I can hear his voice in my head as he nuzzles his face into my neck, inhaling my scent. *"You'll find happiness again, I promise. I love you, Tam."*

TAMZIN'S STORY CONTINUES IN

HUNTING THE FATES

Hunting The Fates is Atlas' story, with a side of Tamzin. Will he finally meet Jacqueline?

https://books2read.com/HuntingTheFates

Sign up to my Newsletter for updates on upcoming books and exclusive content.

https://sendfox.com/melissasilva

www.ingramcontent.com/pod-product-compliance
Lightning Source LLC
La Vergne TN
LVHW050919080826
845145LV00001B/133

* 9 7 8 1 9 9 8 5 0 0 2 5 3 *